SHADOW BEAST SHIFTERS

REBORN

JAYMIN EVE

Jaymin Eve

Reborn: Shadow Beast Shifters #3

Cover: Tamara K
Editing: Amy McNulty
Proofing: Aubergine Editing

To my husband, the possessive bastard.

Without you, Shadow Beast would be missing a few of his personality traits, and that would be a true tragedy.

This book is our love story... if we suddenly woke up in a PNR.

I love you. Most of the time.

JAYMIN'S NERD HERD

Join the group and stay up to date.

The best way to stay up to date with the Shadow Beast Shifters world and all new releases, is to join my Facebook group here:
www.facebook.com/groups/jayminevenerdherd

We share lots of book releases, fun posts, sexy dudes, and generally it's a happy place to exist.

Library of Knowledge

Shadow Beast Shifters

SHADOW BEAST LAIR

FROZEN TUNDRA

DINING HALL

DESERT LANDS

FAERIE

WATCHERS

KARN

SHADOW REALM

VALDOR

HONOR MEADOWS

TUNDERA

BROLDER

DIRECTORY

Frozen Tundra

Desert Lands

Faerie

Watchers

Karn

Shadow Realm

Valdor

Honor Meadows

Tundera

Brolder

Grey lands
Shado
Holister
The
Isle of Rechaste
Glistin
Ashan
Samsan Grove
Dety

Chasm

ordes

Dankor

Trinity

Fraple

The Depths

Green isle

Rodan

Onther islands

Chapter One

A *broken mind and a fractured soul. Was there redemption or relief from the endless darkness? Or would I continue to dwell on the bane of my existence?*

I reread the final line of the book in my hand. A paranormal romance I'd loved, despite the somewhat evil cliffhanger it ended on —I had hate-love for cliffys because I was desperate to know what was going to happen next, but there was also this thrill of the unknown that kept me thinking about the story long after I finished reading.

Either way, it had been such a great book, temporarily keeping my mind off the shitshow of my life.

"Girl! There you are!"

Sucking in a deep breath, I tried not to lose my shit over the fact that someone had discovered my hiding spot by the lake. Not just someone... Sisily Longeran. Former enemy and current frenemy, which was both confusing and annoying. Par for the course these days.

Ever since I'd woken in Torin's bed a week ago with a decent chunk of memory loss, life had been topsy-turvy. Case in point:

Sisily, the shifter who had fucked my true mate in front of me while asking for my death, was now my new "best friend."

With friends like these…

"Meeerrss." She annoyingly dragged my name out as she collapsed next to me. Her eyes rested briefly on the blue typographic cover that sat on my leg. "Really? You're still reading? I don't get it."

She really didn't, and that in and of itself was my first warning that I would *never have been friends with this lunatic.*

"Books legitimately saved my life," I reminded her. "When my dad was killed."

Sisily paled; no one liked to discuss my previous place of torture in the pack. No one liked to acknowledge *that* because I was mated to the alpha now.

I was the alpha-mate.

A title that sent a chill down my spine.

"Torin's looking for you," she said, changing the subject as she ruffled a hand through her mahogany hair. It continued to drift around her pretty face in the light breezes of the spring air, and seriously, how the fuck was it spring? The last I remembered, winter had been choking the life from Torma.

"He's the damn alpha," I snarled. "If he wanted to find me, I have no doubt he could have just strolled out of his own ego and discovered me right where you did."

Torin was trying to wait me out since I wouldn't go near him, sleep in his bed, or otherwise acknowledge his existence until I got to the bottom of what had caused me to forget all of the very dramatic events that had happened to Torma over the past few years.

My memory was patchy, but from what I'd managed to pry from Torin, I was missing more than just a few months. When I'd woken up, I'd remembered my first shift, Torin's rejection, and nothing else beyond that. But that wasn't even where it got really weird because it turned out that all of that didn't happen in the year 2020 as I'd expected. *Nope.* Apparently, just before the 2020 Winter Solstice, Victor, our former alpha, had pissed off the shifter god, Shadow

Beast, getting himself killed and all of Torma locked down in a two-year stasis.

I came out of this stasis with everyone else in 2022, shifted for the first time, and got rejected, which I remembered, but then the rest was blank after that. So, technically, I was missing two years and two months of time, with only one day of memory in there—my first shift and Torin's rejection.

How did any of that make fucking sense? No wonder my head ached consistently as I tried to drag memories back that I believed had been stolen from me. "Tell me again where my mom, Simone, and Glendra are," I said to Sisily, hoping that this time, she would trip up and reveal the lies. "Torin told me that all of Torma was locked in the stasis, so why are those three missing now?"

She leaned in with a smile like we were about to gossip. "It's so weird to me that you can't remember anything from the last few months. Like... how?"

I glared at her, wishing I could forget her existence just as easily.

"Anyway," she continued, not caring that I hated her, "your mom ran away and we think she's shacked up with a loser in the Alikta pack." I found it hard to believe that my mom had sobered up enough to do that, but it wasn't completely out of the realm of possibilities. "And Simone..." Sisily said, wrinkling her nose. "She took off right after the stasis was lifted, on some sort of vacation she had been planning for years. I don't know the details. We were never friends. But she's perfectly fine." This part boiled my damn blood because Simone would never take off on a "vacation" without me. And why the hell was her phone going straight to voicemail? Her parents assured me she was *fine*, just as Sisily had said. They told me they talked to her every few days, and they passed on my worries. They told me Simone didn't want to talk to anyone else while she meditated on her future. Everyone was *telling me all the things*.

It all felt like bullshit.

"And Glendra bailed immediately after the stasis lifted." Sisily sounded sad now; she'd gotten along with Torin's mom pretty well. "I have no idea why, because if the Shadow Beast wanted to kill her too, he'd have done so that night."

Her story remained the same as Torin's. The same as all of Torma's. They repeated it so often, I wondered if it actually was the truth.

Gods, my life would be so much easier if I could just accept it and start building a world here in the pack. I was the alpha-mate and would finally be able to feel comfortable around these shifters. And yet, I just couldn't.

"You would feel better if you allowed a true relationship with Torin," Sisily said, cutting through my dark thoughts. "You're even sleeping in your old apartment. I mean... Meers, we can't have the alpha-mate in a shithole like that."

Her use of "Meers" had me grinding my teeth. "Aw, Sissss," I mocked, "you are such a great friend." My sarcasm was the only thing not out of place in my life. "But it's best if I take my time until my memory returns. I'm sure you... and everyone else... understand that."

She missed all of my snark, her face brightening. "We need a ladies' night out! It's the only way to remind you of how incredibly cool you are. This dreary version is a real downer, girl."

Incredibly cool? Who was this bitch talking about?

"Isn't the pack mixer tonight?"

I was keeping up with pack business, even while trying to avoid Torin with every part of my being. He made my skin crawl, and no matter how much I tried to get on board with my true mate, it didn't feel right. My gut was telling me that there was something hidden in my memories that I needed to unlock. And I needed that to happen sooner rather than later.

My wolf surged up in my chest, her strength fuzzy and unfocused, just as it had been all week. "I'm going to shift for a run," I told Sisily, already yanking my shirt up.

This was the first time in two days that my wolf had shown any life, and I was going to let her out in the hopes that it would give her new energy.

Sisily started to undress as well. "I'll run with you."

I shook my head, my fingers leaving the hem of my shirt to wrap around her forearm. "I want to be alone," I said bluntly, since she clearly wasn't very good at reading between the lines.

Her face fell, while her azure eyes remained hard and sparking with anger. She thought I didn't see through her fake smiles and annoying nicknames, but I saw everything. She hated me, but she wanted the benefits of being friends with the alpha-mate. Sisily liked to have friends in high places.

Unfortunately for her, I had a very long memory. Ironic, considering my short-term memory loss of the last few months, but the rest... I remembered clearly.

I would never run with her as a pack.

"Okay, well, I guess I'll see you at the house tonight for the mixer," she replied with a huff, before turning and strolling off.

Good riddance, as far as I was concerned. Ditching the rest of my clothes, I placed my book and phone on top of the pile, shaking my head at the displayed date and time. Was that why my wolf felt so sluggish? Because our first shift had been delayed for two years? I couldn't come up with another explanation, and I'd spent every waking hour trying to find one.

Maybe someone from one of the other packs would let slip a new piece of information. The pack mixer was Torma's first real introduction back into the shifter world since our punishment. To think the Shadow Beast could just steal years of our lives was... scary. The demon in our shadows, who'd always felt more like a myth than reality, was apparently very real. Not to mention super-hot—according to the female shifter contingent—and lethal as fuck—according to the males. Torma pack had seen and fought him, during which time our alpha had been killed.

This was a huge fucking deal, right? So why couldn't I remember it? Everyone else remembered the day the stasis had occurred, citing their fear and grief at losing time as well. Then they remembered the day we'd awoken, followed by the Winter Solstice about a week later.

The last thing I recalled was going to school and Jaxson terrorizing me, and then the day I'd shifted and had been rejected, but the rest was blank.

I'd read stories about human women who had their drinks spiked, waking with no memories of that night or sometimes a few nights. Their grief and terror over being vulnerable during that time, possibly hurt or raped, had been palpable on the pages. I empathized with that, and the only thing keeping me sane right now was Torin's assurance that I hadn't slept with him yet.

We had been taking it slow while I made him work for forgiveness, which sounded more like me than any other parts of the story. Apparently, waking in his bed last week had only been the second time I'd slept over, baby steps in moving forward and trusting him again. Steps that were completely gone now as I attempted to pry free all my missing days.

A sharp jab of pain in my head told me I'd gone too far in prodding at those blank memories, and I had to back off. My memories did not want me pushing at them, warning me with migraines and near seizure-like attacks. If only it were in my nature to let it lie. Even knowing I would be afforded a nice, comfortable life as the alpha-mate if I just accepted it all and moved on wasn't enough to force my hand.

Whoever had done this to me had given me almost everything my shifter heart had desired because they'd thought it would keep me complacent. And if the target of this memory manipulation had been inflicted on anyone other than me, they might have been in luck.

Who would be strong enough to do this, though? It had to be the Shadow Beast. It had to have happened when Victor was destroyed.

Had I annoyed the beast when he'd been here? My mouth had been known to get me into trouble, and while Torin assured me I'd never even spoken to the shifter god... I must have.

My wolf howled, and I didn't fight her, allowing the change to wash over us. It was slow and painful, which I'd expected since we'd only been shifting for a few months. I mean, it was amazing I could even release her like this at all and not lose control of the Mera side of my brain. It had been that way since the first shift, and I still had no idea why.

Torin acted like it was due to our bond that I'd gotten control so fast, sounding all proud and shit when he said it. About the same way he sounded when he talked about the size of his dick, so it clearly wasn't that hard to impress him.

My wolf howled again as we ended up on four legs, annoyed that I was once again hating on our mate. In her wolf mind, we just needed to accept our position here and be grateful to have such a strong, powerful mate.

If only the human mind worked the same way.

I knew I was being lied to, and my inability to get to the bottom of it when everyone in Torma was telling me the same story was driving me crazy.

It was a very convenient story, one that none of them ever messed up.

That was probably all a normal person would need to accept it, but for me, it had a "rehearsed" feel to it, and until I figured out the truth, I would trust no one in this pack.

Just like old times, since, apparently, my previous place of *pack punching bag* was the one part of my past I would never forget.

Chapter Two

My wolf ran in a frenzy for the first ten minutes, and just as I was feeling a sliver of positivity that she was gaining in energy, she crashed, stumbling forward until we ended up resting beneath a tree. My concern grew, and as I tried to search through her essence for a reason, I had to ask, *What's wrong?*

She whimpered, and there was weakness in her soul as I dug deeper into the bond between us. A howl spilled from us, and I wasn't sure which one of us had initiated it; my wolf soul had never felt more like a separate entity living inside of me as it did today. But truth be told, I'd only known this bond for a week, thanks to my stupid memory loss. Maybe it had always been like this...?

My wolf and I whimpered together, laying our head on crossed front paws, staying in solemn silence for a long time as we searched for peace.

It never came.

Instead, what did come was a huge wolf who was almost as annoying as Sisily. He casually strolled into view, and I had the sense he'd been watching me for some time, like the fucking stalker he was.

Sighing, I got to my feet, but I didn't shift back, not wanting to be naked with him.

The wolf's shiny midnight coat was longer than mine, making him almost shaggy in appearance, which didn't take away from how truly spectacular the new beta of Torma was.

Jaxson Heathcliff.

He used to be my best friend. I hadn't forgotten the way he'd been my rock for so many years, but that had all changed when my father died. Since then, we'd been enemies.

In the past week, I'd only seen him two times, and neither had ended well as I'd screamed about my memory loss and everyone hiding shit from me. He'd called me insane, and I'd repeatedly thought about ripping his throat out.

Speaking of, my wolf growled, spreading our legs into a better position to attack if needed.

Jaxson's wolf didn't care, ignoring my hostility as he bounced forward and nudged me. That was all my wolf needed to shut down our anger, as she nudged him back, wanting to play and frolic with her pack. Me holding us back from pack life was no doubt adding to her melancholy.

I'd never felt this dark and low before, not even during the worst of the pack's treatment. These depressive episodes were... like their own entity, and no matter how hard I worked to claw my way free, it sucked me under every day. It was even worse than when my father had died because at least then, I'd known why. I'd understood the grief.

Today, I understood nothing.

Jaxson tried to roll me over, and I forced my wolf down, sending another growl his way. The sound ripped from my chest with ferocity, and the beta backed off. I was the alpha-mate, but technically, my power came from Torin's position in the pack, not from my own wolf. As the beta, Jaxson only obeyed my will because he wanted to, not because I was more powerful.

Kind of bullshit if you asked me.

There was a swirl of magically charged energy in the air, and then Jaxson was on two feet, his black hair slightly tousled, as his dark eyes locked in on me. He stepped forward, his feet bare, along with the rest of the very impressive body attached to them. Tall and lanky, he was ripped in all the right places, but unlike the previous times I'd seen his body, I felt nothing but a cold emptiness inside. I was viewing him like I would Michaelangelos's statue of David. His form was nice, but it stirred no attraction within me.

With that in mind, I shifted back myself, making sure to keep a decent distance between us. "What do you want, Jaxson?"

He looked taken aback by the abrupt nature of my tone. "It's after five, babe. You know we have that mixer tonight."

My foot was swinging toward him before I thought about it, and the guy probably got an eyeful of vagina as I kicked him solidly in the chest. He flew backwards, which was... odd because I wasn't really strong enough to do that to a male of his size.

"Mera, what the fuck?" he shouted, already on his feet, not remotely injured. "What is wrong with you?"

"I don't know," I bit back through gritted teeth. "All I know is that calling me 'babe' is pissing me off. Stop doing it."

His eyes darkened, their deep rich coffee color reminding me of the old days. They were warm, like they used to be. Part of me wished that whoever had stolen my memories had also taken the ones from when my best friend had betrayed me. Maybe it would hurt less not knowing.

"You can't keep pushing us all away," Jaxson warned me.

Yeah, challenge accepted.

"I don't want to be disturbed."

He crossed his arms. "Tough shit, princess. You're our alpha-mate, and as such, you need to present a united front with Torin at these events."

I was gritting my teeth hard enough to crack them. "We aren't united."

It was clear that Jaxson was here for one purpose: to make sure I didn't make our pack look weak. That was a beta's job, of course, but if Torin was any sort of worthy mate, he'd be here sorting his own shit out.

Couldn't respect an alpha who allowed others to fight his battle.

"Please, Mera," Jaxson coaxed. "It's good for you to start getting back into pack life. It might help jog your memory. Remind you of happier times."

My first instinct was to snap that I had no damn "happy times" in this pack. I'd wanted to escape Torma for as long as I could remember, but somehow, during my missing memories, everyone else I'd cared about had fled, while I was still here.

Had I stayed for a reason? Why wouldn't I have left with Simone? Was it part of the reason she didn't want to talk to me?

It all just hurt, and I wanted it to stop. In truth, Jaxson did make one good point: My attitude was only creating more distance between me and the rest of Torma.

Maybe trying something new would shake me out of this dark mood. Books were masking the pain, but deep inside, I had been hurt. The need to figure out why and by whom was nearly destroying me.

"Okay," I said softly. "I'll be there tonight, and I'm going to make more of an effort to integrate back into pack life."

Those words tasted like ash on my tongue, but before I could second-guess my new life plan, I called on my wolf to shift back. Only she never rose to the surface, instead sinking lower inside until I could barely feel her. I knew my eyes were wide and panicked when I lifted them to Jaxson.

He took a step closer, his face scrunched in concern as he ran his gaze over me. "What is it, Mera? What's wrong?"

Should I confide in him? Truly confide? I had no one else to talk to here, and Jaxson at least had been a good friend to me in the past, which didn't negate the following years where he'd basically acted like an asshole. But I was desperate.

"I think the Shadow Beast did something to me."

He jerked his head, and it was clear that was the last thing he'd expected to come out of my mouth. "What do you mean? When did you see the Shadow Beast?"

I shook my head. "You know I don't remember the time that he punished us all, but I must have been there, right? You all said I was there. What if, during that time, I annoyed him too, and this is the extra punishment I got?"

Jaxson shook his head. "You were there, but you didn't go near him at all. Victor was punished first, and then the rest of us were locked down until he could 'deal with us,' as he put it. You were not on his radar for even a second, Mera."

"Who else would have the power to take my memories like this?" I snapped back. "I'm a freaking wolf shifter—we heal head injuries—so it has to be magic!" I paused, realizing that for the first time, there was new information I hadn't heard already. "What do you mean *deal with us*? Has he dealt with us in any way except releasing the stasis?"

Jaxson blinked at me before shaking his head. "Actually, no, and until you mentioned it right now, I didn't think anything of it..."

My breath started to rattle in and out of my mouth in gasps. "What if *I* was the part he dealt with? What if it was me?"

Jaxson reached for me, but I stepped out of his way, not wanting to be touched. "Mera," he said, shaking his head. "I think you need to calm down. I don't know why you're stressing so hard on this. Even if you did lose a few months, what does it matter? It's sixty days. Nothing happened in that time that would impact you, outside of mating to Torin, and you still have the rest of your life with him. If that was the only punishment, then be grateful and move on."

I shook my head. "You know I can't. It doesn't matter how easy that life would be, I cannot let this rest. Someone stole from me, and I want those damn memories back."

He took another step forward, and I fought the urge to wrap my arms protectively around myself. I'd never been weirded out by naked men before—shifters were always in various states of undress—

but ever since I'd "woken" in Torin's bed, I'd avoided being around the men while naked.

It felt disloyal.

But to whom? Definitely not my "mate," since the strongest emotion I held for him was hate.

"Why do I hate Torin?"

The question was more for me than Jaxson, but he answered anyway.

"Disregarding the years we didn't treat you right," he said shifting uncomfortably, "rejecting a true mate is a near unforgiveable crime. He has a lot of ground to make up if he wants to be worthy of you." As he stared into the forests that surrounded us, a sigh left him. "You probably don't remember, but when I found out he was your true mate, I didn't take it well. I'd thought it would be me. I hoped it would be, and then no one could keep us apart, not even my father—"

My bitter laugh interrupted him. "You keep making these little comments. Alluding to Dean Heathcliff being the sole reason that we're no longer best friends. Shifter up and own your fuckups, Jax! *You* treated me like shit. *You* hurt and ignored and bullied me. Dean, the evil fuck, wasn't important to me. You were. And you let me down."

His curse was loud enough to echo through the forest and slam back into us. "I was a damn kid! My father is a brutal, unforgiving sort of man. I did the best I could. If I was tormenting you, then he wouldn't be, and trust me, his hit is a lot fucking harder than mine."

My next lament died on my tongue. I'd heard lots of rumors about how Dean treated his family, but this was the first time Jaxson had put it so bluntly. Still, it had been too many years. Too many hurts. My pain was buried deep.

"You should have come up with a better way," I said softly, my voice vibrating with the hurt that was always lingering below the surface. "We could have done it together. If I'd known what was happening to you, I would have tried to understand. You cut me out in all ways, and I can't forgive you."

I turned to walk away since I had a long hike back without my wolf's speed.

"Mera!" Jaxson called, and I paused but didn't turn. "Let's go back to what we used to be, please. I know you're hurt, but you have a forgiving heart."

His words burned like acid in my soul. "Sorry, Jax." I still didn't turn. "You don't know me as well as you think. I'm not really the forgive-and-forget type."

Not anymore.

This time when I walked away, he didn't stop me.

Chapter Three

The wolf mixer was in full swing by the time I made it to my apartment, got dressed in the only half-decent outfit I had, and returned to the pack lands. Torin's house was filled with alphas from many of the other packs, as well as a decent selection of single shifters who were all hoping to find a true mate tonight.

If only they knew.

Despite my reluctance in having anything to do with being alphamate, Torin had assigned me more than a few tasks in relation to this little soirée. Most of them involved liaising with other packs' alphamates in regards to the guest list, décor, and food. I'd ignored every request to assist, of course, and I had no idea who'd stepped in to take up the slack. Probably Sisily. I sensed she was still fucking my mate— oh, sorry, *taking care of his needs because his mate was neglecting him*, and I really wasn't mad about it.

As long as someone kept him busy, it didn't have to be me.

My silver sequined dress swished around my boring silver heels as I descended the stairs into the ballroom. It was awash in soft lighting, with strands of fairy lights above and candles on the ground level.

Everything was tastefully done, with gold and silver as the main theme.

Heavy gold curtains were pulled back on the multi-pane windows, showcasing spectacular views of the pack lands, along with an outdoor area for more of the packs to mingle in. We would literally have so many here tonight—the meeting of the decade—that not all of them would fit inside our massive ballroom.

"Mera," Torin said, appearing at the bottom of the stairs, wearing a perfectly fitted black tux. He ran a hand through his dark hair, shaking his head as his awestruck gaze lifted to meet mine. "You look absolutely stunning."

I forced a smile, glancing down at my outfit. The dress had been my mother's; it had sat unused in her wardrobe after my dad had been killed, since she'd had no more balls or mixers to go to. It was modestly cut, with a skinny-strapped top that fell into a slinky silver length, trailing longer behind than at the front. Not really my style, but for this, it worked.

"Thank you," I told him, wishing he would stop looking at me the way he was. Despite the connection I felt between us, his heated stare made my skin crawl.

"Are you ready?" he asked, holding his hand out to me.

I didn't want to take it, but Jaxson's words reverberated through my mind, and even worse, the beta himself was across the room watching me with the same laser focus as Torin. They both needed me to act the part tonight, present a strong, united front, and I was going to give it at least a thirty percent try.

"Touch me anywhere except my hand," I muttered to Torin from beneath a fake smile, "and I will make you wish you could reject me again."

He grimaced, swallowing hard, but didn't argue as he took my hand into his much larger one. I forced my smile to remain in place, even as a vision of ripping my shoe off and stabbing him through the chest with the stiletto heel flickered briefly through my mind.

No doubt I needed anger management help, but if that was the case, there was only one pack to blame for that. They were finally reaping what they'd sowed.

When we stepped out onto the main floor, lots of faces turned our way, nodding respectfully, but it wasn't crowded yet, allowing us to walk uninterrupted. Which, unfortunately, gave Torin time to talk to me.

"At what point are you going to let go of your virgin status?" he asked bluntly—and kind of rudely, since this wasn't really the time or place for a damn sex talk.

But hey, I wasn't shy, and if he wanted to hash it out tonight, then he was about to get some real talk. "I'll never give my body to a shifter until I think they're worthy of it," I said just as bluntly as the alpha. He opened his mouth, and I cut him off. "That doesn't mean I hold myself above anyone else, because I don't. What it does mean is I have a hand and a vibrator, and if getting off was my sole aim, it's more than covered. With sex... I want a bond and a connection. I want mutual fucking respect. I really don't think that's too much to ask."

His head jerked as he took a quick, frantic look around in the worry other shifters had heard my words. Apparently, this was personal business he wanted kept secret, and yet he was the one who'd brought it up here.

Dickhead.

"You always have to fight everything," Torin finally said when he was satisfied that no one had overheard. "Even when we were children, you could never just let it be. Always picking at issues. Digging deeper. Sticking your nose where it didn't belong, which is clearly a family trait. It got your father into trouble, and I just don't want to see you going down the same path. We're mated. That's not changing. I just need to feel a deeper connection with you."

Translation: My "dick" needs a deeper connection with you. Eye fucking roll.

More important than his poor "neglected" penis was the mention of my father. Lockhart Callahan had destroyed my entire life when he'd attacked Alpha Victor, a crime he'd been executed for. But at least his punishment had been over immediately, unlike my mother's and mine.

"Tell me what caused my father to attack Victor," I said suddenly.

For years, I'd never questioned that day—I'd asked Jaxson and Torin one time when I'd been younger, and they'd deterred me from ever trying again by leaving me locked in a prison cell for two days. I'd nearly died from dehydration since I hadn't had my wolf to call back then.

My hatred for the pair should come as no surprise to either of them.

Torin's face paled. "You have to stop digging into the past, Mera. You just have to stop. I don't even know what happened, and I'm pretty sure the only shifters who do are dead. Whatever bad blood was between Lockhart and my father, it died with them. Let's leave it there."

My lips tilted into my fakest smile yet. "Of course, dear. Whatever you say."

Torin was just lucky I was too lazy to reach down for my heel. Because that brief thought I'd had earlier was about to turn into a premonition.

At this point, the bulk of the guests came in from the outside, so our conversation was cut short as we greeted them. The rest of the evening was one of non-stop socializing and talking pack bullshit. The amount of times I wished I'd smuggled a book in here with me so I could escape and read in a corner was about the same number of times I had to gush about Torin, acting like he was the next coming of the Shadow Beast because he'd "saved us" after the dark years we'd been punished.

I loved the way no one mentioned the fact that it was Victor who'd created the need to be punished in the first place. Apparently, only Callahans would be vilified for the sins of their father.

My mood lifted when five true mate bonds were discovered, one right in front of me between two females from Southern and

Northern Californian packs. They'd been so close to each other all that time and hadn't known. I loved that true mate bonds knew no sex or race; it was truly about who was the most perfect fit for your soul. At least I hoped it still was. Torin and I had to be the exception, right? At one time, I had truly believed in the magic of these bonds, and I couldn't quite let go of that, not even today.

Halfway through the evening, I excused myself to use the bathroom, and once I was done, I didn't bother to find Torin again, instead choosing to head outside for a moment in the fresh air.

When the cool breeze hit my face, a fraction of the tension crushing my spirit faded, and I briefly closed my eyes to appreciate the moment of serenity. I scented the shifter a second before I opened my eyes, only just managing not to run into him.

"Sorry!" I said in a rush, taking a step back from the tall man who was not from Torma.

He had dark skin and eyes and looked to be of Asian descent. He could be an alpha or beta from any number of the packs, though, and since I'd taken no time to really learn about the other leaders, I was going to have to try to figure it out by chatting with him.

"Apologies," he said in a deep, pleasant voice. "I don't speak English."

I just stared at him. "You speak perfect English, actually," I said, arching my eyebrows at this peculiar conversation. "I would have guessed you were a native speaker."

His eyes widened, and there was a wariness in the depths as I felt his wolf shifting in his energy. I'd clearly said something to alarm him. "What game are you playing?" he finally bit out.

Now it was my turn to be on the defensive, but unlike him, my lethargic wolf was barely noticeable. "I'm playing no games, sir. Just merely commenting. Now if you'll excuse me, I'm in search of a moment alone."

I turned and walked off, glancing back just one time to see him staring after me, his face creased in suspicion. Seriously, that had been some of the weirdest shit ever, but I already had too much to deal with to worry about it any longer.

"Mera!"

The shout stopped me before I made it into the trees, and I gritted my teeth, unable to keep up a fake smile any longer. Turning, I waited for Jaxson to interrupt me for the second time that day.

"Did I just see you talking to Alpha Dai?" he asked as he hurried up.

My eyes flicked around him to where the other man had been. "Alpha Dai?"

Jaxson nodded. "Yeah, he's from the Tokyo pack, visiting America with some of his members. I just thought it odd because he doesn't speak English, and I know you failed out of Japanese in school."

My eyes narrowed on him as I sorted through my confusion. "He spoke perfect English. If this is a joke between the two of you, it's a really fucking bad one."

Jaxson didn't smile or laugh, and I could have sworn he was as confused as I was. "No joke, Meers. He requires a translator whenever he comes to these things."

He pulled out his phone and pressed a few buttons before the alpha dossier appeared on the screen. Scrolling through the many packs and various details about their members, he finally stopped at the International contingent. Sure enough, right there in black and white was *Alpha Dai, requires full translator*.

"Uh..." I mean, what was I supposed to say to that? "Maybe it wasn't him. I mean, there's no other reasonable explanation, right? Except if I secretly learned Japanese in the two months of memory loss time, all the while keeping it exceptionally well-hidden from everyone who knows me."

I was being sarcastic, but Jaxson didn't even crack a smile. Lifting his phone, he pressed a few buttons before I heard it start to ring. A familiar voice answered in a gruff *"What?"* on the other end.

"Something is up with Mera," Jaxson told Torin. "Get outside and bring Alpha Dai with you."

After he hung up, I resisted the urge to run before my moron of a mate showed up here. It was only the small part of me curious to see if this was all a misunderstanding or not that had me staying put.

Jaxson and I existed in an awkward silence while we waited, and even though he attempted to break it a few times with small talk, I ignored him, staring toward the pack house.

As soon as Torin and Alpha Dai walked out, I went to them.

"Are you okay?" Torin asked when we were close, a look of concern on his face. "I might just kill Jaxson if he keeps up with these vague cryptic messages about my mate."

As he wrapped an arm around me and pulled me close, I tried to figure out why his touch was so abhorrent. Torin was giving me everything I'd ever wanted in this world, a true pack and family life... and it felt so damn wrong.

Leaning forward so that his arm would fall off me, I smiled at Alpha Dai. "Did you speak English to me before?"

The alpha tilted his head, and again he wore a super confused look. "You're speaking Japanese," he said, in what sounded like perfect English.

Switching gears, I faced Jaxson, whom, despite everything, I still tolerated better than Torin. "Did I speak Japanese?"

Jaxson nodded. "Yeah, sounded like it to me."

"See," I said, turning back, only to shake my head and side-eye my oldest friend. "Sorry, what? I spoke Japanese?"

I knew Japanese? Had I actually learned it during my two months of memory loss? As I pressed into that thought, the familiar sharp pain in my head jabbed harder than usual. "How is that possible?" I mumbled through the pain. "I did one semester in school! The extent of my Japanese is *Konnichiwa* and *Ohayou gozaimasu!*"

Alpha Dai blinked. "When you said that, you sounded like an American trying to butcher my language, but before, you spoke to me in perfect Japanese. Like it's your natural language."

"Nope." I shook my head. "Nope. I cannot handle this, I'm sorry."

Before anyone could say another word, I spun on the spot and took off into the trees, desperately craving an escape.

"Mera!" Torin bellowed after me, but I didn't turn back.

The one advantage to tonight's event was that Torin was required to be present and converse with all the alphas. Especially since he was so new to this role; it was more important than ever to establish us back in the pack hierarchies and foster new friendships.

Duty first. Which gave me exactly what I needed: time to escape.

Only someone did come after me, the crashing of bushes and trees loud behind me, as I tore through the forest.

I didn't turn back, though.

If they wanted me, they would have to catch me.

Chapter Four

After a few minutes of free running as fast as I could, with no thought to direction or destination, my wolf finally rose up to lend me some of her speed and strength. My heels disappeared soon after, and I took a second to lean down and tear the train off my dress.

From there, I was sprinting with the wind at my back and the moon shining light on me from above. A howl rocketed up through my chest to escape my lips as I tilted my head back.

There were days I would never exchange this gift of having a wolf soul and supernatural abilities for anything.

"Mera!"

Why the hell was Jaxson always shouting my fucking name? And always with a command in his tone. Unfortunately for his arrogant ass, I was done taking orders from anyone. Even orders silently given in a single word.

I ran faster. And faster.

The trees whipped by as I released the anxiety and stress that had been eating at me for days.

It had just been too damn long living like this, broken, wallowing through the darkness in my head. I needed to rise above it. I needed to be... more?

Words started to form in my mind, familiar words, and as they unfurled, I saw them as if they were literally being written in front of me.

From the darkness, the phoen—

The pain hit me harder than ever, and I hadn't been ready for it this time, my feet tripping over nothing as my brain spasmed violently. Slamming into a tree at that speed sent me flying into the air before I tumbled down a small embankment.

By the time I came to a stop, I was bloody and beaten, the dress nothing more than tatters.

"Mera, shit, are you okay?" Jaxson asked, his voice coming from above me.

I couldn't see him, of course, since I was too busy trying to lift myself up off the tree branch impaled through my right shoulder.

"Stay right there," he said. "I'll be down to help in about fifteen seconds."

Literal bastard was there in fifteen on the dot, helping me tear myself free from the tree. It hurt like a fucking bitch, and I barely managed not to cry out as I waited for shifter healing to kick in and the pain to ease.

"What the hell were you thinking?" Jaxson growled, and it seemed less impressive than what I remembered. "You're a shifter, but that doesn't make you invincible. You can die, Mera, and then what are the rest of us supposed to do?"

A derisive snort escaped me. "Celebrate. You've been trying to kill me off for years; at this stage, you should be grateful that I'm taking myself out. Might be the only way you'll succeed."

The wound in my arm was finally knitting closed, which was no doubt why Jaxson felt entitled to *shake the ever-loving shit out of me.* "Mera, this is not a joke. You're important to a lot of people and I need you to stop acting like a maniac for one minute. I need you to look after yourself."

His words snapped something inside of me. "If I'm so damn important, then where the hell is my mom? Where is Simone? Are you trying to tell me that both of them took off the moment we were finally free of our punishment? What sort of moron would believe that? It's not even a decent cover story. Firstly, my mom is broke and drunk all the time. Secondly, Simone and I planned to leave Torma together."

"Yeah, but you're the alpha-mate now," Jaxson said. "You can't leave, and she has dreams that don't include you."

That stung much more than the branch through my arm.

I mean, I wasn't completely self-involved; I knew Simone had a life outside of me. It just didn't sit right with me that she was completely uncontactable. "She wouldn't go this long without calling me," I finally said. "She just wouldn't. I've phoned dozens of times and texted just as many, and there's never any reply. You know how much she loves her phone. The thing is never out of her hand!"

Jaxson finally started to pay attention to what I was saying. "It's really bothering you, isn't it?"

Fuck, I wanted to punch his stupid face. "*Of course* it freaking is. Are you kidding me right now?"

He ignored that, nodding a few times as if he was sorting it all out in his head. "Tomorrow I'll speak to her parents and find out exactly how they're talking with her. She's required to be contactable, so it won't even be an odd request. How does that sound?"

I wanted to growl. "It sounds like you're patronizing me, but in the small hope you discover something important, I would really appreciate you putting in maximum effort to find her."

And if she was just drunk and shacked up with some man or woman in Bora Bora, I'd laugh at my paranoia while being super happy she was alive. Until I knew for sure, though, I couldn't stop worrying.

"And your mom," Jaxson continued, even though I'd already forgotten about her. Not that it wasn't concerning, but her absence was basically the constant in my life. "Torin has not been that good at keeping track of shifters who leave Torma, but the last record of Lucinda was that she'd been given permission to leave with Alpha Shaw from the Alikta pack in Idaho. I'm sure she'll surface again when he gets sick of her."

I snorted, finally able to move my arms freely, as the last of my injuries healed. "Yeah, sounds a lot like her." Getting permission to leave Torma was a hell of a lot easier under Torin than it had been with Victor. Of course, as per my usual luck, it was too late for that to be of use to me. Especially since I was the damn alpha-mate.

"Come on," Jaxson said, attempting to capture my arm so he could lift me from the ravine. I didn't need his help, though, so I shook him off.

Once we were out of the ditch and back on the main path, the unanswered questions in my head churned harder than ever at me. What had caused my brain to near explode, sending me into the ravine? Had it been those words in my head?

I tried to think about that phrase again, and before I even got three words in, pain slammed into me. Pressing my hands briefly to my temples, I breathed through the stabbing sensation, only able to relax when it faded away. And it only faded when I stopped trying to recall the complete sentence.

It seemed those words were connected to the missing parts of my life. Parts someone did not want me to uncover, but all they were doing was increasing my need to figure it all out.

Someone out there knew the truth. Even if that someone wasn't Torin, there were plenty of other shifters in Torma, and my brain was not going to let me rest until I questioned every single member of the pack.

"You're doing it again," Jaxson said, cutting into my thoughts. "Disappearing into your mind. I've never seen you quite like this in our twenty-plus years of friendship."

I blinked at him, forcing myself to focus on him. *Twenty years?* Yeah, okay pal. More like ten and then we were solid enemies.

"Memories were stolen from me," I bit out. "I can't let it rest, Jax.

I know you've told me to just enjoy my blessings and position of prestige in the pack, but it's—"

"Not in your nature," he finished for me. "Yeah, I know. And... I think it's best if I stop hindering you and start trying to help you. Maybe together we can unravel what caused your memory loss, and then you can finally be happy. Do you want me to speak with every pack member I run into and see if any of them remember anything odd happening around you in the last few months?"

To have him finally step up and support me, gave me a bizarre sense of being part of a pack. The moment I had that thought, a weird flutter hit my chest, followed by an itch on my hand. The combination of the two was so odd that I paused, staring down at my unmarked hand. It felt like bugs were crawling all over it, but they clearly weren't.

"Are you okay?" Jaxson asked, noticing my newest confusion.

I shook my head. "I'm not sure... I just... Your support gave me this feeling of really being part of the pack." A bitter laugh escaped me, for obvious reasons. "At the same time, there was also this unnatural flutter in my chest, and my palm is super itchy."

It sounded even stupider said out loud, and I briefly considered learning to keep the weird thoughts inside my mind, where they belonged.

Jaxson dropped a heavy hand on my shoulder. "You're my pack, Mera. You always have been, and if fate wasn't such a bitch, you'd have been my mate too. I made so many fucking mistakes in how I treated you, but I promise that in my own way, my moronic adolescent brain thought it was keeping you safe from my dad."

I shrugged him off. "Why haven't you killed Dean? I mean, after everything he did to you." And me, if I were being honest. Actually... "I should kill Dean. I'm almost certain that he needs to die for the future safety of myself and other pack members."

Jaxson shook his head, nudging me to keep walking. "While that's very true, you know you can't kill him without reason. You'll have half the pack turning on you."

27

"I could challenge him."

He nudged me again, and if he did it one more time, I was going to practice my murder skills on the son as a warmup for the father.

"You can only challenge for a higher position, and he's beneath you," Jaxson reminded me.

Ah, fuck. Jaxson was right, quoting a rule that had been set in place to protect the weaker pack members. I had no issue with the rule, but it did mean my hands were tied when it came to killing Dean without provocation. And he'd be very careful about upsetting me, now that I was alpha-mate.

I'd think of something, though, or more likely, the former beta would screw up and let his evil side out again. Then I'd have full rights to rip his head from his body.

It was really the least he deserved.

Chapter Five

By the time we made it back to Torma, we weren't talking, but somehow I felt closer to Jaxson than I had in a long time. His offer to help with both Simone and my memory loss was apparently the olive branch I'd been waiting for, to step forward and try to rebuild a semblance of a friendship.

It would take time. Years, if I knew myself at all, but a step forward was a step in the right direction.

Chatter and laughter blasted into us as we arrived on the edge of the cleared pack lands. The wolf mixer was still in full force. My palm itched again, and I rubbed it against the tattered remains of my dress, forcing myself not to think about this weird new development. Had I hit some undiscovered species of plant that shifters were allergic to?

I mean, odder shit had happened, right?

As we stepped into the light, no one even glanced twice at us emerging a little beaten up and dirty. They'd just assume I'd half-shifted and busted my dress, and that we'd been running through the forest. Shifters were often in a state of disarray. Such was the nature of the beast.

29

"I'm probably going to head out," I said to Jaxson, rubbing my palm against the torn side of my dress again. "I think I've had my fill of duty for the night."

Before he could reply, Torin appeared.

I must have let out an annoyed groan under my breath because Jaxson shot me a warning look. Yeah, it probably wasn't normal to detest the sight of your true mate, but despite the connection I felt through our bond, most of me hated his guts. Our mystical bond was not Torin's ticket to a life with me, especially not after the way he'd treated me. Now he had to earn my body, soul, and love.

No woman should settle for less than that.

"Where have you two been?" Torin asked, and his words were clipped as he ran his eyes over what remained of my dress and the traces of blood on it.

"For a run—"

"None of your fucking business," I snapped over the top of Jaxson, who, as always, thought he needed to baby his alpha. "You don't own me. Ask me a question in that tone again and I'll rip your face off... and smile about it."

Torin's eyes darkened, and unfortunately, my words had the opposite effect of my intentions. He took a step closer, and I could tell he wanted to drag me by my hair into his room and finally divest me of my virginity. Once again treating me like I was a damn possession he owned.

"I like your fire, Mera," he rumbled, his eyes wolfing out as he reached for me.

Ducking under his hand, I shot my fist straight into his gut, sending him back more than a couple of steps. "You don't get to touch me." My words were soft and cold, and I knew we were drawing a lot of attention. Not a surprise, since I'd just punched the alpha, doing exactly what Jaxson had warned me against.

I was too far gone to stop now, though. "I'm not your property, and true mate or not, you haven't earned the right to me or my body. Remember that."

Spinning on one bare foot, I stormed away, not glancing back once, despite the gaze I felt burning along my spine. Luckily, I didn't have to worry about whatever Torin was planning because I was distracted by another flutter in my chest and the itching on my palm.

At this rate, I was going to tear my skin off before I got back to my crappy old apartment—

"You're hurting him, you know." Sisily's voice jerked me out of my angry march when I was about halfway into town.

How in all the fucks had she crept up on me like that? I really needed to get out of my own head before I got ambushed; I was rusty at protecting myself these days. One slip up could be a death sentence, and I would not give them the satisfaction.

"Excuse me?"

Even a moron with half a brain knew that "excuse me" delivered in that tone really meant, *What the actual fuck did you just say to me?*

Sisily though, who was apparently swimming in the less-than-half-a-brain category, took me literally, speaking up. "I said you're hurting him. Torin. Making him look weak in front of everyone."

I was laughing before she even finished, gut-hurting laughter that in no way spoke of me being amused. Darkness descended over my vision; Sisily had picked a really bad time to bring this shit up. She looked taken aback as the laughter died in my throat and I took a step toward her. Whatever she saw in my face had her own falling into terrified lines, and with a brief squeak, she turned and sprinted away like her tail was on fire.

I wanted to follow her, but again, I couldn't hurt a lesser member of the pack without reason, and her trying to defend her alpha was no reason. Her words had hit me deep, though, bringing up every memory of how much Torin used to hurt me, with his harsh words and heavy hands, with his dismissiveness and lack of protection against his father. Everyone in this pack had turned a blind eye to Victor's treatment of my mom and me.

And now I was supposed to be their alpha-mate?

None of them deserved me. Maybe that was my current issue...

my current anger. I was alpha-mate to a pack that I wished didn't exist... and I couldn't pretend to half-ass this role for much longer. Once I got to the bottom of this mystery about my memory and what had caused Torma to lose a few years of life to the Shadow Beast, then I would leave this pack behind and forge a new path. One hopefully with Simone in it.

By the time I made it back to the apartment, a plan had started to form in my head.

I'd take Jaxson up on that suggestion of interviewing members of the pack, starting with the higher-ranked ones. Someone had information and even the most insignificant fact could help.

I also wanted to get to the bottom of why my father had attacked Victor all those years ago. I'd always assumed it had been some sort of jealous lover shit to do with Glendra, Victor's mate, who was notorious for stirring the male ego and temper, but maybe there had been more to it.

I was finally in a position to push for answers; only Torin could stop me in this quest, and if that fucker knew what was good for him, he'd carefully consider all moves made around me.

Just like on a chess board, the queen ruled everything.

He'd made a mistake in revoking the rejection because I was the fucking queen here, and I would sacrifice them all to learn my truth.

Chapter Six

At some point through the night, in the middle of my angry musing and plan making, I wrote my six objectives down and left them on the notepad beside my bed so they'd be the first thing I saw upon waking.

1. *Figure out what happened to me in the two months my memory was wiped.*
2. *Search out the catalyst for my father attacking the alpha.*
3. *Determine if Simone is safe and proceed to yell at her for worrying me.*
4. *Find out exactly why the Shadow Beast cursed us to lose time. Did it impact all the packs or only Torma? And why is no one more concerned by this abuse of power?*
5. *Make sure Lucinda Callahan, a.k.a. Mom, is alive and shacked up with an alpha. Then forget about her as solidly as she's always forgotten about me.*
6. *Figure out why my heart is fluttering and palm itching.*

I had zero explanation for number six, my skin showing no signs of any irritation except for the marks from where I'd near scratched it to the bone. In regard to the flutter in my chest. Dr. Google was sure it was an early sign of a heart murmur or impending heart attack, but of course, those were human symptoms. In the preternatural sense, I had nothing.

When I eventually fell into a restless sleep, I tossed and turned through the night, until eventually I woke panting and crying out. The heart flutter and itchy palm was gone, only to be replaced with skin that felt like it was on fire. I ran my hands across my body, letting out a low moan as my overactive sex drive kicked into gear. I slid my fingers into my panties, only... every time I tried to touch my aching pussy, I couldn't quite reach the spot desperate for relief.

Mine!

It was a growl of a word, and it jerked me from my half-sleep so fast that when I sat up, my head spun. I quickly looked around to determine that I was still alone, ragged bedroom furniture my only companions.

As I moved to the edge of my bed, the throbbing ache between my thighs deepened. In desperation, I staggered into the shower and cranked the water on as hard as it could go. Sinking into the small stall, I let the cold stream wash over me. I tried to bring myself to orgasm again, but again, no matter how much my fingers scraped over my clit, I couldn't get close enough to do what needed to be done.

Any drowsiness I felt disappeared the moment I found myself clit-blocked by an invisible entity. "What the fuck?" I muttered, staring down in confusion. It was almost as if there was a barrier on my fucking vagina, and yet the water was hitting it fine...

I let my thighs fall open farther, the beat of the water landing right where I needed it, the chill almost sending me up the wall as it cooled my heated flesh. Soon I was moaning, the swirls of arousals so strong that I was near clawing the tiles in need.

"Holy fuck, Shadow Beast." I cursed and cried out as an orgasm slammed into me.

Why I'd called out to the damn devil of shifters, I had no idea; it had just slipped out in that moment of release. I supposed if anyone was to thank for the pleasure a body could have, it was the one who'd created our race of beings. *Thank you for the clit, Shadow Beast.*

Oh, and the G-spot.

Dude deserved an award of some description. Even if he was the one currently messing with my memories.

As I came down from the high of my orgasm, I reached up and adjusted the temperature, wondering where to slot this additional *what the actual fuck* moment in my life.

I couldn't touch myself.

When had that even happened? I mean, I hadn't tried since waking in Torin's bed because I'd been somewhat preoccupied with the missing months of my life, but my natural horniness was always going to rear its head sooner rather than later, and it seemed that I had another point to add to my list.

7. *Kill the motherfucker who decided I couldn't touch myself to bring pleasure.*

If there was one thing I hated more than any other, it was the loss of my free will. No one was allowed to dictate what I did with my body. If this was thanks to whoever had stolen my memories, be it the Shadow Beast or someone else, I would be merciless when I found them.

By the time I dragged my ass out of the shower, I felt wrecked, but with determination filling my soul, I pushed through. Once I was dressed, I checked my phone, praying that somehow Simone had left me a message during the night.

Twenty text messages blinked at me, along with five or six voice-mails. When I flicked through, half were from Torin and half from Jaxson. Checking in with me. Asking if I got home safely. Chewing me out for leaving the mixer without saying goodbye to the alphas.

I deleted them all and their voice messages without even bothering to listen. I was acting like an asshole, I was well aware of that, but... fuck them. Especially Torin. He didn't deserve my forgiveness.

I always thought the heroines in books I read were far too lenient with the alpha males. They never made those bastards work for the right to be part of their lives, letting their hormones do the thinking instead of their brains.

I would not just be forgiving and forgetting all the years of bull-shit and torment I'd gone through. They owed me at least ten years of their changed attitudes before I'd consider it, and while Jaxson had taken the first step, Torin was not even in the race yet.

Pushing those two assholes from my mind, I left the apartment and headed toward town. Torma really only had one main section of shops, and since I hadn't ventured this way since waking without my memories, I decided it was the perfect place to start my investigation. The main street was well known for its gossip.

As I walked, the heat beat down on me despite the early hour—it was going to be a scorcher today. Our elevation was high enough here that we often escaped the worst of the temps, and considering it was only spring, clearly, the weather was as pissed off as I was.

At least I'd chosen wisely in the clothing department, wearing cutoff denim shorts, a black tank, and flipflops. I'd also gone with the zero makeup mom-bun look, which was the easiest way to tame the absolute mess of hair I had going on. I wasn't sure when it had happened, but my hair was acting as strange as my life, channeling Rapunzel so that it was twice as thick as normal, not to mention down past my ass.

Torin wanted me to cut it. He'd mentioned more than once that my hair was a little out of control, so, of course, I took great pleasure in canceling every appointment he made with our local hairdresser. The fucking arrogance of that alpha, thinking he could dictate the length of my hair. Thanks to his archaic attitude, I would see the ends literally drag on the ground before I cut it to please him. Yep, there I went, showing him the one thing that truly controlled me.

My pride.

As I got closer to town, the foot and car traffic picked up, and every shifter who passed me waved and called out a greeting. My first instinct when pack members came close to me was to make myself small and get off the main path. A survival instinct that I'd no doubt never get rid of. Torma was a trigger for me, holding so many memories that I wished I'd lost. At least I had a plan now to escape; I just had a few little issues to clear up first.

When I reached the street, I stopped at the first shop: Baked Buns. It was a fantastic little bakery that had old-school red brick across its frontage and huge woodfire ovens lining the back walls, so everyone could see the delicious treats baking.

When I stepped through the door, the scents near killed me as my stomach grumbled and growled. Normally, I'd never have the money to spend on treats, not even as the alpha-mate because I refused to accept any of Torin's "support." But thankfully, during one of my tiny little rage-blackouts in my mom's apartment when I'd trashed a bunch of shit, I'd found a packet of cash in an old cushion. Must have been one of my hiding places that I'd forgotten about.

Wherever it had come from, I was now cashed up enough to buy myself a nice pastry for breakfast.

"Good morning, alpha-mate," Brenda, the cheery owner, said as she bustled out to take my order. "We're so blessed to have you in our store today."

Bleh. There went my appetite as an old memory assaulted me. When I'd been about twelve, this bitch had watched with a callous expression as a group of shifters had kicked the shit out of me in the field behind her house, on the east side of Torma. At the time, I hadn't blamed her for not wanting to get involved, but even when she'd hurried off, no help had ever arrived for me. She hadn't told anyone, and that was what I wouldn't forgive.

At that age, I'd been lucky not to get raped; I was fairly certain it was only Jaxson and Torin putting their foot down that had stopped it from happening. I probably owed them for that.

Whatever.

"Brenda, hey," I said to the petite brunette, forcing the dark memories down.

She leaned forward against her front cabinet, all of five feet, petite and pretty. Despite being at least fifty years old, she didn't look much older than me. Her mate was an enforcer, their two-year-old twins absolutely adorable.

She lived the life I'd always wished I could, but now that I was here, it just tasted bitter.

"I'll grab a jam tart, two of the apricot pastries, and a small jar of chocolate sauce," I said, my voice quieter than I'd wanted it to be. Pushing the memories down only got me so far, and both my face and voice acted as mood rings in these situations.

She nodded before hurrying off to package everything up. As she bustled around, I wandered along the cold display, deciding to take advantage of the empty shop. "I have a few questions for you," I called out. "If that's okay."

"Of course," she said instantly, her voice still light and open.

That would probably change the moment she heard my topic of conversation.

"I'm trying to gather information about what happened in Torma after we woke from our stasis punishment. With my memory loss, I'm worried that I've missed something important."

Her head jerked up from where she was sliding a pastry into a white paper bag.

"Has Torin not said anything?" she asked breathlessly, her dark grey eyes wide and shiny. "I mean, he's your true mate, right?"

I shot her back my best fake smile. The one that said we were old friends and confidantes, and she should feel secure in sharing all of her secrets with me. "Of course, Torin and I have discussed it in detail, but he remembers nothing of significance and suggested that I question a few of the more upstanding citizens in the pack. In the hopes that from another perspective, there might be more information out there."

Dropping Torin's name burned my tongue, but I legitimately

wasn't above using his position in the pack to get the answers I needed. I had to get out of Torma soon, before Torin forced his will on me, but I couldn't leave until the mystery was solved.

Someone had fucked with me and I was determined to find out who.

Chapter Seven

Brenda's movements didn't suggest she was panicked by my question, but I felt her unease. The only things that had stopped her from brushing me off, in the hope of avoiding an uncomfortable topic, were my words about Torin encouraging this. No one wanted to go against the alpha.

"In all honesty," she said softly, "I haven't really seen you in town since we were brought back from our stasis. We all figured that you were dealing with your bond, learning how to be alpha-mate."

I paused. "Torin has only been an alpha of Torma for what... two months? Wouldn't he be learning it too?"

She blinked. "It feels so much longer, but yes, I suppose that is correct. No doubt the many years under Victor acclimated him to the role much faster."

The look on her face told me that she really hadn't stopped to think about it, just going about her daily life for the last two months without questioning how the fuck we'd all been frozen for years.

How had none of them lost their minds too at the thought that the world around us had continued moving while we'd stayed the same? In stasis. Vulnerable to any who'd wanted to hurt us.

When I asked Brenda a condensed version of that, she shrugged. "Most of us never leave Torma anyway. And what's two years when we live hundreds? We celebrated the release of our punishment, and now we live our lives. You should just be happy with your gifts, Mera. You're our beloved alpha-mate, and through a quirk in fate, the sins of your family were wiped away in a single instant."

My jaw ached at how hard my teeth were clenched. Everyone was feeding me the same line. *Be happy with what you have; don't worry about the past; move forward and enjoy your newfound popularity.*

I could tell they thought I was being an ungrateful brat who just couldn't stop poking and prodding at the fabric of our pack. But, seriously, there was something majorly wrong here. I felt it so deep inside that it was butting heads with my DNA.

A few other shifters entered her shop then, and I wasn't able to interrogate Brenda any further. In reality, I already knew she held no other answers. Just like everyone else, she hadn't questioned what had happened to us, already back to living her same day-to-day reality. If the Torma shifters had niggling doubts or worries about their time held prisoner, they were far better at pushing them down than me.

When I left the bakery, I ate my pastry—which she hadn't even charged me for because apparently I was *the shit* these days. Wandering into a few other stores, I dropped more questions, but all the answers were the same. I'd been with Torin over the past two months, getting our pack life back in order. Everything normal. No drama.

And yet for some reason I was missing every damn memory of that. Why did no one have a reasonable explanation for that?

As I continued down the street, having exhausted almost all the available store owners, an empty shop caught my attention. At first, it was because I couldn't remember this street ever having an empty storefront, but soon after, it was the oddest feeling that I'd spent a lot of time inside those walls.

When I got no answers from peering through the partially boarded-up windows, I stopped in at the hardware store beside it, knowing Magda, my least favorite town gossip, would know what was up.

"Been empty for years," she said without pause, chewing her gum loudly. "Some sort of water leak that no one could find or repair."

"I could have sworn there was a shop here the last time I came to town," I murmured, staring out the hardware store window toward it.

Magda scoffed, her wrinkles deepening so she looked every one of her hundred and fifty years. "You haven't been into this part of our town for months, and before that, we were all in stasis, and even before that, there was a flood that washed the shop out. Nothing has been there in your lifetime."

"And what shop was it before my lifetime?" I asked, wondering if I'd seen old photos or something.

She paused, her brow scrunching until her eyebrows nearly hit her yellow-blonde hair. "You know, I don't remember."

I pulled my gaze from the other shopfront to stare at her. "What? You've never forgotten a damn thing."

She clicked her tongue at me. "Watch your mouth, missy. Alpha-mate or not, you will respect your elders."

In what world was uttering the word "damn" not respecting my elders? But, for the sake of possible information, I shot a quick apology her way. The older shifters had the weirdest hang-ups, but at this point, I needed her more than she needed me.

"I remember books," Magda finally said, but then her eyes tightened again, like that hurt her to say. "Or maybe I'm wrong. There's never been a bookstore here, so I... don't know."

She wandered off then, looking mildly dazed as I continued to stare at the building. *Books?* That felt... right. The moment I had the thought, my temples were stabbed by invisible knives, and now I was the one walking off rubbing my temples.

Was the abandoned shopfront part of the mystery as well? Magda had acted odd, so it wasn't just me. It was starting to occur to me that maybe the reason I couldn't get anything other than the same "story" from the pack was that everyone else had had their memories messed with too. They might not even have realized because it was subtler than what had happened to me.

Truth be told, even if there were gaps in time for them, they didn't care. They'd fallen into their daily routines, accepting the weird and questioning nothing.

Had that been the plan all along, by whomever had set this in motion?

Had they expected I would just be so happy not to be the shit under Torma's boots that I'd fall into this new life and never question a damn thing?

If that was the case, the culprit had made a few fundamental errors. Firstly, they should have chosen someone less stubborn than me, and secondly, they should have removed my memories of the pack's torment and Torin's rejection. Huge obstacles standing in the way of me falling into pack life.

I supposed removing a few months of time was much easier than removing ten-plus years. I'd have been very surprised to wake up in a twenty-year-old body thinking myself a child.

Why had the culprit had to remove any time, though? If they'd allowed me just to wake with everyone else from the stasis, I'd have been none the wiser...

It just didn't make sense. None of it, and my time in the main street had only helped to confuse me further.

With nothing else to do, I wandered back in the direction of the apartment, restless and bored. Plan A might not have panned out, but there were plenty of letters left in the alphabet, and it was time to move to "S" for Simone.

Simone's parents lived in one of the more affluent areas of Torma. It might have only been a relatively small town, but it was still clear who held positions of prestige in the pack, solely through the land and house size they'd been rewarded with. When I walked through their neighborhood, with the acre-sized lots, huge double-level mansions, and perfectly manicured lawns, I tried not to think of all the times I'd been made to feel like I didn't belong here.

Gerad and Mika Lewison, a.k.a. Simone's father and mother, were two of the worst for withholding the welcome wagon. I couldn't really blame them. Their daughter had suffered for her friendship with me, and even though I'd been too selfish to walk away from someone I loved and needed, I'd always felt guilty about it.

So, no, I didn't blame them, but the scars were there nonetheless.

Their wrought-iron gates were open, so I walked up the path, and just as I reached their door and went to press the buzzer, I heard shouting. Simone's parents were enforcers, but I'd never heard them yell. They tended to favor the silent and deadly style of intimidation... especially her mother, who was of Japanese descent and proficient in a variety of martial arts and fighting disciplines.

Torin had said on more than one occasion that we were lucky to have the Lewison family defending ours, and despite my personal feelings toward them, I hadn't disagreed because they were great at what they did.

The door jerked open before I could decide if now was a bad time to be here, and I found myself face to face with Mika. Her elfin features, which had been scrunched in anger, smoothed into a look of surprise as she ground to a halt. The very dark, blue-black hair she had passed onto her daughter flew around her face as she stared at me.

"Mera," she choked out, blinking a few times before she pulled herself together.

In an instant, every ounce of her fear, surprise, and fury was buried deep beneath a calm sheen of serenity. Her dark brown eyes, also like her daughter's, were now regarding me with a look of respect.

This fake alpha bullshit was annoying.

"What are you doing here?" she pushed. "Is there an issue at the pack house? Why didn't Torin just alert us through the two-way radio?"

I waved her off, shaking my head at the same time. "Oh, no. Everything is okay at the pack house." Or I assumed so since I hadn't bothered to answer any of Torin's messages to actually check in. "Sorry to just drop by, but I've been worrying about Simone. She still hasn't returned any of my calls or texts, and I wanted to find out if you've heard anything new."

Mika swallowed hard, and I could have sworn her lips trembled before she pulled herself together again. "Yeah, she's still doing so well," she said stiffly. "Totally fine and busy with her—"

"Stop fucking lying to me."

My patience ran out the second she gave me the same tired line. Simone was not fine. We all knew it, and I was done allowing my friend to suffer because these bastards wanted to lie to me.

A tear spilled down Mika's cheek, tracing the smooth, brown skin. That was when the panic burst to life in my chest.

"If Simone's in trouble, you have to let me know," I said with force. "How long has she really been gone? Where is she?"

Mika didn't want to answer me, I could tell that, but maybe today she knew I wasn't leaving without a real response. "I don't know where she is, Mera." Her entire body deflated, like that secret had been bursting at the seams of her being, desperate to get loose.

"She ran away just after the stasis was lifted." That part of the story came from Gerad, who appeared behind his mate. "She was here when we went to sleep, and the next morning when we woke, her bed was empty."

Gerad, six-feet-seven and built like a brickhouse, actually took a step back when Mika whipped her head around and glared at him. "You've been forcing me to remain quiet while you investigated her disappearance, and yet you have no issue telling Mera all the details?"

Gerad sighed before shaking his head. As he moved back into the light, I was surprised at how wrecked he looked. Tired and broken, the fine lines around his face aging him ten years. His dirty blond hair stood up in sections, as if he'd run his hands through it a dozen times today, and his shirt was most definitely buttoned up mismatched. He hadn't looked like this the last time I'd checked in, but today he clearly had zero fucks to give.

"I've searched everywhere," he said quietly. "We haven't slept. We hardly eat. We need help..."

It was clear that the argument I'd heard through the door had been about Simone. Simone, who had been missing for two fucking months with only these two fucking idiots unsuccessfully looking for her.

I clutched a hand to my chest. "Please tell me you have at least heard *something* from her in the past two months? How could you keep this a secret? What if she's dead? That would be on both of you."

With each accusation, my words got louder and sharper as my panic attack grew.

My best friend was missing and had been for months.

And I had done nothing to help her.

Chapter Eight

Simone and I were best friends. True best friends.

We had grown up together, and she was literally the only one in this pack to never turn her back on me. That meant it was my duty to ensure she wasn't being held in some creepy fuck's basement, having her toes licked.

Toe fetish was only cool when you were into it, not when it was being forced upon you.

And as the alpha-mate of Torma, it was even more important that we ensured the safety of one of our pack. Torin was going to be furious when he found out about this, and I sure as fuck wasn't about to keep it from him when he had a ton more resources to help track her down.

"We had to protect her place in the pack," Mika said, still making excuses as tears trailed down her cheeks. "I never thought she would leave the pack without permission, but she did. We played it off as a vacation so that she wouldn't be punished upon return. Thankfully, Torin is much more accepting than Victor, and he's just allowed us to update him without pushing to speak with her himself."

Accepting or lazy. The jury was still out on that fuckhea... *alpha whose help I needed.* "We have to tell him now." My tone made it clear that if they argued with me about this, I was going to bring the full force of Torma down on them. "She's been missing for too long. If anything has happened to her..."

If I hadn't had my memories stolen from me, I would have been onto this shit weeks ago. My anger and frustration over what happened had reached a crescendo, exploding in growls and curse words. To say I was pissed was an understatement. I'd woken up in my underwear, in the bed of a man I detested, with no memory of how I'd gotten there or the weeks that had passed since my first change. I'd woken to find that someone had messed with me in the most terrible of ways, a true abuse of power, and now it seemed that Simone was involved as well. Maybe hurt—*or worse*—because of me...

I was finally seeing the bigger picture. "I get it now," I said slowly. "It's all finally starting to make sense."

The Lewisons were understandably confused.

"I've been furious since I woke up," I explained further, "and no matter how much Jaxson and Sisily and everyone else in the damn pack tell me that I should just let it all go and enjoy being alpha-mate, the truth is, I feel like I was completely violated. My life stolen from me. My best friend stolen from me, so I would have no choice but to rely on Torin."

Mika stepped closer. "No, Mera. You cannot think that Torin would ever act inappropriately toward you; he's been nothing but a gentleman."

I nodded. "Uh-huh, sure. Just like the time he rejected me and then fucked Sisily in front of me. A true, *true* gentleman, that one."

Wow, the silence was so awkward that even *I* wondered if I'd gone too far.

"Let's focus on Simone," Mika finally said. "She's our priority."

"Let's go to the alpha," Gerad added, backing up his mate. "Hopefully, Torin has resources above my own because as far as I can tell, Simone isn't anywhere in America. We'd have heard something by now."

A heavy weight settled deep in my stomach, but I couldn't lose it yet. Simone needed me to keep it together and ensure that this was everyone's top priority.

Mika and Gerad were quiet as they led me to their Mercedes G-Wagon, one of five cars in their roomy garage. Including... Simone's old truck?

I hurried toward it. "She didn't drive? Was she taken?"

When I turned back to Simone's parents, their faces were blank. "There was no sign of a struggle," Gerad finally said, and I seriously wanted to throat-punch a motherfucker.

I didn't, choosing instead to spend my time combing over her vehicle for clues, but there wasn't a single thing that stood out. It looked, and smelled, exactly as I remembered. Her truck had nothing to do with how Simone had left Torma.

When I'd exhausted that as a lead, I joined the Lewisons in their car, throwing myself into the smooth leather seats with all the dramatic flair of a toddler who'd had their toast cut in triangles instead of squares. But, dammit, these assholes should have cared more about their daughter's well-being than her place in the pack. It was too late now to do anything except damage control, all the while praying that Simone was okay.

When Gerad exited onto the main road, I decided that I'd never have a better opportunity to question these two, so I leaned forward. "Tell me about my father."

Gerad hit the brakes, all of us jerking against our seatbelts, as he ground to a stop in the middle of the street. A stunned silence followed, which I ignored. "Why did he attempt to kill the alpha?"

Leaning back against the dark, buttery leather, I crossed my arms. "I'm just going to keep asking," I said softly.

"Why are you questioning this now, after all of these years?" Gerad finally muttered. "Why can't you let the ghosts of the past rest?"

I snorted. "They've never rested for me. I suffered every single day for what my father did, and I wanted to ask every damn day for years, but if I even thought about it, I was punished. Now I'm finally in a position where most shifters would think twice about hurting me. So I'm finally asking the damn questions."

"What about Simone?" Mika choked out, reminding us that we'd been heading to Torin for her. I hadn't forgotten, of course, but killing two birds with one stone sounded like a great plan.

"You can drive and talk," I reminded them. "We have plenty of time."

We didn't. It was at most a ten-minute drive out to the pack house, probably less at this time of the day, but they got my point.

"Your father was a complicated man," Gerad said as he set the car in motion again. "Always searching for answers, even when no one asked the question. Right around your fifth birthday, he told everyone that you created a fire in the yard. Using just your hands. No matches. No accelerant. Not even a beam of sunlight."

Mika cleared her throat. "There was evidence of a little fire that day, but it was determined to be from other pups playing with a lighter."

What? Seriously, what?

I must have looked unhinged as I stared between them.

Gerad nodded. "Yes, it was investigated, but Lockhart couldn't let it go. In his later years, he started to believe that you were not his child. He said that you had dark energy, that you'd turned your mother into an alcoholic, tainting her soul. Victor refused to indulge him in his insane ramblings, and your father grew more distant and unstable until eventually, he attacked."

"That... makes no sense," I finally choked out.

My father had been a loving figure in my life. At least in my memories, he had been. Were those early days of my life covered in a rose-colored sheen due to the unconditional love a child had for their parent?

Mika broke through my inner turmoil. "Lockhart had been trying to get Victor to use alpha coercion on all the shifters who'd been present at your birth. But we'd all been observing you as a child, and there was no sign of anything untoward. You were a normal, happy, sweet little girl."

"His request was denied." Gerad confirmed his mate's story.

I wasn't sure what answers I'd expected to get after so many years of wondering, but it really hadn't been this. I'd never expected that the attack had been about me. Not for one second. I'd believed I'd been punished all of these years due to my father's actions, but maybe there had been so much more to it. Maybe some of it had been my fault? Maybe Victor had hated me just a little extra because part of him had wondered if my father had been right.

"My father called me 'Sunny' because of my hair. Callahan hair," I murmured, half-caught in the past.

Mika shot me a commiserating stare. "He called you 'Sunny' for more reason than one. He said you had the power of a burning light inside you. A demon power."

I was floored, trying to merge this new information with the life I remembered in my head. The life before my father's death had been the golden age, but maybe it had simply been Jaxson's presence that had made it brighter. Maybe I'd never really had parents who'd cared.

"Has anyone ever given a proper single fuck about me?" My words were a sad, woe-is-me whisper, meant more for me than any other ears.

But, of course, one of the assholes in this car witnessing my breakdown had to answer. "Simone has always truly loved you," Gerad said gruffly. "No matter how much it hurt her or our family, she would never turn her back on you."

That knocked some sense into me, and I pulled myself from the dark thoughts that had been wrapping around my mind. "We have to find her," I said, the emptiness falling from my voice as determination filled me. Fuck my parents and their bullshit that had been apparently ruining my life since birth. They would get no more energy from me.

It was time for me to focus on Simone. I had to save my one true friend and family, no matter the cost.

My palm itched and my chest fluttered at the thought, and this time, I was going with that being a positive sign that I was finally on the right path.

Chapter Nine

The rest of the drive to the pack house was done in silence. No doubt they were feeling sorry for *poor little Mera*, who was once again getting kicked in the guts even as the alpha-mate.

Despite my best effort to not think about my father, two words lingered just a little longer.

Demon power?

My father had thought I had a demon power. Were demons even a real thing? I mean, outside of the Shadow Beast, who was often referred to as the demon of the shifters, there was no other reference to them in our lore.

Staring down at my hands, I tried to remember ever setting anything alight. Had I been a secret pyro as a child, with a flame obsession that had scared my father to the point he'd truly believed me to be a creature from the depths of hell?

"Could my memory loss be related to what happened to my father?"

Thankfully, Gerad had already pulled up in front of the pack house, so my random question didn't almost send us through the front window of the car this time.

"I know it happened years ago," I continued, "but maybe it's still all connected. Could I be more than a regular shifter, and that is part of what has caused my memory loss? What if my father was right?"

The enforcers exchanged a pitying stare, like they thought I'd finally cracked and were trying to figure out a way to break it to me. But I knew my truth, and there was more to be explored there. I'd been thinking too small, not correlating all of the bullshit in my life.

It was connected. I felt that deep down in my demon soul.

The Lewisons didn't answer, so I pushed into my memories, both childhood and more recent, trying to connect the dots. Of course, the moment I did, a sharp pain slammed into my temples, but for the first time, I didn't release the memories. Instead, I closed my eyes, gritted my teeth, and forced myself to push through. The pain was a barrier to whatever I wasn't supposed to remember. I'd been shying away from it, but fuck, a little brain stabbing was nothing compared to having parts of my life stolen from me.

So I pressed harder, barely managing not to scream at the relentless and intense attack on my entire body. It got so bad that I had to blindly throw open the car door, falling out so I could vomit on the ground. Still, I did not release the hold on my memories, not even as I heaved and clawed at the grass.

I heard shouts, and no doubt Simone's parents were about to be in trouble for seemingly hurting the alpha-mate, but I was too close now to lose focus of my goals. Memories were there—I felt them hovering below the surface. I just had to break through to the next level. Maybe then I would know what path to follow to claim back what had been stolen from me.

Come on! I screamed internally, my wolf howling with me as she rose to try to absorb some of my pain... but she couldn't. This was my fight alone, and I was fighting like my life depended on it.

With a burst of light, I broke through the top layer of darkness, my mind's eye slamming against a barrier woven with light and dark beams. As if rays of sunlight had been bonded to beams of moonlight. They wrapped around each other, crisscrossing until one was almost synonymous with the other.

This was the barrier.

This was what I had to destroy to reveal my memories.

When I mentally reached for it, I was blasted back by an intense heat, which took me by surprise since there hadn't been an ounce of warmth until I'd gotten closer.

"Mera!" Torin's voice was a deep roar as he yanked me up off the ground, and it was at that point that I had no choice but to release my hold on the pain, letting it fade away.

Feeling like a failure since I hadn't broken through the barrier, I at least tried to console myself with the fact that I was still on the right path. Yesterday I hadn't seen the barrier, so that was another step closer to the truth.

"What happened?" Torin shouted, his voice grating on my already aching brain as he pulled me closer. "Who did this to her?"

To an outsider, the alpha's concern would appear genuine, but I knew it was less to do with caring about me and more about losing the mate who was essential to boosting his power base. The most damning evidence was the way he hadn't even looked at me once, choosing instead to spend his time and energy throwing a tantrum because his toy was broken.

"I'm fine," I croaked, tapping him—okay, it was more like a hard poke in the chest—so he would look down. "You can let me go."

He finally registered that I was talking, and as his furious, half-shifted face turned toward me, I met his gaze.

"Mera?"

Who the fuck else would it be? "Clearly."

His lips twitched, and fuck, if my smartass mouth wasn't growing on him. About the last thing I wanted to happen. I wanted him to hate me and stay away from me, but no, he had to be all up in my shining star of a personality.

"What happened to you?"

I wiggled in his arms, reminding him that no one carried my ass around. Thankfully, he didn't fight, placing me back on my feet. "I was trying to break through the barrier around my memory loss," I said matter-of-factly, not missing the angry expression that creased his face.

He wasn't a fan of me *"opening past wounds,"* as he put it.

Too fucking bad. Maybe he shouldn't have inflicted wounds in the first place.

Mika stepped in, and I mentally applauded her bravery because Torin was fuming. Luckily for her, the new alpha wasn't quite as cruel as his father yet.

"We were on our way to discuss Simone with you," she told him, "when Mera collapsed and started screaming. I'm not sure what happened, but I think it's best that we head inside so the alpha-mate can rest."

I scoffed, crossing my arms over my chest. "I told you already, I was fighting against the spell in my head that appears to be holding my memories captive. Someone wants me to remain in the dark, and that someone is going to be greatly disappointed."

The many shifters around us shuffled their feet and cleared their throats, since, apparently, a tiny, innocent discussion about a magic spell made them uncomfortable.

Whatever. I knew my truth, and even if they didn't want to deal with it, it didn't change a fucking thing.

I'd been spelled by a powerful being. A powerful being who'd underestimated how far I'd go to destroy this stasis holding my memories. And thanks to Simone's parents, I now knew that more than just my current memories had been messed with. Memories of my past and my father had also been tampered with, or at least tainted with happiness that probably hadn't existed.

More pieces to my puzzle, and very soon, I'd have enough to know whom I needed to kill.

Torin moved closer to me, and the only reason I didn't step away was because I'd never back up from him again. His heady, musky scent washed over me, stronger thanks to the energy of his wolf riding across his skin, and for the first time, literally nothing inside of me responded. I could barely even feel the bond now.

Was he even my true mate?

The more time I spent with him, the stronger my distaste for him grew.

"How does a true mate bond break?" I asked suddenly.

He jerked back, looking hurt. "A statement of rejection," he bit out, his heavy gaze slamming into me. "From one or both parties. I've also heard that if you don't nourish a bond, it can fade to nothing."

At first, his quick and honest response to a touchy subject confused me until I realized he was telling me so I'd know that the distance between us was my fault. I was the one separating and forcing us apart, and in doing so, the bond was fading.

The first true smile I'd had since waking in his bed spread across my face, and as his scrunched expression faded into confusion, I lifted my knee and slammed it right into his junk. A choked gasp escaped him as he dropped to his knees, shock emanating from him.

I smiled again, feeling this surge of power like I never had before. The mate bond that was holding me back would soon be gone, and that was truly empowering.

"Mera." Torin gasped, dragging himself back to his feet as shifter healing fixed up a couple of busted testicles. "What is *wrong* with you?"

"You were in my personal space," I said sweetly. "Best not to do that again."

Patting him on the chest, I spun on one foot and strolled past a ton of shocked shifters, making my way into the pack house.

Chapter Ten

The pack house was quiet and cool as I walked through the front hall, past the formal dining and living rooms, and back into the row of offices used for business meetings. Since I was the first one in there, I chose the best chair at the head of the table. It was Torin's seat, but he could fight me for it if he wanted.

The alpha strolled in a few minutes later, looking unruffled. He didn't say a word about me randomly kneeing him in the balls or about me sitting in his chair. He just chose the seat next to me, and we sat in an awkward silence until the other members arrived.

Mika and Gerad were first, followed by two senior pack members, Jos and Hench. Burly, middle-aged shifters, they were respected due to their many years helping to run Torma.

They had been Victor's right-hand men, outside of his beta, and Torin had continued the same tradition.

"What is this about?" Jos asked as he leaned toward us, the lights above reflecting off the dirty blond of his hair, which was shaved close to his head.

"I'd like to know that as well," Hench said shortly. He didn't lean forward or otherwise engage; the icy blue of his eyes was the same blue of his wolf, which looked like a snow-white husky when he shifted. His hair was just as white, falling to his shoulders, and I always considered him the most beautiful wolf in our pack. His human side was a right old fuckhead, though.

"Simone is missing," I said bluntly. "At some point just after the stasis was lifted, Simone left her house and hasn't been seen since."

Torin, Jos, and Hench, in near unison, nailed the Lewisons with a glare. "You lodged her as being on vacation," Jos said, pulling out his phone. "I know because I've been asking you for weekly updates, and you've been logging her itinerary."

He spun the device around to show what looked like a GPS map with flashing red dots. I figured that these were supposed to mark out Simone's planned route.

This was the point when Mika paled, her gorgeous brown skin drawn as she sank lower, seemingly defeated. The silence in the room extended, no one willing to be the first to break it.

"We were protecting our daughter. Our family," Gerad finally said, wrapping his arm around his mate. "I figured I could track her down and get her back here before she was punished for leaving the pack without permission. Simone has never done anything like this before, and with no real money or resources, how far could she have gone?"

A sound of annoyance escaped me, drawing attention away from the Lewisons. "What if she didn't run away? What if she was taken, and all of this time you wasted in hiding the truth is what screws up our chances of tracking her down? In the end, you wanted to save your family name, and in doing so, you might have lost your damn daughter."

I was mad. Not just mad but scared, and heartbroken, and lost. Mostly scared, if I was being honest. If anything happened to my best friend, especially if she was in this situation because of me, I would never recover.

Torin cleared his throat, running a hand through his hair agitatedly as he got to his feet. This new development had really thrown him, and I wondered if he was questioning his control over the pack. "Mika and Gerad are to be held in the basement until we have every piece of information about Simone's whereabouts," he said gruffly. "And we will begin an immediate full-scale search to track down our missing pack member. If she ran of her own accord, she will henceforth be banished from this pack, but if she was taken, the full force of Torma will come down on those who have touched one of our own." He lowered his head to meet my gaze. "We will find her, Mera."

I swallowed roughly. We had to find her; there was just no other option.

Torin, who had clearly been waiting for me to respond to his declaration, shook his head and spun on the spot, storming out. In the wake of their departing alpha, Jos and Hench got to their feet to fulfill his orders. Thankfully, neither Mika nor Gerad fought back, the pair seemingly too broken to care about heading to the prison cells below.

I just hoped they had information to help guide the others in their search. Gerad said he had been conducting his own investigation—there had to be something he could tell them.

Hench closed the door behind them, leaving me alone in the room. I had so many questions still unanswered, but it felt like gears were finally turning. All I had to do was figure out where to put my time and attention.

My planning was interrupted as the door opened, and I looked up, half-expecting to find Torin back in my space again. Only it wasn't.

An unfamiliar woman closed the door quickly, her gaze darting around as if ensuring we were alone before she focused on me.

"Uh, hello?" I said, getting to my feet. "Can I help you with something?"

She hurried closer, and I took a moment to pay attention to her. She was tall and statuesque, with perfect brown skin, deep, rich emerald eyes, and long, straight black hair.

Not black like Simone's; it was closer to mine, with deep auburn undertones.

She was stunning. Model perfect. And there was no way she was a Torma local because I'd never forget a face like hers.

"Alpha Wolfe," she said respectfully, half-bowing her head. "My—"

"Whoa, okay, I'm going to stop you right there."

Her head shot up, the insanely long eyelashes framing her rich green eyes, caught my attention as she blinked at me.

"I'm Mera Callahan," I told her. "Not Alpha Wolfe. Or any Wolfe."

Torin would have done well to change his pretentious and frankly laughable family name, but of course he wouldn't. Ego and all that.

She smiled, flashing near perfect white teeth that contrasted with the rich brown of her skin and hair. "My apologies. I've only been in the pack for a month or so, and in that time, you were always referred to as 'the alpha-mate Wolfe.'"

My teeth clanked together, but I managed not to growl in this poor woman's face. "Sorry we haven't met up until now," I said, reaching out a hand to shake hers. "I've been distracted with a personal matter, but I love seeing new blood in the pack."

She grasped on to my hand with a firm grip, and there was a nice moment between us before she stepped away. "My name is Samantha Rowland, Sam, actually, and I'm sorry to track you down like this, but I saw you in town today. I work part-time shifts in Henry's café, and there was talk of you asking about odd happenings around Torma recently." She paused dramatically, and I barely managed not to shake the information from her. Thankfully, she continued without need for violence. "I think I found something you should look at."

Holy fucking fuck. Was this my first genuine lead? My wolf bounced in my chest, and it was probably due to the jolt of intrigue and hope that blossomed inside us. The gossip of the main street was finally working in our favor.

"Can you show me now?" I asked, leaning closer as I worked to keep the excitement from my voice. Best not to scare her off yet.

She nodded, a flicker of curiosity in her face, but she didn't ask me why I was so interested in weird shit around Torma. Probably figured it was an alpha thing.

"Of course," she said. "My full-time job is as one of the new teachers in the pack school. This oddity is in a basement room, in the lower levels, and... honestly, you should see for yourself."

Hell fucking yes, I should.

"Let's go, new friend Sam," I said, linking my arm through hers so I could get us out of this room fast. "While they're all distracted."

Distracted tracking down the most important person in my world, which gave me a chance to continue poking at the mystery of my missing two months. It was essential that I figured it out because I had an uneasy feeling, deep in my gut, that all of it was connected.

Me, Simone, my lost memories, and the new Torma I'd woken up to.

Sam and I made it out of the pack house without running into any other shifters. She was quiet at my side, but it wasn't an awkward silence. Instead, it almost felt comforting. Like she was secretly supporting me without even realizing it.

When we got into her small white sedan, parked at the back of the lot, she wasted no time pulling onto the road toward the school. It was only a few miles away, but that was enough time to practice my rusty small talk. "How are you finding Torma?" I asked as she drove sedately. "Is everyone treating you well?"

She had both hands on the steering wheel, and it was clear she wasn't a massive risk-taker because she never removed her eyes from the road to chat. "It's been wonderful. I petitioned long ago to join Torma, starting from when my mate first rejected me, but it was always a no. And since my pack wouldn't release me to any alpha weaker than theirs, it left me with very few options. For years, I lived in the same pack as my true mate, watching as he created a life with another. It was torture."

For a second, I wondered if I'd misheard her. "Your true mate rejected you?"

She cleared her throat. "Yeah, a long time ago. I'm okay now, but it was pretty rough."

"Yeah, I understand completely," I breathed.

This caught her attention, and for a brief moment, she actually looked away from the road to meet my eyes. "You understand completely? But how? You're mated to the alpha and everyone loves and respects you."

The corners of her eyes pulled into sad lines, and I had the brief idea that she thought I was mocking her. With a shake of my head, I placed my hand on her arm. "When our bond was first realized, Torin rejected me. Quite brutally, actually."

Sam blinked at me, seemingly as confused as I'd been about her words. "But... But you're together now?"

I shook my head. "Kinda, not really. I can't forgive and forget, and with my missing memories, let's just say... There's something rotten in Torma and I am not going to rest until I figure out what it is."

She cleared her throat as she turned her focus back to the road. "I had no idea. The few times I've seen you around, you looked so confident and put-together. I figured you were one of those shifters living the fairytale pack life."

I snorted. "This pack was my prison and hell. I understand your need to escape, far better than you might think."

Her hands tightened on the steering wheel as she breathed deeply. "Rejection is rare," she finally said, pausing for a beat to safely navigate an intersection, "and for someone as strong and capable as you are, I'm completely stunned Torin wasn't over the moon to have you as his mate."

My laughter was dry and cynical as it rasped from me. "My father tried to kill the previous alpha. From that day forward, my family was shit in this pack. Torin wanted to kill me the day I first turned, and the only reason he didn't was because of—"

The pain hit me harder than ever, my brain sliced into pieces as figurative knives attacked with vengeance. Screams shattered the car and it took me a minute to understand they were mine. Sam, who had not been expecting that at all, careened all over the road as she shouted, "What is it? What's wrong? Did you see a spider?"

She started screaming too, and if I hadn't been about to die from the pain, I would have laughed at her apparent fear of spiders. She was a damn wolf shifter; spiders were not a threat to us at all. Alas, logic had nothing to do with true fear.

When Sam finally wrested back control of her car, bringing it to a halt on the side of the road, I managed to stop screaming. "I'm sorry." I got out, my throat aching before it healed. "It was my memory loss... Every time I try to trigger a memory, the pain is so damn bad, I near pass out."

Sam pressed a hand to her heaving chest, the long, shiny strands of her hair completely tangled around her face. "That's truly terrible. I hope it wasn't anything I said."

Straightening, I wiped at the drool on my face, sending up a prayer of thanks that I hadn't pissed myself as well. "It was nothing you said. It's just the mess that's my brain, and whoever fucked with me better *hope* I never regain my memories. Because I'll be coming for them."

My voice lowered into a growl, and Sam cleared her throat. "You're kind of scary. Glad to see your inner wolf wasn't brutally torn to pieces by your father's betrayal and the lackluster true mate you got. Wish I could say the same."

Being called "scary" was a compliment to me, and I took it as such. In truth, my pack's oppression and bullying ways had forced me to evolve into a shifter who gave zero fucks. The same treatment of Sam had had the opposite effect. I mean, I'd only known her all of half an hour, but already I was painting a picture. From the cautious nature and gentle soul to the sedate button-down shirt and black slacks. Whatever wildness had existed in her soul had been burned away, leaving behind a shifter who took no risks.

Was coming to me with this information the first true step outside of her norm in a long time? If it panned out, I would owe her everything. No matter what happened, one day I would help her reach her full potential.

After all, we rejected mates needed to stick together.

Chapter Eleven

We pulled into the parking lot a minute later, and despite her jumpiness from my screaming fit, Sam still managed to lock her car, check all the doors twice, and then follow me into the school.

It was a weekday, so shifter students were everywhere, and it was weird to think that this had been my life not very long ago. When had I even graduated? Was that in the period of time where I'd lost memories?

Another jab hit my head, so I forced the thoughts away. Now was not the time for another screaming and/or vomiting session; I needed to stay focused on whatever Sam was showing me.

She veered away from the main hall, and I was grateful to get off that path so all the shifter students could stop freaking out and doing a double take at the alpha-mate being in their school.

We ended up in the theater wing. "They've closed this section down for renovation," Sam said, "but I had to come in here to find some old school files, and I'm starting to think there's more than just renovations going on."

The closer we got to the basement, the more uneasy my stomach grew, swirling and dancing inside until I had to press my hand to it in an attempt to ease the flow. The energy here was dark, and I could tell from the relaxed expression on Sam's face that she wasn't feeling it. Whatever she was about to show me... it was connected to me. It had to be.

When she opened the door, pushing past the yellow tape that was supposed to keep everyone out, I followed her down the stairs. "I hope you don't take offense to this," I said, trying to distract myself from the dark wisps of energy that were sending my body into hyperdrive, "but what even made you snoop down here? You don't seem like the type to venture into forbidden areas."

She shot a small smile over her shoulder that I saw quite clearly even in the low lighting. "Would you believe that once upon a time, many years ago, I was the child always in trouble for sticking my nose where it wasn't supposed to be? My nature is innately curious, and even though that has been somewhat beaten out of me, this time, I just couldn't resist. Maybe it was fate since I happened to find the one person who might need to know about this place as well."

Fate? I wasn't really one to put faith into an entity that I hated most of the time—hello, Torin? Scraping the bottom of the barrel there. But again, it was either divine intervention or a ridiculously huge coincidence that Sam and I had found each other. Or more like she'd found me, right when I'd really needed her to.

"I'm sorry about your pack," I said softly. "If you want me to beat the shit out of every single one of them for hurting you, just say the word. I'll throw down for a friend." Fuck her mate for taking her spark. I literally needed to start a support group for shifters like us, those who didn't fit into pack life.

Sam's chuckle was a welcome relief. "I'm really glad I met you, Alpha Mera Callahan. You were right to ditch 'Wolfe.' You don't need it."

Okay, so I literally loved this shifter babe. She knew what was up.

We stopped talking when we hit the near pitch-dark ground level, the unease in my body stronger than ever as a faint musky scent invaded my nostrils.

"Smells like fire," I whispered. "And death. Someone tried to cover it up, but the undertones remain."

Sam cleared her throat. "Yeah, I brought another teacher in here and she could smell nothing, but I picked it up too. My sense of smell is my strongest asset."

It was mine as well—another common trait between us.

Sam led me through a small hall and out into the huge, open main room, and the farther we went, the more certain I was that I'd been down here before. I just couldn't recall when or for what.

"Do you see it yet?" Sam asked.

I couldn't see much, so I called on my wolf to rise up and assist me. For once, she responded immediately, adding her power to mine. The darkened room came into clearer focus so I could see exactly what I'd been missing before.

"What. The. Fuck?" I took a step forward. "What happened here?"

Sam was motionless beside me, as if to not disturb the spirits of this place. "I have no damn idea," she whispered. "How is it possible for there to have been this much destruction without the rest of the school suffering from it as well?"

The basement had been burned, black scorch marks across the room, reaching as high as the far-off ceilings. My human eyes hadn't seen the destruction, but my wolf ones saw it all. There was nothing left besides piles of char and blackened fixtures. "I read the pack meeting agendas, going back a few years," I said softly. "No fire here was mentioned."

I'd been trying to find some sort of evidence about what happened to me, but I would have remembered a fire in the school.

"I asked around too," she admitted. "Hence why I knew this was odd. Judging by the damage, this would have been a raging inferno, unable to be hidden. But someone is hiding it, because no one I've spoken to knows a damn thing about a fire in the school."

I nodded. "This was no ordinary blaze. It would have burned high and hot, with zero chance of being extinguished without outside help. Someone knew about it."

That swirling feeling in my gut was growing harder and harder to ignore, and as I walked farther into the room, the scent of old ash filling my nose, I stopped trying to calm the swirls. My gut was telling me something.

Allowing my senses to roam free, I paused at the point where I scented smoke the strongest. Staring up, I noticed there were a few chains hanging from the very high ceiling, but no platform to go with them.

"You think the fire started here?" Sam asked from close by, half-scaring me to death. I'd been so focused, I hadn't even heard her approach.

"Yeah, I think so," I muttered, still trying to see into the dark ceiling. "Those are scorch marks up there, and the damage here looks worse than anywhere else."

When no new evidence from above appeared, I focused on the ground, leaning down to run my hand across the cement. I expected to pick up black residue, but my fingers came away squeaky clean. The dark smudges were just the burn marks that had remained once the ash had been cleaned away.

"What are you going to do with this information?" Sam asked.

I straightened and faced her. "I'm going to follow my gut."

She had no idea what that meant, but she got onboard anyway. "Can I tag along? It's been a long time since I've had an adventure."

"I'd love that," I said, linking our arms again and dragging her back the way we'd just come. "You're the first new friend I've made in a long time. Apologies in advance for the full force of my personality, but if you think you can handle it, you'll never have to question my loyalty."

"I could really use a friend," she said matter-of-factly. "Let's do it."

Sure, we'd just made friends like toddlers in the park, but why did adults have to complicate everything? If you click with someone, be their friend. If they prove they're not worthy of your friendship, bury their body and start again.

It's simple, really.

I had a good feeling that Sam wouldn't betray my instant friendship. Like with Simone, sometimes you just knew.

When we left the school, the swirling feeling in my stomach disappeared, as if it had never been there. There was something really off in that room, and I wasn't going to stop now until I figured out what it was. I'd have to come back tonight when the school was empty so I could really bash around in there, delve into what had happened, and sniff—

"Shit. We should have shifted."

Sam stared at me. "You think we missed something the wolf might have picked up?"

"Definitely worth trying, because there is more to that room, and I'm determined to figure out what it is."

I waited for her to look at me like I was insane, but she just clapped her hands together and nodded. "I'm ready to head back whenever you need. I have classes to teach tomorrow though, so maybe this weekend?"

"What about tonight?"

I expected tonight would be too soon for her to mentally prepare herself, but I couldn't wait any longer. Then she surprised me. "I'll meet you here around nine," she said.

I blinked before nodding overly enthusiastically. "Yes! Perfect! We're going to get to the bottom of this if it's the last thing we do."

Despite my ominous words, Sam's confident smile never faltered. "We will figure it out. Now do you need a ride somewhere?"

I shook my head. "Nah. I think I'll just take a walk to clear my head. I want to be in the right mental space for tonight."

"We've got this," she said, leaning in to pat me on the shoulder. With a final smile, she walked to her car, got in, and drove off slow and sedately, which made me laugh.

I loved women built in shades of grey with contrasts at every corner. There was a mystery to solve in Sam, and maybe, while solving my own life, I might learn a thing or two about my new friend.

Chapter Twelve

Torin came for me that night. I wasn't surprised, especially after the way I'd humiliated him in front of the pack. He'd been pretty restrained not knocking me down then and there to reestablish his dominance, but I'd known his restraint wouldn't last for long.

When the rickety door to my apartment slammed open, Torin marched in like he owned the place. I was already waiting in the living room, threadbare couch at my back. My wolf drifted in my chest, closer to the surface than she'd been for a long time, thanks to the impending full moon.

"Mera!" Torin growled, and he was so pissed, his nostrils flared, hands already half shifted into claws. "Where the fuck have you been? Why aren't you answering your phone? I've checked this place five times today."

I shrugged, not even bothering to reply. It was none of his business.

He took a step closer. "This has to stop."

Now it was my turn to bare my teeth at him. "I reject this—"

Before I could get the words out to finally sever our bond, he dove for me, and I had to shut my mouth to get out of his way. Torin had no right to come at me like he owned me, which meant I had to best him here tonight. It was my dominance that would win.

He was faster than I'd expected, which was stupid of me because the alpha gathered power from those in his pack. I should have gathered it as well, but because I refused to truly seal the bond—i.e., have some really bad sex—I was cut out of the share of power.

"Why do you hate me so much?" Torin shouted, clawing at his hair and face in frustration, cutting lines across his skin that healed instantly. "Sure, I didn't treat you that well after your father's sin, but I was never the worst. Jaxson and I stopped you from being raped. We stopped the members of the pack we could control from stepping over the line. You would have died a million times over if it wasn't for us!"

He was shouting in my face now, his cheeks red, his eyes burning into me with intensity. "And yeah, I rejected you, but I reclaimed you as soon as I came to my senses. You have to understand, I never expected you were anyone other than Jax's. When I was the chosen one, I panicked and acted like a stupid fucking moron. I've regretted it ever since."

He was saying all the right words, but that was seriously all they felt like to me. Words. Empty, meaningless, *say whatever to get his own way* words.

"Being with you *feels wrong*," I said, needing him to understand.

That statement hurt him, his eyes shiny as he stared at me. "We're true mates," he whispered, like those two fucking words solved all the problems in the world.

"We're not."

He blinked about a million blinks. "What the fuck, Mera? Are you insane? We have a fucking true mate bond, and that means you belong to me. Your heart. Your soul. And your goddamn body."

I had been starting to feel sorry for him, but as always, his stellar personality took care of that. "You know I'm right," I said shortly.

"There's no true bond between us any longer. You should make it official with Sisily and save yourself the rejection."

Torin shook his head, coughing out laughter through his growls. "You never were one to mince words. Throw your every thought out there and deal with the consequences later."

I shrugged. "Yeah, that's what happens when you stop expecting to live past your next birthday. There was never any point in curbing my words. It made no difference to how the pack treated me."

"Your father is to blame for that," Torin shot at me. "Not me. I refuse to be punished for actions that weren't my own."

Oh, the irony.

"I heard a story about why my dad attacked yours."

Torin stilled. "What did you hear?"

Oh, yeah, that wide-eyed look of panic told me he had a very good idea what I was going to say. "I heard that Lockhart considered me a demon child. He wanted Victor to use his alpha power to confirm it."

"There was no evidence," Torin said in a rush. "My father would have killed you if there was."

And yet I distinctly remembered Victor calling me a demon... The night I'd first shifted, maybe?

Pain stabbed me, sharp and intense, and it took my breath away as I clutched my head. Torin, the sneaky bastard, saw his damn opportunity and this time when he leapt across the room, I was too slow to get out of the way.

The moment his hands wrapped around my biceps, I started to fight, but his strength far surpassed my own, and when he yanked me forward, kissing me with enough force to draw blood, I screamed and kicked like the devil himself had me. "You just need the bond reinforced," Torin said, lifting his knee and slamming it into my gut in an attempt to stop me from kicking and clawing at him.

It didn't work, instead enraging me further. "You have no fucking right to kiss me," I spat at him. "Or touch me. Or be anywhere *near* me. Walk away now, Torin, before I kill you and take this fucking pack from your family line forever."

He wasn't listening, lust-filled frenzy turning his eyes dark and murky as he attempted to kiss me again. I managed to headbutt him first, his teeth cutting into my forehead, but I had zero regrets.

"*Obey*," he commanded, using his alpha power on me. I felt the tendrils wrap around me, and while my wolf, who had been growling in my chest, settled, another part of me just grew more enraged. Torin was going to use his alpha power to hold me while he raped me? Holy fucking... He needed to die.

"No!" I snapped as fury swelled within me, an almost unnatural power, boiling and simmering below the surface. "*You* will obey *me*."

Torin stopped his attempt at *raping the bond into me*, halting all movements as his eyes glazed over.

"Release me," I said.

He dropped his hands, and my arms ached briefly as the blood rushed back into them.

"Walk out this damn door and never come near me again."

He wanted to refuse—there was a moment when he clearly fought my control—but he had no true power here. My command superseded his, and neither of us had a clue how that was possible.

By the time I calmed down, my breaths no longer rasping from me, Torin was long gone. The burning anger under my skin lingered a little longer, until it too faded. Feeling like I was losing my mind, I rushed from my apartment, heading toward the school. I didn't see anyone on the way and by the time I arrived, I felt much calmer. No less confused, but it was time to focus on what had happened here in the school.

As I stepped out into the moonlight, my wolf stirred listlessly in my chest. Prodding her energy, I tried to draw her to the surface. *Come on. We need to shift, to figure out what's been hidden from us.*

This piqued her interest, and she stretched languidly in my chest before pushing forward. Holding on to her energy, I crossed the parking lot, making my way to the side entrance, where Sam waited.

She was leaning against the wall, looking at her phone, but when she heard my steps, she pocketed the device. "Hey," she said with a smile. "I was worried you weren't going to make it."

"Had a visitor I had to get rid of first," I said, pushing Torin from my mind.

That motherfucker was just lucky he didn't finish what he'd set out to do. Since I apparently had the ability to control him, and with that power, I could make him eat a silver bullet. He'd do well to remember that.

"Want to shift now?" Sam asked, already lifting her shirt. "The moon is fairly high, and I can feel the pull."

"Yep, I'm ready."

I got undressed too, and when we were both naked, I noticed the tattoo that started on her right side and wrapped around her back. From what I could see, it looked like a wolf, but one that was half-shifted into a red-and-silver beast.

It was such a contrast to the prim and proper teacher façade she had going on that I was genuinely surprised. "Amazing tattoo," I said, gesturing to the part of the image I could see. "How did you get it to not heal over?"

Her smile was wistful as she pressed a hand to her side. "Before I turned, I ran away with a human. This moon-loving, crystal-wearing dude who was covered in ink. He convinced me to get this done, and I didn't think it would stick, but somehow he managed it. Must have been due to me not shifting for the first time yet."

She ran a hand over it, and in the weird play of light, it almost looked like it moved under her touch. "Why that image?" I asked. A regular wolf would have been the logical choice, not one that looked like the werewolf of human lore.

"It called to me," she said with a brighter smile. "My beast."

I was going to ask her more about it, but she had started to shift, so I did the same. My wolf didn't fight me for once, and thankfully, her lethargy faded as our bones cracked and reformed into the wolf.

When I was on four paws, shaking off the change, my red fur

bright under the moonlight, Sam padded toward me. Despite our heights being similar in human form, she was a smaller wolf, with shaggy black fur, and the most striking silver eyes. If I had to guess, her eyes matched the silver in her tattooed beast.

She yipped low at me, and I returned the sound, nudging her toward the door. It was thankfully unlocked and slightly ajar, and since I hadn't even thought to check, it was a damn good thing my practical friend was here.

The interior of the school was dark, cool, and quiet, but with the monochromatic wolf sight, I could see everything as clear as in the day. It took us no time to make our way down the hall and into the cordoned-off section of the school. In wolf form I could smell the soot and char before we even entered the theater basement, and as we descended the stairs, it grew strong enough to fill my nostrils completely.

I sneezed a few times, and when Sam did the same, it was clear the sensitive wolf nose was reacting to more than just a long-ago fire.

Something big had gone down here, and whoever had tried to clean it up might have missed important clues.

We just had to find them.

Chapter Thirteen

This time in the basement, there was no swirling in my stomach. Maybe the wolf was able to filter it better, or maybe the swirl had turned into a flutter in my chest, since that was what I felt as I stepped into the room.

Sam stayed close behind me, and I kept my nose to the ground, following a familiar scent. It wasn't until I was near the center of the room, right in the spot that had clearly been hit the hardest by the flames, that I figured out why it was familiar. It had a lavender and aniseed undertone. Two smells I associated directly with one person: Simone.

She had been in here. Either before or after the fire, and the thought that the hints of death that lingered here might be due to her presence almost sent me back into my human form.

I couldn't think like that. I had to stay calm and keep searching, for her sake.

And my own, because if anything had happened to Simone...

Yeah, not a sentence I could finish.

We ended up farther back in the room than I'd gone with Sam

earlier that day. Simone's scents were soon intercepted by a different scent, one that was rich and spicy, and even in wolf form, it curled my toes in a way that was purely sexual. Human sexual, not anything to do with my beast.

It was a smell that, once found, I couldn't release as it dragged me to its origins.

Sam stayed right beside me, probably wondering what the fuck I was doing as I zigzagged across the room, rumbles ripping from my chest.

I just... finally felt like I was on the right path.

More flutters rose inside me, and the pressure in my brain was stronger than ever as I tried to follow memories and scents. I was bracing myself for the usual stabbing head pain, but... it didn't come. Was my wolf insulated from the worst of that as well? Had she been the key all along to figuring this shit out, and was that why she was so sluggish? Maybe someone didn't want me in this form because this form was how I'd get my answers. And that meant we were on four legs until I figured this shit out.

That darkly enticing scent led me to the farthest wall from the entrance. I nosed around, trying to find an opening in the scorched and blackened concrete. Sam nudged me after I'd spent a minute trying to pry this wall's secrets free, with very little success.

She jerked her wolf head away from the wall, and I followed her the few steps back until I figured out what she had been showing me. The bigger picture of what I was sniffing at.

The burned shape looked exactly like a giant silhouette of a person, scorched into the brick. The silhouette was larger than even the biggest shifter I'd ever seen, and I wondered if it was just a random coincidence, or was this the literal outline of someone bursting into the room?

But from where?

The basement had thick brick and block walls. Bricks and blocks that were still completely intact, outside of the blackened outline of a giant. Moving forward again, I placed my nose right in the silhouette, and the flutter in my chest really kicked into gear.

I sniffed harder, and in the next inhale came a whiff of spice and books and... magic.

My wolf tilted her head back and howled, stronger and with more emotion than she'd had since we'd awoken in Torin's bed. Her call was a lament of pain, and I had no idea why, but the feeling of loss was so strong, it almost sent me to my wolf belly.

Beside me, Sam joined in with our howls, spurring on my wolf even harder, drawing up more of our power that had been trapped inside. As our burning energy increased, it pushed past barriers I hadn't even known were there. Power flowed from me until my howls echoed through the basement at an almost-deafening decibel. Sam eventually had to drop down and cover her ears with her paws, and while I didn't want to hurt her, I couldn't make myself stop.

On instinct, I directed the energy flowing from me toward that wall, and as it hit, a fire sprang to life, intense and bright in the dark room. There had been nothing to burn, but this sort of fire was fueled by my rage, with no need for any other accelerant.

Seemed my father had been right about me all along—I was a demon child.

Eventually, I was able to release the howl, my wolf slumping forward. Sam was there, her head under me, lifting me back to my feet, both of us staring at what I'd created.

Right where the silhouette had been was a swirling... portal, maybe? There was no way to tell what lay on the other side of it, since it was cloudy, but it was definitely not a solid wall any longer. Exhaustion pressed in on me as I stumbled forward, but I forced myself to take another step, scared that this portal might close before I found the energy to step through.

I braced myself when my nose touched the swirl, but there was no pain, just a rush of power across my fur. Turning my head, I nodded at Sam, hoping she'd understand that I was thanking her. She returned my nod with a little yip, and I let out a deep breath before returning to the portal, preparing to cross. Whatever lay beyond was my destiny... The truth that had been stolen from me.

I'd finally found my big break in this investigation, and I was not about to waste it.

Chapter Fourteen

I t took less courage than I'd expected to step through a magical barrier into a completely unknown situation. I was that keen to be away from Torma and Torin that honestly, it could have been hell on the other side and I'd still think it was a better option.

When I arrived in a bright, stark-white hallway, I had to blink and adjust my sight, jumping at movement to my right before realizing it was Sam, her wolf so black that she appeared to be a shadow.

Sam! Fucking hell. She was not supposed to be here on this possibly very dangerous mission. I tried to nudge her back through the doorway, but of course, it faded out before I got her more than a step.

I sniffed around the spot, but there was not a shred of evidence that the portal had even existed. My wolf growled at Sam, but she just nudged me, and with an annoyed huff, I moved my focus back into the hallway.

We started to run in one direction, and I wasn't sure about Sam, but I spent many minutes thinking about the fact that a magical portal had brought us here and we had no way to get back. I had no real regrets, except for the fact that I may have condemned my new friend to whatever fate lay in wait at the end of this path. Her choice to return to Torma was gone, though, so we'd just have to hope for the best.

Sam stayed with me as I picked up my pace, the landscape around us never changing. It wasn't until we got a little farther along that I noticed several doorways scattered along the walls. I paused at one, sniffing beneath it, but there was no scent or feel of energy. If anything, they almost seemed like illusions, designed to distract, and with that in mind, I continued forward. My need to know what was at the end of the hall drove me; I'd come back for the doors if needed.

After another ten minutes of loping along, we still hadn't reached an ending, and I was starting to despair that we'd found ourselves trapped in another cage. One much smaller than Torma, but without Torin, so... silver lining.

Just when I was about to give up and start exploring behind the doorways, a swirl of darkness caught my eye. It was a few yards away, and finally, it seemed we had reached the end of this hallway.

As we padded closer, the energy in this area grew stronger, and by the time we were near the portal, it started to hiss and spit power, as if it was malfunctioning. Or warning us not to go any closer. A warning I would be ignoring because I'd come this far on a hope and dream, and instinct told me my truth was on the other side of this hall.

Sam, to her credit, did not even show an ounce of hesitation in following me, and it was growing clearer that the browbeaten wolf-shifter side of her was fading back under the strong shifter she used to be. Maybe we'd find more than just *my* truth here.

The closer we got to the sparking vortex of darkness, the heavier the air felt, until we were all but wading through energy. For the first time, Sam fell back, her wolf whining at the magic coating everything. I could taste it on my tongue, briny and rather unpleasant. Like an ocean during a storm, when all the dirt and muck was stirred up, the blue and green waters turning grey and tumultuous.

Despite this, I pushed on, and unlike Sam, who was held back by some kind of magical barrier, the same magic allowed me to sail right through, sliding off my fur like I owned the damn place. Within seconds, I was mere inches from the spitting, angry cloud of darkness.

I took a moment to examine it closely, looking for an opening or break in the swirling energy. A safe path, if you will, but there was absolutely nothing visible.

If I wanted in, I would have to take this energy on head first.

Extending my neck, I allowed the tip of my wolf nose to brush across a dark swirl, all the while preparing for the worst in the form of pain, death, and magical entombing. As an FYI, for anyone monitoring my thoughts, if there was a choice between death or being frozen into some sort of waking coma, I would take death any day.

The darkness reacted as soon as we made contact, shooting out and wrapping around my wolf's head and chest, squeezing so tight that for a beat, we couldn't draw air in. I didn't struggle at first, allowing this entity to explore, its intense power running across my wolf body before delving deep into my center. Either it was verifying my right to be here, or it was a huge perv copping a magical feel. Either way, I was stuck, unable to move.

Just when I'd almost reached my limit of not breathing, the touch lightened, and my wolf howled on instinct, finally able to draw air in. The energy reacted to that as well, shivering and jiggling against us, and it was so familiar that for a moment a flash of déjà vu hit me.

When had I seen jiggling black smoke before?

It released me, and as the howl died in my throat, I found myself staring at a perfectly normal-looking portal. No darkness or sparking power to be seen.

Sam, who was finally able to approach, reached my side, both of us staring at the lightly swirling grey portal. Sucking in another deep breath, I stepped forward and nosed my way into its midst, encountering no resistance as I stepped through to the other side.

This had to be it... My truth.

I felt it deep inside as my energy rose up and another howl ripped from me, much stronger and more powerful than before. Whatever or whoever had taken my memories had also bound my wolf and powers. I had no idea why or when or how, but I did know one thing for sure.

They'd made a big mistake by not just killing me—because I would never stop until they paid for what they did.

Chapter Fifteen

On the other side of the portal, there was no sign of the white hallway. Before I could take a step into this new room, Sam darted in front of me. Wondering what had her worried, I looked around quickly, finally following her line of sight above our heads.

Oh, shit. The black sparking smoke that had hovered around the doorway was following us. Floating like a cloud of evil, it was actually much calmer than before, its energy now curious versus murderous.

Sam and I exchanged a glance, and it was at this point that I initiated the change back. It was time for us to discuss what was happening here because this was messing with my head. My wolf didn't fight me, and a few minutes later, I was able to stand.

Shaking out my limbs, I waited until the sensation of bones breaking and bodies reforming faded. Immediately, I noticed that I felt stronger here; that couldn't be a coincidence, right?

"Where are we?" Sam asked huskily, rubbing at her chest as she straightened from her shift.

"I have no idea," I said breathlessly because a lowkey excitement had started thrumming through my chest. "To my knowledge, I've never been here before. Never stepped out of Torma into another damn dimension or tangled with an angry cloud of smoke, but at the same time... this feels familiar."

She halted me with a hand on my arm. "I have no idea what happened to you, but can I just say how badass you are, taking this on without a clue of what was waiting on the other side of those magical doorways?"

Badass or stupid. Such a fine line.

"Why did *you* step through?" I asked, reminded that she'd followed when she should have stayed safely in Torma. "This isn't your fight, and you already went above and beyond in trying to help me. So why?"

Sam ducked her head, a long sigh escaping. "Would you believe that my life has been such a miserable suckfest that I actually don't really have that much to lose by following you on your adventure?"

Empathy rose inside of me. I understood more than I wished to. "I think that's part of why I felt such an instant connection to you," I said, shaking my head. "You and I are the same, just raised in different packs. I would literally choose anything over staying in Torma."

"It's better for you now," she whispered, lifting her face, her eyes shiny as the ghosts of her past spilled out in a few stray tears. "You're a strong alpha, and you're respected. You didn't have to beg... fucking *beg* for years to get another pack to take you in. One of the other teachers told me that it was only thanks to Alpha Torin's soft spot for rejected females that my transfer was approved. Otherwise, I'd have been stuck with my old pack forever."

I snorted. "That bastard only has a soft spot because he's trying to make amends for what he did to me, but whatever the reason, I'm happy you were able to escape your pack."

She shrugged. "Yep, but as I said, I'm still a mess over it, so I'm trying to—" She paused, searching for the words. "Change my fate, I guess. And in doing that, I need to stop hiding and living a half-life.

In doing that, I have to take risks. It was what drove me to track you down in the first place."

Nudging her side, I let out a long, calming breath. "I understand you on a level that's somewhat scary, but on the other hand, I love that we're doing this together. I'm scared too, but we've got this. Women can do anything, especially when we stick together. I truly believe that."

She linked her arm through mine, seemingly bolstered by my words. "I believe that too," she said, her voice growing in confidence. "Let's do this. Together, we can figure out why you're here, what the hell happened to this place, and what sort of smoke demon pet we just inherited."

I was struck by the truth that real friends, as rare as they were, could be recognized in how they encouraged us—either via words or actions—to be the best versions, the *strongest* versions of ourselves. And when we couldn't be strong, they were there to pick us up and hold us together.

Like right now, our confidence together was what pushed us to take our first steps into the new unknown we were facing.

Sam shook her head as we observed the carnage around us. "It was a library, right?" she asked.

"Yeah, I'm pretty sure it was," I said, staring from the carved ceilings soaring above, down to the multiple windows that lined the walls. They were cracked and broken now, as was everything else in this place, having been reduced to mere rubble.

Only pieces of white shelving remained, piled haphazardly across the shiny floor. The books that had once adorned those shelves had fared no better, now just scattered pages and torn covers.

"Are you a book lover?" Sam asked, sounding choked up.

I nodded, my head bobbing like one of those stupid dolls. "*Huge* book lover," I said through my tight throat. "I feel like I've stumbled into my worst nightmare, and the only thing that could make this worse is if a fucking clown car drove in, eighteen tiny clowns piled out of it, and then they pummeled me to death using the broken books."

Sam cleared her throat. "Oh, good. I was worried I'd be the dramatic one in this friendship."

"Rest assured..." I choked out. "You have no need to worry on that front."

She actually laughed, and somehow I felt a tiny bit better.

Walking farther into the room, I found myself growing uncharacteristically angry. "Whoever did this is a fucking murderer," I rumbled. "How could they?"

Sam wasn't laughing now. "Yep, a book murderer, and if we find them, I'll help you bury the damn body."

She was dead serious, and I was right there with her.

"Do you have any thoughts on where we are exactly?" I asked because it was clear that we were... a little outside our normal existence. "Do you think we're still on Earth? Or maybe...?"

Sam paused, right beside another pile of broken dreams. "Look, I'm not one to believe in magic, but after today... there's not a hope in hell we're still on Earth. I'd bet my left tit on it."

"My left tit is my favorite," I told her. "But I'd still bet it because I agree with you."

She snorted. "Good to know."

But was it? Because not being on Earth changed the whole narrative here, and I wasn't sure where we were going to end up once we uncovered the truth of this place.

The farther we walked into the broken library, the larger the wreckage was, until we almost couldn't make it any deeper into the room.

"How is there no one here?" Sam asked, pushing up on her toes to try to get a better look. "Do you think they all died during this destruction?"

"I don't know," I said, frustration and confusion warring within me. I'd been so sure my truth was here, but all I'd found was a broken library. Maybe it was an allegory for my brain because right now I felt like I was one step away from being nothing more than what I saw here.

"Maybe we should try to climb over that largest pile," Sam said, stepping closer to kick some of the shelving out of the way. "We shouldn't give up yet—"

She was cut off by a faint sound, a scuffle, near to where we stood. Sam and I exchanged a quick, wide-eyed look, before we both hurried forward. "Hello?" I called, starting to lift books and wooden fragments off the side closest to where I'd heard the sound. "Is anyone there? We're digging you out."

There was another scuffle, and with it came the faintest scent of old moss and earthy soil. Those were not library scents, but rather a living entity. "There's someone under there," I said with urgency, and Sam and I worked frantically to move the items off the pile.

It took us a few minutes to lessen the heaviest part, and by this time, the scuffling was louder. "I really hope it's not a giant rat," Sam said, staring down with a look of unease. "I have my doubts anything else could survive under that much weight. Unless it was small enough to move between the pieces."

If it was a larger being, they would have to be exceptionally strong to survive. Strong and possibly dangerous. Still, I couldn't leave anyone trapped and hurt when I could help; it wasn't in my nature.

With that in mind, Sam and I scrambled to get the final layers of debris off, and much to our surprise, the cloud helped as well, zipping down to scoop up the heaviest objects, its misty substance apparently able to solidify and wrap around shelving, to drag it from the pile.

The physical work helped to keep my mind from wandering into panic territory, though I did find a second to hope that this was a new clue to uncover.

I'd come looking for answers, and at this point, I only had more questions, but as long as we were moving in the right direction, I would keep on pushing.

I had no other choice.

Chapter Sixteen

It took us another ten minutes at least to get the being free. It was not a rat, or a cockroach, or any other critter, but it also wasn't a human or shifter, that much we knew for sure.

Despite her previous fear of what we might uncover, Sam was the first to dive down and help them up. I was slower because I couldn't stop staring at the hairless, three-foot-tall... little dude?

Roughly humanoid, it had gnarled and toughened skin. Despite its small stature, it had to be very strong because there were no visible injuries from being buried under a very large and heavy pile of books and shelving.

When the creature was in a sitting position, it wiped the last of the dust from its face, smiling at Sam before it turned to me. When its huge eyes locked on mine, the dark, unblinking orbs sent trills of unease through me.

Just when I was about to step away, it said, "Mera?"

For a beat, I freaked out before remembering this was exactly what I'd been waiting for. Evidence that I'd been here before. Dropping to my knees, I reached out and grabbed on to its hands, and the firm grip that almost crushed my fingers confirmed how strong the creature was.

"You know me?" I choked out. "You've met me before?"

Our gazes remained locked for a long moment in time before the being nodded. "I know you very well, Mera Callahan, of the Torma shifters."

A tear escaped from me, and I sucked in a shuddering breath, trying to get myself under control, lest I fall down and cry on this poor guy.

The creature smiled at me, a crooked curve of thin lips that strangely calmed me. "And before you ask, my name is Gaster. I'm a goblin of the demi-fae of Faerie, and I identify as male, in what you would understand gender to be."

I swallowed hard. "How did you know I had all of those questions running through my mind...? Wait a fucking minute. Did you just say 'Faerie?'"

His smile grew. "You have not changed, my girl. With or without your memories, you'll always need labels."

The smoke cloud drifted closer, wrapping around Gaster. I leaned away, unsure if it was going to attack or not. Gaster laughed, a rough, grating sound. "Ah, yes, I should have known Inky would find you."

I looked between him and... Inky?

"The smoke cloud has a name?" I asked, my aching brain trying to piece it all together.

"You gave it the name," Gaster told me. "It stuck."

I shook my head. "I don't remember," I breathed. "I don't remember any of this and when I try, my head feels like it's being pummeled in a knife fight."

Gaster pulled himself to his feet, needing only a little help from me. "I have the answers you seek," he said softly. "Just give me a moment to restore my energy."

Answers! He had freaking answers.

My gut had been right, and I owed Samantha Rowland a fucking house on the beach for her help today. Speaking of... "Are you okay?" I asked, noting how pale she looked.

Her throat moved as she swallowed roughly. "I'm not sure. Who is this being you've found?"

I tilted my head. "He said his name is Gaster, a goblin of the demi-fae."

She stared at me. "And you speak demi-fae?"

It was at that point I finally understood why she looked so pale and confused. Gaster didn't speak English, and apparently, I spoke whatever language he did. Just like with the Japanese alpha back in Torma.

Gaster cleared his throat and I looked down to meet his eyes. "The universal translator on the library has been destroyed, along with the Solaris System doorways. We're in deep trouble, and I'm afraid you might be the only one who can help us fix this mess."

"Holy shit," I breathed. "Even speaking demi-fae, I only understood about half the context for what you just said. Maybe you can start at the beginning and tell me everything."

He nodded, wincing as he stepped forward. "I agree, but I'm not sure how much time we really have before it's too late to undo what has been done."

Oh, excellent, more ominous forecasting.

"Does he need any help?" Sam asked, still confused as hell. "Food or water or medical attention?"

I repeated her questions to Gaster and he shook his head. "No, I'm fine. My energy is returning faster than expected, and I think I have the strength now to find you some clothes. When you are comfortable, we can quickly catch each other up on what happened."

I repeated his words to Sam, and she let out a relieved breath. "Yeah, look, I know we're shifters, but at some point, I prefer not to have all of my body parts greeting the world."

An actual genuine chuckle escaped me. "Yep, same."

"Then follow me," Gaster said, already looking more energized as he moved through the debris. His face fell as he took in the destruction, craggy crevices creasing his cheeks. "I was knocked out during the first assault," he said sadly. "Unable to protect my charges. I think the only reason I wasn't banished from the Library of Knowledge like all the others is he missed me in the chaos."

He? Oh, damn, I legitimately had so many questions, but now wasn't the time. Gaster had said he would spill everything that had happened; I just had to be patient. Which was clearly a strong character trait of mine. Along with delusion.

When he finally reached the part of the library east of the main entrance, he started to search through what looked like badly dented storage cupboards. I spent the time waiting for him, filling Sam in on everything she hadn't understood because she didn't speak demi-fae.

Like a normal shifter.

By the time Gaster finally emerged, with long sheets of white material that he helped us fashion into makeshift togas, my friend was completely up to date. And then, when our naked parts were clothed, Gaster led us to one of the very few spots not covered in devastation, gesturing for us to sit.

"I'll translate," I told Sam.

She nodded, looking like a toga-clad goddess. Pretty sure Sam could wear a potato sack and still be gorgeous. "I can wait until the end. I know this is your story and you've waited a long time to uncover this truth."

Technically, it hadn't been that long, but it felt like a damn eternity.

"Thank you," I said, before Gaster cleared his throat, stealing all of my attention.

"You arrived here almost two Earth years ago," he said.

My stomach swirled violently. "Two years?" I repeated, feeling my lips tremble. "When the Torma pack was locked in their stasis?"

Gaster shook his head. "They were in stasis for a few months, that is all. The last two years were normal for them, but clearly, someone has changed the timeline."

I opened and closed my mouth, no words emerging, because I

was too stunned to form coherent thoughts, let alone speech. All of the packs had remembered this new version of the timeline, none of them questioning the small inconsistencies. How was the being who did this powerful enough to change the minds of tens of thousands of shifters?

Sam reacted to the devastation on my face, inching closer to wrap her arm around me. "What did he say?" she bit out. "Are you okay?"

I shook my head, swallowing roughly. "No, I'm really not okay. He told me I arrived here two years ago, and there was no long-term stasis with Torma. Which all boils down to the fact that I'm not missing two months of memories... I'm missing two *years*."

Her brow furrowed as she stared at me. "You know," she said slowly. "I have the memories of Torma being locked down, but a part of me also remembers applying to them during what should have been the stasis. Applying and getting rejected."

There were many holes in this entire fucking situation, but Sam, like all the others, had just brushed off her confusion. I was the only one who couldn't stop picking.

"You were brought here by our master, the Shadow Beast," Gaster continued, bringing my scattered attention back to him.

"The Shadow Beast?" I confirmed, once again parroting him in shock.

A flutter hit me hard in my chest, and it was different to the one I'd felt in Torma. My palm was itching again too, stronger than ever, and in the same moment, my wolf surged to the surface, almost forcing me to shift.

Somehow I managed to wrest her back because we had to stay in this form to ask our questions. "I know the Shadow Beast?"

Gaster nodded. "Oh, yes, very well. You're friends. Maybe more than friends, I think, even though I wasn't really privy to the inner workings of your relationship. But I never saw him treat anyone the way he treated you. You're special, Mera. You changed the beast for the better, and for a powerful being who has spent two thousand years ruling with fear and control, that means something."

None of this felt real, and yet... I believed him. I felt it deep in my chest, where a huge, gaping hole existed. A hole that Torin had tried to fill, but he'd been a poor substitute for what I'd truly lost.

A mate.

"Shadow." I tested the name on my tongue, and Inky responded by wrapping around me.

"You called him that," Gaster said with excitement. "Are you starting to remember?"

I shook my head. "Not really, but it's familiar. Whatever spell was placed on me, it's designed to cause me pain whenever I push at its barrier. I have to figure out a way to break through so the memories return. Whoever created this spell, they hoped I would just settle into my new life and never question the plot holes, so to speak."

Gaster's laughter rasped out of him again. "They don't know you at all. You're forever questioning everything. It's part of your appeal."

At this point, I wanted to hug this little guy, but I refrained, just in case it was offensive here.

"So how did my memories get taken? And what happened to the library?"

This was when he sobered, the odd laughter that I already enjoyed hearing disappearing as quickly as his smile. "You had a powerful spell placed on you," he said, his eyes lowering. "From what I observed, almost everyone who was outside of the library at the time of placing was affected by the spell. Those of us inside these walls were somewhat protected."

I nodded, encouraging him to continue, even as dread built within me.

"Shadow was outside the library," he said in a rush, "and even though he was spelled to forget you, he knew something was wrong. When he returned to the library, he was more beast than I've ever seen him be. He lost control, destroying the library and Solaris System. He didn't know what he was looking for, but he knew something important had been stolen from him. He..." Gaster shook his head. "It was catastrophic, and I have no idea who survived the fallout. Everyone is gone, as you can see, and the doorways have been destroyed. Along with any means to get help from the outside world."

"What is the Solaris System?"

At this point, I'd given up repeating for Sam, but she was good to her word, waiting patiently.

"It was a network of doorways connected to this library." He waved his hand, letting out a long breath. A sad breath. "This was one of the most beautiful and complete knowledge portals in all the worlds. Knowledge that will now be lost for eternity."

Okay, if he cried, I would cry because this was heartbreaking.

"There were ten doors, each leading to a different world in our system of worlds. Including my home world of Faerie."

He repeated a bunch of other names, including Valdor, where vampires of all fucking things lived, and the Shadow Realm, which was where he said I'd been when everyone's memories had been wiped.

"Was Simone here in the library?" I asked, because that was what made sense with everything else I'd learned.

Gaster nodded, sitting straighter. "She was! She was here when Master Shadow released his beast, and I have no idea what happened after that."

My heart thumped loudly, and I pressed a hand to my chest to try to keep it together.

"She's alive," I decided, still refusing to accept any other possibility.

He nodded. "There's every chance she made it out alive. Many escaped through the doors before they were ripped away. And she was with Lucien, the Master Vampire of Valdor. If he could have saved her, he would have."

Tucking my trembling hands under my legs, I fought through the panic. I had no idea what I'd expected to find when I'd started out on this journey. As always, I'd taken it one step at a time, dealing with the information as it came to me, but seriously... *Seriously!*

This was so much more than any shifters should be expected to accept. "Is there any way to return my memories?" I asked, figuring that would fill in all the blank spots and hopefully remove the low level of panic flooding my veins.

"A very powerful being has cursed you," Gaster said, leaning in to examine me closely. I prepared myself for the bad news. "And, while it won't be easy to break through the multiple crisscrossing lines of their power, there might be a way. It's just..." He trailed off ominously.

"What? I'll do anything."

Crisscrossing lines? That had to be the wall of sunlight and moon beams I'd seen in my head when I'd been fighting against the memory spell.

"To break this spell, you have to break as well," he said, ripping the Band-Aid off in one swift yank. "The spell has had enough time to infiltrate into your true self, and to remove it..." No one needed him to finish that sentence.

It really didn't matter to me. Whatever the consequences, I'd take them. "I can't live like this anymore, Gaster," I told him, having no doubts. "Missing all of my memories and life-changing experiences. It's worth the risk."

Gaster nodded, and I loved that he didn't bother to argue with me.

I might not be strong enough, but at least he was giving me a chance.

Sometimes a chance was all anyone ever needed.

Chapter Seventeen

When Gaster left to find ingredients for his spell, I spent my time pacing, stressing, and filling Sam in on the information she'd missed.

"The Shadow Beast?" she whisper-screamed, before shutting her mouth with a snap. She shook her head. "It's too insane to even think about. I don't understand how you lived this life, and it was all taken from you."

"Gaster was very light on the details when it came to that," I said, thinking hard enough to hurt myself, "and I'm guessing it's due to the fact that he wasn't there for a lot of the big shit that happened. I bet he doesn't want to give me any false information."

"Hence why this memory reversal is important enough to risk death, right?"

She seemed unsure. I couldn't blame her, but like our goblin friend, she didn't try to talk me out of it. We were all adults capable of making our own decisions, and it was nice that I didn't have to explain my reasoning to them. They got it. And I sensed that both of them would have made the same decision.

By the time Gaster returned, Sam and I had salvaged twenty

books, the mostly undamaged tomes which appeared to be about one of the great fae wars, were stacked neatly nearby. "Oh, thank you," Gaster cried, hurrying up, his arms full of parchment and jars. "It's beyond devastating what we've lost here. Priceless knowledge from ten worlds and thousands of years."

No lie, that almost made me throw up. Shadow Beast had a lot to answer for, even if he hadn't been quite in his right mind when it had happened.

"Now, are you sure?" Gaster checked one last time as he started to spread out his items on the ground.

"I'm ready," I said with conviction.

I really was because the alternative was walking away from this world without all of the answers I'd sought and returning to Torin and Torma. Hard freaking pass, people.

"I'm going to need you to lie in this circle," Gaster said, and I realized that in mere seconds, he'd managed to trace out a very complex-looking circle of images and symbols in white chalk. "This is called a spell sphere," he explained, "and it will protect you and us from whatever"—he cleared his throat—"might emerge in the destruction of this bind on your memories."

Ominous, but not surprising. Gaster didn't strike me as a being prone to hysterics, and there was no hiding the genuine worry in his voice as he spoke about this *procedure*. The spell sphere was an excellent choice.

Sam reached out and grabbed my hand as I moved past. "You've got this," she whispered. "I know whatever is thrown your way, you'll catch it and throw it back even harder."

I returned her squeeze. "Thank you."

Our eyes met, and while she looked worried, the worry was considerably less than the unwavering confidence in her gaze. She thought I could do this, and I was determined to prove her right.

When I was ready, I stretched out in the circle, finding it the perfect size for me. A tingle of power zapped over my skin, fast, like electricity. Gaster continued to sketch images around me, and as he closed in the final sections of the spell sphere, the energy settled across me.

"The sphere is complete," Gaster said, his voice muffled, like a literal barrier existed between us. "Brace yourself, Mera Callahan."

I closed my eyes and held on for dear life, digging my fingers into the ground. There was little traction, but I still felt like it was an anchor, keeping me in place. Gaster started to chant, the words growing in volume until they echoed throughout the library.

The chant entered my brain, spinning and building in power and volume. Eventually, when my head felt like it might explode and I was on the brink of screaming, Gaster's final word chimed over me like a chord.

A chord that grew deeper, my body vibrating with it, as if every one of my cells was bouncing and picking up speed. My body left the ground, the spell sphere the only thing preventing me from drifting off completely.

"Hold on, Mera!" Sam shouted as the shaking got worse. "You're almost finished."

Trusting that she knew something I didn't, I closed my eyes tighter and stopped fearing the unknown. I gave myself into the spell and allowed it to do its job. The vibration increased until my brain was a jumble. I couldn't remember who I was, where I was, or why I was even there. But I definitely remembered how to scream.

When the pain grew greater than I could manage, screams burst up from my chest and out of my mouth, going on for hours, days, weeks. A pain beyond pain. A broken mind and body. Lines of light shattered through and around me as that shield across my memories was torn to pieces. And the pain went on.

Sobbing.

Screaming.

Lost. Alone.

Shadow... Shadow... Shadow.

Where was Shadow?

My soul raged, in a way I had never felt before, eclipsing even the near complete destruction of the pain in my body. *Shadow Beast.* He was not my enemy, or the being who had stolen my memories.

He was my... *everything.*

Flames raged with me now as my power tore free from its cage, filling the sphere and coating my entire body. With this, the pain faded, and eventually, my screams stopped and I was finally at peace.

A gentle touch on my shoulder shook me from the darkness, and as Gaster said my name, I jerked up in a rush, my head pounding like a jackhammer as more memories were freed.

"You made it through," Gaster said, continuing to keep his voice low, "and your memories will return as soon as your brain heals."

As a shifter, my brain injury should have healed up in seconds, but, apparently, whatever had been done to me went much deeper than usual. It took at least ten minutes for the pounding to stop, and as I finally lifted my head and looked around, the destruction I saw hit me on a level that only in this moment I could truly understand.

"My library." I gasped, and then I was sobbing, my hands coming up to cover my eyes as I tried to suck in deep breaths. When I looked up to Gaster, his expression was as broken as I felt. "I missed you," I rasped. "I forgot you."

He leaned forward and wrapped his arms around me, holding on with about ten times the strength you'd expect him to have. "I missed you too, Mera. But we'll figure out how to fix it."

The memories continued to return, mostly in jagged images, and I had to work through them slowly because the rush was overwhelming.

"We were in the Shadow Realm," I murmured, "and we'd just defeated Ixana, Shadow's mate, who was the one to start the entire series of events two thousand years ago..." My words died off as I found the final key to my story. The final betrayer.

"It was Dannie," I whispered. "Dannie is Shadow's mom, and a goddess born of the Nexus. She tried to save us. She ate a powerful stone from Faerie so that Ixana couldn't use it, but the power corrupted her. Changed her. It turned her into this phoenix-goddess hybrid obsessed with keeping the balance. To her, that meant I needed to go back to the shifters and be the alpha-mate."

The more I spoke about it, the clearer the memories grew. I quickly repeated everything to Sam so she was following along as well.

"A goddess," she gasped. "A goddess who'll still be determined to keep this balance? What are we going to do?"

I knew what I needed to do. What I needed, period. My pack. My real one.

The flutter in my chest burst to life, but this time, there was no fear or confusion that followed. Dr. Google had been wrong; it was no heart attack. I was feeling my bond with Angel. And the itching on my palm in the exact same spot I used to have a purplish mark, was for Midnight, my bonded mist. I'd been feeling my pack, who were missing out there somewhere in the system of worlds.

"Where're Shadow, Angel, Simone, and Midnight?" I asked in a rush. Simone had been in the library, so her memory had likely been spared, but the rest of them had been in the Shadow Realm with me. I scrambled to my feet. "Gaster, please, you have to tell me where they are."

He opened his hands, his face wreathed in devastation. "The only one whose whereabouts I know for sure is Inky. He's clearly been guarding that hallway from Earth to the Shadow Realm the entire time."

Like he'd called him, the mist zoomed down, and this time, when I saw him, the feeling of being followed by an ominous cloud of scary was gone. *It was my Inky.*

It wrapped around me, and I hugged it as close as I could. There was no real substance, but it felt like we made contact. "Inky, buddy." I sobbed. "Oh, gods, how did I forget you? Do you remember everything? Spark once if you do."

Pulling away from me, it swelled up larger and sparked twice.

"Okay, dammit." Even the mists were affected. Freaking Dannie and her overachieving. "But you clearly knew I wasn't a threat because you let me through the doorway."

He sparked once.

It was starting to make sense now. "Inky and Midnight are connected to Shadow and me, so they were lost in the spell, just the same as we were."

I'd been feeling a sense of dread since I'd woken up in Torin's bed, and while some of it had to do with that slimy bastard, so much more of it was because of Dannie. Because of what she had done to me and all of my pack.

"I have to find Shadow."

It was a need filling me up until I might burst from it.

Gaster shook his head. "That's not a good idea, Mera. He destroyed the library and all of the doors from here. The master is a true beast, and... what if you're also destroyed in his anger?"

These were the parts of my story Gaster didn't know because he hadn't been there.

"Shadow will not destroy me," I said with confidence. "Firstly, I'm stronger than you think. I was born of the Nexus... a similar being to Dannie. I'm a match for Shadow."

In more ways than one. Every touch and kiss—our first kiss— burned like a bright light of memory in my mind. Every single moment that had been stolen from me.

"And secondly, I believe he left the hallway to Earth unbroken for a very specific reason, whether he realized it or not. I am the one being who can bring him back."

Gaster held my gaze, but he didn't argue. He nodded, like it all made sense.

"You are the key," he said. "Thank the gods you didn't fall into life back in Torma."

That was when the real truth of what had happened hit me hard. I had all the context now, the memories, the history. "How could Dannie do this?" I whispered, trying to hold tears back. "She knew what my pack did to me. She fucking knew. And she sent me back to them. Back to Torin. If I hadn't trusted my instincts..."

I trailed off at the horror of what might have happened to me if I'd listened to Jaxson and all the others. I would have fallen into bed with the alpha and never known what had been stolen from me.

"The sunburst stone is no ordinary faerie stone," Gaster told me, reaching out to take my hand in his. "Very few could have survived being close to it, let alone taking it into their essence. Corruption was really the only ending for Dannie's story, and I fear that as the stone has time to really root itself into her power, her views on the 'balance' will only grow worse."

In a way, Dannie was a victim here as well, but unless she was willing to repent her ways, she was also the enemy. An enemy I needed my pack to deal with.

"Will you help me track the beast down now?"

"Yes," Gaster said. "Your points are very valid, and I think the thing he raged about losing was you. You're the one who can bring him back to us."

"Damn right," I said.

I'd lost a lot in my life, and what Dannie had done to me topped all of that, but I'd been given a second chance. A chance I would not waste.

For starters, no more pretending I wasn't in love with the Shadow Beast.

Desperately, *desperately* in love.

A beast I had forgotten in my head but never in my heart. I knew now that Shadow was the main reason Torin had always felt like a spoiled, selfish, *weak*, petulant brat.

Shadow Beast was anything but weak.

He was worthy beyond all others, and it was time that I tracked him down... and made that bastard repair my library.

Right after he fucked me silly.

No lie, my heart and my vagina fluttered at the very thought.

Chapter Eighteen

Since he'd been trapped under what remained of my library, Gaster really had no idea where Shadow had disappeared to. Tracking the beast was never going to be easy, and especially not with his recently re-acquired ability to use shadowy energy to move between worlds.

He could be anywhere. Any of the worlds. Worlds I could not get to because there were no doorways.

However, I did have a few clues when it came to his whereabouts, the first being Inky. Shadow and Inky were bonded, and where there was one, the other was close behind. Dannie hadn't taken their memories of each other away, so it stood to reason, Shadow was still here.

With that in mind, I headed straight for the lair, all the while reaching through my bond for Midnight. From the moment my memories had begun unraveling from their cage, I'd searched for my mist, but there was nothing at the end of our bond except static electricity.

I could only guess that my mist was still in the Shadow Realm and out of my reach. Hopefully, once I found Shadow, he'd have all the final answers to the timeline that had begun after Dannie had swirled me back to Torma.

Inky, Sam, and Gaster stayed with me, right until we reached the lair portal. A portal that was still intact despite the complete destruction everywhere else. Hello, second clue.

"This is as far as you can go," I said to Sam. "Shadow is very particular about who enters his lair, and he's obviously a little out of control, so let's not test him today."

She nodded, nervously worrying at her bottom lip. "I understand. I'll stay here and help Gaster ferret out more books that can be saved."

A woman after my own heart. "We'll make the Shadow Bastard fix my library, don't worry."

She didn't laugh, and I didn't blame her. This entire situation was the stuff midlife crises were made of.

Gaster stepped closer, and I read the worry in his orb-like eyes. "Be safe," he finally said. "Don't trust that this is the same being you knew. His power and anger destroyed a library and Solaris System that have been part of him for thousands of years. You have your work cut out for you, Mera Callahan."

I hugged him.

At first, he was surprised, but within a few seconds, his body relaxed against mine. I finally remembered why none of the powerful creatures here liked to hug: because they feared their energy being stolen by another. Gaster, despite his diminutive stature, was a being of great power and intellect, and his reticence when it came to touching was no different to the others.

I was the only one they let into their personal space, and because of that, I gave them hugs as freely as I could. "Please don't die," Gaster said against my shoulder. "Your light makes the world much brighter for us all. I truly missed you."

"I've missed you too," I said, straightening. "More than I can say.

It was like a part of my soul died when Dannie stole my memories, and I won't get that part back until we fix it all."

He nodded, taking a moment to compose himself before he stepped away from me. "Best of luck with your mission, Mera Callahan."

I shot him a cheeky smile. "You got it, Gaster. Also, can you look after Sam for me? Maybe you can find a way to communicate with her?"

"I'll see what I can do."

When I repeated that to my new friend, she waved me off. "We'll figure it out. Miming always works."

Unable to resist the tugging in my center any longer, I finally followed my heart's—and soul's—desire and stepped toward the portal. I had no idea what I was about to find on the other side, but not even a million insane goddesses could have stopped me from walking through.

Inky, the only one permitted to enter with me, stayed right behind me as I reached out a hand. The moment my fingers touched the barrier, a zap knocked me back a few steps.

What in the hell?

Peering closer, I finally noticed that the portal was laced through with tiny specks of fire; Shadow had upped his barriers. Thankfully, my own powers were free now, and I knew exactly how to access my fire.

Without any effort, I drew the flames protectively around my skin, hearing a low gasp from behind me. Sam would no doubt have some questions for me when I returned. *If* I returned.

This time when I placed my hand into the barrier, the zap of electricity raced across my skin like an old friend. I had missed that zap so badly, relishing in the feel of it tingling over my skin and sliding through my body to settle between my legs, hot and heavy and aching.

Shadow.

With the whisper of his name in my head, I pushed harder against the portal's security, until the resistance faded, and I was finally able to step through. Inky remained with me, and it was comforting to have my buddy there.

Especially when the lair came into view.

I'd been expecting the worst after seeing the Library of Knowledge, preparing myself for more destruction, but... that wasn't the case in the lair. Taking a step into the darkness, my wolf rose up to help me see, and it still took me a moment to figure out what he'd done.

The lack of light in here was a combination of shadows and mists, layered over every surface by the Shadow Beast himself. He'd created a web of darkness, designed to trap and destroy any who entered its midst.

My fire, which had died down across my skin, flared again, giving me the ability to both see and cut through the web of shadows. The room was icy cold as I moved deeper into it, and I had the sense that if I were any normal human or shifter, the cold would have killed me.

Even as it was, with literal fire burning around me, my breath still puffed out in a visible cloud before me. Inky pressed closer as we both felt the beating heart of another deep in this cave of death.

Gaster hadn't been wrong about Shadow.

He was no longer my beast. He was the true *beast* of shifter nightmares. The creature who stalked us in the night and destroyed any who crossed his path. And maybe a year ago that truth would have had me turning tail and running like a scared bitch, but after all I'd been through with Shadow, I'd never give up on him now.

I needed him.

Fuck, the *worlds* needed him.

Without Shadow, his mother would probably destroy us all in her manic need for order and control. I hadn't forgotten what Gaster had said... The stone was only going to continue corrupting its host until there was no sign of the Dannie I knew and loved.

If anyone knew how to stop that from happening, it was Shadow. I just had to find him first.

The farther I crept into the room, the colder it got. How the fuck that was even possible, I had no idea, but apparently there was a new level of *frozen nipples in Antarctica* that Shadow had discovered.

"Shadow," I called after creeping for way too long. "Come out of your damn labyrinth of a library and talk to me."

A moment of silence. A moment before a roar blasted through the shelves, the force knocking me back; I would have landed on my ass if Inky hadn't caught me from behind. Straightening, I shook off the lingering effects of beast magic, returning his roar with one of my own.

"Listen up, you cranky bastard. I'm not your enemy," I bellowed, feeling him move closer. I stood my ground. "I get it, Shadow, I really do. I'm fairly pissed at Dannie as well, but your mom isn't in her right mind, so I need you back in *your* right mind so we can help her."

Despite what Dannie had done to me, I didn't hate her. I was hurt, but I also understood that she'd been trying to save us when she'd swallowed that stone. She probably *had* saved me, since I'd been about to grab it, and who knew what that would have done to someone who was half-shifter.

The power corrupting her was not entirely her fault, and she deserved a chance to be saved.

His roars faded as I sensed him stalking closer. The connection I always felt to him burst to life as my fire grew larger, spreading out from me like it was reaching for the beast.

The fire was the only reason I knew when he was about to attack. It deflected the first slash of his power, and as I dove to the side, I slapped back at him with my own energy. As I scrambled to my feet, Inky got involved, swelling up into a large curtain between us. Shadow stepped into the light of my fire, his misty magic sliding away so I could see every naked inch of him.

He was at least ten feet tall. Or somewhere around that. I was shit at judging heights, as had been well documented, but I knew for a fact that his Anubis form stood well above his normal seven feet.

He was still in a humanoid body, with some structural changes so he was stronger and hairier than normal, both of which were totally fine by me.

Wolf shifter, right? Hair was kind of our thing.

The Anubis wolf head was the most foreign part of him, turning him into a being so god-like that it was hard not to just stare at him in awe. My eyes traced down his bare chest, his ink still visible even under the extra hair, not to mention the abs, and... *holy dick gods in heaven.* Someone needed to say a fucking prayer for that bounty.

"You shouldn't be strolling around here with your weapon just flapping in the book breezes," I managed to say, trying desperately not to let breathlessness creep into my voice.

This was a serious situation, with a beast ready to rip my head from my body. It was certainly not the time to be cockmerised, no matter how impressive the specimen in question, or how long I'd been without him.

Shadow tilted his head again, and the way he moved was so animalistic. Just as Gaster had told me... Shadow was more beast than anything else right now.

Inky drifted closer to me again, and I wondered if it was communicating with Shadow or not. Was the beast able to form coherent thoughts, or was it all rage and instinct?

"Any help would be greatly appreciated, buddy," I said to Inky, my skin prickling as Shadow moved closer to me. His energy was electric, and I wasn't so stupid that I didn't recognize the grave danger I was in here. It wasn't the first time I'd been near death around the Shadow Beast, but it was the first time he could not be communicated or reasoned with.

Right?

Was I making a mistake in assuming that just because his eyes were flaming pools of bloodlust and his claws were mini samurai swords that his brain was not still fully functional? Even when the wolf took over, a part of me remained Mera. Remained my human self.

Unless Dannie had done something else to affect him, the real Shadow was still there, just buried under a shit ton of anger and power.

"You probably don't remember me right now," I started in a soft whisper, "but we're friends. Great friends. I'm most definitely in the top six beings you trust, and considering how long you've lived and how many beings you know, that is really quite the fucking achievement."

Nerves had me babbling, but that had always been a way to get through to him in the past, so I went with it.

"You kidnapped me," I continued, "which, by the way, you're not allowed to do with any other shifter. I'm far too jealous and posses-sive for you to drag another in here by their hair. Nope. I might even beast out myself and put bleach in their shampoo at a high enough strength that their hair would fall out. Not all of it, just... like half of it. I'm not a total monster."

He'd stopped moving, his head stilling as his depthless eyes devoured me. It was hard for me to believe I'd forgotten that intense stare.

"You don't remember me, Shadow, but our souls matc—"

Before I could finish my sentence, he roared, a deafening sound that had true power behind it, sending me flying back into a nearby shelf. I hadn't been ready for it, failing to brace myself and stop bones from breaking. Normally, it wouldn't be a huge deal, but the few minutes it took me to heal was all the time the beast needed to attack again. Thankfully, my wolf saw the issue as well, forcing the change on us so we healed in an instant.

Without a glance back, we took off through the library, Shadow right on our tail.

Calling up the fire as soon as the portal came into sight, we dove through. Shadow didn't follow me, but I felt him there, standing on the lair side of the portal.

Dammit, that had not gone as well as expected, but at least I knew what I was dealing with now. And I didn't have to track Shadow down halfway across the worlds. He was here, and now I needed a plan of attack.

Chapter Nineteen

G aster and Sam appeared mere seconds later, waiting patiently as I shifted back. Then, my favorite goblin dug out another sheet with which to fashion a toga for me, and I filled them in on what I'd found.

"He's completely lost himself to the beast." My lips were pressed into thin lines as I tried to figure out what the hell I could do now. "I'm going to have to keep pushing, bit by bit, until I figure out the key to breaking through to my Shadow."

Gaster's face was uncharacteristically solemn. "Are you sure that the man is not lost without hope? It has been known to happen, and I'm not sure that those lost are ever truly recovered."

"He's still there," I said firmly. "After everything he's gone through, I seriously doubt this is the moment he gives into the dark side."

Gaster didn't look convinced. "If what you've said is true, you might be the one thing that Shadow could not handle losing. He doesn't remember why, but he knows deep inside that he's broken beyond repair. From what I heard, Shadow destroyed worlds for you.

He dismantled the Solaris System with a swipe of his power. Literal worlds fallin—"

"Holy fuck." I gasped, interrupting him. "He said he would let the Shadow Realm fall, if it was a choice between that world and me." My eyes met Gaster's. "He said that to me when we were in the realm, but it's just an expression, right? A super sexy, hot-as-hell expression that made me feel all the things. But no one literally destroys worlds when the person they care about is hurt..."

A sad chuckle emerged from the goblin. "You don't understand. Shadow didn't just sever all the connections to the worlds and then hole up in his lair. Since you were taken from him, he has struck a path of destruction through the ten worlds. With enough force that I'm not sure all of them can recover."

Well, okay then. The beast was literal, a good point to remember.

"We can still fix it all," I said with more confidence than I felt. "I'll give him a few hours to calm down because he's a wee bit angry at the moment. But tomorrow morning, first thing, I'm going to be on his ass like a goddamn barnacle until he learns to love me again. If there's one thing I'm good at, it's wearing people down."

I repeated this in English for Sam, and she smiled. "Embrace your strengths, right?"

That almost got a laugh from me. "You're handling this fairly well," I said, impressed with her calm demeanor. "Are you saving up your freak-outs for later? I often do that."

She shrugged. "I'm trying this new thing where I just go with the flow. Sometimes it works; other times I fail miserably. Today I'm somewhere between the two."

I patted her on the arm. "Stick with me. You'll be adjusted to the randomness of life in no time."

My words didn't seem to be reassuring for her, but she didn't argue either.

"If you're going back into the lair, I think it's best if we get some food and rest," Gaster said, falling into his concierge role.

"Is the dining hall gone too?" I asked sadly.

He paused, and it was clear he had no idea. "We should find out."

Stepping through the library, we finally managed to maneuver our way into the dining hall, which, surprisingly, was completely untouched. Robot servers intact and everything. They rushed straight up to us when we walked through the door, like waitstaff desperately waiting for their first customers to arrive.

"Hmm," Gaster said, seeming confused. "I thought the master had destroyed all the magic of the library, but it's still quite strong here."

"I can understand you!" Sam said with a shout before she lowered her voice. "Oh, wow, it's nice to talk after resorting to sign language."

Gaster's face lit up. "Oh, yes, the ability to communicate lowers so many barriers between races and worlds. I will enjoy discussing many of your life achievements."

Sam didn't laugh and quip something like "Oh, that will be a short discussion," like I would have. Instead, she returned his nod, and in as formal a tone said, "I look forward to that day, sir. "

Match made in heaven, even if their formal talk in the dining hall did depressingly remind me of Angel. My best friend who was out in the worlds, with no memory of me.

As soon as I got through to Shadow, we had to track down the rest of our pack.

But first, food.

"Please give me one of everything," I told the server, elated that my appetite was finally back.

The small fae-created robot scurried off, swift and nimble. They were ingenious and perfect for this role, able to balance cartloads of dishes and never mix up an order.

"It was nice of you to order for us," Sam said with a smile, settling into her chair.

Right... "No problem."

Gaster shot me a knowing look, well aware of my love of this place and my ability to eat enough for three grown shifters. But he didn't correct me in front of our new friend. Dude had my back, and I would always have his, no matter what happened in these worlds.

Sam and Gaster continued to converse while we waited, so excited to be given this gift of understanding. It seemed that they had quite a lot in common, especially the way Sam was very well-read in my least favorite genre: the classics.

Gaster was in nerd-goblin heaven.

And all I could think about was Shadow.

I'd never ached for another being the way I did for him. I'd been attracted to Jaxson and other shifters, and my vagina had certainly done her fair share of whining about our dry spell, but that was pure horny-girl-hormone stuff. It was nothing compared to the deep-seated ache that started low in my gut and fanned out through every part of my body when I thought of Shadow.

It was beyond intense, to the point that sitting here and not running back into the lair to be near him, even if he was more beast than person at the moment, took real effort.

"How could Dannie do this to me?"

It was a rhetorical question. We'd already been over it all. We'd already discussed the stone and its many varied ways of corrupting my former friend. But the grief in my chest needed a place to release.

Sam placed her hand on my shoulder, and while she didn't say anything, her touch was comforting to me.

Chapter Twenty

We slept in the dining hall because apparently you could order bedding, toiletries, and other items, and the servers would bring it along. With that in mind, we swapped out our sheets for clean clothing, and I somehow managed not to ask for a vibrator, just to see how far I could push it.

The next morning, after breakfast and finding a bathroom to pee and wash up, I was ready to return to Shadow. In truth, I'd never left Shadow, at least not in my mind. It had been near impossible to sleep knowing he was so close... and yet still so far away.

Gaster and Sam waited near the barrier as I crept closer, and I expected that I'd be unable to venture through without some real power this time, and I was absolutely correct. My beast had ramped up all his securities overnight. Shadow was somewhat predictable when it came to protecting his power base, and his more animalistic form was no doubt worse than ever.

Sparks shot at me when I got closer, but I just brought fire to my skin and sent my power back in response. At the familiar burn across my body, I tilted my head back to enjoy the sensation.

My power had been locked away from me most of my life, but

after being in Torma again, I looked at my energy differently. Knowing the reason my father had attacked the alpha, the reason his paranoia had grown until he'd felt he'd had no choice but to force Victor's hand, had changed my perspective. I still had questions, that I hoped to talk to Shadow about—if he ever returned to conversing in full sentences, that was.

Like, why had my powers been so odd growing up? I'd thought my first shift and release of my wolf had triggered my Shadow Realm side to emerge, but now I knew that there had been a few other times.

It had been grief the night my father had died that had opened a doorway to Dannie, allowing her to leave the Shadow Realm. And then there'd been the night of my first shift, when the grief over my rejected mate bond had allowed me to touch the Shadow Realm, setting in motion the rest of my destiny.

Was grief the key? It clearly wasn't torture or fear, because Torma had thoroughly tested that theory.

Another mystery to add to the endless sea I'd been wading through for years. Even when I thought I had a handle on it, something new would blindside me, and I'd realize I knew nothing.

At least I had my powers today when I needed them, strong and blinding in their intensity, and by the time the fire was near-licking the ceiling of the library, I was able to step through the barrier into the lair.

"Shadow," I called softly, pushing deeper into the mist-strewn ice locker.

It was freaky as hell as I moved deeper into his lair, feeling the beast breathing down my neck, but I wouldn't change it for anything. The "safe" world I'd been dropped in with Torin and the Torma pack had been very clever of Dannie. She had given me everything I'd ever wanted, dreams built in a young child's mind of my future in the pack. Funny how dreams could turn to nightmares in a split second.

Shadow had given me such an advantage in Torma too. I didn't know it at the time, but now that my memories were back, I had pieced together a lot of the odd occurrences that had happened to me with the pack. "You kept your word, Shadow," I called loudly. "The one where you promised I'd never have to be vulnerable again. Torin tried to force his will and strength on me, and he was repelled away. At the time, I didn't know why, but I do now. Your power superseded Dannie's."

He was probably also the reason I hadn't been able to touch myself, since he had strong opinions on that as well, but we'd talk about that possessive piece of bullshit later.

An echoing roar rang down the corridors between shelves, an ear-piercing burst of sound that grew louder and louder until a raging beast was right there, huffing as he stared me down. Shadow looked exactly as he had the day before, a powerful mountain of muscle, man and beast, and I drank him in like I hadn't seen him in years, rather than about eight hours.

"You kept your promise," I repeated, my voice shaking from emotional overload. "Torin couldn't hurt me, no matter what he tried. I didn't have my realm powers thanks to Dannie, but she didn't know that your promise to me was stronger. You kept me safe."

He stalked closer, and this time, I did not run. I stood my ground, prepared for the pain he'd inflict. He towered over me as he reached out with those lethal claws, attached to hands about the size of my entire torso. This beast could disembowel me with a single swipe, and still... I did not move.

Last night in the dining hall, when sleep had been an elusive bitch, I'd debated how to bring Shadow back to me. There were two options. The slow path, where I patiently spent months coaxing him into his humanity, little by little, until I eventually wore him down and he released the beast. This was an option I had neither the temperament nor the time for. Which left number two: all in and hope for the best.

"I missed you," I whispered, the words dragging up from deep in my chest. "I hate that I wasted the time we had together, always keeping my distance. Always telling myself that you weren't mine and I was beyond stupid if I grew attached. I fought the connection, the bond between us because I knew it would hurt like this. I knew it would tear me apart in a way that nothing else ever has, not even the rejection of my mate. And you know what?"

He'd stopped moving; it was the first time his predator stalk had ceased.

Now I took a step closer. "It was worse, Shadow. The pain I thought I'd feel when you finally walked away from me was nothing on what I feel right now. *Nothing!*"

Another step closer, and he could reach me now if he swiped, but again, I didn't care. "Our demons match, Shadow. Our souls match. Come back to me."

Flames grew around him, fast and intense, and any normal being standing in his vicinity would be dead. Not me, though, as I sent my own power out to join his until the swirls of fire carried up into the ceiling above.

"Our souls match," I repeated, the burn of our loss deeper than ever.

In the split second it took for me to blink, I was in his hands, a biting grip around my stomach as he stole me away. Flames continued to swirl around us as death held me in its grip, and I'd never been happier.

Shadow took me deep into the library, way past the point I'd ever ventured in the never-ending hall of shelves and books. His grip on my stomach did not ease, his claws cutting into me at times, leaving behind minor flesh wounds that healed instantly. In his own beastly way, I had the feeling he was actively trying *not* to hurt me. A nice and positive step forward.

Unless, of course, this entire venture was all to keep his prey intact until he reached his torture chamber, where he planned to kill and eat me. But, I mean, why bother taking me away from the main entrance? Plenty of room to dismember a body right there... *and* I really had to stop with that line of thought.

Shadow just kept running, and I didn't fight, allowing him this time to work through whatever he was working through. The beast-man was walking on a thin line, and I sensed he could be tipped either way if I screwed up my next move. If one potential result here was losing him to the darkness forever, I had to ensure that never happened.

The running went on for hours, and by the time he was done, I could see he'd been trying to exhaust himself. Had that been his life since he'd returned to the lair? Running to forget... to not feel?

When he was finally ready to rest, a doorway appeared in front of us, huge, shiny and black. His massive frame fit through easily, leaving behind the icy chill of the lair to enter his bedroom. I'd been here only one time before. Once when I'd been near death and he'd taken care of me. Now, it was my turn to do that for Shadow.

I just had to make sure that he didn't murder my ass in the process.

He prowled forward and I would guess by the general warmth and untouched look in here that this was the first time he'd entered since Dannie had betrayed us. Ignoring the bed, the beast prowled to a thick olive-green rug, and there he curled up, tucking me securely against his chest.

My breathing grew shallower thanks to his tight hold, but I didn't complain. For the first time in what felt like forever, I was comfortable and warm, if not a little overwhelmed at whatever was happening right now. Trying to snap him out of this quickly was not without its risks, and while it was too soon to feel overconfident, we were definitely moving in a positive direction.

I was still alive, for one.

Shadow's beast form had claimed me, treating me like a possession it was quite fond of, and I was almost certain that was progress.

Despite the exhaustion I felt seeping from his aura, the massive body behind me remained tense. Eventually, I managed to free one hand so my fingers could run across his fur and skin, stroking the beast softly. "Sleep, Shadow," I whispered. "I'm going to hazard a guess that you've barely rested since Dannie fucked both of our worlds, but you can now. I'll still be here in the morning."

His tension remained for a beat, and then... he relaxed.

My chest grew tight, emotions forcing their way up until my eyes burned and watered. I beat them down, focusing instead on Shadow. I could deal with my mental scars later. For now, he was my only worry.

Chapter Twenty-One

I never expected to sleep. Firstly, my heart was pounding like a freaking jackhammer in my chest, thanks to finally being with Shadow. And secondly, our energies were buzzing together with the force of a power plant.

The magic in our souls had always been copacetic, taking every chance to mingle. It explained why our connection had been solid from almost the first meeting. Maybe we hadn't recognized it then, but looking back, it had clearly been there.

So tonight, teamed with my emotions, our powers, and the chaos in my head, I figured there was no way in hell I'd relax enough to sleep. At one point, during the endless loop in my head, I found myself desperate to pee. I tried to wiggle my way out of his hold, knowing there was a bathroom nearby. The moment I moved, the beast dug his claws in tighter, to the point of drawing tiny pricks of blood across my bare skin.

Apparently, I was going nowhere.

Shadow shifted our positions slightly, clawing at the already torn-up yoga pants and white shirt I'd been wearing. My clothes were annoying him, and he only settled when one of his large paws gripped my right breast.

Just like that, the beast was holding my fucking tits like they belonged to him.

"Don't try any funny shit while you're rocking Egyptian god," I warned Shadow, my voice rumbly in the semi-dark room. "I swear, I will make you regret it if you do. I don't swing that way, okay? I'm not into furry."

The beast howled, a low, soulful sound, seemingly disappointed by my response. The hold on my breast didn't ease, though, and if anything, Shadow's beast just continued lightly clawing at my clothing until eventually I was all but naked, still tightly held against his chest.

Thankfully, he was satisfied then, never touching me anywhere that would cross my line. I was okay with his tit obsession, and it was nice to relax against him with one of his hands across my thigh and the other on my chest, pulling me into his fiery heat. A hard erection rested against my ass, but again, as long as it stayed on the outside of my ass, I could deal because this was a huge first for us.

We'd never cuddled. Not after sex or when we'd almost died. Never.

This was a gift and despite my best efforts, a few tears escaped, dripping down my cheek to land on his furred arm. Shadow Anubis didn't seem to notice, so I allowed myself this moment to express the deep-seated pain that had been cutting me to pieces for weeks. I hadn't known the reason then, but I did now, and in some ways, it hurt worse than ever.

Sometime later when I opened my eyes, I realized I had fallen asleep, so warm and safe in the arms of my beast. Looking down at the hands covering my breasts, I let out a short shriek because the fur and claws were gone.

Shadow growled from behind me; I'd startled him from sleep. His hold on me tightened, but I managed to roll over to face him. His eyes were lava red as I met his gaze, and there was confusion clouding his expression. "Shadow," I said softly.

He startled, jerking me harder against him. "*Mine.*"

The same word I'd heard in Torma, even when I hadn't known where it had come from. Hearing it again now, the first word he'd spoken to me, had my lips trembling.

"Shadow, do you remember me?"

I tried to touch his face, but he held me immobile, his grip unyielding, no matter how much I attempted to break free. He growled and said nothing more, but I felt his free hand running along my skin as he stripped away the final tangles of my underwear. At this point, my body was fully onboard with this because Shadow was back in his humanoid form, and I was one horny, *horny* shifter, who'd been separated from the only male to ever touch my body.

I arched against him, my brain near going offline at the feel of being with Shadow again. If only there wasn't a small part of me frustrated because he still didn't know me. Not really. All of this was instinct, and while I loved that part, I needed the rest. I was a greedy bitch when it came to my beast.

"Shadow. You have to try to remember me. I miss you—"

I was cut off as his hand slipped between my thighs and found the moisture pooling there. Arching into him again, I groaned as he stoked me, his power following each touch, zapping across the sensitive skin. This was effective in shutting down the last part of me that wanted to fight until he remembered.

Maybe I could just have a little sex first. That wasn't too much to ask, right?

"Mine," he murmured, pressing his lips to my throat, his tongue stroking my skin before he dragged it along to my shoulders, kissing and biting me, hard enough that I was near arching half off the ground. *Motherfucker.*

"Darkor!"

I never used that name except when I wanted to make a point. What that "point" was changed with the circumstances, but this time,

I needed to jolt him from his current task of *very* successfully seducing me into forgetting the shit that had happened between us.

His hand slowed but didn't leave my pussy, fingers still sliding their way through my folds and into my aching center. I was drenched, my pleasure dripping down his hand, and I *really couldn't focus on that right now.*

"Shadow, you're a very powerful god," I gasped out, barely managing to think but knowing it had to be said. "You know something has been missing. You know something was taken from you, which is why you destroyed my library. And don't think we won't talk about that later, but for now, I need you to remember what happened. Your mother did this to us. She stole our memories and our lives. She lost control, and from what I know, she will continue to lose control. Until the point she destroys everything... I can't fix this without you."

His fingers finally stilled, leaving me literally on the edge of an orgasm. I managed to keep from screaming and panting by biting my tongue until I drew blood. Shadow watched me closely, his penetrating gaze seeing everything, and when he lowered his head and swiped his tongue across my bloody lips, I finally broke.

Kissing was our thing. The most special moment that existed between us. For those born in the Shadow Realm, they reserved this intimate act only for their true mate. Shadow had given that gift to me, and ever since, when his lips touched mine, my gut filled with butterflies.

The orgasm I'd been holding at bay by the damn skin of my clitoris unfurled inside of me as I cried out against him. It was a long, slow arc of pleasure, spilling from deep in my center until I felt it through every inch of my body.

With that release, my power burst to life. Usually, that sort of release would result in a torrent of flames around me, but this time, it slammed into Shadow. The force was so great that it tore us apart, and within the same heartbeat, he was on his feet. All seven feet of naked Shadow, his breaths coming in and out so harshly that his chest heaved.

I dragged myself up as well, and as Shadow shook his head a few times, I tried to get my wobbly legs to support my weight. That orgasm had been different to any other I'd ever experienced. Stronger, but not in the normal way. It was more cleansing, almost as if...

The last of Dannie's spell had been expunged from my soul.

"Sunshine?"

My knees hit the ground, a sob shaking my chest as I ended up on all fours, unable to get my shit together. *Sunshine.*

How could I have ever forgotten Sunshine?

How could I have forgotten Shadow?

"Shadowshine," I choked out, and before I could lift my head, tears tracing my skin again, Shadow was there, drawing me up and into his arms.

He held me so tight, my ribs groaning against the force, and I only wished it was tighter.

"Sunshine." He groaned, and then he threw his head back and roared into the heavens. It was a long, rumbling lament of pain. My ears ached when he was done, and I could have sworn that I felt moisture that wasn't my own against my skin, but when I looked up into his face, there was no sign of anything except pure, unadulterated fury.

Shadow's face was a mask of death and destruction. The mask of a being who was about to destroy the world.

And I just might let him.

Chapter Twenty-Two

He held me for so long that time basically had no meaning. Days could have passed and yet neither of us moved. Maybe we were in competition for who could hold on the longest, and for once, it was a competition I hoped we both won.

"I'm going to need you to explain everything to me," Shadow eventually rumbled from above. "My memory is still clouded with events that I believe have been falsely planted there to confuse me."

It made sense that Dannie would have used different methods to mask our memories. We were all vastly unique individuals with differing powers. She was far too freaking smart, and that in and of itself was terrifying because it had only been the spell Shadow had already layered on me, and my own tenacious personality, that had kept her from fully succeeding.

"Dannie, your mother, has been corrupted by the sunburst stone," I said, leaning back to see his face. I kind of never wanted to stop looking at his face now that it was in my life again. "She stole all of our memories to restore the balance. I was never supposed to be created, so she sent me back to Torma to be the alpha-mate—"

Shadow's grip tightened as he slowly drew me up off my feet until we were near eye level. "To Torma? With no memories?"

I swallowed hard because his beast was so close to the surface.

His jaw tightened. "Did Torin touch you?" He said it slowly, without inflection, but the cold detachment was far scarier than shouting could have ever been.

I didn't pretend to misunderstand what he was asking. "He never touched me sexually. I didn't remember you, but I sure as fuck remembered what a piece of shit he was."

There was a slight thawing in his gaze, and the grip lessened enough that feeling returned to my limbs. "Why would my mother allow you to keep those memories when she wanted this plan to succeed?"

I'd thought on this a lot during my endless cycle of overthinking last night. "I have two theories," I said. "One, she still held some love for me, even with her transformation, and in that regard didn't want me to be completely vulnerable against beings who had hurt me in the past."

Shadow's expression grew darker. "And two?"

"Two, the promise that you made to me, where I would never be vulnerable to my pack again, was a strong bond that Dannie either didn't know about or couldn't break. It was what allowed me to remember as much as I did and fight them off when I needed to."

His chest was rumbling now, and with the beast hovering close by, I had to calm the situation. "Shadow," I said firmly, drawing all of his attention to my face. "Thanks to you, I've never touched, fucked, or orgasmed from any man except you."

That was exactly what he wanted to hear, and when his lips met mine, a sigh so deep, it was near a groan escaped. "How the fuck...?" I murmured against his lips. "Dannie must be scary powerful to make me forget you."

Shadow didn't like that reminder, his kiss turning harder, and my brain went on a little vacation from thought. "My beast knew you," he finally said, his voice a husky rumble. "Even if I didn't remember, my instinct knew you were mine. Nothing in any world would have gotten through to me except you, Sunshine. I need you to know that."

I nodded, my lips trembling again. "I know. I felt that so fiercely, and as soon as I remembered, I came for you."

His body stiffened, and it was clear that what I'd just said bothered him. "I should have been strong enough to remember you."

I wrapped my arms tighter around him, holding on with all of my strength. "The only reason I remembered was because of your spell. You did save me... or more accurately, we saved each other." He didn't appear satisfied by this response, so I pushed on. "More so, you did remember me without any outside help. You destroyed every damn doorway from this place except the one to Earth. There was only one reason you'd have done that."

Shadow made a disparaging sound. "Maybe that was for the shifters."

I wrinkled my nose at him. "Don't even try to play. You love me. I knew it from the first time you threw me over your shoulder."

He went very still, blinking down at me, and I wondered if maybe I'd gone too far. I mean, I had been joking around, and while I knew *I loved him*, Shadow had never been particularly forthcoming with those exact words. It didn't matter to me because actions spoke much louder, and his told me that I was important to him.

"Love," he repeated, and I didn't bother to look away or be embarrassed. If he didn't love me, it wouldn't break me. Mostly because he'd get there eventually. My plan to grow on him like some sort of exotic fungus was in full swing.

"Love is a human word," he rumbled. "A human word they throw around with such careless abandon."

Where was the lie? Torin had told me he loved me more than once, and I knew for a fact that he didn't love anyone except his power and reflection. And maybe Jaxson, because... bros, man.

"I don't have a better word," I said to Shadow, "but for what it's worth, I do love you."

His jaw was as tense as the rest of him, and normally, that expression would be worrisome, but I saw that this was shock. Shock that was soon replaced with fire as he cupped my face.

"You're the match to my soul, Sunshine," he rumbled through the power surrounding us. "You are my one. The only being I would destroy worlds for, and I'm afraid I did just that."

I snorted. "Yeah, Gaster is not very happy with you. You're going to have some cleaning up to do when you get out of here."

My library could not be collateral damage in this war. It just couldn't.

"I was no more than rage and cold, cruel intent," Shadow admitted. "I would have killed everyone."

My chest grew so tight. "Do you know what happened to Midnight, Angel, and Simone? And the rest of your crazy band of brothers? You... You didn't kill them, right?"

Shadow's brow furrowed, and I had a feeling he was sorting through memories, trying to figure out what was real and what had been falsely planted by Dannie. I relaxed a little when I saw no devastation on his face. "Simone is with Lucien," he finally said, "on Valdor. And Angel is back in the Honor Meadows. I sent them to their lands, broke a lot of energy barriers through those lands, and then destroyed the Solaris system."

"And Midnight?"

"I have no idea," Shadow admitted, with reluctance. He really hated not knowing everything. "I can't sense it anywhere close by, so maybe still in the realm?"

That had been my thought too. My hope. Because I refused to believe it was gone-gone.

"Can you get the Solaris System back?" I tentatively asked, not sure I wanted to hear the response if it was a no.

I felt zero reassurance when Shadow huffed. "It took me hundreds of years to establish it originally, but I can sense that the base of the power is still intact, and I'm a lot stronger than I was back then, so... I believe I can." His eyes darkened into pits of golden lava. "But before we try that, there's one thing I need first."

My pussy spasmed because she knew what was going on.

Shadow walked me back until my legs hit his bed, and when I was crowded between the massive mattress and an equally massive being, I felt no fear or claustrophobia. *I felt alive.* The parts of me that had been ragged and broken were finally moving back into the places they'd originally been before Dannie had taken a sledgehammer to us.

Dannie.

She was an issue we'd have no choice but to deal with later, but for now, the focus was... elsewhere.

Shadow's hands closed around my waist as he slowly dragged me up his body. I attempted to wrap my legs around him, but he was having none of that, his power holding my limbs. Even as I arched to try to rub my naked parts against his naked parts, desperate to ease the ache inside, he stopped this as well.

His power held me; his hands controlling every move I made.

"I cannot change my nature for you tonight," he warned.

I knew what that one sentence meant. I was getting the full ride, pun intended. An experience that was almost certainly going to destroy parts of me, but it was all good. That wasn't a glib, throwaway statement either. Having lost Shadow once, I would take any sort of physical pain before I'd do that again. Whatever happened today was a gift.

His fire surged, as did mine, and I felt the scrape of his tongue and five o'clock shadow across my sensitive skin as he dragged his tongue and mouth down my stomach, following the line of my body. He held me up off the bed as he devoured every part of me he could touch, and only a god would have the strength to do what he was, using nothing more than his triceps, chest, and shoulder muscles to keep me elevated.

When he released some of his control on me, my hands scraped across his skin, searching for traction, until I managed to slide them into his hair. It was only as I tugged on the short strands that I realized Shadow was no longer in possession of his signature tousled wave. My eyes flew open, and despite his intensely pleasurable journey, which had now reached the junction of my thighs, I forced myself to examine his shorn locks. Now, with the light of our fires burning around us, I saw him clearly.

Holy fuck me sideways.

Shadow was always beyond hot, dangerously sexy, and incredibly perfect, but this new haircut was... damn. It was like every plane of his masculine face was on view for me, giving him a scarier vibe, while taking away nothing of his beauty.

"Your hair," I whispered, sounding like an awestruck teenager who had just met her favorite rock star. "What happened to it?"

He rumbled, power vibrating my clit, and I clenched my legs to try to stave off an orgasm. It was always so fast. Too fast. And despite knowing I'd probably have ten orgasms tonight, I wanted to make this first one last.

I tugged on his hair again, or at least attempted to, my fingers slipping through the short strands. "Shadow, what happened to your hair?"

"I cut it."

Just as I was running that simple statement through my head, he bit into my thigh. A hard, punishing action, which I fucking loved. To return the favor, I wrapped my thighs tightly around his head, waiting for him to take control of me again.

Which he did, his hands closing around my waist as he bit into me again, over and over, across my thighs and along the sides of my pussy. It hurt, but with each bite of pain, followed by a swirl of his tongue, my body forgot everything except feeling the dual sensations. When his teeth finally closed down on my clit, I screamed, unable to stop the heavy swirls of arousal from exploding through my body.

Before I even had a chance to ride out that orgasm, he shifted positions, holding my body above him as he buried his face in my pussy. His happy groan as he tasted me properly was enough to have me crying out again, and as I thanked the fucking gods for this moment, I found myself flat on my back, Shadow crowding over the top of me.

Staring up at him, I felt the swelling of heat in my chest as all my feelings tried to make themselves known at once.

"Why did you cut your hair?" I asked softly.

I needed to know what he'd gone through when we'd been apart. I needed to fill in the blanks of what I'd been missing.

Shadow's expression didn't change, the flare of arousal in his gaze about as strong as I'd ever seen from him. "Nothing was the same without you. I didn't know why, but I knew that I was missing something vital to my survival. I searched, and I destroyed. More than just the Solaris System. I stripped myself bare so I could build myself up again and find the fundamental part of my soul that was missing. Only you weren't there."

Fuck. He might not think the word "love" meant much, but he spoke a language of love without even realizing it.

"Never again," I said fiercely, reaching for him, and for once, he allowed me to drag him down to my level. Our kiss was bittersweet and perfect.

A kiss to soothe and heal.

A kiss to cleanse our pain from many bitter nights apart.

A kiss to break the final dredges of Dannie's spell.

A kiss of love. No matter what my beast might think.

Chapter Twenty-Three

Shadow always kissed like he never wanted to stop. It was part of what made up the beast, and his need to have his mouth on any part of my body... Yeah, I was here for it.

Just the thought that I might have never kissed him again almost broke me. Thankfully, when Shadow's kiss turned harder, more passionate, as his tongue tangled with mine, it was all the distraction I needed to forget everything else.

Lifting me from the bed, he never broke the contact between our lips as he spun us around. I found myself with my back against the wall, his weight pressing into me. Opening my legs wider, I rubbed against him, surprised he was letting me. It was all explained when he slammed up into me, hard and fast. Even as ready as I was, he was so fucking huge that pain and pleasure were instantaneous. Fighting for dominance, both sensations danced on the edge of what I could handle.

Shadow was relentless, thrusting into me over and over. His long, sure strokes had the natural fires between us sliding into my center. My clit swelled and ached, each stroke of Shadow's body against mine pushing me to higher levels of pleasure.

I opened my mouth to scream, but he cut me off with a growl. "No."

It was a command. A domination of my body. "Shadow," I whimpered.

"No, Sunshine," he repeated. "You belong to me. Your body. Your soul. Your heart. Your orgasms."

For a moment, I considered throat-punching him because he was stepping up the dominance thing to new levels, and I really wanted to come. Each time he stopped me, the swirls grew larger inside; he knew what he was doing, even if it was driving me insane.

Whimpers spilled from me as I arched, slamming my head into the wall as the pleasure continued to build.

"Mera," he warned.

"I can't help it," I got out breathlessly.

He leaned down, his teeth closing on my shoulder, all the while he fucked me with animalistic savagery. A part of Shadow had not completely released his beast. And I didn't mind one bit.

Just as the tremble started in my thighs, the one I was starting to recognize as a precursor to the sort of squirting orgasm that I'd never experienced until Shadow, his lips tilted up in a predatory grin. "That's what I was waiting for."

A vibration of his power into my clit sent me screaming over the edge, my body jerking as I came so hard, I lost consciousness for a beat. It went on and on, my pleasure going everywhere, sliding across our bodies.

His chest rumbled in satisfaction, and fuck, if that wasn't one of the most intense orgasms I'd ever had. Before I could catch my breath, he shifted our positions, another classic move of his, since he had the sort of stamina that would kill a human. We ended up on the floor, the thick rug beneath us as his weight pressed against me.

Despite the head-spinning orgasm I'd just had, I was already ready for the next one as his hand slid up my right calf to my thigh. When he wrapped those long fingers around me, he lifted my leg so it was positioned over his shoulder.

I gasped as his hard cock came into contact with my pussy, like they were perfectly lined up and ready to mingle. Expecting him to push straight inside, I prepared myself by gripping the soft material on either side of my body. The thick tip of his cock stretched my entrance slowly, and even as I tried to arch up, his weight prevented me from moving more than a few millimeters.

Before I could ask him *what the fuckery he was up to*, he slid his other hand along my left leg, wrapping it around that thigh, and then it was over his shoulder in the same moment.

"Oh," I gasped. I'd never had sex in this position before, but already, I was excited.

"Fuck, Sunshine," Shadow rumbled as he continued to push inside me, his large size taking time to bury balls deep. As soon as he was fully seated, he was already drawing out his length, then sliding it right back inside, scraping along every damn nerve ending.

It was so deep. The sort of deep that I swore to fuck I tasted on my tongue, and as he continued to move in and out of me, I couldn't breathe. My head was spinning as the next spirals of pleasure built, my nails clawing at his chest now, even if I was unable to break the skin of the beast.

"Mera," he said in his normal snap of a command. This time, I didn't know what he wanted, or at least I thought I didn't until I felt the sting of his power tracing over nerve endings, and I realized he wanted me to return the favor.

Releasing my hold on my energy, I sent it into Shadow. As our fire clashed, there was a bolt of lightning across our skin. Pain and pleasure, fire and ice, and with each surge, I arched higher, allowing Shadow to plunge so deeply into me that the taste on my tongue intensified.

I mean, logically, I knew his damn dick wasn't big enough to make it to my mouth from my vagina. I hadn't failed biology that badly, but clearly, it was deep enough that it was triggering senses all across my body.

"Come, Sunshine."

I was the puppet, and he was the master, but when it came with such intense pleasure, who the fuck would complain? The moans that had been falling in rapid intervals from my lips increased to a near high-pitched explosion as he fucked me into my next orgasm.

When he finished, he did just as I expected, shifting off me to change positions again. Only this time, I was expecting it and had a plan of my own. My domineering beast wouldn't like it, but he was just going to have to suck it the hell up.

Well, I'd be the one doing the sucking, but the analogy remained.

He slid from me slowly, the thickness of his shaft catching along my pussy, all the way until he was finally free. As he reached to move me into the next position he wanted, I was already gone, shifting down between his legs to wrap both arms around his thighs. Before he could issue another command from that sexy-as-sin mouth of his, I wrapped my lips around the tip of his cock.

A groan burst from me as I tasted both of us in that first suck. My cum and his pre-cum was a delicious mix of power and spice and desire. Needing more, I drew the tip deeper inside, my mouth stretched to full capacity to take as much as I could.

For the first time in our relationship, Shadow didn't fight me for dominance, allowing me to taste him in the same manner he'd always tasted me. Probably the dude just really liked getting his dick sucked, but either way, I was enjoying my small scrap of power.

As I got into a rhythm of sucking his knob, stroking his shaft, and cupping his balls, I found my jaw was more flexible than I'd thought. I managed to slide a few more inches along without choking myself out.

At least there was no choking until Shadow laughed darkly, wresting control from me in a heartbeat. He'd been lulling me into a false sense of security, allowing me to think I was in charge, but that had been a mere dream.

He gripped the back of my head and thrust into my mouth, and then he did it again, and I had no choice but to open wide and hold on for dear life as he fucked me. His fire-touched eyes remained locked on me, even as my center throbbed with need. I knew better than to reach down and try to relieve the pressure there.

Of course, all the best intentions disappeared as that need inside me grew, and just as my hand moved down my stomach, Shadow growled. Thankfully, he took pity on my poor horny ass, shifting us enough so that he could lean over and bury his tongue into my aching pussy, all the while never having his dick leave my mouth.

It took less than two strokes in my wet heat before he sucked my clit into his mouth, and I came, groaning around his cock as he fucked my mouth harder than ever. As he drew out my pleasure, Shadow's body started to vibrate, rumbles emerging from within him, and as his dick swelled, he let out a groan. When the first hot burst of cum hit my mouth, I jerked against him, near drowning in the rush of power that I tasted. Shadow was built of so much strength and energy that I felt myself grow stronger as I swallowed him down.

The taste was weird but not unpleasant, salty and masculine, reminding me of Shadow's scent. I found myself licking the last drop clean as I ran my hands over his shaft.

Shadow's tongue didn't stop swirling across my pussy until we were both done. At this point, I was completely wrecked, barely making a sound as he carried me to his bathroom. We showered together under water that was basically near boiling point. Neither of us was bothered by heat; it actually energized us.

I closed my eyes as I curled against him, wrapping my arms around his neck. I didn't need to hold on tight, though, because he never took his hands off me. Like he was afraid if he let go, I'd disappear again. Even when he left me to dry off, and then brush my teeth, the door between us remained open. It was the sort of closeness we'd never experienced. A real "mate" moment that I was struggling to process, even as much as I loved it.

When I stepped out of his wardrobe, wearing one of his shirts, flames burned in his eyes. In an instant, the shirt was incinerated, leaving me naked, blinking like an idiot. "Uh, was there something wrong with that shirt?"

He took two steps across the room, and before I could ask him another question, I was in his arms. "You sleep naked with me, Sunshine," he said, his voice deeper than usual. "I want to feel every inch of your skin pressed to mine. I want your scent and mine together. I want nothing between us."

My chest squeezed. I'd dreamed of this moment when all barriers would fall away. When we'd somehow find a place where we could exist together, just Shadow and Sunshine. Shadowshine.

Maybe for tonight, we'd get exactly that.

Chapter Twenty-Four

Shadow never let me go. His promises were as solid as his fucking biceps, one of which was under my head. Normally, I'd expect a hard surface like that wouldn't really be conducive to sleep, and yet the moment he wrapped me up in his arms, one leg between mine as he spooned me, I'd basically passed the fuck out.

It was the best sleep I'd ever had—to the point that when I was jarred awake sometime later by a raging mist, it took me a moment to orientate myself. At first, all I could see was Inky, swelled up into a huge sparking cloud over our heads. "Are we under attack?" I rasped, looking around the near pitch-dark room.

Shadow lifted his head, looking sexy and sleepy. One thing he didn't look was concerned, though, so it had to be something else that had Inky all ragey.

"A shifter is trying to break into the lair," he said, leaning down to press his nose against my shoulder, drawing my scent in as his hands cupped my breasts. "Should I kill her?"

I groaned because he was doing illegal shit to my body with just that light touch on my skin, but then his words registered, and I tried to sit up. "Fuck, it's Sam. She's probably worried you murdered me and she's here to avenge my death."

She seemed like a solid friend, who would always try and save those she cared about. "I just need to let her know I'm okay," I told him, patting his arm.

Shadow rumbled, in his usual beast way, tugging me into him again. "She can wait."

I wiggled to no avail, and when his teeth attached to my shoulder, in both warning and tease, I found myself rubbing against him rather than trying to get away. Need exploded inside of me, and I wanted him so badly that my core actually throbbed. I wondered if there would ever be a time when the mere touch of his hands and zap of his power didn't make me want to climb him like a damn tree.

"Can you be quick?" I murmured, breathless. "Like, really super quick. Because you know I can orgasm in one minute—"

Shadow pulled me closer, burying both hands into my long hair, as he tightened his fingers to tug on the strands. In the same instant, he leaned in to claim my mouth.

"Only because the damn world needs saving," he murmured, his tongue sliding across mine, allowing me to taste his dark spice. Thanks to our genetics, morning breath wasn't a thing, but I wondered if I'd truly mind it from him. Nothing about this beast was a turn-off for me. At least nothing I'd discovered so far.

When Shadow was done thoroughly devouring my mouth, he moved over the top of me, pulling me around so I was flat on my stomach beneath him. He slid up over me, and as his long, hard length pressed into me, I found myself backing my ass up and biting my lip. Because... damn, I was about to get a good dicking. And I wasn't even mad about it.

"Shadow, you need to stop playin—"

My words were cut off in a jumble of moans as he pushed into me, his cock stretching me as he slid inside in one smooth motion. Because I hadn't really been prepped, it hurt, but at the same time, the pain was so fucking good that I was already rocking back.

Or at least attempting to because he was being the alpha again, controlling the rhythm, pace, and pleasure. The angle we were at was another new one for me. Being flat on my stomach made the strokes feel shallower, the head of his cock running right along my G-spot.

It took about five of those strokes until I was basically dead.

How did he do this to me? Every. Damn. Time.

One of his hands landed on my spine as he thrust in and out, moving just fast enough to drive me insane, but too slow for me to come yet. His hand started to trace along my skin, all the while pressing me firmer into the mattress. Our scents were mingled strongly, and as I inhaled it deeper, my pleasure shot up.

"Holy fuck," I said in a breathless rush. "Please don't even stop. I will pay you good freaking money to just keep doing this forever."

He chuckled, and it was lighter than usual. "You'll never pay me for this or anything else between us, little wolf. It's my job to ensure your pleasure and never leave you wanting."

I came, hard and violently, my body attempting to literally jerk off the bed. If it wasn't for Shadow's solid weight holding me down, I'd have no doubt ended up on the floor.

He picked up his pace, and I came again within seconds because I'd already been so worked up. Shadow followed suit, thrusting inside me a few more times to finish us both off.

My name was a whispered caress on his lips as he turned me over, and even though our bodies were no longer physically joined, I felt our connection lingering below the surface.

"Thank you for remembering us," he whispered, the intensity in his gaze holding me captive. "There's no way I'd truly forget you, but I was so lost in my rage that it might have been a hundred years before I brought myself back. Too long for us to be apart."

"This is real, right?" I said breathlessly. "This shit between us is actually real. Not just me wanting to jump your bones because you're hot."

His lips twitched as the corners tilted up. "I'm starting to under-stand Len and Lucien's fascination with humans. My life was an endless night before you came into it, but now there's fire everywhere I turn. You know how I feel about fire."

It was my turn to grin. "Some might say you *love it?*"

There was more lip twitching, but he just shook his head. "To answer your eloquent question from before, yes, this *shit* is very real between us. My beast has claimed you. I have claimed you. You belong to me, Sunshine."

"Until such a time you say I don't."

We'd played this game before.

Shadow's biceps tensed on either side of my head, and when he lowered himself down, my breath caught in anticipation. "No, Mera," he murmured. "There's no such out available to you any longer. You're mine. End of story or end of life."

I swallowed hard. "My life?"

His lips were almost on mine. "No. The life of anyone who attempts to take you from me."

Jesus. Fucking. Christ. Both of us were about to find out if sexy words spoken in a rumble of Scottish brogue was enough to bring a shifter to orgasm, because *damn*.

He kissed me, and I gave him every part of myself, holding nothing back. There were no more barriers between us, no protections around my heart, no cynicism about this being a short-term thing that I could walk away from.

I'd been kidding myself from the start. There was no walking away from Shadow.

Only death would tear us apart, and we were ready to fight it every step of the way.

Chapter Twenty-Five

Despite the major emotional breakthrough I'd just had with Shadow, there was no time for us to remain wrapped in each other. Sam might only be a very new friend, but she was already important to me. We'd bonded over a huge experience, and it was cruel to allow her to worry.

Of course, there was the small problem of leaving the lair in my current state. "You're some sort of sperm overachiever," I said to Shadow, staring down at the mess that was the bed and me. "I mean, fuck, dude, at some point, it's just overkill. In all the books I've read, they rarely mention the aftermath of fucking a virile alpha male—"

The rest of my sentence was cut off as he hauled me over his shoulder in one swift move, shutting me up quite effectively with a firm smack on my ass. "If you don't want to experience more of my virility, Sunshine, you better shut up now."

I mean... which way did I want to go here?

Dammit. Sam was lucky I liked her.

Shadow cleaned the bed with his powers, energy racing over the surface, removing all evidence of our sex session, but he didn't do the same for us; instead, we walked into his shower. He then proceeded to wash me all over, very, *very thoroughly*. By the time I was done, I'd forgotten my own name, let alone my friend's, but Shadow got us back on track.

"Your clothes are in there," he told me, showing me back into the walk-in wardrobe I'd gotten his shirt from. The shirt that was ash on the floor.

"Oh my god." I squealed when my section came into view. That hadn't been there last night. "All of my clothes are back. Now you just have to fix the library and life will be perfect."

He hugged me, that full-bodied sort of hug that Shadow was damn good at, and I wondered how full a heart could feel before it burst. Turned out, random hugs were a few of my favorite things.

"We do have that small problem of my power-crazed mother," Shadow reminded me as he pulled away.

Ah, right. "Yeah, true. Dannie is just lucky she spent a lot of time keeping me safe when I was growing up. Otherwise, I'd be inclined to drop an atomic bomb on her head and call it a day."

Shadow quietened. "If I thought an atomic bomb would work against her," he said with a sigh, "I'd have already dropped one. Her power is too strong... too unbalanced. We cannot allow her to continue this way without peer or enemy. It's only a matter of time until it ends in the destruction of multiple worlds."

It hurt my heart to hear him talk like that. "She's your mom, Shadow, and she cared for both of us. We have to at least give her a chance to either release the stone's power, or maybe we can just take the stone from her power base...?"

Shadow considered this, and I appreciated the fact that my suggestion wasn't immediately dismissed. He respected my thoughts, and there he went again, speaking love without saying the words.

"I'm not sure she deserves a shot," he finally said. "But if she did willingly release the stone, it would go a long way to making amends."

"I agree," I said, finally paying attention to the clothing selection. Shadow was already dressed in his black pants and a dark grey shirt, and I needed to move my naked ass.

"Do we even know if she's killable?" I asked, pulling on underwear, followed by a white shirt, ripped-up black jeans, Converse-style shoes, and a denim jacket. "Maybe it would take the end of the Nexus, which would end the damn worlds."

"In that situation," Shadow said, stepping closer, "we'd have no choice but to imprison her. If we could create a powerful enough cage."

He wrapped his arms around me, drawing us together. I was really starting to get used to this new side of him, with all the touching and loving and orgasms. If only we weren't discussing the possible end of the worlds at the same time...

"We need our pack," I said, feeling the surety of that. "This is going to take effort from more than just us."

Shadow nodded. "We need those powerful enough to stand at our side," he agreed. "Our pack and friends."

"And they're all alive and well?" I double-checked.

"I banished everyone back to their worlds when I destroyed the doorways. And I can feel all of them *alive and well* except Midnight."

"Are Inky's memories back?" I asked.

"Yes," Shadow said instantly. "The moment your power hit me and broke through my mother's web of lies, both Inky and I were able to restore our memories."

"So Midnight should remember," I said, the true worry I felt creeping into my voice. "It should have remembered the moment Gaster broke the lock on my memories."

Shadow shook his head. "I don't know. My gut says yes, it'll have its memories again, but there's a decent chance it's stuck in the Shadow Realm."

Yes, right. The doorways were gone. "Okay, step one, restore my damn library."

Shadow cupped my face, forcing me to look at him. "I'm sorry, Mera. It was unforgiveable of me to destroy the Library of Knowledge, especially when it means so much to you. To many beings. I have a lot of work ahead to restore faith in me and the Solaris System."

Unable to stop myself, it was my turn for a random hug. "Don't do that," I murmured against his chest. "Don't beat yourself up or let the guilt win. This was done to us, and we had every right to react badly. Together, we will clean it up, and whatever way the final battle falls, we'll know we did everything in our power to save the worlds."

Shadow held on to me for an extra moment, and even if it was only briefly, I loved when he showed his more vulnerable side to me. A side I doubted many... if any, had ever seen before.

Feeling somewhat more settled about everything, we left his room and walked with confidence toward the barrier, only making one small stop for me to check on the fire. It was back where it should have been, in the stone hearth, burning brightly and shooting warmth around the room. Shadow stood beside me, allowing me a moment to get myself together.

"I would do a lot of bad shit if it meant I'd never lose this again," I said, staring into the flickering flames.

He chuckled, a dark and broken sound. "Sunshine, I'd make your bad shit look like Sunday School. There are no limits when it comes to protecting what is mine. None at all. I have and would continue to destroy the foundation of existence if it meant one more day with you."

I closed my eyes and absorbed those words. "I think that's why I love the stories with villains instead of heroes as the main characters," I whispered. "Heroes are limited because they always have to do the right thing. But villains aren't restricted by their moral compasses. They will do literally anything and destroy anyone who tried to hurt those they love. I think, deep down, I've always considered myself a villain. In that way."

"You're my moral compass, Mera," Shadow said, wrapping his arms around me, pulling my back against his chest as we both faced the fire. "As you've seen firsthand, without you, I'm a mindless beast.

There's no hero in my genetics, so maybe we're in the right story together."

"Agreed," I said.

Shadow chuckled, and before I could get even more sappy, he was once again leading me toward the exit. When we stepped through to the other side, Sam was in the process of throwing a damn chair right for the portal. It took me by surprise, and I'd have possibly copped a face full of wood if Shadow hadn't reached out and caught it mid-pitch.

"Shit!" Sam said, her eyes going wide as she took a step back. "Uh, sorry. I was trying to get through to Mera."

When her frantic gaze found mine, she sagged in relief. "You're okay."

Shaking off my guard beast, I hurried toward her. "Yes, crap, I'm so sorry. It took me longer than expected to tame the shadows. Then they decided to mark their territory."

Her gaze shifted between Shadow and me and she did not miss my deeper meaning there. "Best news I've heard all day."

Gaster appeared then, his little goblin's face wreathed in concern. "Master," he cried, hurrying forward. "Thank the gods you have returned."

Shadow didn't smile, but I felt a softening of his energy. He liked Gaster, and more importantly, he trusted him to keep one of the most vital parts of his life functioning: his library.

I was pretty sure Gaster was stronger than he looked—physically and in the magical sense—and was able to hold his own in most situations. It was probably half the reason he'd managed to remain with the library even after Shadow had kicked everyone else out.

We were all lucky to have him in our lives.

"Give me a moment," Shadow said in English and then in demi-fae so that we all could understand. I'd have understood either way, and at least with my memory returned, I remembered Shadow rearranging my brain in the realm, giving me a universal translator in my head. Hence why I'd been able to understand that alpha back in Torma. Poor guy. His confusion made a lot more sense now.

When Shadow strode away, I tried not to pout at the ten feet between us. I was needy, but whatever. After everything we'd been through, it'd be weird not to be a little attached. At least I could still see him as he lifted both hands, the burst of power that left him so strong, it sent all three of us sliding across the floor. I almost went through the portal into the lair again, but just as I was about to, Shadow's head snapped in my direction, and his wicked smile had my panties drowning.

His energy wrapped around me and I stopped moving, once again caught up in the force of the Shadow Beast. His fire followed that blast of energy and then an inky darkness seeped from his skin. Fire, energy, and literal shadows surrounded us, and it was like the start of a bad joke because I had no idea what else was about to walk into the room.

At least I felt safe enough wrapped in Shadow's power, even if it was a dick move to lock me down again. "What's happening?" Sam whispered. "Why aren't you moving?"

I could still talk, thankfully. "Shadow is feeling a little possessive right now," I said dryly. "He's not really allowing me far from his hold."

She looked between us again, her lips trembling as she tried not to laugh. "Sounds like fun. Do you actually know what he's doing over there?"

"He's repairing the library," Gaster said.

Sam gasped and clapped her hands. "I understood you."

Gaster's smile was broad. "Oh, that's wonderful news. The universal translator is back in effect. Hopefully, the rest can be returned as easily."

I would have crossed my fingers if I could manage to move my hands. Of course, I could have fought against his hold, but it wasn't worth interrupting such an important task just to exert my dominance. Returning the Library of Knowledge to its former glory was essential to the well-being of my soul.

"What were you trying to tell me before?" Sam asked Gaster, excited to freely be able to communicate with him. "It felt super important, and there was no time to run into the dining hall to find out."

Gaster's smile was gentle. "You were stacking Faerie history with Valdor history, and I didn't want to hurt your feelings by undoing all your work. I was trying to show you the marks on the books. That's how we catalog them for the shelves."

Sam blinked at him. "But your face was so serious..."

Gaster nodded. "Oh, yes, knowledge is the most sacred of gifts we possess. It must be treated with the sort of reverence that speaks of its importance."

When her wide eyes turned in my direction, I was trying to hide my smile. "He's into books," I said cheekily.

Gaster waved a finger in my direction. "And are you not, Ms. Shifter? You spent most of your waking hours in here sneaking books off the shelves, thinking none of us would notice."

My smile turned into laughter. "Oh, Gaster. I knew you indulged me, and I was very careful to always place them back in the correct position. Respect the library and it will respect you."

He was beaming, like an adorable little ray of sunlight. "You're a true blessing, Mera Callahan. We have all benefited greatly from having you in our world."

My chest went tighter as my eyes burned; it meant so much to hear him say that. I'd grown up a pack burden and outcast, so to now find myself respected and appreciated... It was an overload on my fragile emotions. I mouthed *thank you* to Gaster and he nodded, but then we all had to shut up because Shadow was stepping up his game.

His power wrapped around Gaster and Sam, locking them down in the same manner as I was. They both started to protest, but only until the next explosion of energy left Shadow. Flames burst free from his body in an impressive arc, coating everything in shades of red, gold, black, and amber. The colors of the Nexus. The colors of Dannie's phoenix. The color of my wolf when she burst into flames.

Creation power.

His fire whipped through, clearing the old, followed by his shadows, rebuilding the new. Through my connection to Shadow I felt him tiring. A rare occurrence for one as strong as the Shadow Beast, but I wasn't too worried. He knew his limits, and we were in no immediate danger today, so it was best to try restoring the Solaris System before we went to war.

Chapter Twenty-Six

It took Shadow half a day to bring the library back into working order, and when he was finally done, he was barely able to stand. I personally liked the beast on his knees, but this was neither the time nor the place to take advantage of that. Instead, I attempted to haul his heavy ass up, dragging him to the newly reestablished seating area so he could sink into one of the cushion chairs to recharge.

Sam stayed with me, but Gaster had already hurried off to check if everything was as it had been. From what I could see of my library, it looked just as I remembered pre-Dannie, so I spent my time focusing on Shadow.

"Are you okay?" I asked, kneeling beside the cushion he was sprawled across. He tried to move forward, but I pushed him back. "You basically just rebuilt an entire travel system, maybe give yourself a second."

Shadow's eyes darted toward Sam, and I knew he was unhappy about being this vulnerable around an unknown shifter. I mean, we all knew he could kill her with a blink of his eye, so there was no real danger to him, but it was part of his nature to distrust a stranger.

"I'll recover in a few minutes," he rumbled gruffly.

Reaching out, I took his hand but didn't push for anything else. Sometimes you just needed a little support when times were hard. I had no idea if Shadow had ever had a person like that in his life, but he certainly did now.

The moment our skin connected, the fire of our powers rose together, visible between our palms. Shadow tilted his head in a way that indicated he hadn't expected that. "Your power is restoring some of mine."

The moment he said that, he pulled away, and despite my best attempts to hold on, there was no fighting his strength. "Let me help you," I protested.

The rumble in his chest told me everything he thought of that statement. "I won't drain your power to restore mine. There's no immediate danger, and I'll recover shortly."

Gods save me from stubborn beasts.

"How did I even do that?" I pushed. "Share my power with you?"

His expression gave nothing away at first, but when I continued to stare him down, he released a long breath. "We've formed a bond," he said, giving no indication how he felt about that. "At some point, the sort of true mate connection that's common in the Shadow Realm and among shifters has settled between our two energies."

I eyed him closely, keeping my expression neutral, even though my heart was slamming against my chest. I'd been feeling a connection, but I hadn't realized it was a *true mate* one. "You don't sound very happy about that," I attempted to joke. "But I'll have you know I was picked first for every sports team up until the sixth grade. I'm an excellent choice."

His lips twitched. "That's your sales pitch? For an eternal true mate bond? You got picked for sports?"

I crinkled my brow as I tried to think of something else. "Uh, is that enough? I can probably make some cooler shit up?"

He shook his head as his expression finally thawed. "Sunshine, there's no being in any of the many worlds I've traveled who is worthier than you. But I do worry that with our fates so entwined, if I fall, then so will you. I cannot live with that."

Unsurprisingly, the possibility of me dying with Shadow caused not even a blip of concern. "Dude, if we go down together saving the world, I'm okay with that."

He didn't look happy with that statement, but I gave zero fucks. My true feelings about death had been established long ago, and now I was all in for this crazy ride. Every part of it, good and bad.

"Let's just not waste any more time worrying about what might be," I continued. "We know there's a battle to come, and... maybe we won't lose. Sticking with my sports analogy, I've been a dodgeball champion on at least three separate occasions. The balls I have to dodge this time are just bigger and scarier."

"That's what *she* said," a familiar voice joked from behind us.

Spinning, I almost tripped over myself before scrambling to my feet so I could run, ugly-snot crying toward my best friend. Simone caught me as I sobbed against her shoulder, my relief at seeing her healthy and alive too much to be contained.

When we finally pulled apart, I noticed Lucien nearby, his blond hair a little longer, while his bronze skin and piercing green eyes were as familiar as ever. "Ah, *ma petite*," he murmured, stepping closer. "We've been worried about you."

Simone shot him a dark look, and that was all I needed to know that all was not well between my best friend and the enigmatic Vampire Master. "Lucien would not allow me to return," she bit out. "He said that until Shadow was able to restore the library, it was not safe to travel through any of the normal means. I've been imprisoned in his stupid castle, locked away for fear of the vamps eating me." She raised an eyebrow. "And not in the good way, apparently."

Lucien's face was wreathed in frustration, turning his surfer good looks into a more formidable and scarier façade. *Shadow Beast three?* "You're the most hotheaded, frustrating, insufferable..." He trailed off, clearly having run out of adjectives to describe Simone.

"Annoying?" I chimed in helpfully and she elbowed me.

"Don't encourage this asshole of a vampire who couldn't sparkle if his damn life depended on it."

Lucien muttered something about her life and its value before he pushed past us and strode over to Shadow, who looked relieved to have one of his trusted friends back in the library. They started to talk, and I knew Shadow would be filling Lucien in on everything that had happened.

Which gave me a moment to catch up with Simone.

"Are you really okay?" she asked, pulling me closer, like she couldn't believe we were finally together. "What the fuck happened? One minute you were heading off to the Shadow Realm, and the next, Shadow was back here raging like a beast, destroying everything. Not even his friends were safe."

Her words broke at the end, and she had to swallow a few times before she could speak again. "No lie, I thought you were dead. I figured that was the only event that would set off your beast-man, and it's not cool that I had to think that, Mera."

She wasn't exactly mad at me, but I could tell that more than once, she'd cursed my name. "Lucien didn't know anything?" He hadn't been in the realm with Dannie, but even Gaster had heard rumors.

She sniffed. "That bastard tells me what I *need* to know. Not what I want to know. All he said was to have some faith, and you're stronger than I think and would not have fallen so easily."

"This is going to be a long conversation," I told her. "We best find a seat."

I dragged her back to the beanbag chairs, pulling her down beside me. "Can we order food from here?" I asked Shadow. "Because I really need some food."

He nodded. "I will feed you," he said, "just relax and let me take care of it all."

I blinked at him, and fuck, if I wasn't feeling some kind of thing about being taken care of. I mean, it wasn't like I was ready to hand in my independent woman card, but having him fetch me food was almost a complete role reversal, and I was into it.

"Mera," Simone snapped, "I'm going to need you to start talking."

"Yeah, yeah," I said, "hold on to your hair. I'll tell you everything, but first..." I waved Sam closer. "I want you to meet the shifter who helped me get back here and ultimately restore my memories so I could bring Shadow back from the brink of Egyptian godhood. Samantha Rowland. Sam."

Simone grinned as she reached out a hand to Sam. "It's so nice to meet you. And holy hell, you are super gorgeous."

Sam's lips curved into a genuine smile. "Thank you, that's quite the compliment from someone as beautiful as you." When they were finished shaking hands, Sam pulled a cushion closer so we could all chat. "And it's really great to have another somewhat familiar face here."

"It's like we're bringing a little of Earth into this fantasy world," Simone said, looking pleased with herself as she leaned back and laced her fingers across her flat stomach. She was dressed in the sort of outfit I'd never seen her wear before: blue flared harem pants, a white top with similarly flared sleeves, her long hair drawn back in a tight bun. Sam hadn't just been blowing smoke up her ass to return the compliment; Simone was looking beyond gorgeous after her time in Valdor.

What had happened to her there? I knew there was more to the story than just being locked in Lucien's castle. I'd get all the details one day, if we managed to save the world in time for girls' night.

"So, remember Dannie?" I said, since Simone was once again glaring at me, ready for my story.

She nodded. "Yep. Scary shifter who owned a bookstore."

Fighting a smile, I continued. "Well, yes, and it turns out that she's actually a little more than a scary shifter with a penchant for paperbacks."

Hitting the most important points, I detailed all the shit we'd gone through in the Shadow Realm. From Shadow's former mate, to my unusual birth and rebirth, finishing up with what had happened when I'd crossed over to the Grey Lands, and Dannie had made her ill-informed decision to change our fates.

I'd been so intent on telling the story that I only noticed halfway as more and more familiar faces joined us in the sitting area. Len, Reece, Galleli, and Alistair were all there, along with other members of the ten worlds.

"And then I woke in Torin's bed," I finished with a huff, "thinking it had only been a few months since I turned as a shifter, remembering nothing from my time with Shadow."

This was a part of the story I hadn't specifically told Shadow before, and I wasn't at all surprised when he leapt to his feet, his fatigue gone as flames whipped out in stormy arches.

"Mera." He growled, his voice far deeper than normal. "What happened with Torin?"

I waved off his fire, even though I secretly wanted to bathe in it. "Nothing happened; I already told you that. Even without all of my memories, I knew he was a piece of shit. I spent most of my time avoiding him until eventually I had to slam him in the nuts to really drive the point home." I smiled sweetly. "Even nuts as petite as his felt it."

Shadow's dark expression remained. "Remind me to kill that entire fucking pack when we get a spare minute."

I tilted my head. "You say the sweetest things."

He grumbled, retaking his seat, and before I could open my mouth again, he reached out and hauled me from my cushion onto his lap. The words died on my lips as I tilted my head back to meet his gaze.

"Mine," he said softly.

Dammit, who knew I was such a hussy for that one possessive word? Because I was fairly certain my panties could swim out of here. When I finally managed to tear my gaze from his, I found Simone grinning like a maniac at me, with Sam slack-jawed as she shook her head.

I shrugged, shooting them both a small smile. Apparently, we were not hiding this relationship, which had the possessive shifter side of me unimaginably happy.

Of course, a desert god had to go and pop my blissful bubble. "What are we going to do about Dannie?" Reece asked, crossing his arms to showcase how huge his biceps were. He was dressed in his usual tan-and-brown fatigues, suitable for war if the occasion occurred. His dark hair was closely shaved to his head, with even less length than Shadow's, and if it weren't for the deep blue of his eyes, he'd basically be Shadow's twin. In my opinion, those two were the closest of the six, even if all of them were close to Shadow in different ways.

"We have to kill her," Lucien said, his voice rougher than I'd ever heard. I wasn't sure if it was this situation or Simone who had this effect on him, but he was clearly bothered. "No one can be that powerful and remain unchecked. The balance she's so desperate to keep... well, she's the one throwing it off."

Len nodded, also uncharacteristically somber. The silver-fae had not taken the loss of the sunburst stone well, especially since his prediction of it falling into the wrong hands had come to fruition. "In her quest to continue to bring balance," he said softly, "she'll only bring destruction. My family's stone is not inherently evil, as some stones tend to be, but it was filled with a millennium of power. Too much for any to handle. There's no telling how that has changed them both."

"Wait," I said quickly. "How are you not all still affected by Dannie's memory spell?"

I'd only just clued into the fact that they'd all been in the realm when we'd been spelled, and therefore, should not be here now.

We were all under her influence. I wasn't the only one who jumped when Galleli spoke in our minds. *But Shadow freed us from this burden when he restored the pathways.*

I stared at Galleli of the Honor Meadow, and he looked exactly as I'd seen him the first time. Huge gold wings tucked behind his back, simple black pants, and no shirt. The only difference was his hair. It used to be longer, hanging down his back in intricate braids. Today, it was shaggy across his forehead, with only a little length on the sides and top. It made him look younger and maybe a little less intimidating. Had they all coordinated new haircuts or was this an extra from Dannie, when she'd been messing with our minds?

It was kind of cute.

"Wait, if everyone's memories have been restored," I said with a new thought, "then where are Angel and Midnight?" I reached through the bond for them both, getting a flutter and static electricity in return.

Shadow ran his hands across my arms, his touch soothing. "We'll figure out where they are," he told me. "Neither is easy to kill, and that must mean they're out there, unable to return for some reason."

That didn't sit right with me. What in the worlds could be strong enough to stop either of them from returning to the library? I had a bad feeling that this was still to do with Dannie, and I wasn't sure we were ready to take her on yet.

For my bonded friends, though, I'd be there in a heartbeat.

Chapter Twenty-Seven

The food showed up soon after, and even with everything on the platter being my favorite—speaking love without the words was apparently Shadow's specialty—I couldn't enjoy it like I normally would.

None of us enjoyed it; instead, we were a sober bunch of beings as we attempted to concoct a plan to beat an unstable goddess.

"Would the physical stone be gone now?" Sam asked after we'd thrown questions around for an hour or so. "Absorbed into her energy completely?"

Len shook his head. "Absolutely no chance. It'll have settled inside, finding and forming its own base within Dannie's energy, but it's still whole and complete."

"Could we cut it from her?" I asked. "Like... open heart surgery, but the god version."

The fae took a beat to consider this because clearly that very "human" way of thinking had not been forefront in his mind. "I guess, hypothetically speaking, if we could capture Dannie and subdue her energy long enough to pierce her skin... Yeah, probably not."

I glared at him. "Not helpful. There must be a way to remove the stone. How do you bond them to your family? Or is it to a single fae? I'm assuming not in the same manner Dannie used."

"Absolutely not," he said in a hard voice. "It's forbidden to take one into your energy as she did. It more often than not ends in death through an overload of power. If any try it and succeed, the family come together to kill them."

"Why aren't they coming together to kill Dannie then?" I pressed quickly, wondering if we'd overlooked a powerful ally in this war.

Len shook his head. "Fae deal with Faerie business. The stone is now the Shadow Realm's problem, and in that regard, they'll have nothing to do with it."

"It's everyone's damn problem," I replied with a huff. It was the end of the worlds. Plural.

Shadow's chest swelled against my back. "Forget the Fae," he said harshly, "they're too caught in their own politics. We'll be the ones to deal with this. The ones to kill her to save the worlds. Let's focus on building up *our* power base so that we have a chance at containing her in a cage of energy... a prison. If we're strong enough, we can bind it to her and then it will drain her power so we can remove the stone."

"Remove it as Mera suggested?" This was from Alistair, who leaned back all calm and collected, oozing serenity despite the current topic of conversation. His blue green curls were shorter as well, in the friendship-bro haircut thing they had going on.

"If the cage siphons enough of her power," Shadow said gruffly. "Then yes, we can physically remove the stone. We'll have to act swiftly with no hesitation."

"I can give us some extra protections," Len said, rising to his feet. "My family is in possession of the largest collection of *elotran stones*, which will protect minds from any manipulations. If Dannie tries to remove memories or plant false ones again, these stones would counter her magic."

Right, fuck. That was good thinking on his behalf, and it was fitting that the fae would unknowingly be helping us anyway.

"Thank you," Shadow said, looking between his friends. "There are no greater warriors I'd want at my back."

"All for one and one for all, right?" Len said with a wink. "And on that note, I'm off to gather the stones, and whatever other power I think might help."

The others got to their feet as well, a few of them dropping a kiss on my cheek—ignoring the beast's rumbles when they did so. Lucien even chuckled as he slapped a friendly hand on Shadow's shoulder before he joined the others in heading toward their respective doorways. "We'll meet back here in two days," Reece called, as swirls of dust and the scent of an electrical storm rose up around him. "Bring every weapon in your arsenal."

The others saluted to confirm before they faded out of the library as stealthily as they'd arrived. Leaning back against Shadow, I forced my breathing to calm, hoping that the power and strength I felt in our pack would be enough to beat the ultimate goddess.

"You feel stronger," I said, shifting to see him a little better. "What should we do to prepare while they're gone? Oh, and when is the official ceremony to induct me into the group? Because I think we're all in agreement that I'm basically the leader now."

Shadow's hands, which had been on my waist, slowly slid up my body, over my breasts, leaving behind aching nipples. He closed those long fingers around my throat to tilt my head back. "Mine, Sunshine. You belong to none of them, no matter how badly you love the pack life. Do you need a lesson in remembering?"

I wanted to moan, but this was not the time or place. "Promises, promises," I whispered, lifting myself so my lips could reach his. "Always with the promises, beast."

His chest rumbled, hands moving back to my tits, but before he could drive me completely crazy, I all but threw myself out of his lap.

Ignoring the dark flames in his eyes, I straightened my clothing. "We have no time for that," I reminded him, wishing I didn't sound like I was panting. "We need to do our part in this war."

The flames around him grew, but he didn't argue with me. "I'll have Gaster organize from this end," he said with a nod, on his feet in the next instant. "While he's doing that, we should head to the Honor Meadows and see if we can track Angel down."

I wasn't sure I could have loved him more until he'd said that. Until he'd made my needs a priority, even with all the other bullshit we had going on.

"What can we do to help?" Simone piped up, reminding me that we weren't alone. Damn Shadow and his ability to eclipse everything else in the room, even my best friends.

"Yes, I want to help!" Sam added, leaning forward. "I'm too far into this journey to stop now."

Giving them my full attention, because they deserved nothing less, I focused on Simone first because she looked upset.

"Are you okay?" I asked her, ignoring her previous question.

Her jaw was rigid, but she managed a smile. "Just a stupid vampire, nothing to worry about."

Ah, Lucien. My friend was feeling all the things about his sudden departure, especially since he hadn't acknowledged her before he left.

"Talk to me," I said.

She shook her head. "Girl, there's nothing to talk about; it's not even worth our next breath. Let's discuss how Sam and I can help you."

Sam nodded, looking far too relaxed for someone who'd just stumbled into this insane fantasy world mere days ago.

Before I could figure out what their role would be, Shadow cleared his throat. "You both need to go back to Torma," he said bluntly. "War is about to go down, and neither of you is equipped to fight in it. Mera would be devastated to lose a friend, and in that regard, I want to send you where you're safest."

The moment he said that, I knew it was the right decision.

Simone disagreed. "Yeah, nope."

Shadow stared down at her, and I almost laughed. My poor beast was so unused to being defied that it took him by surprise when it happened. Unlike when I did it, though, he might kill Simone.

I stepped between them. "Simone," I said softly, "I can't have you in danger. Seriously, I would lose my brains. And while I know you're a total badass, you can't bring claws to a god fight—it just won't work." Her lips trembled, and I reached out to take her hand. "I promise I'll come to Earth as soon as we handle Dannie."

"What if you don't?" she whispered. "What if I never see any of you again and I just have to assume the damn worst happened? Again, Mera! I've already done that once this year."

"I agree," Sam added. "You're already important to me, Mera. I'm going to be worried as hell if I don't hear anything."

Shadow laughed dryly. "If we fail, the worlds will fall. Even Earth." The Shadow Bastard was nothing if not blunt. "So I wouldn't worry too much. We're the only chance anyone has, and we can't effectively do our jobs when we're worrying about those weak and vulnerable."

Both of the ladies were offended by that, and I couldn't blame them. Weak and vulnerable were not admirable shifter traits, but in this sort of "god fight," Shadow wasn't wrong.

"I concede to this with one stipulation," Simone finally said. "That if you get a chance to send me and Sam a message or smoke signal or misty communication, you do it. Let us know you're okay."

Shadow paused, and it was clear he was thinking about the best way to grant this request. "I have an idea," he finally said. "I'll be right back."

He strode off into the library, and all of us watched silently until he disappeared from sight.

"Phew," Sam said, letting out a long breath. "He's intense."

Simone snorted. "Mera doesn't seem to mind."

"Yeah, not even a little," I said with a laugh, shaking my head at my obsession with that beast. "I keep having to pinch myself to believe this is even real. Just wish there wasn't war hanging over our heads."

Simone's joking smile disappeared in an instant as she hugged me hard. "I'm so scared for you," she said against my shoulder. "I think I'd rather be here and die, than stuck in Torma imagining the worst."

I shook my head. "Girl, your death is my worst nightmare. I couldn't do this knowing you were in danger. Just go to Torma, and... be careful there. You need a good cover story because they think you took off without permission. Be wary around Torin as well; he's still the same evil dickhead pretending to be an alpha." I looked between Simone and Sam. "Stick together."

"I've got her back," Sam said. "I know how to escape from a pack without detection, so if we need to run, we will."

I had to hug her as well, my new friend who was already starting to feel like one of the pack. "I'm sorry to have dragged you into this, even if I'm not sorry to have met you," I told her when I pulled away, "and if we all survive this, I promise to make it up to you."

She waved me off. "Are you kidding me? Meeting you was the best thing that ever happened to me. There's this whole damn world that I never knew existed, not to mention all of these new supernatural creatures to learn about. Before I met you, I was lonely and sad all the time. I'd take the risk of death over an empty life any damn day."

"See," Simone said smugly. "We both feel the same, and I think you should let us stay."

I didn't bother to argue; she already knew it was a done deal, but it was in her nature to fight until the bitter end. Before she could try again, Shadow stepped into view, holding what looked like a piece of parchment in his hand.

When he got closer, it was clear how ancient the parchment was, made from a material far thicker and sturdier than normal paper. "Here," he said, handing one sheet of it to Simone and the second sheet to me. "These are magically-connected parchments. It's fae magic, and Len left these in my care. If you write on one, it will appear on the other, until such a time that the words are read. Then it disappears. Keep it on you at all times."

Simone looked down at the parchment, her eyes wide and glassy as she clutched it to her chest. "Old school texting. I love it."

"Yes, it's perfect," I said. "I'll send messages through the parchment and you can pass it on to Sam."

A tear spilled down Simone's cheek, sliding along the smooth skin. "I love you, Meers. Please don't die. I honestly can't live in this fucked-up world without you."

Dammit, now I was about to cry too. "I promise to do my very best to remain alive so we can bitch about men and eat junk food."

Shadow rumbled, sounding pissed off. At first I thought it was my comment about bitching, but then he said, "Mera's life is the most valuable life in any of the worlds. I will die for her, as will our pack."

Simone looked relieved by this, and I could understand why. Shadow was scary and intimidating at the best of times, but when he was like this, he literally sent shivers down my spine.

With one more hug for them both, I followed them into the white hallway, waving as they were led to Earth by my beast.

"They're going to be okay, right?" I asked Shadow when he returned to me, sans two shifters. "With those assholes in Torma? What if they get hurt there?"

Shadow's smile was darkly evil. "Torin is about to learn a lesson about touching my wolves without permission. If he oversteps at all, he will suffer. Rest assured, Sunshine, your friends are safe."

I hugged myself into his side, holding on as tightly as I could. "Thank you. For everything. For you."

It was a weird thing to say, but I just felt this overwhelming gratitude to know Shadow. To have him in my life. To share parts of him that no one else did. My need to express that burst from me, but he handled it smoothly.

"You're my Sunshine, and I protect that with all of my power."

Swoon again. My mate had moves today.

As we strolled along the white hall, my eyes were drawn to the doorways. "Are my shadow creatures still here?" I asked, slowing. "The ones I pulled to Earth?"

"They are," he said, "safe from my mother's wrath."

A terrible thought occurred to me and I had to ask it. "Can we use their energy in this fight?"

Shadow's eyes darkened to a deep, burning ember, and I was pretty sure I wasn't going to like his response. But then again, what else was new?

Chapter Twenty-Eight

"We can use their energy," Shadow said, "as it has the potential to power our own in the fight. But... wouldn't that go against everything you stand for? Do you think you'll be able to handle the fallout of what might occur if their energy is used up?"

Fallout if their energy is used up...

I knew what that meant, and since I'd intimately felt the death of many creatures when I'd been bonded to them, I knew I'd react very badly to it happening again. But we were talking about the end of the worlds here.

"I don't think we have a choice. Dannie is *so* much stronger than any being we've ever faced, right?" This question was more relevant to him since he was a few thousand years old and immensely powerful. My history was with the Torma, who were basically worms on the totem pole of power.

Shadow nodded. "I haven't truly feared another in two thousand years, not since coming into my powers and bonding with Inky, but my mother... She has me very aware of her presence. I don't enjoy this new awareness."

Unlike the rest of us, he wasn't used to being the underdog.

"What happened to you in those first few moments after Dannie manipulated all of our memories?" I asked him. He'd told me bits and pieces, but there were a lot of missing details.

All the sex had kind of gotten in the way of the talking.

No. Regrets.

Despite the well-lit hallway, his face was awash in shadowy planes. "After we left you down in the caverns, I ended up in the castle, trying to figure out friend from foe. Most of my family was gone, but that didn't mean there weren't a ton of messes to clean up. In the midst of that, there..." His brow furrowed. "It was a swift wind that expelled everyone from the castle except me. The wind entered my mind, and maybe if I'd reacted faster, or had been more prepared, I could have fought her mind manipulation."

He shook his head. "She took me by surprise, and everything went dark. When I came to, the sort of rage I'd never experienced before slammed into me. I vaguely remembered burning down buildings and leveling mountains until my friends got to me. We were all confused, remembering each other but knowing that we'd been messed with. After that, my beast took over, and I destroyed everything I touched, including parts of the worlds and the Solaris System."

My throat was tight, and even though I'd been the one to ask, I almost wished I hadn't. Thinking about that time made me feel sick and broken. "Dannie was clever," I rasped. "She didn't take it all away; she just changed the narrative enough to get what she needed from us. I mean, Torin was waiting for me in Torma, and I was his true mate, so it was easy to slide me right into that life, leaving you free to rule the Shadow Realm, as you were meant to."

If the cut of his jaw was any indication, he was not a fan of this reasoning. "She wasn't that clever. She should have expected that neither of us would roll over into our new lives. You had no true history with Torin, and then to cover it all up by pretending that all of Torma had been locked in a stasis—"

"Which almost worked because you literally did have them locked in stasis for a while when we were in the Shadow Realm," I reminded him.

And why the fuck was I defending Dannie right now? We weren't in a school debate where I had to prove my point. Dannie had fucked us hard, sans lube, and we had every right to be angry as hell at her.

"What happened to your true mate?" There'd been no mention of Ixana and I wanted to know where that bitch currently was.

Shadow met my gaze, the gold in his eyes bleeding into red flames. "She had her memory wiped and ended up in Torma."

It took me an embarrassingly long time to understand what he meant. And it wasn't like he'd spoken in code or anything. It was just... *fuck*.

"*What?*"

He shook his head at me. "I won't say it again, Sunshine. You heard me the first time."

"You consider me to be your true mate now." My words were slow and confused.

His scoff indicated that he was already annoyed with this line of questioning. "I don't consider shit. You are my mate. Chosen and true. The bond between us would not exist otherwise and since both of us have two sides to our souls, it's not even a far leap to understand how we're bonded."

I waved both hands in front of me, fairly certain he was insulting me again. "Far leap or not, it's a huge step for you to make a statement like that, and I don't need no '*I won't say it again*' bullshit, thank you very much, Shadow Bastard."

His lips twitched. "How's your ass feeling, Sunshine?"

My mouth went dry. "Uh, I mean, I'm all into sexy subject changes, but that one seems like a relatively extreme segue."

His lips curved further. "It's not as far a *segue* as you might think because if your smartass mouth doesn't stop soon, I'm going to test out your ability to enjoy pain with your pleasure."

I stepped into him. "Promises, promises." I said that more than was probably healthy, but whatever. He apparently had no fucking clue how into this side of him I was.

His power wrapped around me, and I was dragged slowly up his body to receive a firm slap of his huge hand against my ass before he wrapped his fingers across the muscle and kneaded it. "We have to find your friend," he told me softly, "and Midnight, and save the world. That's the only thing that's saving you from being tied to my bed for the next month."

His hold on my ass tightened, and just when it was about to reach the level where I might have had to tap out, his other hand slipped down the front of my pants.

Oh, wait, I wasn't even wearing pants because apparently his magic was that freaking awesome. It could strip me in a single thought. Luckily, we were still in the white hallway, without a bunch of onlookers to witness my destruction via orgasm.

Shadow's fingers found my damp heat, sliding inside, and curling up to hit my G-spot. At the same time, the other hand on my ass stroked across my flesh.

I arched into him, the low heady feeling of a decent orgasm already building deep inside of me. "Shadow, please," I moaned.

There was no time, as he'd already stated, for anything in depth, but he couldn't start this and not end it. He slapped me again, and at the same time pumped those fingers in my pussy harder and faster. I was screaming before the first swirls of my orgasm hit, his hands giving me a pleasurable pain that tipped me over in an instant.

"You like that, Sunshine?" he murmured.

I wanted to say *no* because this arrogant asshole was already too sure of his sexual prowess, but I also wouldn't lie to him. Whatever he was doing felt so amazing that I couldn't feel my legs, or my lungs, my breathing shallow and unstable. Not to mention my heart was slamming into my chest with enough force for a heart attack.

"Whom do you belong to, Sunshine?"

I sobbed and his fingers slowed. "You!" I burst out. "I belong to you."

The tilt of his lips indicated that was the right answer. His fingers moved again as he used them to fuck me harder than ever, and this time, the swirls exploded and I came with enough force that I managed to bite through my lip, drawing blood in my excitement.

"Who is your true mate, Sunshine?"

"You." There was no hesitation in my voice. Shadow owned every part of me, and I would take whatever Dannie put us through just to have these moments with him.

"You are my true mate," he confirmed as he kissed me, the slight copper of my blood between us. "You're mine in all ways, and for that, Torin is dead when I have some time to waste. I'm already anticipating the day we never speak about that bastard again."

"Yes," I moaned, still riding the final swirls of my orgasm. "You possessive beast."

He didn't deny it, just slowly removed his fingers from inside me before he lifted them to his mouth and tasted each one. Swear to fuck I almost came again just seeing that.

"Come on," Shadow said, his magic returning my clothing and cleaning me up in the process. "We can collect your creatures once we know there's a need for them."

I'd completely forgotten that was the reason we'd stopped in this hallway in the first place, but with that statement, Shadow brought us back to our reality.

He moved toward the library entrance, and it took me a moment to catch up since my legs were firing on half their normal cylinders. It was only the thought of Angel and Midnight that had me pulling myself together as fast as I could.

Interlude or not, it was time to focus on finding my friends and pulling our pack together. We'd need every member to have a chance at defeating Dannie in this final battle.

Chapter Twenty-Nine

My legs remained wobbly and weak even after we entered the library. Seeing it all whole and unbroken was a great boost, though, restoring my equilibrium. Full shelves and the small army of goblins were a few of my favorite things, and I had to take a moment to appreciate it all.

"Mera?" Shadow called back, noticing my pause. "Are you okay?"

"Yeah—" My voice broke, and he narrowed his eyes, concern filling his face. I waved him off. "Seriously, I'm fine. Just really happy."

The furrow in his brow smoothed. "Ah, I understand. I promise to look after your libraries," he said, knowing now what had me a hot mess. "No matter what happens, they'll be protected as long as I live."

I threw myself at him, finally able to trust that he'd catch me. "Thank you," I murmured, pulling away. "I'll let you in on a secret, though. They're in my top ten favorite things, but they're not number one."

He kissed me, like he couldn't help himself, and I was kind of falling in love with these random bursts of affection. "It's no secret," he murmured.

Is that right? "What or who do you think is number one?"

I mean, no one was going to say themselves, right?

"Me."

Okay, sure, no one other than an arrogant Shadow Bastard. And while he wasn't wrong, he could at least fake some humility.

"You're definitely in the top ten," I said, forcing my voice to remain even. "Along with Simone, Angel, Midnight, Inky, the library, and the lair. All the shadow creatures as well, along with the five morons you call best friends. And Gaster. And Sam—"

He cut me off with a sardonic burst of laughter. "Math isn't your strong suit, is it?"

I smiled sweetly. "Some of you occupy the same spot in the top ten, so my math is actually quite correct."

He shook his head at me. "I'm not sure my math and your math are the same sort of math."

I thought on this. "You're probably right, but that doesn't mean my math is wrong."

I was fairly certain he muttered *actually, that's exactly what it means*, but there was no time to confirm and chastise him because he had started to lead me through the library, stopping only when we reached Angel's door.

"How will we find her?" I asked as he reached out to swing the door open. "And what happens if I need to pee?"

Because honestly, I'd drunk a lot of water at lunch, and my bladder was feeling decidedly uncomfortable. Shadow really should learn to check that no one needed the bathroom before we set off to another world.

"We'll go to Angel's family land first," he said, somehow not managing to sound annoyed with me. "Thanks to your bond with her, it should allow you entry again. And if you hurry your ass up, you can use the bathroom right now before we leave."

My smile could have lit up a dark room. "Thank you! Seriously, thank you."

I sprinted off, heading toward the nearest facilities. It might have been weird to have bathrooms in a place like this, built of fantasy beings and other worlds, but the truth was, most of them needed to use a bathroom for varying reasons, most of which I did not want to know about.

When I was done, I returned to find Shadow in the same spot, all but guarding the open doorway into the Honor Meadows. "Everything okay?" I asked, noting how hard he was staring into the swirling white abyss that existed on the other side of the doorway.

At the sound of my voice, his focus returned to me. "All good," he said with a nod. "I was just checking out the Solaris System since it's still coming online from my reboot."

Despite the many beings already making their way along his paths between worlds, there were clearly parts of the system not quite up and running yet.

"Did you find any issues?" I asked, not really expecting any because Shadow made no mistakes.

He hesitated, and I frowned at him. "There's an issue?" I asked.

Now he was the one frowning. "There's a foreign entity coating the surface of my magic," he said slowly, like he wasn't quite sure if he was reading it right. "It's so light and thin that it's barely noticeable, but it's not mine. It doesn't appear to be affecting the general function, but I will have to look into it when we return."

He didn't want to leave it be, but at the same time, there was no way in hell he'd let me head into the Honor Meadows on my own. "Will everyone here be safe until we return?"

"Yes." This time, he was surer. "There's no malevolence in the presence. It's just foreign, and since this is built from Inky's and my energy, it's obvious only to me that there's a foreign beat in the heart."

As if it had heard its name, Inky swirled down then, wrapping around Shadow.

"Can Inky feel it too?" I whispered.

Shadow nodded. "Yes, and Inky thinks it's best if it stays here and investigates."

I felt better to know that someone would be keeping an eye on it. "Fine with me, as long as you don't think we'll need Inky in the Honor Meadows."

Shadow shook his head. "If we run into a situation that you and I can't get ourselves out of, there's very little Inky could do to help. I can think of only one being with enough power to worry us, and it's the one I call 'Mother.'"

That was good news... if you tilted your head and squinted at it. I mean, I was all about silver linings these days, and the fact that I wasn't currently in Torma with Torin meant everything from here on out was good news.

Inky faded up into the ceiling, and I imagined it spreading out through the mechanics of the library. "Stay safe, buddy," I called after it, just as Shadow nudged me toward the still-open doorway.

The Honor Meadows felt the same as they had the last time I'd stepped through. Warm, inviting, and ancient in a way that I couldn't fully describe. I just sensed it deep in my own magic.

"This world truly fascinates me," I said when we were standing in the long field of gold, the only part of Angel's land I'd been to. My wolf rose up at the memories, and I was relieved to feel her strong and content in my chest again. Back with our true, *true mate*, we were once again whole. My wolf might have been team Torin for a while, but after witnessing her melancholy the last time around him, it was clear who we'd both chosen.

Our beast.

"This is one of the more ancient of the lands," Shadow told me, his steps silent as he moved through the ankle-length golden grass. "It's definitely the basis for the human's perception of Heaven, and I believe it's most probably due to those who heard stories from their 'guardian angels.' I know Angel told you some of her family's history and work on Earth. I was the one to nudge them in that direction, as an additional safeguard over humans and shifters."

I was near speechless.

It wasn't as if I was particularly religious, and certainly not about angels and gods and the devil as such, since I'd always worshipped the Shadow Beast—still did actually, just in a different way now. But I knew how strongly humans felt about their religions, and the reverences they held for their gods. I didn't blame them, either, because the world was damn dark, and to have faith in something greater, even if it was mere flickers of hope filling that darkness, was worth a lot more than what was tangibly returned to them. Shadow had helped shape some of that hope, and I felt very insignificant in comparison.

"Do all the transcendents go to Earth?"

Shadow shook his head. "No. Their big-picture role is like my mother's with the Nexus. To keep the balance. To do that, they must travel between all places, holding evil at bay and protecting those who are destined to do great things. They sense where they are needed to be through meditation and their own personal psychic abilities." He stood taller, the light here casting a perfect tint of gold over him, turning a god into something greater. "There aren't many transcendents left now. Maybe a few hundred thousand, and as you can imagine, they're stretched thin."

Maintaining balance would be a thankless fuck of a job, and with all the worlds, a few hundred thousand wouldn't go far. "Why are they dying out? I thought they were immortal."

Shadow's expression didn't give a lot away, but his eyes were as brilliantly gold as the light around him. "As the worlds' evils grow stronger, it weakens them. Then there are the wars. Dannie is not the first we've had to go up against when it comes to those who believe they deserve more than their share of the power. This might be the worst, but there have been many before. Angel's entire family was killed in such a battle, and it's only her pure strength, tenacity, and the inherited power she got from each member that allowed her to break free and return to the Honor Meadows before she, too, was claimed."

"She told me that saving their family power is the most important part of their culture."

He nodded. "Yes, nothing else stands above it. Each family here has a unique power. It's why the balance is growing further and further off-kilter, as more of the family lines and abilities are lost."

Poor Angel. My heart still ached for her tragic story, and knowing she was out there alone again, thinking she had no family left, was a weight pressing me into the ground. "We have to find her," I said, spinning on the spot, like she would appear with that movement. "Can you feel her here?"

Shadow breathed in deeply, the mist tattoos on his arms moving, as they often did when he channeled his power. "This land is so imbued with her energy, it's impossible for me to tell her specific location. We're going to have to push through the magic, peel off the layers, and see if an Angel falls out."

I gulped. "That kind of seems like a great way to get attacked. I mean, have you seen her curved blades? I really like my insides to stay inside. For aesthetic reasons."

Shadow drew me along with his power, low chuckles spilling from his lips. "She will never hurt you, Mera. Angel might not remember you, and I might not be able to penetrate the magic of her land to release her memories, but when she sees you, your connection will remind her. I'm sure of it."

He sounded sure, but then again, he always was confident. Maybe if I channeled some of that confidence, I'd feel the same way. With that in mind, I forced my anxiety down and followed him across the land.

When he ground to a halt, I ran straight into his back, but he must have expected that since he was already twisting to catch me before I bounced onto my ass.

"There's a break in her power grid here," he said as he set me on my feet.

Before I could ask what the fuck that meant, he reached down to the golden land, and as he ran his fingertip along a small section, it sliced open, like a knife through paper.

Was he shitting me right now? "Peel away the layers" had been a literal statement.

He was going to take us into the beating heart of Angel's world.

Chapter Thirty

There was no adequate way to describe the sensation of stepping through the fabric of a world, and when we emerged under the first layer of Angel's territory in the Honor Meadows, I was basically speechless. Again.

A rarity that amused Shadow to no end.

"In time you'll come to expect that much of what you see is an illusion," he said, chuckling at the gobsmacked expression I wore. "We all wear masks and use power to disguise parts of ourselves."

I swallowed roughly. "Yeah, I mean, I know that in theory, but to see a world turn from a twilight expanse of golden fields into a sunlit realm of clouds and waterfalls, after you cut through that golden field layer, is not really an everyday occurrence. I mean... *how in the actual freaking illusion are they doing this?*"

It was as if Shadow had peeled a layer of a painting away to reveal a completely new scene below. Or maybe it was like peeling an orange to find a pineapple below. This layer looked, felt, and smelled different to the one above, and I was really starting to understand the many layers of Angel herself.

"It's just magic," he told me. "Your eyes see what you're told to see, and it's only if you look closer that you'll notice the delicate edges waiting to be peeled away."

I thought on this as I followed Shadow along a white fluffy expanse of cloud, marveling at how we weren't plummeting through it. "Would my wolf have seen the edges?"

He looked back at me. "Not when you were first here; you were resistant to the truth. But today, you could see it all if you allowed the true power within you to rise up."

"Part of me is still weakened by my wolf side, isn't it?"

We'd never spoke explicitly about it, but I'd pieced it together from what Dannie had said, and what I also felt inside. I was a hybrid —that much was true—but I could be so much more than. I could be like Dannie; I just didn't know how to take that step to becoming that Nexus-born being. I wondered if I might have to figure it out to before this battle was done.

"No part of you is weak," Shadow said gruffly, "and your potential knows no limits. Continue to evolve, and you'll be the strongest of us all."

I couldn't imagine that ever happening, but it was a nice thought.

Shadow picked up his pace, and I noted that the waterfalls around us seemed to stream from above the clouds. The way the light sparkled off the teal-tinted water made it look so damn enticing. Right up until a few unfamiliar creatures splashed through the strands, looking like a hybrid of a unicorn and shark, with a sparkling gold-tinted horn, pearlescent skin, and very sharp fangs.

"The cogarish," Shadow told me. "They're native to this world. Their horns are used to reinforce a lot of the armor the transcendents wear—when the cogarish dies, of course, since they're revered and protected here."

"How many different creatures live in this world?"

Shadow shrugged. "There's no way to tell. The layers hide everything, but as far as I'm aware, the only true sentient beings are the transcendents. Otherwise, it's just these smaller creatures."

"Do the different families here fight with each other?"

Shadow considered my question. "Again, their secrets are their own, but I don't believe petty squabbles are part of their makeup these days. Their evolution is old and near flawless."

Flawless. I liked that. Maybe there was a chance one day, if humans and shifters got their shit together, that we, too, might one day be perfect.

Shadow continued on, only stopping when he reached a particular sparkle of light, and as he had done before, he cut through the layer, taking us from the cloudland into one of water. Huge bodies of water that we used our power to walk above.

"Angel can live in any of these levels?" I asked. "Are they all real?"

He looked around, seeing and smelling everything I did. "Is anything truly real? Or is it all a product of our imagination?" Before he bent my brain further with his philosophical questions, he continued. "But as far as I know, each layer here is as real as the one before."

To test this, I reached down and ran my hand through the water. It was wet and cool, leaving a residue of liquid on my fingertips. When I touched those fingers to my lips, it tasted a little briny.

"How is it that you still don't understand the danger of putting a foreign object in your mouth?" Shadow asked with a shake of his head. "For all you know, the water here could kill you in an instant."

I gawked at him. "You didn't say anything when I had your dick in my mouth. Where was your concern then?"

He blinked, and then he laughed, a deep, rolling rumble that had many parts of my body sitting up and paying attention. When he finally stopped laughing at me, he stepped forward and cupped my cheek. "I'd kill my mother just for the fact that I might have never heard your inane chatter again. You don't think before you speak, and it's... refreshing."

Forcing myself to swallow the thick swell of emotions, I managed a smile. "She will never take this away from us again."

He nodded, pressing a lingering kiss to my forehead, and... how was that so freaking hot? I would swear I felt it in my vagina, if the flutter there was any indication.

He turned and walked off before I even had a chance to pull myself together. "Wait," I called after him, hurrying to catch up. "You didn't confirm that the water won't kill me?"

"I didn't confirm that my dick won't, either," he called back over his shoulder. "Guess only time will tell."

I muttered under my breath as I splashed after him, my magic keeping me mostly dry. Shadow didn't slow until he reached the next layer, and this time, we stepped into the water, popping out into a new layer.

I straightened to find that this level was what I'd liken to the Amazon jungle. It was humid, filled with millions of plants and trees, some towering over us, others bushy and thick, and the scents. An overwhelming number of foreign smells filled my nose, making my head spin for a second before I filtered them out.

"This is the layer she lives in," Shadow murmured. "I can feel her energy now that we're here."

The flutters in my chest went haywire, confirming that the jungle level was the one. "It's insane. I literally couldn't feel her in our bond until we got here. I'm starting to understand Angel's fascination with your mate's maze house in the realm."

Shadow let out a rumble of annoyance, and I had to work hard not to smile. Riling him up was too easy, but I really had to stop mentioning Ixana. Mostly because it still hurt to think about that dumb bitch of an ice queen.

"What actually happened to Ixana?" Okay, yeah, maybe I'd stop after this question got answered, since the last time I'd asked, he'd deflected me rather cleverly.

"She was interrogated and disposed of."

Oh... okay then. "Short, sweet, and to the point, I see."

He shrugged. "Sweet might be a stretch, but in the end, her crimes were beyond redemption. And she held no remorse—not even as broken as she was after losing the stone she'd been bonded to for a thousand years. She said she would still do it all over again."

"How did she even find the stone in the first place?" I asked as we started to move through the jungle.

He took a second to answer, focusing on widening the path as we walked. "During her last confession, she admitted that it was her bond with me." His fury spilled out in his tone. "She kept tabs on me during my years exiled, knowing whom my friends were and what alliances she could manipulate. Apparently, I grew more powerful than she'd expected, and that was to be used to her advantage." A few trees singed around us, but he managed not to burn the forest down. "I have full access into Len's territory in Faerie; Ixana could tap into that through the bonds we had with each other from birth. Using my bloodstone as added backup, she figured out how to infiltrate and steal the sunburst stone during one of the Faerie festivals."

Probably another sex festival because they were all-consuming when they hit Faerie.

"How is it that no fae was guarding the stone?" Even during a festival, an object that important had to have been secured.

Shadow paused, his face almost unreadable in the shade of nearby trees. "There were fae guarding the stone, but they disappeared when the stone did. Ixana wasn't too coherent in the end, but the general vibe of her plan was seduction followed by betrayal. Len was relieved that she hadn't taken the rest of his stones, but I knew she wouldn't. She only needed one weapon and would not waste her time on anything else."

He recognized the single-minded focus of his former chosen mate now.

"It's hard to believe she had the brains and fortitude to do everything she did."

No doubt there was more to the story that she hadn't revealed, but it really didn't matter. The end result was the same, and now we had to deal with the fallout.

He scoffed. "Her family helped her plan it in the early days, until she went rogue. She's the entire reason we even made it back into the Realm. She released the spell and opened the doorway."

I stumbled, since that was the first I'd heard that. "Seriously? I didn't break through when I called the mists and creatures?"

He shook his head. "When she felt your surge of power and the exodus of mists and creatures that you called to Earth, she knew there was another Danamain out there who could be manipulated into completing her plan. So she dropped the spell."

Disappointment rocked me hard, and I couldn't hide my forlorn expression.

"What's wrong?" Shadow asked, pausing in the middle of parting twenty fern-like plants.

I rubbed a hand over my face, trying to pull myself together. "I don't know. I guess I liked being the one person who helped you get what you wanted and needed most. It was a nice feeling to be useful to someone as powerful as you. And now you're telling me it was still that dumb bitch, and I never outsmarted her at all?"

I'd done nothing in that final fight. Shadow had fought Ixana, Dannie had swallowed the stone and stolen the power from her, and I'd... gotten myself kicked back into Torma with my memories wiped. That didn't sit well with me because I was no damsel in distress.

I wanted to be on equal footing with Shadow.

"Sunshine," he said huskily. "You have no idea what you've done for me. Trust me; it's much more than opening a doorway that I wished was still closed. You fought through the memory spell, saving us all. I don't think you need to worry about your worth."

That was true. "We do make a great team, and I'm glad that we were both strong enough to reject the 'perfection' Dannie gave us. I could have been alpha-mate, and you could have stayed and ruled the realm."

"I have rejected my position of Supreme Being," Shadow said with no hesitation. "I've built a new world for myself, with you, and there's no room in my life for the realm."

Holy shit. That was... huge. He was rewriting his destiny, and he made no apologies about that. "The libraries are mine," I said huskily. "I will straight-up *fight* you for them."

His lips quirked as he wrapped an arm around me, dragging me higher so our mouths could meet. Heat poured off both of us as my tongue slid out to trace across his. I couldn't be more addicted to the taste of this guy if I tried.

"Let the battle begin," Shadow said against my lips, and I knew then, with absolute certainty, that this most perfect of true mates was going to challenge me every step of our relationship.

Fuck, if I wasn't beyond excited for our future.

Instead of grinding against him as I wanted, I just wrapped my arms and legs around him and hugged him tightly. "Sleep with one eye open, Beast," I whispered into his ear, as if imparting sweet nothings. "Those libraries are mine."

His chest shook as he let out a deep chuckle, starting to walk again while I was still wrapped around him. With each step, my need to rub against him grew as tingles of pleasure swirled low. "I can smell your arousal," he murmured.

I sighed. "Yep, that's me, always horny around the Shadow Beast. But we seriously have to find Angel, so you better put me down."

With reluctance, I released my hold on him, and he set me on my feet, both of us focused again on finding our pack mate. If there was anything our conversation had just shown us, it was that we had a lot of future to look forward to, and that meant we needed every power at our disposal to take Dannie down.

There was no other option.

Chapter
Thirty-One

The jungle was surprisingly quiet. I'd never been to the Amazon, or to any place with more forests than Torma, but even in the sparse sections of land back home, there had been a lot of wildlife.

Here there was nothing. The silence itself somehow deepening the farther we traversed, and despite the many unanswered questions still running through my head, I didn't voice them.

It felt wrong to speak.

"Angel likes silence," Shadow reminded me when we'd been walking for half an hour without saying a word. Clearly, he had no issue breaking through the energy she had over her land to keep it quiet. "She's designed this part of her territory to be a tranquil oasis, an escape from the rest of the worlds."

"I feel it."

The layers of Angel were definitely reflected in the layers of this world she'd built here. Maybe one day my power would create the perfect world for me... Then again, maybe it was already there, in the Library of Knowledge and the lair, both of which I loved.

"We're finally getting somewhere," Shadow said. "Her true presence is stronger here than anywhere else we've been so far."

I pressed a hand to my chest again as the flutter kicked harder than ever. Following this was a strong burst of emotion. Rage first, and then the tiniest spike of panic. Angel had just realized there were strangers in her midst, strangers with strong powers, and she had no idea how that had happened.

I felt her energy searching through ours, cataloguing the threat, and when she paused on Shadow, there was confusion and curiosity. Shadow, she remembered, but no doubt she was wondering what the hell he was doing here.

Angel appeared a moment later, dressed for battle, in black molded armor that closely followed the lines of her body. The dark outfit blended beautifully into the mahogany of her hair and amber in her wings. No being had ever looked more like an angelic celestial than my Honor Meadows best friend. Hence the nickname.

"Shadow Beast," she snarled, marching forward. "How dare you enter my domain without my permission? How did you even get around the securities? I didn't feel you until you were almost upon me."

Instead of attacking first, she was smart enough to ferret out the breach in her security so she could ensure it never happened again. Meanwhile, I was fighting the urge to run forward and wrap my arms around her. I'd missed her so much, and even as I pressed a hand to my chest, I couldn't stop the huge swell of power beating at me like a drum, right in the spot she'd first touched me to bond us.

Her gaze jerked to mine, boring into me as she too pressed a hand to her chest. We examined each other, and while it was clear she had no memory of me, she felt the connection.

"What is happening?" she snapped, stepping closer. The curved blades appeared in her hands, making it clear that she was more than a little threatened by our presence. We'd invaded her tranquility. Her peace. We'd stepped foot where I would hazard a guess no other had since her family died.

And while she might have learned to trust Shadow during her time bonded to me, that time was no longer in her memory. "Can you break through Dannie's spell on her?" I whispered to Shadow.

He shook his head. "Not from this distance. She's too powerful here in her dominion."

"Speak up!" she commanded, the air crashing around us in tune to her voice. "Or I will attack, and even the Shadow Beast cannot stand against me here, surrounded by the power of my family."

His eyes met mine. "It would be close," he admitted reluctantly. Which in and of itself told me everything. My girl was a total badass.

I stepped forward to draw her attention while remaining near Shadow because there was no way he'd let me out of his protective circle. "You don't remember me," I said, projecting my voice, "because our memories were manipulated by a powerful goddess, but I'm Mera Callahan. I'm a wolf shifter slash goddess of the Nexus. And you and I are bonded because we're family. *Treasora.*"

She paled, her hands trembling until her blades visibly shook. "You lie."

I smiled sadly, hating this distance between us. "You feel our bond. It has been calling to me for weeks. Even when I'd forgotten everything about you and this world, the flutters in my chest never stopped."

Her head jerked as she shook it, like she was trying to clear her thoughts. "I'm too powerful for any to touch my mind. I protect that above all else. And I would never have bonded to one not from my world. We are warne—"

"Warned against it," I finished for her. "Yeah, I know. But you trust me. You didn't want your family line of power to die with you, though if I have anything to say about it, you'll be outliving me anyway, so it's a moot point."

Shadow's pissed-off grumble from behind broke through, but we ignored him.

"Angel," I said, allowing her name to drift across in a whisper. "I call you 'Angel' because you're the most beautiful, angelic being I've ever seen. You remind me of Earth's version of a guardian angel, and I know your family filled that role in the past."

Her eyes widened, and I had all of her attention now.

"If you allow me to touch you, I can release your memories," Shadow said.

She snarled again, any sliver of trust that had been building gone in a flash. "You would touch me to steal my power. Or plant the very memories you want me to have. The odds of me allowing you to ever touch me are zero."

"Great work," I muttered to the beast, wanting to sigh at the backward steps we'd just taken.

"I don't need her damn power," Shadow rumbled. "Since I returned to the realm and bonded to my stone, I'm stronger than I've ever been, and if Angel removed her head from her ass for five minutes, she'd see that."

And there he was, my Shadow Beast, nailing people skills since the dinosaur days.

Thankfully, Angel, who was also ancient, took a moment to consider his words and examine his power. When her eyes closed, I knew she was assessing the truth of what he'd said. An increase in power was a tangible measurement, giving our story some credibility.

"You are stronger," she said, her gaze once again on us. Her expression remained wary, but there was curiosity there as well. Angel was ancient and world-weary, and more than a little broken, but deep inside, there was just a being who loved fiercely and deserved the same in return.

If she took the risk here, she would discover the inbuilt family she had in us. Her treasora.

Her family.

As that word shimmered in the air between us, she locked me in those depthless eyes. "Did you just speak in my mind?" she asked.

I shook my head. "We're bonded, and while I can't speak in your mind, sometimes the emotions or words cross through our connection."

Her denial of our bond didn't emerge this time. "I know you," she whispered. "I've been feeling so lost, in a way that I haven't felt since my family perished in the final battle of the meadows. I couldn't understand why, after all of these centuries, I was back in the pit of despair. What could I have lost again when I had nothing left of any value?"

Her words cracked me open and left me bleeding, tears falling down my cheeks as she spun her tale of hurt and loss and emptiness.

"Mera was who you lost," Shadow said bluntly. "We all lost her, and apparently, she's the humanity that holds us all together."

Before he even finished that somewhat sweet statement, Angel leapt forward. I expected Shadow to react defensively; it was his nature, after all, especially when she was still armed. He didn't move, though, and I remembered his earlier words about her never hurting me. He obviously had faith in that, and I did as well because I didn't even flinch when her blades glided up to rest against my throat.

Shadow's chest rumbled, but he remained where he was. The only thing saving Angel in this moment was the lack of aggression in her face. "I'm going to touch you now," she said softly. "If I feel even the slightest tingle of Shadow's energy near my own, I'll end both your lives."

Shadow added a scoff to his rumbling, which Angel ignored, focusing on me. With one blade remaining at my throat, the other faded into nothing so she could press that free hand against my chest.

The moment our skin connected, there was a burst of power that flowed between us. The past, present, and future that had been stolen by Dannie tumbled around like weeds in a swift wind until both of us were swimming in our bond.

Angel gasped, a choked and shattered sound. The other blade faded out in the next second as she wrapped her arms tightly around me. Just like with Shadow, the rare hugs I got from these god-like creatures were treasured above any power or gold. They made me feel safe, and loved, and strong; they made me feel like I had a family.

"Dannie is going to die," Angel said hoarsely, and fiercely. "She stole from the wrong beings, and I don't care whom she calls brethren —her blood will spill."

Her rage was tangible, tasting like bitter oranges on my tongue. And while no one argued with her, a part of me still hoped our original plan would work, and that there was a chance to save the Danamain.

Chapter Thirty-Two

"You must follow me," Angel said, when she was done with our hug.

She turned and walked off, and I exchanged a glance with Shadow, knowing we didn't have a lot of time. We'd planned to meet the others back in the library in two days, and I had no idea if time moved differently between Honor Meadows and the library, but even if it didn't, the clock was still ticking.

When Shadow didn't argue, I had to assume we were still good on our deadline, which allowed me to enjoy observing Angel in her natural environment. Not to mention I had about fifty questions to ask her.

"Go on," Angel said with a smile when I caught up to her. "I might not remember everything about you yet, but the snippets I have through our bond are memories of you questioning everything."

I laughed, reaching out to link my arm through hers, just like old times. "See, the thing is," I said, "I'm like twenty-ish years old." I'd lost track of the specific age with all the world-jumping and memory lapses. "You're all thousands of years old. The worlds are brand new to me, as is magic and... basically everything else. I need to know about it all, and with the way my life is going, we might all be dead next week. There's really no better time to ask."

"That makes sense," she said softly. "But I'll have less talk about your death, thank you. If anyone's time is up, it's mine. I've lived too long as it is, and I'm tired."

I ground to a halt, and surprisingly, she stopped with me. "I'll hear none of that talk," I mimicked back to her. "None. You signed up to be my family, and with that comes a certain set of responsibilities. No sacrifice. No loss. No death. Understood?"

Shadow chuckled, and I narrowed my eyes on him next. "Same goes for you, mate."

Angel forgot whatever wise thing she was about to say, which was probably something like: *Death is not the end of family.* Instead, she was fascinated by my utterance of the word *mate.*

"You're the mate of Darkor?"

I gritted my teeth. "Shadow and I have somehow formed a true mate bond. Without any actions on our behalf, and he assures me that it means our Nexus sides are fated to be together."

Thankfully, even with sketchy memories, Angel followed along well.

"Ixana?" she asked Shadow.

"Dead."

Why waste words when you could answer with just one... Shadow's motto in life.

One word was enough for Angel, though, who just shrugged as she started to drag me along with her. We walked for a few minutes in silence, and I marveled at the array of grey and green and gold plants that surrounded us.

Some were familiar, others not at all, and I'd hazard a guess that Angel had modeled the different species after plants from various worlds when she'd created this level.

When we entered a small clearing, we stopped outside of a dwelling. Excitement at maybe seeing her home shot through me.

Everything I knew about Angel was based on our life outside of her world, but I was finally getting a sneak peek.

The outside of her home was nondescript, blending into the plants around it. The layered boards were gold, accented by stone and wood in shades of green and grey. It mostly looked like a cabin that had been claimed by nature. There was no visible entrance, at least not until Angel pressed her hands to a mass of intertwined vines on one wall.

Energy flowed through her fingertips, and the vines responded, twirling and slithering like snakes until there was an opening big enough for even Shadow to walk through without ducking his head.

Inside it was as I'd expected. Simple, practical, with a few select touches of Angel. A shimmery wall of armor, with many varied colors, including gold, bronze, silver, and a deep rich maroon set that looked ancient and heavy. "I can call this armor to me from any place in any of the worlds," she told me when I stopped to stare at it. "Also, the weapons."

Even Shadow was impressed when we reached the next wall in her main room, which was covered top to bottom in weapons. From swords to small blades, axes and other lethal chop-off-your-own-arm items, there were so many, I couldn't take them all in. Each one was mounted upon what appeared to be bone, displayed to perfection. "They sit on the remnants of our enemies," Angel explained.

Remnants of her enemies? Bone was correct.

"I remember some of these," Shadow said, leaning in close, but not too close that there was any chance of him touching her items. If I knew anything about ancient Honor Meadow weapons, they did not like to be handled by those who were not family.

"When our bond is complete," she told me, "you'll be able to call any item from these walls."

Now *that* was exciting. Except... "You don't have to die first, right?"

She actually cracked a smile. "No, the wall can be called by more than one. Any who are in our bonded family are gifted with these ancient battle materials."

Okay, then, sign me up.

When we were finally able to tear our eyes from the wall "art," we moved farther into the cabin. Angel led us into a lounge room containing a few wooden chairs. "I like to carve in my spare time," she said, gesturing for us to sit on the intricate pieces. "They're stronger than they look."

That was probably meant for Shadow because they looked plenty strong to me. I was the first to sit, and before Shadow could move to the bench beside me, Angel stepped in front of him.

"Free the rest of my memories," she said in a rush. "I've been able to release some through my current awareness of the spell, but... the being who cast it is too strong for me to best their energy completely."

"All of us needed help to remember." I piped up from my spot. "Nothing to be ashamed of." They both shot me a glare and I shrugged. "Just trying to help. I figured it's tiring being a badass all the time. It's nice to let others support you on occasion."

Angel had actually imparted that advice to me in the realm, which she may not remember.

Their glares didn't cease. "Completely not tiring," Shadow said bluntly.

"Agreed," Angel added, and I just smiled because they were adorable... and scary. Always scary.

Shadow wasted no time placing his hand on her forehead. Angel closed her eyes briefly, and I felt the burst of power that came from them both, near knocking me off my seat. Angel flew across the room, her wings shooting out to stop her from slamming into the walls. Scrambling to my feet, I was prepared to jump between them if a battle broke out, but Angel just shook her head a few times, finally meeting my gaze. "Mera."

She'd known me before, but until this moment hadn't truly known, *known* me. I ran toward her because of course we had to hug again, both of us holding on for many minutes.

It had been too close to almost losing them all.

When we were all hugged out, we sat and caught up. I quickly got her up to date on what had happened on Shadow's and my side after Dannie, and where we were at now.

"What's the plan to defeat the Danamain?" Angel asked, leaning back in her chair, mulling over everything she'd heard.

"Shadow's friends have all gone to their worlds to gather their most powerful spells, energy, and artifacts," I said quickly. "Len has some stones that will hopefully prevent her from stealing our memories again, and the others are bringing their strongest weapons and abilities to the table. We need the firepower to trap her in a prison, which will drain some of her energy. If that works, we'll attempt to remove the stone from her... in whatever way necessary."

"Mera is hoping that she'll release it on her own," Shadow added, "always trying to save us, even when we're barely redeemable."

He wasn't just talking about his mother. "I would never give up on you," I assured him, squeezing his hand. "And while I'm mad at her as well, I believe Dannie deserves a chance."

Angel tilted her head, probably considering my words. "The stone itself is neither good nor evil. It was just too much power for her to handle. She wanted to return the balance to how it had been before Ixana. Before Shadow was expelled from the realm. Dannie's logic was flawed, though, because the path of destiny was long changed from that time." She waved at me. "Take Mera, for example. Until Shadow was exiled from his world, Mera's path did not exist in the cosmic plan. Her life came about to match the new Shadow who would emerge from the flames of the wreckage of his last life. There's no turning that back, which was why neither of you embraced the world Dannie tried to create for you."

Shadow nodded, reaching out to drag me closer to him; he'd hardly let me out of his sight or hands since we'd found each other again, and I was one lucky shifter.

"Not even with her current power could she change our fates,"

Shadow said. "She was only muddying it up, but thankfully for all of us, Mera is too damn stubborn to accept that sort of subterfuge."

I found myself feeling strangely proud. Sure, I'd had some help from Shadow's spell, but those niggling doubts and inconsistencies wouldn't have meant much without the stubborn part of my personality forcing me to dig deeper until I uncovered the truth. I never gave up. My time being the pack's punching bag, of refusing to roll over and die, had prepared me well for my future.

A future that was now in grave jeopardy.

Hopefully, a few of my other life skills would come in handy because I was not ready to lose my current fated path. Not when it meant losing Shadow and the rest of my pack.

Yeah, hard pass, Dannie. Hard fucking pass.

Chapter Thirty-Three

With Angel up to speed and the countdown clock still ticking, we decided to head back to the library. "I'll take some energy from the layers of my ancestral power," Angel said as we left her cabin. "I don't need as many levels of protection as I have, and if we all die because we lack the power to best Dannie, it'll be useless anyway."

She had all of my attention now because I really wanted to know how she planned on taking energy from a "layer" of her world.

She didn't touch the forest level, leading us back to the spot we'd first entered it. "This is a main connective point," she explained, motioning to the exact area Shadow had used to step through. "From here, I can take as many layers as I need."

A blade appeared in her hand, shimmery and gold, with small spirals of smoke wafting from it even though nothing burned. Angel lowered the blade and sliced it into the ground. It parted the same way it had for Shadow, but there was one difference. For Angel, every layer appeared like pages in a book, allowing her to rifle through and select from them.

"Holy shit." I gasped. "How many layers do you have?"

We'd crossed three to get to her, and I'd assumed that there weren't many more than that, but from what I was seeing...

"Eight hundred and seventy-four," she said succinctly. "Varying in worth and power."

She reached out then, grasping on to a level of water that existed below her forest land. "This level is a good start," Angel said, pulling that water page up toward her until there was a grating sound of her tearing the page free.

"What the fuckery?" I muttered, staring at the shimmering piece of "land" she held, no larger than a piece of printer paper.

Angel winked at me, and then she opened her mouth and... ate the freaking page.

I mean, sure, I expected a lot of humans and shifters had eaten some paper before, but this was taking "eating paper" to an entirely new level.

"What does it taste like?" I asked.

Was that a weird question? It felt like it might have been a weird question.

Angel paused in the process of ripping out the next shimmering layer of land, tilting her head to meet my gaze. "There's only one way to find out."

She tore a small corner from the glowing level and handed it to me. "We're bonded, Mera. This won't hurt you, and the best way to learn is by doing."

Holy shit. Excitement shot me forward, and I didn't hesitate to take the corner from her. When it hit my hand, it felt like I held a boiling stone. The texture was smooth, and it sizzled against my hands but didn't hurt me. And the power... it filled me with heat, like that of my fire, but also different. Ancient and heady, it pushed and pulled at my essence, and I swallowed roughly in an attempt to pull myself together.

Shadow leaned closer, drawn in by my power, just as I always was with his. His eyes were flaming orbs, eating me up, and I ended up both weak at the knees and horny like no one's fucking business.

"Eat it, Sunshine," he said in that deep rumble of his voice. "Swallow that power down."

Motherfucker. His words were saying one thing, while his eyes reminded me of our last dance in the bedroom when he'd come in my mouth and I'd felt a burst of power from tasting him like that.

Clearly, our few times together since our memories had returned were not enough to make up for our time apart. Of course, we had that small matter of saving the worlds to deal with, but if we couldn't manage to fit in at least six to ten more quickies during this mission, the world might just be on its own.

Never taking my eyes from Shadow's, I lifted the section of power Angel had torn off, and pushed it toward my mouth. It slid down my throat, like a thick, hot cocoa, as sweet and delicious as anything I'd ever tasted.

The heat that followed spread and bloomed throughout my body until I felt like I'd swallowed a drop of sunlight. "Your power will take a minute to accept the offering," Angel said from the side, and no lie, I'd almost forgotten she was there. Between the heat and Shadow, my mind was consumed and occupied to its fullest degree.

Her advice was solid, though. Within seconds, the warmth faded everywhere except right in my center, where my own flaming power existed alongside my wolf. My wolf wasn't too sure about this new power, to be honest, but she didn't fight it, either, nudging against it with curiosity before resuming her position of calm watchfulness inside.

When the power settled, I shook myself in an attempt to put everything back in its place. "That was... interesting," I said, energy threading my words. "I've never felt anything quite like that."

Shadow and Angel both watched me closely, in that unblinking way I was coming to see all immortals had. "You don't feel odd?" Angel pressed.

Ominous words, but deciding to humor her, I pushed deeper into my power, examining the new drop of sunlight in there. "Not really,"

I said. "Just lots of heat, but it's always hot in my energy, so no huge difference."

Shadow and Angel exchanged a look, and I didn't like it when they did that. It was very hard to take these ancient beings by surprise. When a surprise happened, it usually wasn't a good one.

"What were you expecting the power would do to me?" I asked, looking between them. "Since that was clearly an experiment."

Angel wrapped an arm around me, her wings shooting out behind us. "No, seriously, it was definitely not an experiment. Neither of us would ever allow you to try anything that could harm you. It's just... the lock on your power. I keep waiting for the moment you burst free and become everything you are capable of. You're born of the Nexus. Your power is about as raw as it comes, as are the layers of my land here. The two together..."

Ah, I understood what they'd been waiting for. "I think because I was reborn as a hybrid shifter, there's a part of me that can never be awoken again. I'm not pure, but I'm okay with that. My shifter side is what allowed me to leave the Shadow Realm and be part of the other worlds."

Angel nodded a few times. "Yes, yes. You're right, and with that in mind, I best fill my well of energy so we can be on our way."

She went back to the layers of her land, continuing to eat through them like she was a starving shifter who'd just finished her first change. I'd never actually seen her eat before, but this she definitely enjoyed.

"Where are you storing it all?" I knew she filled her regular strength through meditating with the land itself, but this had to be so much more than normal. So where was the extra going?

"I'm layering it upon my skin," she rumbled, tilting her head back as a burst of light expelled from her mouth. "I'll take as much as I can."

"Until now, Angel refused to power herself using the extra energy," Shadow said dryly, "for fear that others would consider it an act of war."

She scoffed. "They'd have stood no chance against me, but you are correct. I can no longer tolerate war. It was easy to allow the power to rest here, providing me with a safe haven that none could infiltrate."

No wonder she'd been so shocked at our arrival. The thought that her sanctuary was so easily infiltrated must have filled her with a level of fear that would have felled a lesser being.

When Angel took her final layer of power, she was literally glowing, sparkles of gold falling off her skin like glitter. "We must return now," Shadow said, and he wrapped me up before Angel could touch me. "Mine," he added for good measure, nailing the angel-faced beauty with a glare. "Even as powered up as you are, I will destroy you if you claim Mera again. The first bond is bad enough. Don't make it any worse."

I was missing something here, but there was no time to ask. Angel's eyes flashed to a deep molten gold. "Don't push me, Shadow Beast," she snapped. "You cannot lay full claim to Mera, since there's more than one bond connected to her energy. Mine, Midnight's, Torin's, and now yours."

I cleared my throat. "Look, I fully intend to murder Torin, so you can scratch his ass off that list. If I'd had my memories in Torma, he'd already be dead."

Shadow was pissed, flames sliding up and across his body as he pulled me tighter into his chest. "Mine, Melalekin. Last damn warning."

Because I was messed up, his words had me purring like a damn kitten. Shadow had always been possessive, but it used to be in the way of an object he didn't want others to play with. Now it was the possessiveness of a shifter with his true mate. The sort that spoke of a deep-seated need to protect his heart and soul to the bitter end, destroying any who got in the way.

I was into it, no lie, but now wasn't the time. We had bigger enemies to fry.

"Guys, we really don't have time for another clash of the immortals," I said, looking between them. "Figure out how to divide me up later."

I understood their stance—I'd literally kill any who tried to remove our bonds. But our best chance at defeating Dannie before she destroyed the world was to be united. "We have one chance to take Dannie out before she realizes what we're doing," I reminded them. "There's no time for any other battles."

Angel and Shadow exchanged a long, power-filled stare-off, and I could tell that there were "words" being spoken, just not out loud. The tension that filled the space was thick and heavy, and as much as I wanted to interfere again, I allowed them this moment to mentally duke it out.

"It is done," Angel finally said, her voice deeper but still musical in nature.

"Let's return to the library," Shadow said in reply to her obscure statement. "We have a battle to plan."

And just like that, it was done. Apparently.

Chapter Thirty-Four

No one spoke as we climbed through the layers of Angel's world to the surface. When we reached the top level, where the beautiful golden fields remained unchanged, Angel took a few minutes to ensure all of her securities were in place.

"Is there any danger to your family land with the loss of power?" I asked her.

She shook her head. "Not at all. I've taken a mere fraction of what I hold here. It's too much power, really; power that should have been spread across many family members. But with all of them gone, the responsibility falls to me." She patted the ground, sealing up the final cuts in its essence. "I can pull more from here if needed, even at a distance. It's slower and not as effective as taking it in the manner I just did, but if we need it, there's more power."

That was good to know, even if I was praying we'd never need it.

Once she was satisfied with the securities, Angel followed us back to the library. Shadow was quiet, and I felt the brooding simmer of his energy. Our connection was new and hard to read, but I sensed that he was starting to mentally prepare himself for what was to come. Fighting against your mother was no easy task, but Dannie really hadn't left us much choice.

I loved her too. She'd been more of a mother than my own.

A twinge in my chest reminded me that my "real" mom was dead. I'd spent weeks thinking she'd run away from Torma, when all of that time, she'd been buried in the pack lands. The loss felt somewhat raw and new, but it was still built on "what ifs" rather than true grief.

What if we'd gotten our shit together and tried to form a relationship? Or what if she'd stopped drinking and started caring? Truth be told, I'd never really known her as a proper mother, and I wondered if maybe all along it had been because she'd felt no real bond to me. The child who was only half shifter.

I'd been forced into her world through the machinations of a goddess. I'd hated my mother for a long time, but maybe all along, I should have cut her some slack. It was too late now to know if her drinking and hatred of me had been thanks to Dannie and my hybrid nature. But it didn't stop the questions from crossing my mind.

"A few of the guys are back," Shadow said, drawing me from my heavy thoughts. "They're waiting in the lair."

Angel's lips twitched. "It's actually cute how you've adopted her Meraisms. Maybe you two are true mates after all."

Shadow shot a rumble of angry energy her way. "Nothing about me is cute, *Angel*."

He deliberately emphasized her name, like he was reminding her that she was also using the moniker I'd given her. Another "Meraism," as Angel had put it.

"Touché, my friend," she said. "It grows on you, her refreshing way of addressing the world. Sometimes I almost forget how jaded I am."

"You are both just super old," I reminded them, hoping to lighten the mood. "Don't be too hard on yourselves."

Shadow had me in his arms so fast that my head spun. Or maybe that was just the result of being held by him like this.

"Your smart mouth is about to turn your ass red," he murmured close to my ear, the hard length of his body pressing into mine as his power surrounded me.

"That would be quite the skill," I managed to choke out.

"Not at all," he replied easily. "Just count yourself lucky that right now, we have places to be."

I pouted. "I don't consider that lucky at all, thanks very much."

Flames sprang to life in his eyes, and I could see the battle he fought. One day my ability to bring him to the brink of losing control would bite me on the ass. Only time would tell if I liked it or not.

"Come on," Angel snapped, reminding us that we truly did have somewhere to be.

The library was bright and open, bustling with beings from all different worlds. "You brought it back to perfection," I said to Shadow, my voice thick. "It's exactly as it was."

"Nothing can ever be exactly as it was," he said, looking around, "and it's going to take some time for the library to find its true power again, but I've set it on the path. Sometimes that's the best you can do."

His words struck a chord within me, and it took me a minute to work out why. It was how he'd talked about the library... like it was his child. He'd created and nurtured this offspring the best he could, giving it all the skills needed to grow and flourish in the world. Now it was time for it to find its own way forward, with Shadow there in the background as a support system.

Kind of made me think that part of the reason I loved this particular library so much, outside of a lifetime obsession with books, was because of its ties to Shadow. *My mate.*

Before I could get too mushy over all things Shadow, Inky swirled down from the ceiling above, spreading out before us. "Inky!" I exclaimed. "Did you figure out what was wrong with the library?"

The mist twirled around Shadow, and I could tell they were talking. Angel and I waited patiently... Well, at least she did. I started bouncing on the spot in anticipation of bad news.

"It's Midnight."

I lurched forward at those words. My heart was pattering like crazy because until this moment, I'd thought my mist was still stuck in the realm. But to hear it was in the library, and had been the entire time... I wasn't prepared.

"What do you mean it's Midnight?" I said in a rush. Inky wrapped around me, offering comfort, which did not bode well for the information coming my way.

"Midnight is the kink in the library," Shadow said. "It's infiltrated itself into the creation energy I used to bring this system to life and is causing the disruption."

My heart hurt, a giant squeeze that was legitimately more painful than what I'd felt over my mother's death. No doubt I needed therapy or some shit, but I couldn't help that my mist was already more important to me than my birth mother. "How do I... I mean, what can I do to fix this situation? How do I free Midnight?"

Shadow pursed his lips, those sinful lips, but for the first time, I was too distraught to get distracted by him.

"From what Inky sensed, Midnight has integrated itself completely into the system, and the odds of easily untangling all of that energy are low. The only one who might have a shot is you. Can you reach Midnight through your bond? Convince it to release its hold on the library?"

Closing my eyes, I mentally followed the path of our bond. A path that had sat mostly dormant, even as my memories had returned. *Midnight? Can you hear me?*

A sharp vibration of energy shot back at me, not exactly hostile, but definitely not up for a friendly chat. I recoiled, unable to find a way to break through to my mist. At least I did know our connection remained, but it had been changed.

"It's not up for a friendly exchange at this time," I said sadly, opening my eyes and releasing my hold on the bond. "I mean, why did it even return here? Wouldn't it have made more sense to stay in the realm it's from, especially without memories of me?"

Shadow took a moment to converse with Inky before he passed the information on to me. "Inky believes that it was drawn back through the Solaris System looking for you. Only it didn't remember you and ended up bonding to the shattered power of the library."

I had to hold back my tears again, thinking about my poor Midnight just aimlessly searching for its bonded one, only to find the closest thing and settle. "Dannie has a fucking lot to answer for," I growled huskily. "She managed to screw so much up, and it's only by the grace of the damn gods we've come as far as we have after her manipulations."

"Grace of no fucking gods," Shadow shot back. "It was your stubborn ass. Now let's head into the lair; Midnight will find its way to you. If there's one thing I know for sure about Mera Callahan, it's that she's impossible to resist for long."

He strode off, Inky wrapped around his shoulders, and I exchanged a look with Angel. "He just keeps using love words," I whispered to her, "even if he won't say the actual word itself."

She smiled, tugging me against her side. For non-hugging beings, they'd certainly come around to the concept fast. "You should have known that he was going to love you from the first moment he didn't murder you for smarting off at him. The Shadow you know is not the one most of us do. He never suffers fools or any form of disrespect. Not even from his friends, but with you... he almost encourages it."

"It's a lot like winning the damn lotto."

Angel actually let out a chuckle. "Like winning it twice."

Couldn't argue with her there, and it was nice that I didn't have to explain my colloquial sayings to Angel. Her years as a guardian angel on Earth had prepared her well for our friendship.

We hurried toward the lair portal to find Shadow had already stepped through. Just as I went to follow, I had a thought that jerked me to a halt. "You can't go in there," I said with urgency. "Wait here and I'll tell Shadow he has to allow you entry."

Her expression softened. "I appreciate you looking out for me, but Shadow and I have already reached an arrangement. For the time being, I'll be allowed into the inner sanctum of Shadow's life and power."

"Really?" I blinked at her. "He's usually very selective about who's allowed into the lair."

Angel let out a deep breath. "Yes. And it's only because we both love you. That's why he trusts me."

The glow of her powered-up skin was near blinding as I pressed my face into her neck. "I love you too," I murmured. "And even though Shadow won't say the words, I've never felt so blessed to be loved by you guys."

Her face softened. "Words are not worthy of the emotion, but I lived among humans long enough that I've never quite shaken the need to hear them. So thank you."

Angel didn't give me time to get caught up in my feelings, dragging me through the portal and into Shadow's lair. As she'd predicted, there was no security trying to expel her; instead, she remained at my side as we strolled toward the firelit seating area, warmth washing over us as multiple sets of eyes turned our way.

We were the last to the party, and since the party was once again six powerful, sinfully sexy men, I was more than a little happy to have an extra set of tits on my side.

This merry band of psychos needed our perspective.

It was time for six to become eight.

Chapter Thirty-Five

I'd never spent a lot of time—outside of battle, that was—with Angel and the group of gods whom Shadow called his pack. As we made our way into the inner circle, I got to observe them in a more subdued setting, and I noticed something fairly odd.

Angel greeted Len, Lucien, Alistair, and Galleli politely, a certain level of mutual respect clear between all of them. Similar to how she treated Shadow when they weren't fighting over me, of course. All of them had a history, one that was clearly filled with shared experiences and respect.

But here was where it got weird... She didn't even look at Reece. I kept waiting for her to acknowledge him, even if it was only a simple head nod, but she was flat-out pretending he didn't exist.

Well, well, well... What's happening here?

At first, I thought he was ignoring her as well, but then I caught sight of him watching her from under hooded eyes. Eyes that flashed with the sort of burning anger I often saw in a pissed-off Shadow. Reece's eyes were a blue fire, the part that burned hotter than normal flames.

Shadow the second strikes again.

But why?

What the heck was up with the animosity between Angel and Reece? Had something happened in the realm that I'd missed? Or was this much deeper than that? A past event I wasn't aware of?

Had I ever seen them together before? If I had, I hadn't been paying attention at the time.

"Sunshine," Shadow called, forcing my attention away from the weird tension between my friends. For a beat, I felt like he'd cut me off in the middle of my favorite drama show, until I remembered that we were trying to save the world.

Drama would have to wait.

He was already seated, as were all the others, including Angel, so I hurried across to my mate, all but dropping into his lap. He pulled me farther across him, and I wasn't going to lie—there was a huge part of me that wished everyone else in this room would temporarily disappear. Being close to Shadow always sent my mind in one direction. South.

But there was no time for slutterbrain today.

"Did we all achieve what we set out to do?" Shadow asked, and this was just enough distraction to get my mind out of my vagina.

Len leaned forward in his chair. "I have the stones to protect us from future memory disturbances." The firelight reflected off his hair and skin, making him look paler and blonder. He shone like Angel, seeming much more powerful than he had when he'd left.

He parted his long, silver trench coat to reveal an entire vest of gems. "I also gathered every extra gem and spell we had. I don't know if it'll be enough, but if this doesn't help to take her down, then I don't know what will."

His eyes flashed toward Angel, who was perched on the edge of the couch, her wings tucked neatly behind her. "Looks like you brought extra power as well," he said to her. No one had missed her new golden glow, and I wondered if that was part of the reason Reece was so huffy.

Angel shrugged. "It was just sitting there unused. I promised I would never go into battle again, but in this situation, it would be a greater crime to remain on the sidelines."

A few of them nodded, except for Reece, who just looked more pissed than ever, crossing his arms as he silently glared. I was lowkey obsessed with watching those two now because there was something going on. What that something was, I had no idea, but I had to find out soon or I'd lose my mind.

Lucien sat forward from where he'd been sprawled, and I was surprised to see that he was still fairly subdued, no telltale smile on his face. "I've also powered myself from the ancient lines of magic my family protects. It's not the same level as Angel, but I can hold my own."

Reece finally made a sound, a deep rumble. "No one is at the same level as Angel," he bit out, "except for Shadow. Here's hoping this time she uses it for the greater good."

Okay, yep, it was happening, people. Bring on the dramaaaaa. I turned my wide-eyed gaze to Shadow, lifting my eyebrows to ask him *what the fuck was going on*, but the bastard just shook his head.

Shook. His. Freaking. Head.

That was just... unacceptable. How dare he leave a girl hanging when there was some sort of beef between our friends? Was this a new or old feud? Had I been so caught up in myself and Shadow over the past year that I hadn't bothered to notice? Or was it just that here, with no other distractions, and Angel's powers on display, Reece couldn't hold his tongue?

"You know nothing about me, Reece," Angel snapped, and her annoyance was subtler, but it was there. Her eyes didn't turn into flames; instead, they deepened into a rich pink. "I fight for those worthy. Mera is worthy. You should think on that before you let the past cloud your mind beyond salvation."

I was practically jittering in my chair, and since my chair was a set of hard-muscled thighs, there was no surprise to feel one very large cock pressing against me as I all but vibrated on his damn lap.

I patted his shoulder to remind him that now was not the time. The drama channel was on.

With a low groan, Shadow's firm hold over my thighs stopped my movements. His lips brushed near my ears. "Stay still, Sunshine, or I will be the one helping you forget business that isn't yours."

I clicked my tongue. "Ah, my poor sweet Shadow. You don't know me at all if you think I'm leaving *that* alone. There is just so much to unpack, and I have time."

I didn't have time, but I would damn well make it.

Angel stood then, distracting us both. "My power is mine alone," she told the room, even though we all knew she was talking to one giant desert deity. "Mine. And it always has been. What I've chosen to use it on should not be a factor that keeps you awake at night. Be grateful the burden is not yours, especially since inheriting it required my entire family to fall."

She turned and walked off, her wings spreading out protectively behind her. "I'll see you in the morning, Mera," she called back.

Shadow didn't argue with her, so clearly there was no plan to do anything else tonight. Apparently, we had one more night before all of us went up against the most powerful being to walk the worlds. That thought alone sobered my excitement over the intrigue of Angel and Reece. Tomorrow, we'd be in a fight for our lives, and I sensed deep inside that not all of us would walk away from this battle.

A fact that scared the absolute shit out of me because I could not lose anyone. Not again.

I wouldn't survive it.

Chapter Thirty-Six

The room felt emptier and colder without Angel, but at least Reece stopped acting like a fuckwit, which told me his mood had been all thanks to my gorgeous friend. More specifically, my gorgeous friend at full power.

No one allowed me to pry further into the situation as we focused on war talk. "We cannot delay heading to the Shadow Realm," Shadow said, still holding me down by my thighs, his very healthy erection wedged between us.

"We're going to head into the Shadow Realm tomorrow?" I confirmed.

I felt him nod behind me. "Yes. We may have to practice some spells first, but after that, we will make our move on the realm."

"Do we want to maybe go in stealthily?" I pushed for more information. "Or are we just guns blazing, racing across the realm until we find her?"

Alistair chuckled, the cool and calming nature of his energy caressing the room, keeping us all relaxed. "As interesting as the guns blazing visual is, Dannie might actually come to us. If she senses your energy, she will seek to rectify the situation."

I felt Galleli's essence a beat before he spoke in our heads. *I've been observing her energy from afar. Taking into account the fluctuation of the realm's power, Dannie grows in both strength and confidence. Her need to restore balance and order will destroy everything, but she truly believes she is doing the right thing.*

"I have sensed the same," Shadow said gruffly. "And while Mera hopes to convince my mother to release the stone on her own, I think she's too far gone. I believe we need to create a fortress of binding power. It's what we'll practice to achieve tomorrow."

There was a heavy, almost stunned silence in the room then, but he sure as hell had all of their attention. "I know you spoke of a prison circle, but... the fortress?" Len shook his head. "I mean, I expected you to come in hard, but that's... harder."

I sat there without a single clue what this fortress was, waiting patiently for someone to explain.

"The fortress is forbidden," Reece said, sounding fifty percent less of an angry fuck than he had with Angel. "It could kill us all and destroy the realm."

Well, shit. That didn't sound good.

"We've all created one before," Shadow said, not denying what Reece had said. "And we know there's nothing else strong enough to contain the Danamain long enough for her powers to be stripped away. It's our only real hope."

"Maybe it won't come to that," Lucien said, clearly trying to sound hopeful. Trying and failing. "Mera's plan is still solid. Dannie was reasonable at one point in time, and maybe with enough of us to give intervention a try, we might get through to her."

No one looked convinced. Not even a little, but we needed the hope.

"We have a Plan A and a Plan B now," Shadow finally said. "We can work with that."

The others got to their feet, since it was clearly the end of his speech. "All of you rest up," he continued, "and keep your powers as flexible and close to the surface as possible. We're going to have to be at the top of our game tomorrow, which will start with fortress training."

His friends nodded, trusting in him and his plan. "We'll be in the library if you need us," Reece said. "All of us will remain close tonight."

Shadow agreed, and I was taken by surprise when he stood, dragging me up with him. Probably so that everyone didn't see his raging hard-on.

"We'll meet you all later in the dining hall," he said. "For those of us who need to eat, it will be one last chance to fuel up."

My stomach rumbled, and I was more excited than I'd ever admit, to know I had one last feast in front of me. Of course, all thoughts of my stomach vanished when the guys turned to leave.

Maybe it was the firm grip of Shadow's hands on my hips, biting just enough that I could feel his imprint across my skin. Or more likely, it was the fact that while I knew we were going to have sex the moment they walked out the door, I didn't know the how, where, or what Kama Sutra position he was going to put me into. The unknown was enough to have my knees weak, breaths short, and panties wet.

Shadow's chest rose and fell behind me, his grip unyielding, and I started to mentally urge the others out of the lair. Were they moving in slow motion?

Just when we were almost clear of witnesses, Lucien turned back toward us. Shadow's chest rumbled, but I elbowed him. We could wait a few more minutes, since the vampire looked like he had a lot on his mind.

Some of Shadow's tension eased as he focused on his friend. "What is it, Lucien?" he asked, sounding like he actually gave a shit. I mean, he did care about his friends, but he was also rocking dick-brain and if I knew anything about that condition, it made it difficult to focus.

"Is Simone okay?" The question was directed at me, and I blinked. I hadn't expected that; I should have expected it, but I hadn't.

Patting my pockets, I wiggled until Shadow put me down. "Hang on. Let me check."

I finally found the parchment, but of course I had no pen on me. "Use your magic," Shadow murmured, close behind.

"Right, right," I murmured before I placed my fingers on the ancient parchment, willing words to appear.

Simone, are you okay, girl? We found Angel and will head to the realm tomorrow.

Lucien remained quiet, even though I felt tension emanating from him. The parchment lit up, and I held it tighter watching as the words I'd written faded away.

"What does that mean?" I asked, tilting my head to see Shadow.

"She read it," he replied shortly.

Okay, excellent. That was excellent news.

All good here. Words glowed on the page, and I followed as she wrote them. *Torin is acting weird and confused, so the pack is a bit of a mess, but that's an improvement. You stay safe. You hear me? I love you, Meers.*

My hands shook for a beat, and as soon as I read her last word, it disappeared off the parchment, which I placed back in my pocket.

"She's safe," I told Lucien. "Back in Torma. Earth is the securest place for her to be."

His eyes flashed, the green darkening. "That pack is trash," he said bluntly. "They need to be wiped from the face of the Earth."

He was upset, and I *really fucking needed to talk to Simone.* Where had all of this tension between my friends come from? Maybe I was finally noticing because my own tension with Shadow was somewhat resolved.

"She has the power to protect herself now," Shadow said bluntly. I wasn't surprised when his next words were, "Is there anything else, Luce?"

My mate was nothing if not an impatient bastard. Lucien finally seemed to register the position Shadow and I were in, especially the way he held me against his body. A ghost of a smile appeared on the vampire's face. "Nothing else for now. As long as she's safe, my responsibility is over."

I had my doubts that was the truth, but neither of us called him out on it. He waved before strolling away. "See you two tonight at dinner. If either one of you can walk, that is."

Then he laughed, the sound only fading away when he exited through the portal, leaving us alone in the lair.

"Inky, guard the door," Shadow said softly, and the mist wrapped around us a few times before it drifted off, disappearing from sight as well.

Then it was me and Shadow.

Anticipation sent bubbles through my veins, making me feel lightheaded. I had a brief moment where I wondered if I needed to check into Sex Addicts Anonymous, but considering Torin had left me as dry as the desert, I knew it wasn't sex I was addicted to.

It was sex with Shadow.

The Shadow Beast, demon of the darkness, and plunderer of my vagina.

Okay, that sounded wrong, but sometimes wrong was the exact kind of right I needed.

Which also made no sense, but who expected sense when one was about to be fucked by their mate? Their love? The plunderer of their vagina?

Because we were going with that.

Chapter Thirty-Seven

Shadow's flames appeared first, and as much as I wanted to turn and see the fire in his eyes, his hold kept me immobile. Not just his hold, but also his power.

"You never fight me here," he rumbled, and dammit, why was his voice sexy enough to curl toes? "You have power beyond almost any other, and yet, you've never tried to fight my hold on you when I touch you like this."

He was talking and walking, and I was burning alive in the most delicious way. "Why would I fight?" I croaked, trying to remember what words even were. "You give my body so much pleasure that at times—and this is no lie—I feel like I might die from it. I gave up control to you that day in the Shadow Realm, and despite thinking that would be a onetime thing, I find that... I don't mind it so much now. I get to be strong in every other avenue of my life except—"

"Except with me." He interrupted, needing to take control of my words as well. "This is why we're true mates; beyond anything you could have had with Torin. We build each other up, making each other stronger by embracing who we are. Torin wanted you for your beauty, strength, and brains, but only in a way that enhanced his. You were his trophy mate, his prize. A male of strength will get on his knees for his woman and know that it doesn't lessen him in any way. Torin was too weak and stupid to see that, and he never could have honored you as you deserved."

My body was on fire, my panties drowning, and I needed Shadow to do exactly what his words were promising. I wanted him on his knees. Easing the ache that no one else in the world could except my beast.

"I love you," I told him.

His hands came up to cup my breasts, his power holding me against him. "I am honored to be your mate."

He was still avoiding the L word, but somehow what he did say felt like the same thing. Or stronger. Because for a being like Shadow, honor was everything.

I'd expected him to take us into his room again, but I should have known that conventional sex wasn't Shadow's jam. He wasn't into weird shit like cucumbers in my lady parts, but he also never headed straight for a bed.

We ended up in a part of the lair I'd never been to before, and it was here that Shadow's power fully released me, allowing me to turn on the spot to take it all in.

Pushing past the comfy-looking couches, I was immediately captivated with the view. "Windows," I whispered. I hadn't known that any parts of this lair had windows, but here we were, surrounded by the most beautiful night sky I'd ever seen. There were stars, scattered outside of the twenty-foot-high paned glass, seemingly so close, I felt like I could reach out and touch them.

"Is this real?" I breathed, feeling overwhelmed and awed, standing on the edge of the universe. It reminded me of Faerie, but in a way, far more intimidating.

"Does it feel real?" he asked, his hand sliding across my side as he pulled me into him.

I nodded, finally tearing my gaze from the stars so I could look up at him. "For the first time in my life, everything feels real."

His eyes held me, the intensity there enough to draw forward my soul as he cupped my face. It wasn't in Shadow's nature to be soft, not in touch or mannerisms, but as he pressed his lips to mine, it was with the gentlest of pressures. He turned me so that both of his hands held my face, cradling it like I was precious, and maybe this was the point my heart finally burst.

The kiss started slow, a sensual sweep of our tongues. There was no rush—we had no reason to hurry this night—and in that, we savored every taste. Of course, we hadn't actually had personality transplants, so it was no surprise that within minutes, hormones kicked in and that slow, romantic kiss turned more passionate.

I groaned into his mouth, rising up on my toes to get closer. Shadow used his power to drag me higher on his body, and I wrapped my arms around his neck. His hands slid down my hips, gripping the flesh of my ass, holding on as he rocked me against him.

Kissing Shadow was maybe the best thing I'd ever experienced in my life, and I could happily do this forever without ever tiring of it. He kissed like he fucked, with so much intensity that it sizzled in the air. Shadow had officially ruined me for all other men, but since I planned on having him stick around forever, I was okay with that.

Our kiss grew even more frenzied, my back pressed to the thick glass, which was the only thing separating us from the universe outside. When I was about ready to start begging, my aching pussy grinding against him, Shadow lifted his lips from mine.

"You taste like life, Sunshine," he groaned, his eyes heavy lidded as he stared down at me. His lips were fuller than ever, thanks to our kisses, and with his hooded eyes and a half-fucked stare going on, I was a goner.

Wiggling against him, I yanked his shirt up, stripping it off him. Normally, he'd use his power to get us naked, but today we were savoring this, for reasons that I was not going to think on.

He removed my clothing piece by piece, kissing along the naked skin, like he was discovering it all for the first time. His actions clouded my head, but I hadn't forgotten my plan to be the one to give the first pleasure this time. He was always so generous with that very skilled mouth and tongue of his, and I wanted to return the favor.

I just needed to make my move before he had me forgetting my own damn name.

When we were finally naked, I pushed myself higher, pretending I was about to steal another kiss, and instead, I snaked my hand out and palmed his cock. Sliding my fingers halfway around the thick shaft, I stroked his knob. Shadow groaned and I took that as a sign I might be about to get my wish.

Stroking him again, firmer, I leaned down and kissed the hard planes of his stomach, defined abs presenting an easy path to trace with my tongue. His cock was calling me, so once I'd had my fill of tasting his skin, I dropped my head and licked right across the slit, savoring the salty bead of moisture there. I didn't stop with that, licking him again and again while my hand continued to stroke his shaft. My experience with this was fairly minimal, but I found going on instinct and listening to his groans rarely led me astray.

It was quite the task to get my mouth over the thick head of his cock—he was so hard that I wondered if it actually hurt him—but I was determined to take more than I had before. My wish was to make him come from this act alone, but he had so much damn stamina, I doubted my jaw would ever last the distance. Practice made perfect, though, and I was excited to start training.

"Sunshine," Shadow rumbled.

I wasn't sure if that was a warning or just a random groan of my name, but before I could figure it out, his power washed along my body. He took control of every part of me except my hand and mouth, since apparently, he wanted me to continue what I was doing.

Shadow groaned again, and then his power tightened, and I almost gasped as my body started to move. At first, I thought he was pulling me up toward him, but... no, that wasn't right. He was rotating me like a damn clock hand, and by the time he was done, I was upside down, his cock still in my mouth.

Dude was lucky I hadn't bitten the damn thing off with a move like that. Before I could yell at him, his hands gripped my ass and thighs, and he plunged his tongue into my pussy. As I moaned, he thrust against my mouth, forcing me to take his cock deeper than ever.

Blood rushed to my head just as he sucked and bit against my clit, sending me screaming, which allowed him to mouth-fuck me even deeper. My head swum, probably from being upside down, but also from whatever he was doing to me as he devoured my pussy.

I'd never in my life thought that you could do a sixty-niner in this manner, and in between screaming and sucking, I was wondering what other fancy foreplay he had up his sleeve.

When he plunged his tongue into the dripping heat of my center, swallowing down my pleasure, it was so damn good that at one point, I forgot to suck. Like, he was destroying me and I wasn't sure I'd ever recover.

As I had that thought, one of his fingers slid inside me. Then a second. Then a third, and as he sucked on my clit, he pumped those fingers into me, sending me screaming around his cock.

The moment I screamed, he took advantage of my open mouth, and then I was drowning in his dick. It was a good drowning, and as soon as I caught my breath, I focused on sucking as much of his length into my mouth as I could.

But dammit, Shadow's tongue was such a weapon that the moment I found my rhythm, he was sliding his fingers over my G-spot, building me higher until my thighs vibrated out of control. When I came in a huge fucking gush, I swore he chuckled darkly.

Bastard took too much pleasure in bringing me pleasure... and why was he so damn perfect?

Every time I came, he managed to get his dick farther down my throat, until I was literally choking on it. Needing to breathe, I pulled away, popping my mouth off at the end with an extra hard little suck. He released a pronounced groan, and that made me want to do it again. And again.

I started sucking him hard and deep before letting my mouth pop off the end, only losing the rhythm when his tongue and fingers started on me again. The upside-down part, which had freaked me at first, didn't even feel weird now. Maybe all of my blood had gone where it needed, or my body had adjusted to the change, because I barely even noticed I was upside down.

I lost my rhythm again when he flicked his tongue across my clit, and I could focus on nothing except the pleasure shooting through me. His fingers joined his tongue, curling up and sliding over that spot that was both of our favorites, and the buildup was so stupid good that when I finally came, I was screaming and jerking against him, my body no longer mine to control.

Basically a normal day when it came to sex with Shadow.

Despite my best plans to make Shadow come through the power of my mouth alone, today was not to be. When he was finished devouring my pussy, leaving me completely spent, he finally allowed me to return the right way up, pressing me back into the icy glass of the windows.

My head was spinning thanks to a bunch of orgasms and the rush of blood. Or maybe it was Shadow's body pressed against mine, every nerve ending firing.

"I won't let her take this from us," Shadow promised, his hands on my face again, those eyes locking me in so I couldn't speak or breathe. "She might be my mother, but the moment she tried to destroy our bond was the moment my loyalty to her died."

He kissed me before I could reply, and I tasted myself on his lips, the memory of my last orgasm taking over every other thought in my head. His power lifted me higher on the glass, and he thrust up, the thick head of his cock pushing inside slowly.

I expected Shadow to fuck me hard and fast, like he did in the past. Slow lovemaking was not really his thing, and that was okay with me, since I was usually so thirsty for him that I had no patience to wait. In my inexperience, though, I hadn't realized one very important part of slower sex. The intensity of the buildup.

It swirled in my gut, low and heavy, pulsing within me. This thrum of pleasure, sending me into the sort of euphoria that I would normally associate with drug use. It had to be damn illegal to feel this good. It had to be.

"Shadow," I moaned, leaning forward to kiss him, our tongues clashing in time to his thrusts. He changed positions then, shifting my legs up over his arms so he could brace his hands on the window on either side of me. This new position allowed him to slide in deeper, each slow thrust gliding across my favorite damn spot.

He kissed me again, and there was no way to keep an orgasm at bay when I was tasting Shadow. The moment his tongue caressed mine, the intense swirls inside exploded, sending figurative stars behind my eyelids to join the literal ones in the sky around us.

I cried out, moaning as the spiral of pleasure shot me higher and higher until I was sure I'd transcended to the next plane of existence. Nothing felt real, and Shadow dropped his head so that his lips rested near my throat, thrusting harder and faster, his breathing short and hard as he groaned and jerked inside of me. He dragged it out, continued to move inside of me until both of us had ridden out the longest, most intense orgasm to date.

What Shadow did to me went against the laws of nature.

Chapter Thirty-Eight

It took both of us a long time to come down from the high of sex among the stars. Even after Shadow slid from my body, he continued to hold me. We were both a mess of cum and all the aftermath of a good fucking, and honestly, before actually having sex, I'd never imagined I would enjoy the sticky mess that followed.

If anything, I wanted more of it. "I won't let Dannie take this from us, either." I reiterated what he'd already said, ensuring the fates knew I would fight them every step of the way.

I finally had the sort of happiness I'd been desperately seeking for years, and fair warning to any who thought to take it from me.

Shadow breathed me in, and I loved that there was so much shifter within him. "She underestimated us," he continued. "Our power and strength together... and our bond. She doesn't understand having a pack or family, and this is what will give us an advantage."

"An advantage is good, even if I'm still hoping we can reason with her."

He didn't knock my hope down, but I knew that he believed Dannie was too far gone for reasoning. Maybe my hope came from all the books I'd read where the main characters went through some super bad shit, but there was always a happy ending to look forward to. Sure, this was real life, but so far, my journey had been a classic paranormal romance, so maybe I'd get my happy ending as well.

Shadow ran his hand over my body slowly and far more intimately than was probably necessary to clean us up. When he was done, we settled into one of the chairs, watching the stars. I was starving, but there was no way I'd drag myself away from this moment. Not even for food.

Shadow was quiet behind me, cradling my body against his. "What universe is it?" I asked sleepily.

"Mine," Shadow replied, the burr in his words stronger than usual. "The one I created to form the Solaris System. This is what connects all the worlds and powers the library. It's from here I drew energy to reform the pathways. Thankfully, I managed not to destroy this in my rage."

That woke me and I turned to see his face. "Does anyone know that this is what lies behind the power of the system?"

He shook his head. "No one comes back here to the center of my 'machine,' so to speak, and I have never trusted anyone enough to share this secret with them."

Well, if that wasn't enough to make a girl feel... *loved*.

I returned my gaze to the stars, still not really sure what was out there. It was clearly a power beyond anything I comprehended, a magic of universes, and the delicate balance of it was on the verge of destruction thanks to Dannie.

"You can't use this in our battle against Dannie, either, can you?"

Shadow's breath released slowly, pushing against me as he sighed. "This is the sort of power that the sunburst stone contains, but if I were to utilize it in a way that could defeat Dannie, I would risk all of the Solaris System, and the worlds, since I decided to connect them into this energy. And there's also a risk that I might lose myself, just as Dannie did."

He had started to call her "Dannie" instead of "Mother," and it felt a lot like he was distancing himself from her already. Preparing for the inevitable.

I ran my hands up his arms, savoring in the touch of our skin together. "You already feel so much more powerful with your full energy of the realm. Will you be able to keep this power if you are no longer planning on being the Supreme Being?"

His expression was hard to read, but I didn't miss the flash of grief in his eyes. "I will have to pass the mantle on at some point. They'll have their own stone, though, since it's unique to the being it chooses. So, no, I won't lose my powers."

"You didn't really need the boost," I said, my eyes closing briefly as exhaustion pressed into me. "But how will you choose the right one to pass it onto?"

"It will be difficult," he said. "If they're not worthy, then that could be as catastrophic to the realm as what Dannie is attempting to do. As we discovered with Ixana."

It was a lot of pressure for him. Generally, the realm chose, but in this case, it might have to be Shadow himself who selected the next Supreme Being and if he chose wrong, he could condemn his people to being ruled by someone who might use the stone against them.

"Don't worry about it tonight," he said, sliding his hands into the long strands of my hair. He tightened his grip, pulling me up to meet his lips. I went willingly, letting out a soft breath when we kissed.

Our kiss deepened, as always happened, and without thought, my body twisted into a more comfortable position. I straddled Shadow, my already wet center pressing into him. His fire filled my core first, and then he entered me in one hard thrust. There was resistance. There was always resistance with someone Shadow's size, but no lie, that was almost my favorite part. That first burning stretch.

Kissing like our lives depended on it, I let my body move on instinct against him, going with what felt good. In this position, it basically all felt good, and even though there wasn't a huge range of movement, I got into a rocking rhythm. Shadow's hands cupped my breasts, his thumbs playing with the hard peaks of my nipples, stroking over and over, sending shivers through my already over-aroused body.

I rocked harder, moaned louder, and relished in the pleasure of this moment with him. When he'd had enough of letting me lead the pace, he released my nipples and placed his hands on my hips, lifting and holding me in place so he could slam up into me.

"Shadow, fucking fuck," I cried, my body starting to quiver as the first thrums of a heady orgasm made itself known. We'd had sex not that long ago, but somehow, with Shadow, it always felt like the first time.

"Hold on, Sunshine," he growled, and he spun me in a heartbeat, his fucking magic once again doing the impossible of keeping him buried deep inside even while we shifted positions.

We were now in a modified reverse cowgirl, so I felt every thrust of his length, almost instantly losing my battle to draw out the orgasm any longer. I came hard, my body vibrating and jerking against him, and as my muscles relaxed, Shadow pushed even deeper until I swore to fuck I could taste that dick in my mouth. Dude was rearranging reproductive organs down there, but that was cool. I'd heal whatever he threw my way.

When the stars finally faded out from my vision, orgasm two was building, and as my over-sensitized pussy clenched around his length, he was the one to groan, his pace picking up at the same time.

"You were made for me," he said in his deep brogue. "There's no other, Sunshine. Not now, not ever."

His words were a love poem, delivered Shadow-style, and it made me love him even more. If that were possible. "True mates," I whispered, my throat tight with both emotions and an impending orgasm. "Through this world and the next. For eternity."

We both came then, like eternity had been a trigger word, and no lie, my heart was literally hurting. I loved him so much that I could feel it in my chest, like a tangible thing. A tangible thing that we had to protect no matter the cost.

Chapter Thirty-Nine

We stopped by Shadow's room to clean up, and after, I dressed in perfect-fitting jeans, a white tank, red hoodie—Shadow's color, of course—and some comfy slides. The quality of the clothing was second to none, and I took a real moment to give thanks for my mate.

This beast had style.

"Come on. You need to eat," he said when I stepped out of the bathroom, my hair brushed and braided, the thick rope falling almost to my ass.

"I need a haircut," I said, flicking the length over my shoulder. "I have no idea how the hell it got so long, but it's not the most manageable style when we're on the run and going to war."

"You're born of the Nexus," he told me. "Your energy is that of a creation goddess. Sure, it's a little muddied by Dannie's meddling, and I know you're not at your full potential, but it's enough that you will find new changes within yourself constantly."

I shrugged. "The hair isn't really a big deal. I can always cut it." Now that Torin wasn't making the decision, there was no reason to keep trying to grow it to my ankles.

Shadow's lips tipped up in a sexy smile, and I was trying really hard to remember what the hell the conversation was about. "There's a decent chance that if you cut it off, it will grow back instantly."

Of course there was. My hair was as stubborn as I was. "Might just leave it in a braid," I said with a sigh.

"Your hair is spectacular," he rumbled. "The red draws me in, reminding me of my fire, and I just want to bury my hands..."

He trailed off, but ten to one both of us were thinking of our last sex session, where he'd had a very decent hold on my hair.

"Fuck," I managed to get out, and he just laughed.

"You need to eat," he said again.

But did I? Really?

Managing to hold onto my pout, I followed him toward the lair exit, where we found Inky, doing exactly as Shadow had asked. Surrounding the portal to the library, giving us extra privacy.

We'd needed these uninterrupted moments together. "Whenever we have a spare second, we should have sex, okay?" I said to Shadow, taking him by surprise.

"Sunshine?"

I shrugged. "Look, we might all perish when we go up against Dannie. I'm realistic enough to know that she's Solaris System powerful, and we might all be squished like bugs in the first minute of seeing her, so I want us to find moments to love on each other. If we can."

His eyes softened, but he refrained from laughing at me. "Firstly, I will never be a bug," he said seriously, "and secondly, we will have all the eternities together, Sunshine. You're mine, for now and always."

The *always* part was a nice addition to his growled statement.

When we stepped through to the library, it was as busy and bustling as it had been the first time I'd seen it. Night and day held very little meaning to the beings who ventured here from the worlds, especially since all of the time zones, weather, and hours in the day varied between the ten worlds.

It might have been nighttime in the library, with the view outside the windows dark, and the lovely chandeliers and lights above illuminating everything, but that didn't mean it was night everywhere else.

Shadow greeted almost all of the beings he saw by name, and it was the usual crowd, mostly from Brolder, Valdor, Faerie, and Karn. Everyone returned his greeting, bowing their heads, and it wasn't just a show. They might have feared the Shadow Beast, but they also respected him.

A lesson my former alpha, Victor Wolfe, should have learned. Our pack had lacked a true heart because of him, and his son looked set to continue the tradition.

When we entered the dining hall, the noise hit me first, and I actually stumbled. Or would have, if Shadow didn't wrap his arm around me, keeping me on my feet.

"You'd have to be the first clumsy wolf," he said with a shake of his head.

I growled at him. "I'm not clumsy; I'm just easily startled."

He raised both eyebrows, looking like a smug fuck. So of course, I had to add, "If there's a flaw in the wolf design, you should take it up with the creator."

Mic. Drop.

He didn't take offense, though, because he had no chinks in his armor. He just ruffled my hair and led me along the rows of tables toward our pack. As soon as that table came into view, the noise in here made sense; Shadow's friends were riling everyone up.

"Len ingested so much of the poppy flower," Lucien said with a snort of laughter, "that he thought he was in his garden, but he was really running naked through his family's celestial moon party. His mother chased him with a chailis cane. She meant business."

Everyone laughed, even Len, after which he shrugged. "Look, I wasn't even five hundred years old at the time and I have regrets. I have many regrets about how I chose to spend my youth."

Not even five hundred. *Youth?* Like that was a damn teenager.

Many other beings had gathered around to bask in the glow of the "gods" who ran this world. They filled all the chairs, except for the few around Angel. Maybe it was the way she glared at any who tried to slither into her personal space, or more likely it was the intense glow she emitted all powered up that warned them not to mess with her.

This was how it had always been with her in this dining hall. Separated. Alone. Untouchable. Everyone had heeded her warnings except for me. I'd fucked that up from the first moment I met her, but my mistake turned out to be the very best thing I could have done.

"You're looking very relaxed," she said when I dropped in beside her, Shadow taking the seat on the other side of me. Angel had managed to keep two spots free for us.

"You're not," I shot back, noting how her hands clenched, as if she wished her blades were in them.

"These lugheads had to choose my section of the dining hall to set up camp," she seethed. "I told them to move on, but at risk of wasting my energy, I can't literally move them."

It was a large dining hall. They could have sat anywhere, but they had chosen to crowd into her spot. Not just crowd, but bring in dozens of other beings, all of whom would normally give Angel a wide berth.

"Whose idea was it to sit here?" Shadow asked her, leaning back in a relaxed manner, watching the antics of his idiot friends.

Angel glared daggers at him, even though he wasn't looking her way. "Reece, of course. I thought we'd given up on this stupid dance years ago, but apparently, he still has a need for punishment in his system."

Shadow finally met her gaze, his stare as hard as hers. "You should consider yourself lucky that he ignored you for the last few millennia. You know how long his memory is. He rarely forgives and never forgets."

She scoffed. "I did consider myself lucky. But what has changed? I was perfectly content with the 'pretend we don't know each other' thing we had going on. He's messing with the status quo."

Shadow turned his gaze toward Reece, who was sitting at the farthest table from Angel. "It's your power," Shadow said. "It reminds him of long-ago events. Lives lost. Hearts shattered."

Angel went super pale. Super, super pale, and I elbowed Shadow quickly so he would shut up and give her a break. Then I threw an arm around my best friend, maneuvering the hold so I didn't crush the feathers of her wings. "Don't worry about Reece," I said. "If he wants to be a petty asshole about shit that happened millennia ago, that's on him. You're above that, especially while we have to focus on saving the damn world."

"I can hear you, Mera Callahan," Reece shot out, his voice hard and clipped. "And you should not speak about what you don't know."

Shadow slowly got to his feet, and the noise died off near instantly. My beast didn't have to say a word because the flames that sprung to life, followed by the darkness in his expression, did all the talking for him.

Reece stood slowly as well, and for a moment, his fury faded into sadness. "Sorry, old friend," he said formally. "I did not mean to speak in such a tone with your mate. It's just..."

Shadow's flames lessened. "I understand," he said. "But understand or not, if you ever speak to Mera like that again, I'll enjoy making you regret it."

Reece gave a short, sharp nod. "As it should be." He turned to me. "Apologies, Mera. I'm not myself today. I think I'll seek some mental guidance before we depart tomorrow."

Without a glance at Angel, he turned and walked off, never looking back once.

The room felt smaller and emptier without his large frame and even larger energy presence, but some of the tension eased at least, and that was worth the trade.

Angel even seemed happy, ordering food with me when the robot servers rushed by. Shadow didn't order anything, but he did smile at the six dishes I requested.

"I wondered where all the salmon and beef were going," he said with a low chuckle.

I shrugged. "Look, I'm not gonna lie, the food here is amazing. And a lot of it is similar to Earth food, so I feel right at home. My favorite is the stew, though. My god—"

His glare cut me off, and I shrugged. "It's a turn of phrase, damn you," I said. "Stop editing my words."

He leaned back in his chair, arrogant as fuck. "I'm the only god around here, Sunshine."

I wrinkled my nose. "It was 'god' with a small 'g.' So it could be referring to anyone. Maybe it *was* referring to you."

He leaned over and kissed me, hard, not caring that almost everyone in the room stopped talking again and took a moment to stare at us. I didn't care, either, mostly because I forgot all about them the moment he pulled me into him, his tongue stroking greedily against mine. "Yes, Sunshine. Me and only me."

My head spun and my reply was slower than normal. "Goes both ways, Shadow."

He nodded. "It does."

That shut me up. Now all of us were silently staring at the beast who ruled us all.

Chapter Forty

Before I could combust from the mere weight of Shadow's scorching gaze, our food arrived, and I was once again thankful for the gift of food and all of its delicious distractions. Angel's face lit up when they placed her usual tray in front of her, and it was one of those rare treasures that sent my heart into happy flutters.

She must have noticed me looking at her with a stupid goofy smile, which oddly had a dark cloud descending over her features. She went from angelic beauty to badass-who-would-kill-you in a heartbeat. "What?" I said, looking around for the threat.

Angel actually growled, drawing my gaze back to her. "No one will take my family from me again." Gold glittery power fluttered off her. "Dannie made a grave error in judgement, and even though she's Shadow's mother, there's no redemption for her."

My throat was dry, and when I tried to swallow, I couldn't make it work. "She might release the stone," I managed to say.

Angel's expression did not soften. "I'm not sure that's enough."

My face crumpled, and Angel dropped a hand on my shoulder.

"For you, and only you," she said, "I'll give her the chance. Maybe she'll convince me to allow the option of redemption, but I need you to prepare yourself. If she's anything like the many powerful beings I've known, she won't stop until we destroy her."

Shadow closed his arm around me, pulling me away from Angel. "You'll find no resistance from me. Mother or not, she's gone too far."

It hurt to think of them destroying Dannie because she was basically the only mother figure I'd had, and maybe, a part of me understood why she'd swallowed the stone to save us all. I wasn't okay with her choices, far from it... I was fucking furious. But sitting here tonight, with our pack once again whole, I just wanted it all to stay like this. War was the path that would tear us to pieces.

Shadow and Angel were not like me, though. Their pride was strong, and their need to remain dominant meant they could not tolerate anyone messing with the magical balance.

I, on the other hand, knew when it was best to just get out of there and thank the fates it hadn't been worse. Hopefully, I could convince the others that there was no dishonor in all of us walking away alive.

Everyone at our table focused on their food after that. Unsurprisingly, Shadow, Galleli, and Len had ordered nothing, but Alistair did have a fishy stew, its scent interesting but not unpleasant. Lucien only got a drink he sipped at occasionally, which I assumed was blood, but maybe I was stereotyping vamps there. I actually had no idea what they consumed for energy, and I'd add it to my list of questions to ask when we had the time.

"Eat," Shadow ordered, interrupting my observation of the table.

"Yes, sir," I smartassed, snapping my heels together.

His eyes held a warning, but there was no fixing me at this stage, so I smiled cheekily and went to work on the multiple meals I'd ordered. As optimistic as I was, there was still a chance tomorrow was our last day, so I'd chosen all of my favorites.

Once I started to eat, I found I was ravenously starving, stuffing my face until I felt like I was about to burst. Leaning back, I sucked in a deep breath, my lungs mildly uncomfortable by how full my stomach was.

Len let out a low burst of laughter. "That was damn impressive," he said, shaking his head like he couldn't believe what he'd just seen. "I knew shifters could eat, but... where do you even put it all? You're tiny."

I tried to smile, but I was just too full. My eyes had been bigger than my stomach and now I was paying for it. When my gut swirled, I wondered if I might vomit up everything. I must have gone a little green, because Shadow reached out and brushed a hand over my braid, the soothing heat of his power settling my stomach.

"Would you like dessert?" he asked, his voice vibrating with humor, even if his face didn't show it.

I thought about it. Despite what Shadow had just done, dessert would probably push me over the edge again.

"I'd like to try chocolate," Angel said suddenly.

My head snapped toward her. "Seriously?"

She nodded. "I feel this is the best time to give human food one last chance."

Great, so she had that ominous feeling too.

"You're right, there really is no better time," I said.

Shadow waved a few of the robots over. "We need chocolate," he told the closest one. "Bring everything you have that's made from the chocolate of Earth. Cake, bars, drinks—all of it."

If robots could get excited, this little one was doing it, lighting up and squeaking as it hurried off. "Everyone who can eat chocolate and not die will be trying it," I said with a laugh.

Lucien leaned back in his chair, hands behind his head. "I heard chocolate was deadly to dogs. Are you trying to knock Shadow off?"

My lips twitched. "Look, I know firsthand that chocolate doesn't kill shifters, but no lie, I did consider testing the theory on Shadow, especially when I first arrived here. Unfortunately, the bastard doesn't eat."

"Oh, I eat," Shadow replied seriously. "My favorite meal is right here in this room."

It took me a second. An embarrassingly long second.

"That shade of red is nice on her," Len said. "Matches her hair."

I wasn't red from embarrassment, despite Shadow all but talking about eating me out in front of all of his friends. If anything, this public claiming of his was far better than love words, though I wanted those as well.

I was greedy.

The red in my cheeks was the heat of my arousal. It had hit me hard and fast, and with enough intensity that I was barely able to stop squirming in my chair. Shadow knew that because he knew the scent of my arousal.

Before I self-combusted or embarrassed us all, about twenty servers reappeared at our table, their arms full of dishes.

Wow. Shadow *might* have gone a little extra on dessert, considering half the beings here would probably have one taste and throw up or die. These immortals with their "energy transference" instead of food lifestyle were so dramatic.

The only ones at our table now were the main pack, all their hangers-on having disappeared back to their worlds. Which left just the seven of us to be involved in this dessert taste test.

Humans adore these? Galleli asked.

I nodded. "Oh, yes, chocolate is well loved. We have it in many different strengths and styles, but it's always a hit."

I leaned in and breathed deeply, savoring the scents from the closest plates and sighing at the rich cocoa that invaded my nostrils. "Looks like we have cake, mousse, dipping sauce, ice cream, and dark, milk, and white chocolate in an array of styles." I lifted my head to see more. "Cookies, dough, crumble, and... oh my freaking god, they have doughnuts with chocolate sauce and Nutella filling."

Since my arrival here, more and more human food had appeared on the menu. Shadow's doing, of course, since he was the one controlling this space, and I couldn't help but feel completely touched by all the little extras he gave without asking for thanks or acknowledgement.

Ordering one of everything had no doubt been for me as well, and I needed to do better in letting him know how much it meant to me.

"Thank you," I whispered, turning my head to meet his gaze. "I see what you do. I appreciate it. I appreciate you."

For a split second, he looked completely taken aback. Not just taken aback, but... lost.

The Shadow Beast had no idea how to handle gratitude.

No one had ever noticed the good in him, and granted, they'd have had to look closely since he so effortlessly embraced the darkness. But these slivers of light that filtered through the cracks in his shadowy soul were so blindingly beautiful that they took my breath away.

"There's nothing I won't do to make you happy, Sunshine," he told me, his eyes holding flickers of fire. "You only have to ask."

I was going to be seriously spoiled if he kept this shit up, which would only make me all the more insufferable. Maybe I should do some charity work to even it out; I was fairly certain it worked like that.

"What should I try?" Angel asked, distracting us as she leaned over to sniff at a few of the dishes. "Give me the absolute best."

I leaned over with her, weighing them up before I started to rearrange the plates into one long line down the middle of our table. "This is my favorite," I said, pointing to the rich devil's food chocolate cake. The sort with thick, creamy frosting, and a cake so moist, you could see it glisten before you had a taste. People could hate on the word *moist* all they wanted, but when it came to cakes, there was no better descriptor. "And I've lined the rest in my basic order of preference, but to make myself very clear, there are no bad choices here."

Next to the cake was the chewy cookie sandwich, with smooth

vanilla frosting in the center, then a chocolate crumble cake, with a gooey mousse filling, followed by a triple deck chocolate block, showcasing the best of dark, milk, and white chocolate.

Angel lifted one of the utensils provided and scraped off the smallest sliver of the first cake. She cleverly knew to take an even distribution of frosting, cake and cream. Overloading on one aspect destroyed the full experience, in my expert opinion.

When she lifted the sliver to her lips, she smelled it first, her face crinkling. "It's an odd scent," she said. "Almost earthy." Her tongue darted out, and why the fuck I was holding my breath, I'd never know, but this felt like a pivotal moment in our relationship.

She licked at it first, and I saw her nose flare.

Leaning back in case she was going to hurl, I waited for her next move. The whole piece went into her mouth and she swirled it around for a beat before letting it settle on her tongue. Then she swallowed it.

A moment's silence followed.

She was the only one brave enough to taste anything yet, and I knew more than one at this table was waiting for her opinion. Angel was the guinea pig in this experiment.

"Wow," she finally said, her eyes meeting mine. She smiled broadly. "I can taste some of the undertones that I imagine most wouldn't, but... it's good. It's really, really good." She clapped her hands together. "I finally found my thing, thank you!"

Her hug was immediate and enthusiastic, and I wondered if maybe the chocolate was going to affect her in another way. It did have a calming, somewhat euphoric effect on humans... Maybe it would do the same for Angel.

Before I could run away with those thoughts, everyone went into action, reaching for plates of food. "Dig in," Len said loudly, drawing attention as he grabbed some cookies.

Even Shadow chuckled as they started to experiment with the dishes. My heart was so damn full as I watched them laugh and screw up their noses when they found dishes they didn't enjoy.

It was pure fun escapism. One last moment together.

Whatever happened tomorrow, this night meant everything to me.

I would never forget it.

Chapter Forty-One

It was later than expected when we finally made it back into the lair. If we weren't literally going into battle in the next few hours, I had a feeling we'd have talked with our friends all night.

Was this what family and pack life were really like? If so, I'd seriously been missing out. Even before my father's death, I'd never experienced anything like that, and that might be the first real truth I recalled from my childhood. It had always been cold.

"What are you thinking?" Shadow asked as we strolled toward his room after leaving Inky guarding the lair entrance.

"I had a lot of fun tonight," I said honestly. "I've never sat around in a group like that. Usually, I avoided anything to do with gatherings because it was hazardous to my health."

Shadow did not like it when I talked about my life in Torma, but I wasn't one to bottle that shit up. I didn't dwell, and I didn't think of it a lot, but I also wasn't about to pretend it had never happened. To me, that wasn't healthy, and for my own mental health, I had to talk it out.

"I mean, I do remember the early years, before my father decided that I was a demon child who needed to be torn apart by the alpha, but even then, I was lonely."

Shadow's expression grew darker. "I know you told me about your father briefly," he said, "but I'm going to need you to elaborate again. Now that I'm in my right mind."

"You want to know why he attacked the alpha?"

Shadow nodded, and I experienced a warm burst of emotion inside—he cared enough to ask for more information. "Apparently, it started when I was five," I started, before going on to detail everything I'd learned from the Lewisons, and my own theory that my Nexus side would escape when it was about loss or protecting loved ones and not about protecting myself.

Shadow listened intently, his hand on the doorframe of his room that had just appeared before us. "You're definitely geared more to altruism than self-protection," he agreed gruffly. "Hence why the abuse toward you never tapped into your Nexus side. You're too strong of mind and body. You can handle anything thrown at you—fuck, you handled everything I threw at you, all the while tossing it right back in my face. But when your loved ones are hurt, that's when you crumble."

He knew me better than I realized. Shadow saw everything, and he was too smart not to piece together. "I've thought about this a lot, especially when I was trying to recall what triggered my first bout with fire power."

"Did you remember?"

I swallowed roughly because I had recently remembered.

It was a painful memory for me, but I'd tell Shadow. "I'd blocked this out because at the time, it was so traumatic for my young mind," I said softly, "but I've had to force myself to delve into the past recently, and with that, the memories returned." I swallowed hard and he reached out and took my hand, but didn't say a word, allowing me to speak in my own time.

"I had a pet rabbit from the age of three." I sighed. "My parents apparently allowed me to roam free through the woods, and somehow, I found a brown bunny. No one in Torma had pets because Victor had an issue with wolves befriending food, but I was too young to understand how serious his rule was. I visited my bunny every day, and for two years he was my friend, until one time we played too close to the house and an enforcer caught sight of it."

They'd killed him. Just an innocent animal who'd made a mistake in trusting me.

"It was my first taste of loss. I didn't handle it well." I swallowed roughly. "I still don't handle it well. We can't lose anyone else in this war... We just can't."

Shadow stared at me for this extended, heavy moment. The connection between us thrumming wildly, like a baby bird taking flight for the first time.

"I can't promise that you won't lose anyone," Shadow said, leaning into me, his nose scenting along my cheek. "But I *can* promise that no matter what happens, you won't face it alone. We'll fight together and give it everything we have."

His words were comforting and ominous at the same time, but I understood why it was a promise he couldn't make. None of us knew what would happen when we faced Dannie. But at least we had one last night before our final battle.

Shadow and I entered his room, and I had to pinch myself at how couple-y we were tonight. He led me into the bathroom, where he ran the shower hard and hot, dragging me under fully clothed. He leaned over to kiss me, and I was already pushing myself up to meet him, my hands scrambling against his shirt so I could rip it from his body.

We were naked in seconds, and he was inside me in the next second, the heat of the water almost cool compared to the flames of our power. Every time we joined like this, there was a solidifying of our bond, and I was starting to understand how this mate bond truly worked.

Torin and I had the initial pull, but that would never have been enough. We were missing the fuel to fan the fire. Shadow and I were filled with fuel and spark and flames, and our fire grew stronger every day.

Moaning, I clawed at his shoulders as the orgasm hit me. The first of many, and by the time we finally got clean and crawled into bed, we were only going to get a few hours' sleep.

Lucky, we were supernatural creatures because I wasn't giving up the sex for sleep. No freaking way.

FAR TOO EARLY THE next morning, I was dragged out of bed by a very naked Shadow. He deposited me in the wardrobe and told me to get dressed, and maybe it was my sleep-deprived state, but I honestly couldn't hear a word he was saying around that hard cock he sported like a weapon.

"Mera," he said again, his tone both biting and amused. "I need you to focus, Sunshine."

I groaned, my tongue darting out to moisten my lips because it was really thirsty in here... No wait, hot. It was really hot in here.

"I thought we weren't leaving until later today," I mumbled, my eyes still staring his dick down.

"We need to practice the fortress of binding circle this morning," he reminded my addled brain. "It's the strongest prison that can be formed, but it requires a skill and coordination that can take months to perfect. We have hours."

I nodded, and his dick nodded with me. Or... did he just straighten up? Because I was fairly certain that even Shadow's dick didn't have an ability to bob around independently from the beast himself.

"Sunshine, have you heard a damn word I've said?"

I finally managed to tear myself away from where I'd been cock-merised, blinking up into his golden eyes. "Yes, right. Circle of death. Got to practice. I mean, what exactly does one wear when creating a circle that might possibly destroy us all? Red?"

Shadow's irises filled with flames, the gold swallowed in an instant. "Red works for me."

I was just taking my first step toward him, all cylinders of my brain and vagina firing and ready to go, when his power held me immobile, stopping me in my naked tracks. He strolled toward me, and I managed to plaster a glare across my face.

"Sunshine," he drawled. "We don't have time for what your scent is begging me for, but since you tempt me like no other has or ever will, I can't leave you naked and pleading."

His hands skimmed along my sides, and when he sank to his knees before me, his magic lifted my body so my pussy was level with his face. The moment his mouth attached to my clit, his lips and tongue sliding over them in the most delicious dance a mouth could do, I cried out and managed to push through his power to thread my fingers through the short strands of his hair.

In general, it bothered me that there was always so much giving of pleasure and never time for me to give back, but I was starting to see that was Shadow's way. And only an idiot would complain about *his way*.

The orgasm, which started as an early morning slow build, quickly turned into a steam train, slamming into me much faster than anticipated. I screamed, my body jerking as my head hit Shadow's wall of power behind me. My mate didn't ease up as I rode out the orgasm, and when the flicking caress of his tongue increased on my clit, and his fingers slid into my pussy, I screamed again, rocking against him faster and faster, like that would help deal with the sensation.

It didn't help, or at least it didn't prevent the next orgasm, and I was so fucking satisfied when he finally swallowed the last of my release. His tongue cleaned me more thoroughly than any shower ever could. My eyes closed as he released me, and I sank down to the floor completely wrecked.

"I'll see you outside, mate," he said, his gaze heated and possessive as he stared down at me before he turned and left.

Well, fuck.

On weak, wobbly legs, I managed to pull myself up and find an appropriate outfit for saving the world, which included a red tank, black jeans, black biker boots, and a thick, fur-lined black jacket. My shirt and hair were the only two pops of color in my somber ensemble, but that felt appropriate. I also shoved my parchment in my pocket after shooting off a quick message to Simone.

In the bathroom, I used the facilities, brushed my teeth and hair, and braided back the thick strands one more time. After leaving Shadow's room, I reached through my bond to Midnight, hoping that by some miracle, my mist might be ready to talk. I got angry static in return, and no matter how I attempted to get through to Midnight, there was no give in its barriers.

I'd been trying so hard not to mourn over what had happened between us, hoping that it would work itself out in time, but I couldn't shake the feeling that I was losing a part of myself I'd never get back. The ragged trails of our bond, which were all that remained between my mist and me now, were enough to almost destroy me.

I couldn't let that happen yet, though. I had to focus on Dannie, and maybe, once we'd sorted out her shit, I'd have the time to figure out a plan to pull my mist from the library system. With that in mind, I hurried from the lair, making my way into the Library of Knowledge.

The others were already gathered in the largest open space near the center of the room. Angel was there, quietly waiting off to the side, her molded gold-and-black armor fitting every inch of her body to perfection. Her hair was braided as well, much neater than mine, her wings tucked behind her.

Reece was once again part of our group, but he was on the opposite side of the room to my best friend. His eyes were on Len and Alistair, who were bickering over the best way to position themselves for this to work, but I sensed that Reece was very aware of Angel and every move she made. His fury and deep-seated resentment toward her had gone nowhere, still seeping from the desert deity as he crossed his arms, one shoulder nudged into a nearby shelf.

Shadow distracted me with a scorching gaze as he took in my outfit. I shot him a sassy smile, but before I could torment him further, the group noticed my arrival.

"Mera's here!" Len exclaimed. "Let's get started. We're wasting daylight hours when we could be hunting a Danamain."

Galleli gave me a very respectful nod, similar to how he'd greeted Shadow. I returned the favor, hoping one day he'd respect me for more than just being Shadow's mate. One day I'd prove myself and my worth to him.

"Okay, you're all going to have to explain exactly what happens today," I said, forcing myself to sound calm and determined. "Because I've never heard of a fortress of binding power, and I don't want to be the weak link that will fuck it up."

There was a beat of silence, like they couldn't decide who was going to break the news to me. Shadow ended up being the one, since they were likely guessing I'd take it best from him.

They'd guessed wrong.

"We believe it's best if you sat this out. Your power is too similar to Dannie's, and she might be able to figure out how to counter it if it's part of the fortress."

The smile that appeared on my face was not a nice one. "You're her actual son, Shadow, so maybe *you* should sit it out and I'll take one for the team."

If they came at me with a legitimate reason for why I'd be a negative influence on this cage they were creating, I'd listen and respond accordingly. But I just knew this was about Shadow trying to protect me.

I loved him for it, but that wouldn't work in this sort of war. We didn't have the manpower to leave anyone behind, especially when it was a woman. Womanpower was always the most important. Pretty sure there was a meme about that somewhere.

Shadow released a deep breath. "Okay, how about... you have no idea what you're doing and you might get yourself or one of us killed." This time, he was blunt and honest. "As I told you earlier, it would usually take months to perfect this sort of cage because it has to be completely secured on all angles. Even the smallest sliver of a gap between our energies and Dannie can burst through it. We've all studied and trained in this sort of shielding before. You have not. And your power isn't even fully available to you as the two sides of your essence fight for dominance."

I swallowed roughly. *Dammit.* There he went with that legitimate reason I'd been searching for. My wolf poked her head up as well, as if she wanted to remind me she was part of our dual nature causing this issue.

"Okay, I concede to your reasoning here," I said stiffly. "When my involvement affects everyone else's safety, I understand why it's best I'm not part of it."

I stepped away, moving out of the main space, allowing the others to fall into a natural circle, like they'd known all along where the strongest team would stand.

Angel ended up beside Reece, and I waited for someone to suggest they move apart because that was a total explosion waiting to happen. But no one did. Apparently, when the world was at stake, those two could act like the grown-up, ancient immortals they were.

The seven of them joined hands, and there was an instant ricochet of power that sent me back a few steps. I wasn't the only one, books and goblins flying around me. Luckily, the demi-fey were tough, taking their impromptu flying lessons in stride, not missing a beat as they got back to their feet and started to gather up books and paper.

A deep vibrating ding echoed through the library, originating from the center of the circle of power that was starting to build between the seven. I found myself moving forward, drawn into their energy as they began building a visible and intertwining cage of power.

As more of the energy grew, golden lights twining into each other,

I understood why Shadow had been so worried by this task. Each strand of power had to be painstakingly created and then woven, one at a time. Shadow was the first and when the full rotation of his golden cord was complete, it was Reece's turn, followed by Angel, followed by Len, and then so forth. Over and over, in the same order, they wove their power into this complex blanket of energy, until there was a half-formed golden dome rising above their heads.

"Enough!" Shadow bellowed.

It cost him to speak through the fortress, his voice echoing around the entire library. The others in the circle relaxed, and then one by one, they withdrew their power. It seemed that when it was intertwined, the only way to pull it back was to untangle it in the same manner.

"That was actually a really good first try," Gaster said, appearing at my side and near sending me out of my skin.

"It looked impressive," I admitted, my eyes on the group. "I'm guessing if even one of them falters in concentration, though, it could fuck up the entire thing?"

He nodded. "Oh, yes. The strands look innocent enough contained like they are, but it's similar to when electrical wires cross each other. It only takes one wrong connection for a surge of power that could kill all seven of them."

I hadn't been that nervous, but I was now.

Thankfully, they managed to untangle their power with no incidents, and after a quick discussion about ways to finesse what they'd done, they started it all over again.

I settled in to chew off my nails, all the while hoping no one would kill themselves before we got to the realm. Dannie would love it if we took ourselves out first.

Here's hoping we didn't make it that easy for her.

Chapter Forty-Two

By the time they were done with their practice, they were somewhat confident that they could call up a strong enough fortress to contain Dannie. After, we all took a moment to refuel, and then it was time to head to the realm.

"Make sure you have all of your power and crystals," Shadow said, his voice lacking real emotion; he was in warrior mode, his beast side having taken over.

I didn't have anything to bring with me, so I spent my last few moments trying to call Midnight to me, but the stubborn mist continued to cold shoulder me. I knew our bond was still there, but it was weak and frayed, thanks to Dannie. I wondered if I was destined now to only feel my mist here in the Library of Knowledge.

"Here's your gem," Len said, appearing right before me, distracting me from Midnight. "Wear it against your skin and never take it off. Okay? This will give you layers of protection around your mind."

He held out a shimmering purple stone attached to a silver chain. The stone was about the size of a grape, raw and stunning, with many multi-faceted shades of violet, plum, and dark magenta hidden in its unpolished depths.

"Thanks," I said softly, reaching for it. The moment I made contact, he whispered something that even my translator spell didn't understand. A jolt of power shot up my arm, and I barely managed not to drop the stone.

"Just needed to tie it to your energy," he said with a smile.

I narrowed my eyes on him. "A little warning would not have gone astray."

Len's smile was wide and perfect, the shimmering silver of his entire being so otherworldly that for a moment, he was a god. Or at least the way I'd always imagined a god looked before I'd met a bunch of them. "Where's the fun in that? Since you're one of us now, you need to learn that there are no warnings in our world. You jump in with both feet and hope the predators don't eat you."

For some reason, that made me think of Shadow, and it was no surprise to find his gaze on me. His flash of teeth was definitely predator-like. "I think I can handle it," I murmured, turning back to the still-smiling fae. "And thanks for welcoming me to the team."

The merry band of assholes had turned from six to seven, and since that had been my aim from the start, I was okay with giving myself a pat on the back.

When everyone was ready to leave, weapons in hands and stones around their necks, we headed to the realm doorway. Angel and Shadow remained close to my side, Inky above us, and the other five guys behind.

"Whoa," I said, staring at the door. "When did it change?"

It was no longer black, as it had been the first time the spell had been released. Instead, it was a murky grey, similar to the Grey Lands before we'd restored life back into them.

"I'm not sure," Shadow replied. "Probably around the time I lost my humanity, but it's a clear sign that the realm is out of balance."

"Possibly even dying," Angel added without inflection. It was often hard to tell if she was concerned or afraid when she was in super warrior mode. Today it was probably both.

At least it was for me.

No one said anything else about the worrying shade of grey on the door, already well aware we were stepping into a different realm to the one we'd left weeks ago. That poor world had already been suffering thanks to Ixana, and now it seemed Dannie had stepped up to make it worse.

We had to set it right, or the land of our birth would become a mere shell of itself.

Shadow wrapped an arm around me, holding me close to his side as we crossed through the portal into the realm. "I'm taking us straight to the Nexus," he said as he stepped into the mistiness that surrounded the realm entrance.

The mist lasted for about a minute, and as it faded, the land fell out from under us and I didn't even have time to shriek when we dropped into the water. Icy cold stole my breath as I plunged deep. From my last time in the realm, I remembered that the bodies of water here were called "The Depths," and they were filled with many scary-ass creatures I never wanted to meet.

Shadow and I popped up at the same time, and he looked around, his brow furrowed. I followed as well, noticing that the waters were dark and murky, vastly different to the last time I'd seen them, and the sky above was gloomier as well, almost as if the light were fading.

"I directed us to the Nexus," Shadow growled, his jaw rigid. "This isn't right."

Angel burst out of the water nearby, her wings shooting wide, droplets scattering as she flew about twenty feet above. In the same instant, a huge creature followed her up and out of the water, looking like one of those dinosaur crocodiles with a body as big as a blue whale and a long snout filled with razor-sharp teeth.

It tried to snap my friend up like a tasty dinner treat, but Angel was having none of that shit, smacking it down like a naughty toddler.

The creature fell back into the water, learning its lesson about taking on my friend.

"What the fuck?" I gasped, my eyes drawn down to the very murky water beneath us. I couldn't see anything, and my mind immediately went to the worst-case scenario of what lay below.

Shadow laughed, his power wrapping around me as he drew us up and out of the water. "They know better than to try me," he said with confidence. "Even if this world is following none of its regular rules, I am still the Supreme Bein—"

He was cut off by a snapping sound, and we both looked down to see the baby version of what had just attacked Angel hanging from his leg. The pause was near comical; the look on Shadow's face one of pure astonishment.

I really shouldn't have laughed, but a snorting chuckle escaped before I could stop it. Shadow glared at me, but no matter how hard I tried, I couldn't keep my amusement on the inside.

"Are you okay?" I choked out, trying to force my lips into a straight line as we both looked down again.

If Shadow hadn't been *Shadow*, the creature would have bitten his leg clear off. As it was, when it started trying to gnaw on it like an old bone, more laughter escaped from my tightly pressed lips.

The beast shot me an annoyed stare, and I held both hands up, my lips now pressed so tightly that they were starting to go numb. "You do you, Supreme Being," I managed to get out.

He shook his head like I was a supreme idiot, all the while attempting to shake off the baby croc-o-saur. In the midst of that drama, we were joined by his friends, each of them able to float above the mass of water, except for Alistair, who was helped out by Inky.

"Aw, look, Shadow got himself a friend," Lucien said, smiling at the carnivorous creature straight out of Jurassic Park.

"We should keep him," Reece drawled, his lips twitching. "He's cute."

"Let's call him 'Chomp,'" Lucien added.

"I vote for 'Champ' because look at him go," Len added. "Little fighter never gives up."

Shadow, who was apparently done with all of our bullshit today, gave up trying to "gently" remove the attachment. He burst into flames, which did exactly as he hoped. With a squeak, the creature of the deep released its hold, dropping back into the water, and as an added bonus, all of us were dried in a blast of fiery hot air.

The moment of amusement had been welcome, but there was no more time to avoid the reality of the fucked-up situation we were facing. "What did Dannie do?" I asked, searching the skyline but finding nothing but water.

"The Depths have risen," Angel said shortly, the gold of her molded armor barely visible in the unnatural twilight of the sky above us. "She's using the creatures of the deep to hide and protect the Nexus and its power."

The reality of this slammed into me like a bullet. "Are all of my land shadow creatures gone?" I managed to ask through my burning throat, laughter now far from my mind.

Shadow lifted his head, his eyes closing as he sent power into the world. "I feel a gathering of power to the east. Maybe close to the lava chasm in the Concordes. There's a decent chance that Dannie has taken the creatures there since they're her children. It would be a last resort to destroy them."

"*You're* her child," I shot back at him, rage welling up faster than I could stem it. "I was all but a daughter to her. And she thrust us out of her world and away from each other without a second thought."

She didn't kill you, Galleli reminded me. *And she* could *have without a second thought.*

His common sense halted some of the molten rage powering through me. "Yes, you're right," I said, sucking in a deep breath. Galleli had given me a sliver of hope that my creatures might still be alive, which I held on tightly to. "Let's go find her."

Inky formed a huge transport blanket to take us to the Concordes. No one wanted to use their energy to get there themselves because even though we were all powered to the hilt—me less so than the others, but I was part of the team, so it averaged out—we knew we'd need every ounce of our strength to best Dannie.

As we started off, all I could think about was my creatures, wondering if they were okay. "We forgot the shadow creatures in the prison realms," I said suddenly, remembering that we'd been planning on bringing them through as a power backup.

Shadow grasped my hand, calming my racing heart with that one simple action. "You can call them whenever you need. You bonded the lot of them to you in that school basement, and if you need them, they'll be there."

"Midnight too," Angel added from where she was perched uncomfortably on the edge of Inky. She did not like to be carried, in any way, and I wouldn't have been surprised to see her fly off soon. "I believe that when you really need your mist, the true strength of your bond will destroy the barriers between you."

Her eyes held memories of our time apart, and how she'd been resistant to me at first.

"Hopefully, it won't come to that," I finally said. "Hopefully, Dannie will be reasonable."

They all thought I was being naïve, and maybe I was, but that didn't mean I was ready to give up yet. Dannie the Wanderer had been part of my life since the day I'd been created in the Nexus, and then for much of my time as a shifter. She had never let me down until she'd swallowed the stone, so that had to mean if we could get rid of the stone, the true Dannie might once again return to us. Come on, paranormal romance story arc. Don't let me down now.

Chapter Forty-Three

The water was never-ending. So vast and smooth, it was only as I caught sight of all of the bitey beasts in its depths that I found my stomach roiling with nerves. What if there was nothing left in the realm at all? Dannie might have sunk every land mass, taking with them all the inhabitants of the realm. How, even with power warping her mind, could she think this was a balanced world? It just made no sense.

I wasn't the only worried one, the silence tense as all the powerful beings kept watch from the various sides of Inky. Thankfully, before I could overthink and freak out further, Shadow exhaled roughly, and with a wave of his hands opened a small portal in front of us. "We don't have the time to spare," he muttered, even though they'd all silently agreed not to waste any energy. Apparently, when it was a choice between time and energy, Shadow was making the hard calls.

The Concordes appeared below us and thank the gods it was not underwater. At least not the parts where we were, right above the lava chasm. Shadow had brought us to Trinity, the land of his birth, and the territory closest to the mists of the chasm.

Inky slowed as it dropped down toward the castle that had been

Shadow's childhood home. It appeared to be somewhat intact, but every building that had been around it was leveled into nothing more than ash. This was the destruction Shadow had wrought when he'd lost it. Even the great forests that had surrounded and protected his family home were no more.

He'd left most of the castle, but everything else around it was dust.

I watched my mate closely, but whatever he was feeling was well-hidden behind his stoic façade. He appeared to be a calm and watchful god, preparing himself for whatever his mother might throw at us. I wished I could compartmentalize on that level, but at least I knew I'd be able to pull him free of this when we were all done. When *my* Shadow could return and feel all the feelings.

Inky landed, but no phoenix goddess appeared. It was eerily silent as we stepped off the mist, all of us closing in ranks, waiting for someone or something to jump out at us.

I kept my energy close at hand, my wolf restless for a change; we knew we were stepping into what would be a fairly epic final battle.

Shadow moved forward first, and it was so empty here compared to my last experience with the grounds around the castle. That day there had been a battle, with Ixana's soldiers trying to give their leader the time she'd needed to sacrifice my creatures to power her stone and create her own Nexus. Her bullshit need for power was why we were in this position in the first place because—

It hit me then, and I gasped. Shadow was at my side in an instant, his expression fierce as he wrapped his hands around my biceps. "What's wrong? What do you sense?"

"She's doing exactly what Ixana was trying to do," I murmured, finally understanding. Shadow lifted my chin so I had to meet his fire-strewn gaze. "Dannie is creating her own Nexus. One that incorporates the mists of the chasm, along with the previous Nexus, and the power of the fae stone. She wants a Nexus that she will control as the highest power."

The moment I'd said it out loud, I felt the truth of it deep in my soul. In the place inside of me that had been born of the Nexus too. The swirls in my stomach since we'd stepped onto the land here were not just nerves over this battle... I was feeling Dannie's power. The Nexus power.

Shadow stared as if hoping to find the lie in my words, but we both knew he wouldn't.

"There's no reasoning with her," he finally bit out, warning me. "If she's gone this far, then she's lost to the power of the sunburst stone."

"The stone was not designed to be contained like this," Len said from where he stood off to the side of us. "It's why the loss of it has been a never-ending stressor for my family. The amount of power it is capable of holding makes it a formidable weapon. It was imperative it never fall into the hands that would use it as a weapon instead of a defense."

Angel crossed her arms, her face drawn. "Dannie's issue is that she merged it with her own power. Whatever reasoning she possessed was lost the moment she allowed a foreign energy to morph her own. Every being in this world has a counter. It's a balance and checks game we all have to play, but suddenly, Dannie has no checks."

"Actually," Lucien said with a scowl, "she does have one. *Us.* We're fairly formidable together and I believe *together*, we have a shot at ending her reign of terror."

"Only if the fortress of binding works," Shadow rumbled. "We have to weaken her first. And then we take our shot."

No one said anything more, just nodding their agreement with Shadow's plan as we started to move again, making our way further into the grounds of the royal compound.

"She's close," Shadow murmured, warning us when we were closing in on the castle. "We should start forming the fortress now so that we can send it forth as soon as she comes into view. We'll have mere seconds to take her by surprise, and in that time, she cannot break our formation."

Everyone nodded, no one disagreeing that this attack had to be timed perfectly or she would destroy us before we even had a chance to use the fortress. And since we were her only "check," as previously stated, it was imperative that we didn't fall before giving it a real shot.

Another thrum of power hit me in the chest, trailing down my body. It was the strongest burst of Nexus energy I'd felt since stepping into the realm. My wolf started to whine in my chest, her unease over that power growing. From the first time we'd entered this world, my wolf had been stronger and more out of control, and now I was starting to recognize her anxiety for what it was: She was uncomfortable with the Nexus power. My shifter and Nexus sides had been forced together, and for my wolf, it was unnatural.

With this knowledge came a surge of guilt that my beautiful wolf soul was trapped inside a being who should never have been a shifter.

She whined again, and I sent comforting thoughts toward her. We didn't really talk to each other like we had the first time we'd shifted—now it was more of an emotional exchange—but we were always connected on a deep level. I felt her. I loved her. Even as I knew that I should never have had her.

"Are your creatures okay?" Shadow asked, no doubt wondering what the current expression on my face was about.

"Don't worry about me," I said, waving him off. "Focus on the fortress you're in the midst of building." The fortress that was dangerous enough to destroy everyone.

Shadow shot me a familiar look. It was his *you're acting like an idiot* expression. "Can you feel them?" he pressed.

I closed my eyes and dug deeper into the power surrounding us. "Possibly," I finally said. "There's a lot of energy here, and it feels like Nexus energy. So it could be Dannie or my creatures." Or both. "Maybe she's sacrificing them for the power too?"

"Dannie should know better," Angel said, her voice a little ragged from trying to weave the fortress strands. "She's the mother of creatures, and no true mother would sacrifice their children for power. Her soul is corrupted beyond repair."

They were all preparing me, and how could I argue with the truth in front of me?

Reece's energy swirled around me, a dusty dry wind that I sensed could turn into a force of nature if needed. "You're not alone, Mera Callahan," he said in his rumbly voice that reminded me of Shadow, while still being unique to the desert god. "We don't have packs in the desert lands, but we do have dynasties. Family units. Shadow is my family, and now... so are you. We will fight with you today, and if we die, there are no regrets."

"Dammit," I choked out. "You're not supposed to make me cry before we go into a life-and-death battle."

His chuckle was strained, as it was his turn to weave a strand of power. Reece reminded me so much of Shadow, and I wondered briefly if the desert lands had their own version of a true mate bond. If so, I'd bet ten to one that if Reece found his "mate," he'd be as possessive as Shadow.

There was a reason I called him Shadow the Second, after all.

If we survived this, maybe I'd get a chance to find out.

Chapter Forty-Four

Their fortress of binding power was half done by the time we reached the castle. Dannie's power was the strongest here, a veritable itch under our skin we couldn't scratch. Unlike with Ixana, though, who had rushed into creating the final parts of her Nexus through a mass sacrifice of creatures, Dannie appeared to be doing it the old-fashioned way. A slow build of energy.

Had she started her Nexus the moment she'd messed with our memories and expelled us from the realm? Maybe that had been her plan all along, and she'd simply pretended it had been about the balance. If that was the truth, letting her go would be far easier... She was already lost.

When we rounded the largest side of the castle, heading toward the entrance that led into the lower chambers, I was hit with all the memories. Within those chambers, with its deep pool of lava from the chasm, was where I'd lost my creatures.

"Is she in the lower chamber?" I whispered, hoping I wasn't about to alert an angry Nexus goddess to our presence.

"I don't think so," Shadow rasped, sounding more strained than he had the last time he'd spoken. It was definitely clear that the larger the fortress grew, the harder it was to control the energy. "Her power essence is closer to the main chasm."

"Her energy is strong," Lucien said, forcing the words out. "She's taking on the full power of the leicher mists as she weaves herself into a power source with no equal."

My next breath escaped in a defeated manner. "She was way more resentful of those mists than the ether. The mists who spat out the royals." Royals who had taken her creatures and fucked up the realm. "I bet she'll find it fitting that they'll form part of her Nexus, which she'll completely control."

"She's missing the entire point of balance," Angel stated, and no one was going to argue with truth.

"Has the true Nexus been destroyed?" Alistair asked, sounding less serene than usual. "Was that her first step? I swore I felt it in The Depths, but... can there be two Nexuses?"

"One cannot be destroyed until the other is born," Shadow said without hesitation. "Otherwise, there'd be no realm left for us to stand upon."

"He's right," I said quickly. "I feel the other Nexus still thrumming within my power, but it's weakened. Its power is bleeding out of the cracks Dannie left within it."

We were moving slower now, the fortress nearing completion. When we finally made it to the side of the castle with the chasm, the red of the lava came into view, and... *What the fuck?*

There had been no real warning about what we were going to see, and to my shame, I found myself captivated in a way I never remembered being before. Not even with Shadow.

"How did we miss that from above?" I choked out.

Stunning ribbons of gold and red had shattered across the sky, filling it with the sort of beauty that could make grown men cry. Wherever I looked was another pattern and shape, sparkling in the low light of the new realm sky. The one true illumination left in this world.

"She hid it from us," Shadow said, emotion finally threading his tone.

The "she" became apparent as we got closer, her body in the center of the kaleidoscope of power and light that had fragmented across the chasm. Dannie. Only it wasn't the Dannie I'd known from Torma. Or the phoenix hybrid Dannie who had stolen our memories and changed the course of the realm and all the worlds.

She had changed again. Evolved one last time.

It was hard to truly understand this evolution while she was covered in swirling tendrils of power, the red and gold shooting off her body in a thousand swirling arcs and beams. So bright and mesmerizing. I wasn't the only one staring like we'd just found the first oasis.

"She's literally *becoming* a Nexus," Angel breathed. "The metamorphosis is almost complete."

Like a damn caterpillar, Dannie was about to become the Nexus butterfly, and if that happened, it would be too late. We couldn't defeat the power of creation.

I took a step closer, and even though Shadow growled, he couldn't break the fortress to stop me. Inky wrapped around the front of me, as if to halt my forward progress, but neither of them needed to worry. I wasn't going to do anything stupid; I just wanted to get a better look at what we were facing.

Hello, Mera.

I froze, my hands trembling as I pressed them to my head. It wasn't like when Galleli or Midnight spoke in my mind. Dannie's voice erupted as a vibration of power within my own, and with that zap of energy came the knowledge that she could destroy me with a single thought.

I see you have proven stronger than ever expected, breaking through my memory spell.

I swallowed roughly. *You should have known I'd pick at every little inconsistency. I don't settle, Dannie. I never have. My fight might be small, but it's consistent.*

She sorted through my words, mulling over them, all the while continuing her journey to the next stage of power enlightenment.

"The power is growing," someone shouted from behind me, but I couldn't turn away to see who. I was too busy not succumbing to the seductive lure of the goddess before me.

Stop it, I said with force. *I do not belong to you, Dannie. You cannot drag my power into this.*

The chuckle that followed was low and heady, and not in my head. She was speaking out loud now, and it seemed that was for everyone's benefit. "You should not have come here today," she said slowly, swirling and swirling on the spot until the magnificent light of her power twirled back inside of her, and then it was just Dannie there, floating and glowing in the sky above. "I've already set everything in motion, and none of you are strong enough to stand against me."

The others couldn't move, still weaving their fortress, which seemed to be of no concern to this version of Dannie. A version that was now a complete hybrid of human and phoenix. Dannie was red and gold, covered in both flesh and feathers, with huge wings extending from behind her back. She was naked, but you couldn't see anything around the feathers that trailed down her chest and over her middle, flowing out into a long tail. Her face was hybridized, with human eyes, a beak-like nose and mouth, and a high-reaching plume that stretched across her head and down her spine, forming part of the tail.

The phoenix lady.

It wasn't weird to see her looking this stunningly powerful; it felt natural to me, and I wondered if she could have changed into this version of herself even before swallowing the stone.

When she drifted closer, Shadow's power whipped up behind me, and I knew he was about to do something stupid. No doubt because he was pissed about me being a few steps in front of their group. With that in mind, I gave into Inky's nudging, backing up a few paces to stop just before I touched Shadow—the fortress was almost complete, and I wouldn't be the reason they had to start all over again.

"My memories of you are fond," Dannie continued, "but I'm no longer the Dannie you knew. I have a mission now, one that is essential in controlling the balance on a larger scale. A scale that will ensure the yin and yang of the universes are never in jeopardy again. In that regard, no fond memories will save you."

Len sighed dramatically. "I really miss the days when the bad guys just tried to kill you without pretty speeches. If you've heard one, you've heard them all."

For some reason—probably stress—that struck me as extra funny, and I barely managed not to laugh out loud and make the situation worse.

Dannie's eyes flashed, and when they filled with red and gold flames, it was a reminder that this was Shadow's mother. Not that he appeared to care as he wove a prison to steal her strength. Dannie also had zero fucks to give about her son, since she was clearly about to attack him.

Her timing was excellent, with the seven only a few strands away from having a complete fortress. If she shattered it now, they'd be destroyed.

I couldn't let that happen.

In a split-second decision, I decided that it was on me to be the distraction.

Stripping off my clothes, I allowed my wolf to surge up, and with her change came the flames of Nexus power. This burst of energy drew Dannie's full attention, just as I'd hoped.

Shadow roared my name, but we were fighting to win here, and that required all of us to play our parts. This was mine. *Cage her*, I shot back at him, hoping those words would get through our bond.

"Thread faster," he shouted. "Reinforce it for the final transition."

Since I'd heard him, so had Dannie, who immediately lost interest in my flaming wolf, focusing her attention once again on the circle of power. She went for them, ribbons of energy building around her as she prepared to attack.

Nice try, bitch, but not on my watch. My wolf shifted direction, and when Dannie floated over the land, I launched myself at her. If I could give them a few seconds of time, it might be the chance they needed to take her down.

Come on, wolf. Let's do this.

Chapter
Forty-Five

Ninety percent of me had expected Dannie to move out of my reach, so I was somewhat shocked when I made contact, claws digging into her soft feathers. On a regular being, my claws would have torn through in an instant, but there was nothing regular about Dannie.

Her body felt soft, but beneath the façade of softness, the rest was stronger than any substance I'd ever come in contact with. Nothing would tear through her in this state, and I had a split-second freakout wondering how we could possibly steal the stone from her, until I remembered the fortress was designed to weaken her.

That had been the *entire* point of this dangerous spell in the first place. We could not get the stone from her without her energy being weakened, hence why I was acting as a distraction.

"Mera, my sweet Mera," she trilled, her hands coming up to wrap around my wolf neck. "Why do you so recklessly throw your life away?"

I shifted back in an instant, surprising her when I chose to return to my physically weakest form. Her second surprise came when I shot a blast of power at her, and she loosened her hold enough for me to get away. I would have landed hard if Inky hadn't caught me, the mist then raging up into a sparking barrier between us and the goddess, giving the others the last few seconds they needed to finish their cage.

On Shadow's command, they gathered the cage in their hands, ready to attach it to the goddess. Dannie let out a loud chuckle; it was the oddest bird-human sound as she watched the golden coils swirl around them.

"You need to listen to us," Shadow said, and for the first time, someone had all of her attention—the son she might still love deep down. "You can fix this. You can reject the stone from your energy and allow the true balance to be restored. The fae magic you use has no place in the Shadow Realm."

She paused, tilting her head, a look of consideration creasing the corners of her eyes, obvious even on the bird face. "The power it holds is from the realm," she chirped in her power-laden voice. "Power that was stolen from my creatures. Stolen from the mists. Power that I will be able to return when I am the only one who controls it. You must see that this is the best solution for the realm... and all of the worlds. What if another Ixana happens?"

She'd retained her logic, which hurt, because my Dannie was still in there. And the thought of trying to destroy the Dannie I'd known in Torma was breaking me.

Shadow didn't seem to be burdened with the same worry, his previous statements nothing more than another distraction, giving Reece a chance to weave a tiny sliver of the fortress net around Dannie's tail.

The long, stunning plume of her feathers was bright and ostentatious... and possibly her downfall. With a substance to grip on to, the fortress spell settled into place, and a burst of gold released the seven powerful beings who'd worked tirelessly to constrain her.

Dannie's amused expression faded as she felt the power of their cage wrapping around her body. It was so fast that before she could lift her feathery red eyebrows, it was up to her neck. The strands tightened, cutting off her air, and when her head disappeared, I let out a breath, pulling myself to stand. My healing had already kicked in, and by the time I got dressed, any aches from my tiny battle with the goddess were gone.

"Did it work?" I asked, hurrying toward the others, surprised to see that Shadow still held one of golden strands.

"We just need to get the last link secured," Reece grunted out. "She's fighting harder than ever."

Together, they pressed in with the final strands, and as it settled against Dannie, I had a brief moment of thinking we'd won. But the moment was over before we even had a chance to celebrate.

A sliver of red light escaped from the golden strands close to Dannie's face, and before any of us could even react, she channeled her power so effectively that the fortress shattered, sending all of us flying. As I braced myself for impact, I ended up caged in strong arms that took the impact of the blow.

"You okay?" Shadow asked, his face close to mine.

I nodded. "Yeah, but fuck. *It didn't work!* What do we do now? She's too strong to take the stone from without weakening her first."

He was on his feet in a heartbeat, holding me against him. "We try again," he said quickly. "We learn where we went wrong and ensure it doesn't happen twice."

Angel huffed in closer, her wings springing free in an attempt to block us from Dannie's view. "We're bleeding energy, Shadow. I esti-mate we have one more shot in all of us."

"That's all we need," Shadow said fiercely. "We're fast learners."

"One last time," Lucien said.

"We've got this," Len added, pulling more of his crystals free.

Galleli was on board as well. *Let us begin.*

With no time to waste, they formed a circle, preparing to weave another fortress. A stronger one.

Dannie, who was still floating nearby, seemingly none the worse for wear after exploding from her cage, tilted her head back and laughed. "My Darkor, you never used to be so stupid. You cannot best me."

Her power rose up above her, and I knew she was going to destroy them before they had a chance to build a cage to fight her again. There was no way I could distract her for long enough to stop that.

Just as she sent her energy toward us, Shadow reached out and grasped on to my hand, tugging me into him. The world tilted out from under me, and then we were somewhere else. Shadow had moved our location, which had used power we probably couldn't afford to lose, but at the same time, if he hadn't moved us, we'd have been blasted to pieces by an angry goddess.

"Will she follow?" Angel gasped, her wings looking duller than they had been earlier, the gold of her skin all but gone.

Shadow didn't answer, too busy zapping us through to another location, this one above the water somewhere.

"She's clearly following," Reece said dryly. "Maybe you should focus on using some of your family power to speed the process along versus asking inane questions."

Angel's body was vibrating, whatever gold power had been left in her briefly puffing off her skin before she got herself under control. Reece's words were mean and unfair—we were all in a shitty situation—but Angel didn't bite back.

Which bothered me. "You need to chill with that, Reece," I said shortly. "These are unprecedented times, and we can't all be expected to act how you think we should. Let's just focus on staying ahead of Dannie and weaving the cage again."

His eyes flashed, and as he opened his mouth to hit back at me, a raging beast appeared over my shoulder. Even though I couldn't see Shadow's face, I knew he was warning his friend to be very careful about what he said next.

This was the second time Shadow had stepped in when I really didn't need him to. I appreciated the support, and the way he spoke love without saying the words, but we'd be having a chat about me fighting my own battles one day very soon.

If we made it out of the realm alive.

"You're right, Mera," Reece finally bit out, some of his rage fading. "It's neither the time nor place, and it's best to focu—"

His words were cut off as Shadow zipped us away again, and I was starting to worry that my mate was going to run out of energy soon. Through our joined hands, I sent as much of my power as I could into him, and Inky pressing into his other side was hopefully doing the same.

"I heard your words when you were in your wolf form," Shadow murmured near my ear, his gaze on our joined hands. "And I feel the beat of our true mate bond in my chest. Stronger than ever."

The sort of warmth that could only be described as near orgasmic flooded my body, and I sighed, wishing I could just wrap myself around him, kiss those decadent lips, and never come up for air. Before I lost myself any further into that fantasy, Shadow used the energy I'd shared and zapped us to another location. One with land.

"It's the outlier islands," he said shortly.

This had me looking around with more interest since I'd only ever seen them on a rough Inky map.

Shadow pulled us away from the edge of the sand and water, and farther into the mainland. Unlike the Concordes, there were no visible lava fields here; it was very jungle-like, with a thick and dense foliage, humidity sending moisture across my skin within seconds of walking.

"She'll hopefully have some trouble tracking us here," Shadow said, sounding strong and sure, but I felt his fatigue through our bond. "Inky, can you form a barrier around us as well? We need to finish this final cage. No mistakes."

The mist rose up, bursting into a huge covering, which would hopefully block some of our energy from being traced. As soon as Inky was in place, Shadow released my hand, gesturing for the others to form a circle again.

"I'll be the lookout," I said softly, stepping away. "I'll warn you the moment I feel her power closing in."

"Don't try to tap into her power, though," Alistair warned me. "She's bonded to you, through your Nexus origins, and she will feel it if you search for her."

I nodded. "Don't worry. I won't do anything to jeopardize us."

Behind me, their power settled into the land as they started to weave their second fortress. A quick glance was all it took to see that this time each strand was thicker and brighter. As Shadow had said, they'd learned from their mistakes, and if this was our last shot at stopping a war, they were giving it everything they had.

Taking my part of the whole process seriously, I strolled around the perimeter, tamping down my energy so that I didn't inadvertently give us away. My senses were on high alert, and I felt the moment a foreign spark of power drifted closer to the circle.

I didn't panic and neither did Inky, so it was clear we'd both felt the same thing. This power wasn't the Nexus goddess; it was the locals of this outlier island. Their jab of energy was both curious and a touch hostile as they attempted to understand who had invaded their territory.

When they moved closer, I positioned myself so they'd have to go through me first. A flicker of unease thrummed along my bond from both Shadow and Angel, but there wasn't much they could do except trust in me. In the power I contained.

Trust me to be a contributing member of this pack.

I'd been excluded from the fortress due to my youth and inexperience, and while that stung, I understood their reasons. But it didn't mean I was helpless.

The locals were close now, hiding in the trees, and while I couldn't see them, I felt their power. When one finally stepped into view, I understood why they'd been able to hide so well. They were camouflaged, and not just in the way that their clothing had been designed to blend into this landscape, but also their skin, hair, and other features.

The one before me had brown and green skin, the two colors almost splattered together to form a perfect jungle vibe. It allowed them to blend near seamlessly into the environment around them.

"Hello," I said, the translation spell helping me to communicate with them. "We mean you no harm."

They stepped closer, and I had no idea of their gender, of course, but the bare chest was male-like. For what that was worth.

"Why are you here?" Rumbly words holding more hostility. "With the Supreme Being?"

Before I could answer, there was a rustling near the local's feet. I could see nothing there, not until the creature unfurled itself and rose to stand a few feet above me.

I blinked, confused. I was fairly sure it was a sprecker, only heavier-set and... scarier than any of the ones I'd seen before.

"I thought you didn't keep creatures," I asked, turning to the locals, feeling stupidly betrayed by them. "I thought you rejected the way of the royals."

The local being and the creature looked at Shadow, and I could see them judging my judgement of them, since I was mated to the head royal. But we weren't like the others in the Concordes.

Both Shadow and I agreed that the creatures were not vessels to be used for our gain.

"The shadow creatures are our friends, not our possessions."

The local's words rumbled in the winds, strong and sure. With it came a true burst of joy; I hadn't misjudged them.

"I'm born of the Nexus," I said, taking a chance that this was the way to get through to them. "The mother of shadow creatures, and I want to free them from the life they've led on the mainland. Shadow agrees with me, and since he's the Supreme Being, there's hope that we can change the course of the realm's future."

The being and his sprecker friend examined me closely, as the other locals crept forward. "How will you defeat the original mother?" the first one asked me, head tilted as if examining me for lies.

I waved to my pack and their half-done fortress. "That's what we're working on now. Sorry to bring it to your lands, but we needed to hide from the phoenix, and your energy is so strong here that it'll hopefully be enough to confuse her pursuit of us."

There was a beat of silence, and then they all sprang into action, ducking and diving back into the foliage. I blinked in shock, wondering what had spooked them.

"She approaches," one hissed from nearby. "We must protect the barrier."

I felt her then, a moment after they had. Dannie, moving on swift winds, was tracking us the old-fashioned way. By literally following the magic trail of Shadow's jumps.

Spinning, I hurried to Shadow and the others, prepared to fight her if it gave them the time they needed to finish. I wasn't on my own, though, Inky lowering to be at my side, puffing out as sparks flashed through its center. The locals hadn't abandoned us, either, reappearing with silver stones in their hands, which they held above their heads and started to chant. Their words were loud and fast, and I felt the power they were calling.

A cloak of energy drifted down over all of us. I shot a quick glance at my pack and the fortress, and I blinked at what the locals had done. My friends were camouflaged, taking on the form and appearance of the foliage around us. A quick glance at my arm told me I was rocking the same forest-color palette.

Holy shit. They had hidden us using the magic that protected their island.

The locals were helping us stand against Dannie, and I sent out a quick prayer that we'd have enough time for the final strands of the fortress to be complete.

It was our only chance; Dannie wouldn't allow us to escape again.

Chapter Forty-Six

The circle of camouflage pushed us closer together until I was basically standing at Shadow's back. Inky drifted up above us one more time, adding its own protections, layering what the locals had started.

I wanted to shout my thanks to them, not to mention hug them all, but with Dannie closing in, my sole focus was on not drawing any attention our way. Tamping down my energy was number one, followed by shutting the hell up.

Dannie would find Shadow and me easier than any others, and while Shadow couldn't do much to hide himself, still painstakingly threading energy through the fortress of binding power, I could make myself as close to human as possible.

As if to prove me wrong, I heard, "You can't hide from me," as Dannie flew into sight, the shining light of her phoenix form washing over us. "I know you're here, and I promise that if you come out, I'll make your deaths fast. I'll also ensure your energy is distributed to the right worlds. You'll rest peacefully within your ancestral magic."

Got to love the reasoning of a morally corrupted being. *I'm going to kill you no matter what, but if you don't resist, I'll ensure that it's fast and your energy returns to its rightful place. It's the least I can do.*

Really fucking big of you, Dannie.

She glided closer, the flame-covered wings flapping slowly, holding her aloft. "There's really no need to fight me. You can't win, and I think you all know that. You should have just stayed away and enjoyed the lives I so graciously granted you. But you didn't. And I cannot manipulate your minds again, as you've protected yourself enough that I don't care to try to get around it."

Fuck yes. Threats aside, it was beyond exciting that Len's stones were working. Faerie stones for the win, finally, since it was kind of what had gotten us into this mess. But I would not blame the victim here—this was all on Ixana and Dannie.

Dannie, who'd apparently had enough at this point, sent out a strong burst of magic, decimating the camouflage shield like it was nothing. The locals went flying, which had my temper exploding, my vision turning red.

Flames sprung up around me as my fury grew over Dannie tossing innocent beings around like they were pieces of trash.

I lashed out, and a strand of my power hit the phoenix, sending her back a few paces. She recovered in an instant, rising up again, her flames larger than ever. My power, still thrumming strongly through my veins, allowed me to rise up as well, flames coating my skin in the familiar dance of magic.

Dannie and I faced off against each other, and I was certain that the others were screaming at me from the ground, but there was no time to worry about that. My head was in the game, all other distractions blocked from my mind as I dragged from the depths of my being as much power as I could.

"I wanted to save you," I roared at Dannie. "I fought the others, who wanted to kill you straight up!" My voice grew louder and deeper. "I told them you were a good person deep down, and that the stone was the corruption. Not you. I fought for you and your life, and this is how you repay me?"

She drifted closer, and maybe it was wishful thinking, but I could have sworn she was displaying a touch less hostility. "Give up the stone, Dannie," I begged, hoping that name would remind her of who she was to me. "Release it and allow it to return to the Fae Realm, where it belongs. You're already amazing and powerful. You already keep the balance. You don't need anything else."

There was no way for her to truly frown, not with the beak that made up a large part of her face, but her eyes were definitely frowning. "I failed before," she said. "I tried to protect everyone, and I almost lost my son and... you. I almost lost myself. Fighting the stone brought me close to the sort of true death that not even a Nexus born can recover from. If that happened, the Nexus would have fallen. You're no longer a being able to bring the balance, since your soul is shared with a shifter soul. It's only me, Mera, and I must take this responsibility seriously."

"You can do it without the stone," I said, putting every iota of my belief in her into those words. "Trust me, you don't need it or the boost of power it gives you. You're now the one throwing the balance off, and deep down, you know that."

I'd been doing so well, but of course, foot-in-mouth disease had to kick in as I'd said the exact words she didn't want to hear. Maybe it was her own guilt, or maybe I'd reminded her of her mission, but either way, that was the moment I lost her. The moment she stopped listening to my reasoning. The moment her resolve grew.

She spread her wings wide, the flames bursting out of her from all angles, near engulfing the entire forest area around us. The heat scorched me as it blasted past, but it was a fire built of my own power, so I wasn't burned to a cinder, unlike the rest of the foliage. It crumbled in an instant, leaving behind a land that finally held a resemblance to the lava fields.

The forest blackened, ash crumbling all around us, even filling the sky until the only light that remained was the golden glow of the fortress. Shadow, despite his exhaustion, managed to shoot a blast of energy at his mother, knocking her back. I joined him, sending my power into Dannie, and between the two of us, we forced her across the clearing.

We knew there was no way to best her, not like this, but that hadn't been our aim. Our aim, once again, was to give the others the extra minute they needed to finish the fortress.

By the time Dannie flew back toward us, the flames around her the largest I'd ever seen, Shadow was ready and waiting. Gathering up the finished golden strands, he flung them at his mother using every last ounce of his power and strength.

When Dannie was almost coated, she let out a cynical laugh. "You'll never win," she squawked, the vibration of her power felt for a brief moment before the last strand of the golden spell locked into place.

I hurried to Shadow's side, just as he collapsed to his knees, barely able to hold himself up.

"It's got to work this time," Angel murmured, bringing to my attention the fact that all of them were on their asses, having given everything they had, and then maybe a little more.

I hated to see them so broken and defeated, but it would be worth it if this cage worked. We needed it to work.

Wrapping myself around Shadow, I shared as much of my energy as I could, all the while keeping my gaze firmly locked on Dannie in the golden fortress. So far, it was holding, with no slivers of light breaking free.

For many minutes, we watched the prison, the eight of us still and silent in our blackened section of forest. I wondered at what point we could relax and expect that this time it had worked.

"I think we did it," Len rasped out, managing to pull himself to stand so he could straighten and clean his silver jacket. Lucien stood as well, wiping ash from his face, exhaustion pulling at his perfect features. Even Shadow turned to the others, preparing for the next step.

I was the only one still staring at Dannie. The only one who refused to be lulled into a sense of false success. Not until there was not a shred of doubt.

Just when I was satisfied and about to turn away, the tiniest speck of light caught my eye as it crept out of a sliver of the prison, right near her left hand. My blood iced in my veins as I took a staggered step toward her.

No! No, no, no, no, no, no! Fuck.

It hadn't worked.

Our last effort was about to fail, and none of them had an ounce of strength to try to prevent it from happening. *Except me.*

I had no idea if it was possible, but I'd learned from watching them weave this cage multiple times, and this was my chance to prove that I was strong enough to do this. Darting forward, I pulled up the deepest, strongest parts of my energy. The parts that burned like the center of a volcano, molten and intense, and when it filled my hand, I pressed it against the sliver of light that had already started to spread as Dannie poured her energy into the weak spot.

Shadow's roar shook the land, and with that one guttural, broken sound, I understood that what I'd done... the choice I'd made... was not going to end well for me.

Clearly, there was a reason none of them had tried to reinforce the fortress last time when she'd broken through with her fire energy. A reason they knew and I did not.

"Mera! Stop!"

"It will drain your energy!"

They were all shouting, but it was too late. There was no way to prevent this from happening; my palm was already fused to the golden light, the power that had been in my hold now a tether linking me to the fortress itself. A fortress sucking my power into itself, draining me in an instant.

It took from me what it needed to secure the prison, and I was helpless, unable to pull away or resist its strength. By the time Shadow got to me, there was barely even a shred of conscious thought in my head.

Exhaustion forced my eyes closed as the fortress of binding power did its job, binding my powers and using them to bolster itself. It stole the essence of my being, sucking it down greedily and without remorse for the life it stole.

In my desperation not to die, I clung to the bonds in my chest. Shadow. Angel. Midnight. The creatures. My connection to them was the one thing still tethering me to this world, but even with their immense power, it wasn't enough to stop the inevitable.

I dragged them down as far as I could before understanding that this was killing them too.

Maybe under normal circumstances, the bonds would have saved me, but Shadow and Angel were weaker than they'd ever been, Midnight was no longer my mist, and the creatures were too far away. So, facing the risk of destroying us all, I found the strength to let them go. The strength to accept my fate.

Contentment flooded through me at the thought that at least Dannie would be stopped. My wolf howled one final time in my chest, and I hugged her soul to me so that we wouldn't leave this world alone. *Always together*, I whispered. *I love you.*

She whimpered but didn't fight. We knew that our energy, as it turned out, was exactly what they'd needed in their cage to truly secure Dannie. It was the last gift we could give the worlds. The last gift we could give our loved ones.

We could die for them, and I would hold no resentment in my soul for it.

When the power was gone, my heartbeats slowed, and as they finally faltered, I was released from the cage, falling back into Shadow's arms. His hands and power were the last touch on my body, and the last breath I took was mingled with his as he pulled me close, desperately trying to save me with whatever strength he had left inside.

It was too late, though. *Love...*

My heart stopped before I could finish.

My time was done.

Chapter Forty-Seven

Shadow Beast

For two thousand years, I'd been the raging beast who'd walked in shadows. Alone. Always alone. I'd learned to rely on no one, to trust very few, and to ensure that above all else, I protected myself.

Then Mera Callahan had appeared, busting into my damn life, and touching the deepest recesses of my dark soul. She was an incessant ray of light, never ceasing, never giving up space in my head, and every single time she upset the balance, I wanted to fucking kill her. To save the heartache I knew she would bring to my world.

At least three times I'd held her life, her precious, delicate life in my hands, and each time I'd been too fascinated and struck by the unique tendrils of her essence to do what needed to be done. She'd challenged me when no one else had, and for that, I'd spared her.

By the time I'd recognized that this fragile creature, with her smart mouth and innocent soul, was to be my undoing, it was too late to change our fates. I craved her with the sort of intensity that would have scared the life from her if she'd been aware of it.

Mera thought she knew my desire.

She knew nothing. I wanted to possess her mind, body, and soul.

Every damn part of my Sunshine belonged to me, but like always, the fates had other plans.

I'd felt the sneaking tides of time running out for us, and even as I held her closer, binding our souls in a way that only a true mate could, they still came for her.

The mate to my soul. The fire to my fire. My Sunshine.

Before I could tear through the binding that held her, the fortress claimed its victim.

Fire exploded from within me as I struck at the golden prison, not caring that my actions could free the creature below. The fortress had Mera's power, and I wanted it back.

I spared no thought of the greater good, the concept not mine to claim. I was greedy in my love, and I would burn the fucking worlds to the ground to keep Mera with me.

My Sunshine who had sacrificed herself, her power and future in a bid to save us all.

With her limp body clutched in my hands, rivers of fire and mist and rage flowed freely from me. Any exhaustion I felt was long gone as I dragged this power up from the realm, claiming energy that was my birthright.

Destruction built within my veins and I willed it on.

The rumble of the land beneath me was the first indicator that I was tearing the Shadow Realm apart, plucking each string of mist that formed its foundation and watching each one fall. Not caring as this world broke, I tucked Mera into my side, using my free hand to reach for the Danamain. No longer would I ever refer to this abomination as my mother; she'd lost that right—and her life—the moment she'd hurt Mera.

The roar spilled from my lips as I tried to destroy the caged Danamain, but another entity blocked my way. With my vision filled with fire and shadow, I'd missed that the fortress was no longer existing on its own.

A layer of security surrounded it.

Midnight, sparking and zapping, striking everything that got too close, except for the second part of the security: Mera's creatures.

"She called them," Angel cried, her voice cracking as she too fought to get closer, blades in hand, grief tearing at her face. "When she pulled on our bonds."

Her pain was real, but mine was destructive.

I'd been too slow to save Mera. To save the worlds.

I'd been doing everything in my power to save them, but now, as far as I was concerned, they all deserved to burn.

My true beast form rose up to take control, our roar sending all the beings around us to their knees. And it was here they would stay.

This world belonged to me. The Solaris System belonged to me.

They would all burn.

My land raged with me, trembling until it was impossible for any who stood upon it to remain upright. Lava burst up, the land itself cracked, and I tilted my head back, letting more of the power flow from me.

They would all pay. For touching her. For bringing about this event.

When Mera's empty vessel finally disintegrated in my arms, a guttural sound escaped me, sending forth another whip of my destructive power.

Without my Sunshine, there was only darkness.

I was darkness.

And I would destroy everything.

Chapter Forty-Eight

I'd come close to death more than a few times in my life. And since meeting Shadow—a.k.a. being kidnapped—death had hovered close by, waiting for its moment to steal me away.

Why this time it had succeeded was anyone's guess. Maybe it was just my time. Or maybe I'd hastened the process with some ill-thought-out ideas and actions, but whatever it was, when the last of my energy faded into the fortress of binding power, I died.

For real.

My soul and power were torn from the vessel, and I had a brief glimpse of Shadow raging, his power whipping around the lands, flattening them in the wake of his despair before I was gone from that realm and speared into another.

This new realm was warmth, a gentle fire compared to the blazes I'd felt in my short but tumultuous life as a shifter.

Here, I floated in the primordial ooze of creation. The womb of the universe. It was so perfect in its perfection that I was content to exist in the gentle glow.

At least until a light, which was just a little brighter, burning a little hotter, drew me closer. With no physical body, I moved with thought, sending my essence into that bright beam that called me. When the light surrounded me, clarity returned.

The light brought with it memories. Memories of Angel, Simone, and Midnight. My pack. The Shadow Realm. My libraries and all the shadow creatures.

Beings and places I truly loved and would miss.

But above all of them.

Above all else.

There was Shadow.

My Shadow Beast.

The growly bastard was the other half of me, the best piece of my damn soul. Knowing that our story had been cut short destroyed me so thoroughly that for a brief moment, my soul flickered in and out of existence in an attempt to end the pain.

The womb of the universe rushed in to help, soothing, and I calmed as those memories were swept out of the light. Or at least the womb attempted to remove them, but I could not let go.

I refused to forget.

As I drifted farther into the light, the memories were stronger than ever. At one point, the illumination was so strong that it felt like I was blinded and drowning in the intensity, but this was also where I saw it all clearer than ever.

I could stay in my safe womb and enjoy the gentle fire, or I could embrace the pain and the darkness and feel the flames on the outside.

It was my choice. Only it really wasn't a choice at all. I'd take the burn any day over the safe, gentle existence. After all, I was built of fire and passion, and I'd never be satisfied with anything less.

Excruciating pain threaded through my essence as I gave myself to the light, and like all rebirths, it got worse before I got better, until eventually, I tumbled over the final edge, sliding free.

Reborn.

Chapter Forty-Nine

As I emerged from the Nexus, miles below The Depths that surrounded it, I found that once again, I was changed. *Reborn*. Into my true self this time, a being built and layered from the multiple lives I'd already lived.

I knew myself, maybe better than I ever had, recognizing my new perfect mesh of wolf, phoenix, and shifter. The Nexus had taken the best and strongest from each, weaving them together to create my true form.

Flames surrounded me, despite how deep I was in the water, lighting up the endless darkness. Not just the darkness, but the many, *many* creatures that encircled me.

The old Mera would have near died of fright, but I no longer feared any born of the Nexus. I embraced them all, from the hugest of prehistoric-looking monsters to tiny darting specks of fluff.

Reaching out, I placed my hand onto the snout of a creature nearby that resembled a crocodile crossed with a megalodon, my hand barely even as large as one of its five nostrils. A thrum of connection between it and me sprang to life.

They were mine. An urge to touch every creature and seal their essence within my own hit me, but just as I reached for the next, the ground rumbled, shaking even those of us in The Depths.

My head snapped up, but I was too far below to know what was happening in the realm. All was not well, that much I did know. Power ripped from me, sending out swirls of fire-touched energy, which did not hurt my creatures, but it did allow me to feel my connection to the realm and Nexus.

When I rose up, so did the land that Dannie had done her best to bury. My rebirth from within the Nexus "womb" had repaired the cracks she'd left in the power, and it was time for all of us to rise. From the ashes of our former selves.

The sea creatures swirled protectively around me, and I wondered how I could have ever feared them. They were just like the abervoqs and other land creatures—misunderstood. Yes, some of them were ferocious and killers, but that was survival. Once their natural food sources—and the health of the realm—returned, they would be no threat to any who weren't a threat to them.

You couldn't punish them for surviving.

As I got closer to the surface, the instability of the realm grew far more apparent. This did not come from me or my power base, though; there was something or someone else out there tearing the structure of this world to pieces, scattering the mists and leaving raging fire behind.

Urging the Nexus to rise faster, I was determined to stop this new threat. We hadn't fought so hard to save this world, only to have it destroyed now.

As I burst up from the water, my new fire wings spread out wide to hold me in the air. When I took my first breath of air, I felt large parts of who I used to be slide into place. The old and new merging together. With that, I knew exactly who was responsible for the destructive force.

My mate.

Shadow! I screamed along our bond, sending a burst of power with it.

The bond thrummed back to me, as strong as ever. It hadn't been destroyed when I'd died because bonds were deeper than skin. They were a part of our souls, and that part had been reborn with me. If anything, I was stronger and more myself than I had ever been.

Except for my wolf soul. No longer could I feel her sadly languishing within me; instead, we were merged into our best and strongest selves.

Shadow! I called for him again, knowing that he would hear me. We would always find each other. The rumbling of the land's foundations eased, and I soared up higher, my sea creatures following in a large mass of scary below.

Staring down at them brought to attention my reflection in the water. With no distorting, the water here showed me exactly what had emerged from the Nexus. What I'd been reborn as.

Flames coated me head to toe, as stunning fire wings extended behind, looking very much like Dannie's phoenix ones. The rest of me was wolfish, though, reiterating my feeling that I hadn't lost my beast, not exactly. I was her and she was me, and we were a fire beast who looked like a mix of Shadow's Anubis form and Dannie's original phoenix. Minus the beak.

For a brief moment, I wondered if I was going to look like this forever, a creature of darkness and light who was cool and scary, but not the version of myself I was most familiar with.

Not to mention waxing was going to be a super bitch with this much fur.

With that thought, a "Meraism," as Angel would put it, my power eased, and a wash of heat slid across my body. As it faded into the soles of my bare feet, my reflection now showed me once again looking human. A human who was maybe a little taller, a little curvier, and with hair even more wild and out of control. The wings didn't fade with my wolfier side, but I found I wasn't unhappy about that.

The strange new appendages on my back flapped without effort or thought, lifting us even higher above The Depths and Nexus, which was starting to reform as the waters sloshed away from the red and gold lands.

If someone had told me I was going to grow wings overnight, I'd expect to be clumsy and weak using them for the first few times, but there was no transition period at all. They flapped when I wanted to move, and as I sailed smoothly over the water, I instinctively knew how to catch wind drifts and glide along.

It was as if I had inbuilt knowledge of wings, an evolution of those who were born of the Nexus.

Those of us who could never die, for we would always be reborn if we chose to enter the light.

This was another truth I knew, along with the fact that my rebirth had unlocked the final tendrils of my strength, an elemental power of creation that I hadn't been able to access before now.

In the place my wolf once rumbled was a pit of energy, and it felt like Inky and Midnight. Which made sense since the true Nexus was the point where the leicher and ether mists collided and created life.

I was a product of that.

And this product was on her way to find her mate and save the goddamn day.

Chapter Fifty

I felt him before I saw him, his raging energy so widespread and strong that it hit me before he did. This spurred me on faster, desperation to see him again filling me until I could barely breathe. We could have opened portals and moved between the layers of energy in this world, but instead, we chose to come at each other the old-fashioned way.

Like a goddamn romantic movie. All Shadow needed was a boombox over one shoulder and some unsent letters clutched in his hands, and we'd be our own Hallmark Channel special.

As his power grew stronger, I reached out to drag mine along it, wanting to feel the sparking flames. I barely got a second of touching in before his energy wrapped around me, caging and locking mine down, dragging me toward him.

I could have fought back, and I might have even won this time—okay, probably not, because Shadow's level of badassery was unmatchable—but I didn't even try. Powerful or not, my soul belonged to Shadow, and I wanted him to claim and possess it, exactly as he was currently doing.

When he came into sight, I found his eyes first, those twin pools of flames spilling from the irises and down his cheeks. There was fire everywhere, but since I'd been born of the same flames, it only made me feel at home.

He didn't say a word as he continued to drag me into his orbit, his very naked orbit, which I only had a second to notice before his rage captured my full attention again.

Shadow was spilling pure, unadulterated power. He'd lost control, ready to destroy the worlds because I'd died. It was probably narcissistic to jump straight to that conclusion, but my mate had spent two thousand years *not* destroying shit, even when he'd suffered plenty of losses. I was the catalyst that had changed it all. The one who'd finally put a chink in his armor.

And I was owning that shit because I'd landed the freaking Shadow Beast. Take that, Sisily, you dumb bitch. You only got Torin.

Apparently, a metamorphosis-style rebirth didn't make me less petty or more mature, but that was okay. My way of looking at life had gotten me this far, and for that, I'd never curse it again.

When Shadow's hands finally landed on me, his grip unyielding in its desperation as he pulled me into his chest, I sank into him, not even caring if he crushed my new wings.

We were twenty feet in the air as he held on to me like I was the last anchor in this world, heat and rage spilling from him.

"Shadow," I murmured against his chest, unable to lift my head from the strength of his hold. I loved it, though, the feel of being caged against him, his scent filling my nostrils until I could smell nothing else, our powers mingling strongly. "Shadow?" I repeated. "What happened?"

I knew what had happened in the moments before I'd died, but I had no idea what had gone on in the time since I'd returned to the Nexus.

"You left me," he rumbled. Chills traced along my spine as sparks of electricity hit me in time to his thundering voice. "You left me, Sunshine, and the world went dark."

His voice broke, and I fucking lost it, crying like a damn baby.

One of Shadow's hands came up to my face, and without saying a word, he wiped my tears away, still cradling me against him.

Comforting me even though he'd been the one suffering.

Hurting Shadow had never been my intention, and even though we were together again now, I knew in those moments he'd believed I'd been dead, it would have been truly devastating. As it would have been for me if the roles were reversed.

I tried to say something, to offer comfort or an apology, but before I could, his power eased up enough that we could pull back to see each other. "You were reborn," he said. "I feel the change in your power, see the fire wings you sport, and yet, you're still my Mera."

I tipped my head back—the extra addition to my height did bring me a little closer, but I would always have to look up to the Shadow Beast.

"Third rebirth is the charm, right?" I joked, but it was clearly too soon since he didn't even crack a smile. "Tough crowd," I murmured before hurrying on. "My shifter and Nexus sides have merged. I have another form like you, but it's just a Super Saiyan powered-up version of this, with a wolfie face and some phoenix fire."

And now he was looking at me like I was an idiot, and since this was our familiar dance, I wanted to cry again... this time, in happiness. "You almost destroyed the Shadow Realm," I said softly. "Should we talk about that?"

His jaw was rigid, his muscles under my touch trembling. "This world stole you from me, Mera. There was darkness and there was pain and I cared nothing for the rest. It deserved to be rubble and maybe from the ashes—"

"The phoenix would rise," I finished in a whisper. "All along, that saying meant more than I could have ever expected—"

It was Shadow's turn to cut me off, his lips pressing into mine as he devoured my mouth. The kiss was heavy, filled with pain and unspoken hurts, tempered by this sheen of pure joy at once again being alive and together.

It had been close. I had legitimately died trying to save them all.

Ironic, since apparently, my death would have destroyed the realm anyway, through the rage of one pissed-off Shadow Beast.

When we pulled apart, I had to ask him, "Would you really have ended this world? I mean, I'm sure you're aware, but if you had succeeded, you would have not just taken out Dannie, but also our pack and... yourself."

He shrugged. "The others might have survived, but anything born in the realm... yeah, it was end game for us. Dannie was just a bonus, but the real truth is that I go where you go, Sunshine. Right or wrong, you and I exist together... or we don't exist at all."

Fuck, Shadow spoke love without saying the words better than any being I knew.

This time, I kissed him, using my power to lift me so I could wrap my arms and legs around his body, our naked skin sliding together as I pulled his head toward mine. As the kiss deepened, our energy mingled, and for a second, I felt him in my mind.

For a second, we were one.

It was only then that I understood the big deal they made about kissing here in the Shadow Realm. Having just touched Shadow's soul, I wasn't sure I'd ever think about kissing and its connective forces the same way again.

Rocking against him, I was hit with frustration that there was no time to seal this new soul-bond with some good old-fashioned sexing. We were already naked, and it would have been so easy to slide onto his impressively hard cock, but today we were rocking PG-13 since we still had a world to save.

"Come on, Sunshine." Shadow growled, clearly having the same thought. "The others are waiting for us."

He moved back far enough to magic up a pile of clothing in his hands before he all but threw them at me, his energy dressing my body faster than I could have done myself. Comfy sweats and sneakers covered my sensitive skin, and I still had to marvel at his skill in choosing just the right outfit for me. Even if I figured out how to create my own clothing one day, I was fairly certain Shadow would still be better at it than I was.

"Tell me about Dannie," I said, watching as Shadow dressed himself as well in the same manner. "Did the cage work?"

His fire flared again at the mention of his mother, and clearly, he was not ready to talk about what had happened yet. "Your energy sealed the fortress," he finally rumbled. "It drained you until you shattered like ash in my arms."

Fuck. Seriously, fuck.

"I'm so sorry. I didn't know," I said, wrapping my arms around him again. "I promise I would never have touched it knowing that I'd hurt you like that. I wanted to stop Dannie too, but it was a stupid risk."

He let out a curse. "In hindsight, it was the best choice to make. She remains caged, and I believe it's slowly draining her. But if you ever take a risk like that again, I will punish you so thoroughly, you won't be able to sit for a week."

My lips twitched, and I managed not to encourage this line of thinking. Not today.

"Draining her is good," I told him. "So now we just wait until she feels weak enough, and we release the cage, hold her down, and tear the stone from her?"

He nodded. "Yes, we'll have no choice but to free her long enough for one of us to rip her to pieces. And in regard to that, there's one problem only you can help us with."

Before I could open my mouth to ask what the hell he was talking about, a flash of amber over his shoulder caught my eyes.

"Angel," I breathed.

My rebirth had allowed some of my shifter frailties to fall away, and with that came a new, clearer vision when I looked at beings like Shadow and Angel. They were so much brighter and more brilliant to me now. The shine of their power and strength filled my eyes and my heart to the point where it felt a touch overwhelming.

"I have to go to her," I whispered to Shadow, seeing the shattered desperate face of my best friend as she flew toward us.

"I'm only sharing because she was as broken as I was," Shadow warned me. "And only for a few minutes."

I leaned in and pressed my lips to the right corner of his mouth. "Thank you, mate."

As I went to pull away, he tightened his hold on my waist, and when I lifted my gaze, expecting another possessive warning, I instead got a slow, sexy smile. "I love you, Mera Callahan," he said without hesitation, that smile softening as he gave me another piece of himself.

"I love you too," I choked out. "For what it's worth, considering how you feel about *that overused word*."

Now he chuckled, finally releasing me. "I've decided that it's not the word, Sunshine, it's the depth of emotion behind it. When we use the word 'love,' it becomes ours. We will claim it."

I had to laugh. "Arrogant Beast."

He wasn't wrong, though. Love was ours to claim.

Chapter Fifty-One

Angel held me with the same force Shadow had. The same desperation. The same sense that neither of them had expected to see me again. "I'm so sorry," I said over and over. "I didn't mean to hurt you."

She wasn't talking. She was just clutching me, her head buried near my neck as the simmering strength of her energy rocked into me. Our powers didn't merge like Shadow's and mine, but the bond between us was stronger than ever, energies frolicking like old friends.

After some time, she pulled away, her eyes haunted. "I can't do it again," she said, her voice barely heard. "I can't lose another member of my family."

I swallowed roughly, holding on to her biceps. "Well, I have some excellent news for you." I looked at Shadow, who was just behind me. "For you both. I can't really die. It appears those born of the Nexus can be reborn of it if they choose."

Angel choked out a sob. "What if next time your soul is tired and decides that it's time to truly rest?"

Shadow's rumbles filled the air. "There'll be no next time," he snapped. "No more chances. We end this once and for all. Today."

Angel stopped him with a shake of her head, her spectacular amber wings wrapping around her protectively. My own wings moved into a similar position without any real thought from me. "It might not be today," she said. "We have to recharge our power, and there's no better time than while the fortress is draining her."

"Wait!" I said, whipping around to Shadow. "You said before that there was an issue with releasing the cage and removing the stone? What issue?"

"It's best if you come see for yourself," he told me, and now I was rocking some full-blown professional-level anxiety. Rebirth had clearly done nothing to help with that.

Coming back from the dead really should include a slight reprieve from the drama.

For five minutes at least.

SHADOW TOOK us through a pocket of energy, and when we stepped out on the other side, we were once again in a familiar, burned-to-a-cinder outlier island. I noticed a few new cracks in the ground to go with all the ash, but thankfully everything else appeared to be intact.

Including our friends.

"Look at you," Len said, clapping his hands together, a true smile on his face. "Reborn into the fiercest of beings. Powerful and beautiful. Shadow has his hands full."

None of them showed any sign of concern that they'd almost died via one raging beast. Instead, they hurried forward and hugged me tightly, their only visible heartache from the way I'd almost gotten myself killed.

"We failed you." Reece's voice was low as he dropped his head.

"No, you didn't!" I said in a rush. "Not even a tiny bit. I had a choice to make, and I'm really sorry for hurting you all."

"You achieved what we couldn't," he replied, finally meeting my eyes. "Dannie would have destroyed us all, so we should be the ones thanking you. Your sacrifice was what we needed to best her."

"We didn't take Shadow into account, though," Lucien added with a laugh. "He just about achieved the impossible and dismantled a fucking world in his fury. Not that any of us were surprised; we were ready to ride out the storm and hope that whatever emerged from the destruction was salvageable."

I didn't like the sound of that, but unfortunately, I couldn't make grown-ass gods promise not to take risks like that again. The bastards got to make their own decisions—bad management, if you asked me. And that was maybe a little hypocritical considering what had happened with my last solo decision.

Potato potahto.

"What changes did your rebirth bring?" Alistair circled me, my flaming wings bright in the near-night dark sky, catching his full attention. Wondering if I could tuck them away like I had my wolfie-phoenix side, I imagined them fading into my back, and with a small pop, they disappeared.

"Whoa," I said, not even remotely answering Alistair since we were all discovering my new abilities in real time. "Wings," I murmured, and with the thought of needing wings again, they were once again on my back.

"Utterly fascinating," Alistair whispered, shaking his head, my fire reflecting off the blue-green pigments in his curls. "You're part phoenix."

My smirk was instant. "You haven't seen anything yet."

I called up the full force of my new power, which shot my height up over six feet, my skin rippling out into red and gold as my feathered, flaming wings grew larger than ever. I then topped it all off with my wolf-human face.

The shock was instant and complete and... I liked it.

There was no name for me. No previous knowledge of one who was a wolf phoenix, but here I was, and I would not be apologizing for my newfound state.

Shadow, who so far hadn't allowed me to stray far from his side, cupped my wolf-human face. "Perfection," he growled. "My true match and mate."

He shifted in an instant, and then he was Anubis, towering over me. My power went nuts, our bond near visible as energy strummed between us. It was neither the time nor the place to lose ourselves in that, so we had to pull away and focus on the others.

Our pack continued to stare at us, shaking their heads as another Egyptian "god" popped into existence, and they weren't the only ones as the locals crept out of wherever they'd been hiding.

Shadow and I wore our flames differently—mine were mostly trailing along my wings while his ran across his arms, but we were clearly imbued with the fiery power of the Nexus. When the locals bowed down before us, as if we were literal gods, I felt a twinge of unease in my chest.

This sort of blind worship didn't sit well with me, but I knew it was the only way for them to comprehend the truth of what we were. To slot us into a category so they could understand and not fear us.

"Please stand," I said, my voice deeper and stronger than in my other form. "You don't need to bow. Not when you were brave enough to help us against the Danamain. We appreciate your help."

They didn't straighten immediately, but they did eventually resume their upright positions, the closest ones finally meeting my gaze. They held it for a beat before giving me a single nod, then turning to leave the clearing. A hushed sort of chatter followed, and I heard enough to know that they were marveling at what they'd just witnessed.

A great sense of imposter syndrome hit me, but I decided not to have a midlife crisis yet. I'd save that for after we dealt with one power-hungry goddess.

Shadow and I released our power to return to our human forms, and he turned his back on the others, blocking me from sight so I could dress again. At this rate, I was going to drain his magic just by needing new pants every ten minutes. I made a note to try to learn how to create clothing myself.

When I was dressed, I turned to look for Dannie, experiencing a brief moment of panic at not immediately seeing a visible golden fortress. It wasn't until I moved further into the clearing, following her energy, that I found her... surrounded by an army of shadow creatures? Snarling and braying, they formed a veritable barricade between us and the goddess, who was also hidden by a dark mass—

"Midnight!"

My call broke Midnight free from its position around the gold prison, and through our bond, I felt the repair of all those tattered ends. The cool mist washed over my skin, solidifying us strongly.

Mera.

I missed you, I said at the same time.

We both let out a low hum of contentment, relishing in the bond for a few precious moments. *I didn't remember,* Midnight finally said, sparks flying across its dark misty form. *I forgot our bond, and then I was part of the power of the library, unable to break free until you called me.*

This was the issue that Shadow had wanted me to see. The issue I'd left in the wake of my death. When I'd pulled on my bonds in my dying moments, I'd dragged all the beings connected to those bonds into the realm. More specifically the outlier island.

Our bond was always stronger than yours to the library, I told Midnight. *The library could not hold you, no matter how deep you were entrenched in its magic.*

So very true, Midnight said, before it suddenly swelled up, sparking and shooting harder than ever. At first, I thought we were under attack, but then I saw Inky had moved closer, startling my mist. The pair swirled around each other, hesitant at first, and then... holy fuck me, I was going to cry.

They hugged.

A misty hug, with jiggling and sparking, and obvious signs they were happy to see each other again. Shadow let out a low chuckle, moving in to wipe my tears away. "Still my Mera," he murmured. "Your rebirth is the greatest gift I've been given, and I would take any form of you in my life, but to know that you're still your true self brings me a sense of relief."

"You are still Mera," Angel confirmed, pressing into my other side. "I feel the exact same pull toward you that I felt the very first day you collapsed into the dining room chair near me."

A snort of laughter escaped me. "Sweeping is hard. I really hated sweeping."

Shadow smiled, my torture clearly a fond memory for him. The bastard. "I couldn't have made a better choice in breaking you."

"You wish, asshole."

At this point, our bickering was foreplay, but again, no time for that fun.

"How long will the cage hold her?" I asked, gesturing to Dannie.

Now that Midnight was relieved of guard duty, I was able to see the glowing cage. It was still, no sign that the any part of it was alive, but I knew Dannie would be fighting under that fortress. She was stubborn and strong in every form.

"It will only hold another few hours," Shadow said. "She was stronger than we anticipated, having already taken steps toward becoming a Nexus, and if you hadn't been here to reinforce the strength of the cage, it would never have contained her. No matter how well we weaved the fortress."

"Is it really weakening her?" That had been the original goal, after all. The only goal, because if it wasn't successful, we'd never get that stone from her.

Lucien let out a low laugh. "It feels like it is, but we haven't been able to properly check with all the shadow creature guards."

Oh, right. My creatures. The ones I yanked out of the prison rooms in my dying moments.

Come to me.

The call was effortless, breaking them from their formation as they strolled toward me on two and four and many more legs. None of them fought as the wild ones did; instead, they moved like a solid unit of trained soldiers.

Leading them from the clearing, I directed them toward a large open field, one that still contained pockets of forest. Untouched by an angry Danamain. A sanctuary until we could end the dangers in this world for them.

My protective instinct toward the creatures was stronger than ever, and I hoped that I'd find other survivors from the Grey Lands as well when we were done with Dannie.

I had to believe she wouldn't have killed them all, even as corrupted as she was, and that meant they were out there waiting for me to find and save them. When that happened, they could join their brethren here.

Safe at last.

Chapter Fifty-Two

By the time I'd loved on my creatures and returned to the main group, the others had done a thorough investigation into Dannie and the fortress's current effect on her.

"She's weaker." Shadow confirmed. "Much weaker if what we're sensing from her is correct."

"That's great news," I said in a rush.

Moving closer, I reached out, stopping myself just before I made contact with the gold, just in case I broke it somehow.

"You can touch it." Reece chuckled. "The spell is locked on now until we release it or she breaks free."

I returned his smile with a shrug. "Yeah, I don't always follow the rules with that sort of shit, so best to be safe."

There was no argument from anyone. Apparently, my run of *interesting luck* was the one thing we could all agree on. Lifting my hands, I ran them across her, tracing the humanoid shape of the golden cage.

She did feel weaker. The only spot that I got a decided flare of power was right near her chest.

"The stone has not weakened," I said. "What's the plan to extract it from her?"

Everyone here looked a hell of a lot better than when they'd been all but sprawled on the ground, but they also didn't appear to be back at full power. Would we have enough energy to finish the second part of this plan?

"I say we allow Dannie to break free because it's costing her extra energy to do so," Angel said, her warrior mind engaged. "When that happens, we must pin her down so that one of us can cut the stone free."

"I vote we move the final part of this battle off the outliers," I said before anyone else could speak up. "The locals and creatures don't need to become collateral damage in this war."

Of course, if we failed, no one would be safe, but that was something for future Mera to worry about. As far as I was concerned, we had a more-than-decent shot at beating her now.

Weaker Dannie; stronger me; recipe for success. Right?

"I agree on both fronts," Shadow said. "And with that in mind, link hands. I will get us back to Trinity, and to the castle."

The moment we joined up—Shadow keeping one hand on Dannie—he zapped us through to the side of the building near the chasm. The others broke apart as soon as we landed, Reece and Angel most noticeably, moving to opposite sides of the large open area.

Inky and Midnight flew up above us, still choosing to stay close together.

"You all recharge," I said, "because we'll need all the power we can get to hold Dannie, even in her weaker form."

"Where do you think you're going while we recharge?" Shadow asked, sounding casual, but no one was fooled.

"I'm going to search for my creatures," I said. "The ones from the prison realm are reasonably safe in that outlier island, and if any more of their kind are trapped here, I want to send them through as well. Preferably before an angry bitch of the Nexus breaks free."

"The outliers are advanced in their treatment of the creatures," Angel confirmed. "I think that's a great plan."

It really did feel like that was the safest place to leave them.

"You will not go without me," Shadow said shortly, his tone brooking no argument.

Midnight wrapped around me as I smiled at my stubborn mate. "I know you're exhausted, Shadow. You can recharge; I'm just going to have a sneaky look around. I'll be fine."

Leaving us to it, the others settled in around the Dannie-fortress, doing their best to recharge and boost their energy in the short amount of time allowed for it. Len pulled out some gems, while Lucien drank down small vials of... let's call it wine. Wine was good.

I wished I had wine.

"Mera," Shadow rumbled, drawing my full attention back to him. "The last fucking time I left you alone, you were stolen out from under me. Then you died. It's cute that you think I'm ever letting you out of my sight again."

He wasn't joking. There was no ounce of give in his voice or tilt to his lips to indicate that he was *mostly* kidding. Now normally, that sort of attitude would freak me out and I'd start a fight for a little distance. I'd never craved a codependent style of relationship, valuing my independence above all else. But it wasn't the same with Shadow. I wanted to be around him all the time. I wanted us to be a team and protect each other. Eventually, no matter his stance today, we wouldn't always be literally attached, but maybe a small part of me wouldn't mind if we were. Until death stole us or whatever.

You cannot die, Midnight reminded me.

As far as we know, I agreed, *but there's always someone inventing a new way to break shit. Not to mention, Shadow can die, and where he goes, I go.*

There was a moment's pause. *Technically, Shadow is born of the Nexus energy as well. There's a possibility that he would also be able to be reborn.*

It hurt my chest and throat and... every damn part of my body thinking of him dying, even with a possibility of his rebirth. *Let's not test the theory*, I finally murmured.

Midnight wrapped around me once more before sailing up higher, drifting with Inky in a comforting cloud above. "You two stay here and keep an eye on Dannie," Shadow said to our mists. "Alert us if she shows any signs of breaking free."

The pair ducked down to weave around and hug us before they once again resumed their watch from above. The bursts of warmth in my chest at having Midnight back in my life were comforting. That niggling unease of our damaged bond was finally gone.

Shadow reached for my hand, and as we started to walk, our bond thrummed between our joined palms. I wondered how I could feel so joyous when there was still so much shit that could go wrong. It seemed I was embracing the moment, and in that moment, I decided to not feel guilty about it.

"This is nice," I said, swinging our hands. "And I'm almost tall enough now that it's not too uncomfortable."

As I had that thought, I managed to shoot up another few inches, nearly reaching my wolfie-phoenix height. The rest of me hadn't changed, though, so that meant... "I can shift my height," I choked out, blinking in stunned silence.

Shadow's low laughter wrapped around me in the same warming comfort that Midnight gave me. "You can change into a phoenix wolf and used to shift into a literal wolf pup," he said, pulling me closer. "This is the same concept."

Yeah, I knew that in theory, but the height shift felt so much weirder.

"I think I prefer my regular height," I decided, and as I had that thought, I returned to five-feet-eight.

"You're perfect at any height," he told me, "but in truth, I'd prefer to be the one who reaches the high shelves for you."

Aw, fuck, that was almost romantic. Pushing myself up on my toes, I allowed him to drag me up so we could kiss. "You got it, babe," I whispered.

"'Babe' is only just better than 'dude,'" he grumbled before he took control of my mouth, and I forgot my own name until we pulled apart.

Then I remembered what he'd said. "You don't love 'babe?' What about 'snookums?' 'Honey bunch?' 'Sweetie pie?' 'Cutie face?' 'Buttercu—'"

"Sunshine," he warned. "We might be true mates, but that doesn't mean I won't punish you."

"Yes, please," I said, nodding enthusiastically. "I'll take two."

A firm slap on my ass, and my body was covered in goosebumps as I involuntarily jerked against him, craving everything we didn't have time for right now. "We better freaking survive." I was the one grumbling now.

Shadow pressed his lips to my neck, breathing me in, and I had to close my eyes and take this one last moment with him. "Shadow-shine," I whispered. "I was always rooting for us to win."

"And win we did, Sunshine," he said, breath brushing over my skin.

Dammit, there he went again. Who would have guessed that my Shadow Beast was a secret romantic? Very, *very* deep down.

Chapter Fifty-Three

We were on a countdown clock, and since I wasn't too keen on Dannie busting out of her prison before I found the creatures and could wrest control of them back to me, I moved forward with a laser focus.

Shadow, true to his word, remained as a giant ball of fun at my side, silent and deadly, his attention on what lay ahead as well. The fact that he would soon take part in destroying his mother was not an ideal situation, but he would not hesitate or shirk his duties. He never had.

"Can you feel them?" he asked as we got closer to the castle entrance.

I hadn't been inside this part of his home before, and I was curious to see what was on the other side. "I feel something. There's a huge gathering of energy behind here," I said as we paused at the massive entrance doors. They looked to be barred on our side with long, metal planks, and I wondered if the other side was the same, or if Dannie had just done this to tie the creatures in.

Shadow flicked his hands and the planks, which no doubt

weighed a damn ton each, were jerked out of their cross-barred placement and flung into the fire-razed land behind us.

The doors opened easily, making it clear that the intention had been to lock them in, not keep someone out. Definitely the work of a Danamain.

When it was open, we stepped into a dark, dank room.

My eyes adjusted fast, but with the persistent low light of the realm now, there wasn't a whole lot of free natural light to pick up the smaller details. To counter that, Shadow's flames lit up, and I did the same. When it came to Dannie, it was safer to be totally sure we weren't walking into any traps.

As soon as we had light, it was immediately obvious where the damp smell in this room came from. The front entrance was coated in what looked like moss, grey and brown moss that had grown across the walls and furniture before dripping down to coat the windows that lined this front entryway.

"Don't let it touch you," Shadow warned, his voice an annoyed snap. "It's a lot like the tar that almost killed you last time we were in the realm. Only this is worse. The porous underside of this creature is filled with razor-sharp needles that dig into your skin to suck your energy out."

"It shouldn't infiltrate my skin now," I reminded him, while still sidling closer because the thought of being coated in a layer of bitey moss... Yeah, no thanks.

"No risks, Sunshine. No more damn risks."

I nodded because it was a good plan.

As we walked through slowly, I was relieved to see that the moss was wary of our fire and didn't venture closer. It slid across the walls, showing just how quick it could move to attack any normal being entering or leaving this castle. A second layer of defense, in Dannie's insane plan.

"She must have had a reason to keep the creatures locked in here," I said softly, finally breathing freely once we'd made it past the entrance. "Something to do with her plan once she had the Nexus complete."

"No doubt they would form part of her new world," he said shortly, before focusing on the next obstacle in our way.

I did the same, eyeing the window-lined hall, which was clearly a thoroughfare into the rest of the castle. It looked fairly innocuous when we first stared down it, right up until Shadow sent a small ball of power along it and a bunch of arrows fired in unison.

"What the fuck?" I exclaimed, shaking my head. "This is due to all the times Dannie made me watch *Indiana Jones*. She loved the ancient booby traps." The bitch had created her own pyramid of disasters to keep her prisoners in their cage. It was fitting that she herself was also in a cage.

Shadow wasn't worried about this hall, his power shielding us as we walked along. This particular set of traps was definitely geared toward regular inhabitants of the realm, not those of us who were a touch more powerful.

"This is really not as impressive an *Indian Jones* adventure as I expected," I grumbled to Shadow as we made it through the hall. "Just... moss and arrows. Not very inventive."

His chuckle was low. "One day, in the very near future," he said, his deep voice a caress on my senses, "you and I will spend a week in bed, where I destroy your body, and in between, you can let me be part of this world of movies you enjoy. Like *Indiana Jones*."

I coughed. "I legitimately heard nothing after the *destroying my body* part, but it doesn't even matter what you said. My answer is yes. Always yes."

"Now you're getting it, Sunshine," he said with a small smile.

Shaking my head to clear the lust from it, I focused again on what was awaiting us next, but it appeared that Dannie had run out of boring ideas after the first two.

The next room was an outdoor courtyard. In my head I was arranging the castle layout, seeing that the outer thoroughfare of a hall led around the outside, while at the center was this large, open space with no roof and plenty of room for recreational activities.

This was the gathering point for all who made their home here. Market stalls and socialization and parties. Made sense that this was where we'd find them—not just my creatures, but thousands of royals and freilds and other inhabitants.

I blinked at the sight, not expecting to see so many Shadow Realm beings here. And clearly, they returned the sentiment, gaping at the two fire-coated weirdos who had wandered into the middle of them.

The murmurs were immediate, and I noted how bedraggled they all looked. Thin, dirty, and more than a little broken. Dannie hadn't killed them yet, but she also hadn't treated them like anything other than trash waiting to be tossed to the dump.

"We have to help them," I whispered to Shadow, barely able to look at their poor faces, terrified but also resigned. They were preparing for the worst.

"Yes," he snapped, seemingly unable to get more words out through his anger. At least until he said, "Are your creatures here as well?"

"I don't actually know. I feel their energ—" I didn't get to finish my sentence because that was the moment they crept into view. Maybe I'd somehow called them with those words, or maybe they'd just been slower to appear, but as the hundreds of shadow creatures made their presence known, my power exploded.

I hadn't done anything to initiate the explosion, the power reacting of its own accord, in a similar way to how my wolf used to occasionally burst free from my skin. This time, it was the change, washing over me so I went from human-looking Mera to phoenix wolf Mera in a heartbeat, flaming wings and all.

Shadow's chest rumbled, his energy reacting too, as he shifted into his Anubis form, flames still surrounding us both. Our clothing was destroyed again, the energy of our shift always leaving us naked, but in this form the extra hair covered us.

There was a beat of stunned silence, and then the royals rushed forward, bowing and chanting at us. They called us "Nexus gods" and offered up every sacrifice one could think of in worship. I had no idea what I was going to do with fourteen thousand barrels of "gre gre," or what gre gre even was, but apparently, I was going to have more than enough of this unknown item coming my way soon.

As immensely uncomfortable as this entire situation made me, I didn't belittle their actions or beliefs in any way, nodding and thanking them before focusing my attention on my creatures.

My wings spread out farther, the flames shooting into the air behind me as I stepped forward. Thankfully, everyone got out of my way so I didn't have to stress about accidentally burning a royal.

Come to me.

I called the creatures, as I had so many other times. The ones who had been visible stepped forward... followed by so many others. The hundreds quickly turned into thousands, all of whom must have been squished in the very back of this deceptively huge courtyard.

I opened my arms, and even though there was absolutely no way for me to reach around the group, my power didn't have the same limitations. It crashed over them all, like a wave, and as it touched their essence, my bonds to them clicked into place.

Like a mother with her children, I offered them love and comfort and the promise that while I was alive, I would do everything in my power to protect them. My creatures had not had that for a very long time. Dannie had lost her way years before I'd been born—probably around the time she'd broken the rules and fallen in love with a royal. For that, though, I could never be upset with her. She'd given me Shadow, and without him, there'd be no me.

I'd give her a pass on that falling in love part... the rest, though, she'd have to answer for. "I'm going to take you somewhere safe," I told them in a whisper of power. The creatures brayed and called and bellowed out into the world, finally showing life and excitement and their animalistic nature.

"You're taking them to the outlier island?" Shadow asked in his deep Anubis voice.

I nodded. "Yes, it is best to leave them there while we have to fight Dannie."

Shadow moved forward as if to open a doorway, but I stopped him with a hand on his arm. "I don't want you to expend any more energy," I said quickly. "Do you think I can attempt to open it?"

My well of power inside was raging like a storm. Overflowing, overwhelming, especially in this current form I was rocking, as a giant wolf-bird. This version of me was so much stronger than I'd ever been. Torma would not have had it so easy beating the fuck out of me if I'd been able to access this form back then.

I had a thought. "Are my scars gone?" I asked Shadow. "Did you notice?"

"I notice everything about you," he said shortly, "and yes, your skin is unmarked from your shifter life."

An odd feeling filtered through with that knowledge. I wasn't sure how I felt about my "clean slate." My scars were part of who I was, memories of what I'd survived, and knowing they were gone now settled uneasily within me. It seemed rebirth always had consequences.

Shadow brushed a hand over my cheek, bringing me back to him. "Your strength will never fade. You don't need the scars for everyone to know you survived—not just survived, but flourished."

I let out a deep breath. "You're right. I know my truth, and that's all that really matters."

Shadow looked like he wanted to drag me up his body and remind me that he also knew my truth, and every other part of me, but somehow, he refrained. "You can open the doorway, Sunshine," he said, keeping that enigmatic gaze locked on me. "There's nothing you can't do."

He had faith in me. Far more than I probably deserved, but it was the confidence boost I needed to close my eyes and reach for a doorway to the island we'd been on. I pictured it in my mind, threw some power at it in the hopes that would work, and when I opened my eyes again, there was a swirling portal. Well, fuck. It seemed my new energy was going to baby me through these early skills, filling in the blanks itself when I fell short on knowledge.

It was a nice change from my usual bumbling through life approach.

"I need to check with the locals first," I said to Shadow, moving closer to my portal. He stayed right on my ass so we stepped through together.

The locals appeared in an instant, bowing down to us. "We need your help," I said softly, having no time to sugarcoat it. "We have many creatures, royals and freilds. Not to mention other realm inhabitants who need somewhere safe to stay while we fight the final battle. Will you take them in?"

No one answered for a beat, and I wondered if they were going to refuse us. I wouldn't blame them after the way the royals had treated them, but it would make the situation a touch harder.

A being with the greenest skin I'd seen so far stepped forward. "We will. We've never been their enemy, even if we chose to live a different way of life. If they can accept that way here, they are welcome to stay as long as they need."

Relief and gratefulness for their gracious attitude had my voice wavering. "I will let them know, and thank you."

We moved back to our portal, which remained strong and unwavering. I felt no strain in my power from what I'd done, and I had the sense that I could leave the portal there forever and it wouldn't overtly affect me. It was damn impressive, but there was no time to give myself a pat on the back. I had to get my creatures and all the others to safety.

I called the shadow creatures through first, and they were somewhat orderly as they journeyed from the royal compound into the island. All too soon, they filled that field the original creatures had gone into, but the locals found more space for them, looking absolutely delighted by all their new friends.

"Which outlier is this?" I asked Shadow, having wondered but not asked until now.

Shadow took a second to look around again, like he'd not even given it a second thought until I asked. "I aimed for the largest that was away from Trinity," he said, his brow wrinkled. "Samsan Grove, possibly."

In the great scheme it really didn't matter, as long as it wasn't the mainland, where Dannie would focus her attack first. But it felt a little more respectful to at least acknowledge the name of the locals who were assisting us.

The ones who had given us a shot at taking down the most powerful goddess to walk the worlds.

Samsan Grove had shifted the odds in our favor, and now it was time for us to do them proud.

Chapter Fifty-Four

It took longer than expected to usher thousands of creatures and hundreds of locals through to the island. When they were finally done, Shadow and I couldn't hang around, knowing Dannie might be breaking free at any moment.

He assured me that our mists would send out an alarm, but I was worried it'd be too late by the time that happened.

Before we left, though, I had one final task to complete. "The creatures are free now," I said, in my booming wolf-phoenix voice. "Royals are not to bond or use their energy in any way, or the outlier locals have full right to stop you with every weapon at their disposal. And then when they're done, *I* will come for you."

I felt the royals' momentary fear before all of them shouted their promises and swore to never hurt a creature again. Dannie had already somewhat sufficiently broken them in the time she'd had them locked away, so I felt confident that my orders would be obeyed.

"Is there any way we can leave the outlier locals a way to communicate with us?" I asked Shadow. "On the slim chance there *is* trouble?"

Shadow's expression was grim. "I wouldn't worry about it. The battle with Dannie will be over fast. If we lose, they all lose, and if we win... we will remove the royals from here and back to the mainland before there's chance of an uprising."

Right. That was true and depressing, but at least I didn't have to stress about a hostile takeover while we were busy fighting the goddess hellbent on destroying it all.

"We must go now," Shadow said, gently bumping me toward the portal.

I nodded, taking one last look at the island, which was now a few thousand inhabitants larger. It felt cozy, somehow, and I didn't really want to leave, wishing I could stay and help the locals, who were already taking care of the mentally and physically fragile royals.

"Dannie has a lot to answer for," I said shortly. "Do you think your royal compound was the only one she did that to?"

Shadow didn't answer until we stepped through the portal, which vanished as soon as we were back inside the castle. "I think she probably has this entire world locked down in one way or another," he said, creating some clothing so that we could change back and get dressed. "Until the next part of her plan comes to fruition."

"Yeah, I agree," I said, pulling on my pants and boots. "Knowing Dannie as I do. I mean, her next part was clearly to create a Nexus that she controlled, but what after that? What was she going to do with them all when she finally achieved her peak status as goddess supreme?"

Shadow let out a low breath. "Impossible to know, but one thing is clear: This realm would definitely not be as it was."

We were dressed now, so he pulled me into his side, leading us back through the creepy, booby-trapped castle and into the main grounds. When our pack came into sight, the fact that they were all on their feet circling what was clearly Dannie's prison had Shadow and me picking up speed.

She's starting the process of breaking through, Midnight said in my head, since we were close enough to communicate now.

"The prison is cracking," Shadow said at the same time, clearly having spoken to his mist as well. We started to sprint, knowing we had to be by their side when Dannie burst free.

Midnight met us halfway, scooping us up and all but catapulting us across the smooth grounds so we landed in the circle of warriors.

"Just in time," Lucien said, flashing fang as he waited, unnaturally still. He was a predator, a master vampire, and I was curious to see him in action. All of them. The greatest and strongest of their worlds. And every one of them I was honored to stand with and call "friend."

The gold cage started to vibrate, heat rising from it until we were all sweltering, stuck between the lava chasm and Dannie. None of us moved a muscle, except to internally prepare ourselves. I allowed my power to fill me, turning into a winged, flaming wolf-bird, once again destroying clothing. At this point, I should just remain naked between shifts.

"The moment she bursts free," Len murmured, his silver cloak billowing out from his motionless form, "use your powers to lock her in place, and I will call the stone to me. It's bonded to my family and has been for many more years than Dannie's held it. I should still have the greater tie to it."

I loved having a plan. It gave us a focus, and thanks to the many, *many* times Shadow had held me against the wall, locking down my arms and legs, I had a decent idea of what to do to hold Dannie in a similar manner.

It wouldn't be as much fun for her, though.

She was about to understand that the biggest mistake she'd made in the last few months was not swallowing the stone. Or stealing our memories. Or betraying everyone who had ever loved her.

Nope.

Her biggest mistake was not killing us all when she had the chance, because it was her day of reckoning, and we were the ones delivering it.

The light grew brighter around her, the heat as well, and I was so fucking jumpy that I almost pissed myself when Angel moved a millimeter beside me, her wings brushing mine. My tiny shriek and stumble forward broke some of the tension as multiple amused smiles crossed faces.

"You can take the woman out of Earth, but—" Lucien was cut off when an explosion of energy knocked us all back from the fortress.

My wings extended, stopping me before I skidded into the lava chasm, and then two flaps later, I was back in the circle, surrounding an extremely pissed-off-looking Dannie.

Dannie, who had changed again.

Whatever humanoid parts of her that had been there before were gone.

She was a full phoenix, standing as tall as me.

Her beak opened, and a loud screech emerged, which eventually turned into words. "You made a grave mistake," she bellowed, flames shooting off her as the ground trembled. "It will all fall now, and when I rebuild, it will be a better world and future."

None of the others seemed that concerned, moving in closer, their energy humming in the air as they prepared to attack. I did the same, but no lie, my gut was twisted in knots at what was happening. What the fuck were we going to do if she was still too strong for us?

Before anyone even got a chance to find out, Dannie did the opposite of what I'd expected and angled her wings to drop between us. It took me a beat to understand why she'd done that, and it was only when her clawed foot tapped against the land and the rumble increased that I figured it out. She was doing exactly what her son had attempted not that long ago.

Destroying the Shadow Realm.

Before any of us even had a chance to attempt to lock her down with our power, the chasm exploded, spitting out flames that would tear through almost everyone here. With those flames came a truly terrifying sight, clawing their way up from the lava below.

"She's resurrecting the dead," Alistair said, his hands clenched tightly in front of him. "All of those lost to the lava mists."

"Fuck."

That one word was from Shadow, and I knew that meant this was bad. No, not bad. Cata-fucking-strophic.

"How many beings have died in the chasms?" I asked, my wings the only thing keeping me standing as the ground tremors worsened. "Outside of all the creatures."

"I believe it was a regular punishment here," Angel said, having to lift herself off the ground now.

"Yes," Shadow confirmed. "Sacrifice into the mists is common."

Now it was my turn. *Fuck.*

The others had to lift themselves up as well, Inky and Midnight doing their best to shield us all from the shooting spurts of lava attempting to take us out. Lava that didn't bother me or my power, and knowing I might have the only shot, I darted forward, blasting Dannie with a bolt of pure energy.

We had to stop her before this army of undead reached us. They'd clearly be very hard to, uh... kill, giving her a true advantage. My power was deflected by a bolt of her own, and she countered with a strike back at me.

I'd been ready for it, swiping it aside, surprised that she did feel much weaker. We had to finish this shit before she had time to recharge, and that meant I could not stop now.

I attacked with force, and every time her power hit me, it was like a sledgehammer to my gut, but I was fueled by such anger and determination that I barely let it faze me. My determination to save my loved ones added a ferocity to my attack that she was missing.

Her movements slowed, and when she got her shield up a second too slow, I was able to hit her at full power, slamming her against the wall of the castle, the force sending feathers flying around her.

"Give up the stone, Dannie," I shouted at her. "Give it up and have a chance at redemption."

At this point, I noticed that Shadow was at my side, but so far, he was allowing me to take the lead in this one-on-one battle. It cost him to do so, if the tense expression on his face was any indication, but his faith in me was too strong to break his resolve.

Love. He spoke it at an expert level.

Dannie laughed, a screeching, chill-inducing sound, and I blasted her again, but she managed to slip free. She might have been weaker, but she was far from fragile, especially as her literal zombie fire creatures exploded across the land. There was just so much to unpack about what was going on here. Not time for that, though.

Shadow joined me this time, the two of us using our energy to try to contain her, all the while Dannie stepped up her game, sending out her long tail feathers to strike at us. I had no idea what was going to happen if they hit us, but thankfully, Shadow was able to cut them off before we had a chance to find out.

At one point, he managed to bind her powers—he was an expert at that after all—but she only laughed again and broke free even faster than she had when I'd held her against the wall. As she got loose, I slammed her as hard as I could, and Shadow's power increased at my side until my skin hurt from the hot blast of his energy. But together, we were holding her. The only problem was that Len couldn't get close enough to attempt to remove the stone. The fae was trapped in the middle of Inky and Midnight, who were shielding all of our friends from the lava and creatures. And they were almost losing the battle thanks to powerful mist-driven zombies.

It had been a mistake to bring her back to the mists, but then again, maybe she would have used the creatures against us on the island. Dannie always had ten plans to fall back on, leaving the rest of us scrambling. Not one of us had expected she could do this, though, and there was no contingency plan for her secret lava army.

"This was where she was funneling her power in the cage," Shadow bit out, pushing more power against the phoenix. "Her army needed to rise at the same time she broke free. That fucking stone is giving her near unlimited power."

"Hence why we need it freed," I groaned, my words barely audible.

For the first time since my rebirth, I felt my energy waning.

"I'm here." Len's words whispered through our ears, carried on his fae energy. "Hold her for a few more minutes, and I'll work my Silver Magic on her."

A few more minutes; it sounded so short when someone said it, but the reality of holding a raging, powerful phoenix goddess was akin to a human trying to hold a bull still for a few minutes.

Impossible and deadly.

Shadow joined me in his Anubis form, powering himself up further. Dannie looked between us and let out a squawk, shaking her head. "Neither of you are natural," she managed to say through our hold. "I broke the balance with you both. A balance I must repair."

It was a warning that this time she would not hesitate to kill us, but who the fuck was surprised by that? We all knew she had learned her lesson in leaving threats alive. Only one side of this war was walking away today.

Shadow and I gave it everything we had to hold her, and I thought we were going to make it, right up until she drew on whatever she had left in her stone, blasting us back. I stumbled, but Shadow caught me before I could go too far.

"We need the others," he said near my ear. "All of us have to hold her for Len."

At that, Inky and Midnight swirled closer, bringing with them the others from our pack. The two mists raced at the goddess, slamming her against the side of the castle again, with enough force that the stone and brick shattered under her.

Our mists were not as strong as the wild and free version, but they were also not to be underestimated. Unfortunately, the moment they went for Dannie, the lava creatures went for us.

Can you form a protective barrier against the dead army? I asked Midnight. *Give us a chance to get the stone?*

It swelled up larger, sparks flying around it. *I can hold them for a few minutes. Maybe more if Inky helps.*

Do it.

The pair released Dannie, who zapped out at them with her

power, but she was either too slow or off-kilter because she missed them completely, her energy shooting into the lava chasm.

Or no, wait, that must have been her plan all along because the second her energy disappeared over the cliffs and into the abyss below, a huge raging wave of red fire rose with it.

Great. Molten tsunami.

"Go!" I screamed to Midnight. "Get the barrier up so we have a chance."

I barely got my last words out before Dannie's power slammed Shadow and me into the ground. We hit hard, and if I had been a straight-up shifter still, all my bones would have shattered. As it was, the pain strongly pulsed through my body as she continued to press against us, driving our bodies into the crumbling and broken castle grounds.

How the fuck was she so strong? It just never ended, and even with the cage having drained her as intended, there was still too much for us to counter.

Len had warned us about the stone, and what would happen if it fell into enemy hands, and I couldn't think of a way to win against her, not when so many of us were losing strength. Digging deeper, I searched for a way to push back again, but there was no give in her attack. No weakness to manipulate.

At least none until our friends finally let loose. Giving us the sort of support Dannie could have had if she hadn't tried to be judge, jury, and executioner all on her own.

Reece, whom I really hadn't seen in full-on action before, blasted across the clearing in a literal wall of sand and dust. His power always reminded me of a desert storm, and now I could see why. He stood at the center of it, his energy extinguishing some of Dannie's as he sent her flying in his cyclonic sandstorm.

Shadow and I were up in an instant, and we joined the desert deity, using our powers against her once more, finding a hidden strength neither of us knew we had. Desperation and adrenaline were the reasons human women could lift cars off their babies. Today we were the desperate ones, and we were using it to our full advantage.

"She's weakening," Shadow roared. "But not enough to tear the stone free. Not yet."

"One last attempt," Reece bit out, his voice a rumble like the storms he had raging around us. "All of us. All of our power. Hold nothing back."

The others fell into line, Midnight and Inky still giving us some breathing room from the creatures, but that wouldn't last long. This truly was our last shot.

Our one chance to save the world.

Chapter Fifty-Five

The eight of us faced the phoenix. Maybe this was how it should have been all along, our power versus her power. No games or prisons. No conversations or attempts at redemption.

I didn't regret allowing her the chance to save herself, but that chance was over now. Now we had to play for keeps, and I would hold nothing back.

Len held back, since he was saving his energy to remove the stone, but the rest of us shot power into her focusing on our individual strengths and magics. The strongest aspects and skills of our races. Reece with his desert power, dry as it ripped against our skin like magical sandpaper. Alistair's was water-based, but his water turned into large weapons he shot at Dannie in the form of icy green swords, pointed spears, and other missiles. So far, none were penetrating the shield she had formed over herself, but it was all working to weaken her. Angel had her blades, moving up close and personal, slicing and dicing against Dannie's power, moving like a freaking ninja so that the goddess could never touch her.

Lucien zipped around super-fast, his vampire strength and speed allowing him to pummel into the shields, searching for weak points, and when Dannie winced more than once, I knew that he was finding targets. Galleli still didn't speak or make any sounds at all, but he was flapping his wings above Dannie, staring down with a look of complete focus on his face.

Everything okay? I quickly asked, worried that he might have spotted something.

Her mind is strong, he replied. *But I will continue to try to break through to take control of her.*

Awesome. Good luck.

Mentally, I pulled away, allowing him to focus, all the while having a minor freakout that he could take control of minds. As handy as it could be in this situation, there was always the worry that one day he might use it against us.

But, I mean, all of us were powerful, not just Galleli. We were the checks to each other's power, and that was why our group was so strong and well-balanced. Which meant I had nothing to worry about. On that front at least.

"The shield is falling," Shadow roared, and his flames were near twenty feet high as he continued to dig at the barrier around the phoenix. At first, I thought he was talking about that shield erected by Dannie, but unfortunately, I was wrong.

It was the mist shield.

Dannie had just been protecting herself long enough for her army to break free. Damn her and her intelligent battle-ready mind. Next time we fought an arch-nemesis, I wanted one who was stupid. It was only fair.

The army raged at us en masse and we all fell under the assault. Dannie added to that by offensively blasting her power into us, sharp and powerful assaults that penetrated into the center of my power. It hurt, and I cried out as I struggled to cut the tie she'd created by tethering her attack directly into my energy.

I expected the others would be doing the same, only to break free and find all of them were being crushed under the fire army and

Dannie's attack. Our mists were holding back what they could, but it wasn't enough.

"Stop!" I screamed, shooting myself into the air, blind rage at my loved ones being attacked driving me. Shadow roared at me too, and I knew he was working to save our friends and get to me, but he couldn't do it all.

The power inside of me exploded, a nuclear blast that shot me into the sky, my fire wings flapping powerfully as breaths sucked in and out of my mouth in loud rasps. It was pure rage fueling me since I was exhausted and broken, but maybe rage would be enough.

Dannie and I collided in the air, and that was the first time anyone had been able to touch her. Her feathers were icy cold under my clawed hands, despite the heat she was channeling in her flaming tail and power. "You feel empty," I screamed in her face, digging into her with all my strength. "Your soul is gone, Dannie, and there's no way to come back from that."

Those flaming eyes flashed at me. "You know nothing about souls, child. Or sacrifice. You have been a selfish brat from the first moment I saw you in Torma. A disappointment. But I decided to give you a chance to grow into a being worthy of the legacy you carry." Even on a bird face, her disgust was obvious. "You continue to fail. You continue to be unworthy. Your parents thought it, your true mate thought so, and so do I."

Her words hurt. She knew how to use them as weapons, hitting at my soft, vulnerable belly. But there was one truth she couldn't take from me: Shadow Beast was my true mate, and he had not rejected our bond. He'd fought for it.

We both had and I was no longer that poor pathetic pup from Torma.

"You can't take me down like that," I said softly. "A few months ago, it would have worked, but I'm not the same being as I was then. I did best your mind control, and I will best you again now."

I'd been building power in my center, every ounce I had, in preparation for the attack that she was about to send my way. Only she once again went for my vulnerabilities and continued to use her power against my friends. The tethers she held to them, the ones they couldn't break, were killing them. At least the ones who were easily killable, and the others would soon have their energy stripped away until there was nothing left.

I tried to stop her, sending out my power in a bid to break those tethers as I'd done for myself. But it wasn't enough. I couldn't take her on alone, and my small attempts were just delaying the inevitable. Dannie was powered by a stone that could build and destroy worlds. Its power was near never-ending. Our attempt to best her had always been a long shot, and dammit, we'd given it all we had.

"You know you can't win."

She saw it in my face, and I schooled my expression, unwilling to admit defeat yet. I had to hold on to hope, for it was the strongest motivator that there was.

"It will not hurt, and you'll all be together," Dannie told me softly, and there was a warmth under my touch finally. She still felt something, even if it was crushed beneath the ice in her soul. "Don't fight any longer."

This approach worked differently to her last attack because this time it was true. My family was hurting. They were broken and bloody and burning alive. I couldn't allow that to keep happening, and if I couldn't beat her or save them, what was our other option?

Never stop fighting her, Sunshine.

His voice was in my head, his love and strength surrounding me, and I squeezed my eyes closed for a beat knowing that Shadow was right. *Fuck.* I did not lie down and die on command under a bully hurting me. I'd never done that, and I wasn't about to start today. Torma had unknowingly been preparing me for this fight, and I would not waste their training.

Streams of light and fire burst from me, but unlike my last attack, which focused on brute force, this time, I went for a different strategy. Distract, deflect, and detain.

Drawing on the strength of Shadow, Midnight, and my creatures, the bonds I had to them fueled my power. I only took enough to boost my own strengths as I wove my power around Dannie in long beams of light.

Angel, my beautiful best friend, tried to reach out to me through the bonds as well, but she was weak. Instead of taking, I sent power back to her, the connection between us stronger than ever. It was so strong that when Dannie saw what I was doing and changed her attack to focus solely on Angel, I felt the full force of her crushing blow.

I screamed as Angel's presence flickered in my mind, each beat of her lifeforce fading as Dannie decided to take her out and remove one of my strengths. No matter how hard I held on, there was no way to counter the goddess.

Angel, I sobbed, holding on to her with all my power. *Pull from your land. Take all the energy. Fight her.*

The touch of her mind was so strong and calm, the ancient being that she was did as I said and used the last of her strength to draw on her ancestral power. It was at this point that I felt some hope, right up until a burn of power shot down our bond. *Take this, Mera. Take this and finish her off.*

Angel gave me the strength of her family. Strength that could have saved her life, but she knew without it, we'd all be dead against the might of this goddess. In that moment, I didn't care though.

"Angel, fuck, no!" I screamed both mentally and through our bond. "Save yourself."

It's too late, Mera. My power base is fractured and I'm leaking my life force. I can't replenish it fast enough, and this power would be wasted. Use it to save the others. Save yourself.

I tried to pull away from Dannie, but she wouldn't release me. And with more power funneling into me as Angel faded from this realm, a scream built in my chest. Hopelessness crashed into me and I was crying and screaming and fighting, but there was nothing I could do.

It's my time, Mera. You saved me and now I can repay the favor. I'll be at peace, with my family. You need to let me go.

No.

I was an ungracious stubborn asshole, but I couldn't do this. I couldn't let her go.

No, I repeated. *If you fall, so do I.*

Angel chuckled, a whisper so weak, it crushed my heart into a million tiny pieces. This was our last moment, I knew it even as I fought against the inevitable. But how could I accept that I'd never hear her laugh again? Or sit by her side in the dining hall, teasing her about her love of smelling apples? I'd never hear her formal talk when she was ready to kick ass. Or see her warrior outfits as she palmed weapons like she'd been born with them in her hands.

This was our last moment, and I knew that even if we won against Dannie now, I'd lost.

I love you, I told her because there was no time left. Our bond, that fluttering feeling of home and family in my chest, was nearly gone.

I love you, treasora, Angel whispered until her voice faded out. Death had stolen the last of her, leaving the rest of us to mourn in its wake.

Chapter Fifty-Six

My scream of rage burst from me, and everything went dark and red and broken. My fury and pain were relentless in their assault. The only thing that kept me from losing it completely was the knowledge that Angel had gifted me this power to save the world.

Her death could not be in vain.

Channeling my wrath, I focused one part of my attack on Dannie, sending her spiraling across the sky with a sharp strike. Another part of my energy went to the remaining members of my pack, blasting the lava army back into the depths of the chasm, and freeing the mists who'd fallen under their attack. I then repaired and rebuilt my pack's broken bodies, washing away burns and fixing fractured energy bases. I could do all of that, fight the phoenix and drown in grief, because I was a woman.

We multitasked well.

Dannie came at me with full force, but her assault brushed off me like water droplets. Reaching out with my strength, I wrapped my power around her throat, and for the first time, she was helpless against me. The power I used was not the burning flames of the mists, but the ancient heavenly power of the meadows.

As I flew closer to her, weapons appeared in my hands, and as I stared down at the curved blades, my eyes burned. Angel's favorite weapons. Her last assistance in this battle, and fuck, it was fitting that they would be what ended this once and for all.

"This is for Angel," I rumbled at Dannie. "Angel, who sacrificed herself to save us and all the worlds."

My blades swiped through her shields, moving as if extensions of my body. I only had to think of what I wanted to do and they were slicing with speed and grace.

"Mera, please," Dannie said, and there was real fear in her birdy eyes.

"You will find no mercy here," I told her, my voice vibrating and unfamiliar.

Dannie held her hands up, but I was done waiting. Slicing again, my blade landed deep in her chest. I knew where to hit, feeling the stone's power, and the moment I opened her up, a bright light emerged, blinding the world with its intensity.

Len was at my side now, his Silver Magic wresting the sunburst stone from her chest. It came to him willingly, disappearing into a small silver container that went into his coat.

I jerked my blade free from the phoenix's chest, and there was no sense of satisfaction or success.

Dannie's eyes met mine, and there was a softness there that hadn't been before. "I'm sorry, Mera," she whispered, and for the first time, I felt she meant it. "So sorry."

Those were her last words before she crumbled and plummeted, slamming hard against the ground. Feathers shot everywhere and by the time we landed beside her, there was nothing but a few stray feathers remaining of the Danamain.

"She's gone," Shadow said, his arms around me as he held on like I might disappear too.

Like Angel. My eyes filled with tears as I lost my wolf-phoenix, turning back into a chick who'd lost her best friend. A chick whose insides were tearing her apart.

Midnight wrapped around me, followed by Shadow, the pair keeping me together.

When I finally straightened, Shadow pressed a kiss to my forehead. "She went out as a warrior," he murmured. "Don't take that from her."

I trembled, looking at the spot where Angel had fallen. There was nothing but her armor there now, and I had no idea where Honor Meadow beings went upon death. I'd find out when I was mentally able to handle it.

"I will return the stone to Faerie," Len said, interrupting when he couldn't wait any longer.

Shadow held up a hand to stop his friend before he disappeared. "Take Inky and Midnight with you." His eyes briefly met mine. "If that's okay with you, Mera? I'd just hate for anything to happen to Len or the stone until it's locked away again."

I nodded, unable to process my feelings, but knowing he was right. "Yes, that's a good idea."

Midnight dove closer to wrap around me. *I'm sorry for your loss, Mera*, it said, offering support and love. *But I will protect the stone, so it never happens again.*

I swallowed hard. *Thank you, friend. It just hurts.*

Midnight seemed to understand, as it lifted me off the ground for an extra strong hug. Inky joined in, the pair of them loving on me the only way they could. For a moment, it helped, and I brushed my hands through their sparking centers as they set me back on the ground.

By the time Len placed a kiss on my cheek and disappeared from the castle grounds with the two mists, I was once again trembling and on the verge of losing it. Grief was a never-ending torment on my soul.

"Sunshine." Shadow drew my attention. "You need to release some of the power back into the Honor Meadows."

I heard his words but didn't move.

"If you continue to hold this level of energy," he tried again, "it will corrupt you as the stone did with Dannie."

And still, I couldn't make myself release the last part of Angel still with me.

"Mera!" A snap of command. "Come back to me, Sunshine. Step away from the darkness and return to my side."

Technically, I was at his side, but I knew what he meant.

A sob wracked through me as I dropped to my knees, my hands digging into the ground as a scream built. "It hurts," I choked out. "It's killing me, Shadow."

He got down with me, wrapping his huge frame over the top of mine as he cradled my body. "I know," he said huskily. "I feel your pain and my own, but you're not alone. I will hold you together until such a time you can do it yourself. Fall into me, Sunshine. *Fall. Into. Me.*"

For once, I did exactly as I was told. The scream faded when I collapsed against my mate, and he drew me into his lap, rocking me back and forth until I could function again. Shadow was the strong one today because I just couldn't do it for myself.

When my heartbeats had calmed and I was able to focus, Shadow helped me to properly return the energy into the Honor Meadows, both of us building layers until I was only in possession of my Nexus energy. Then he lifted me, cradling my body in his arms. "You saved us, Sunshine," he said as he pressed his lips to my cheek, and lips, and shoulder. "You saved us and the worlds and your creatures. You're the fucking hero today, and we will honor you and Angel's sacrifice."

"Angel deserves it," I said listlessly. "She gave too much, as always, and it's not fair."

I waited for his usual *Life isn't fair, Sunshine,* but he never said a word. He just held me closer, keeping me together as he'd promised.

Chapter Fifty-Seven

At some point, Shadow got us both dressed again, our friends well and truly having seen every naked inch of us as we dealt with the fallout of losing Angel. It was something I'd have joked with her about, but now, I just got to feel her absence stabbing in my chest.

"We should check the Nexus," Lucien said, reminding us that this wasn't quite over yet. "Dannie may be reborn, and we need to assess her threat level."

This broke through my grief. "Maybe I shouldn't have released the power?" I asked, looking between Shadow and the others.

My mate shook his head. "She's no match for us without the stone, and it was too risky to hold that much energy."

That provided some relief, and I thought of what might happen when we saw her again. "I hope she doesn't choose to return," I admitted. "Because I'm not sure we can allow her to remain free. Not with her need for power."

"Her rebirth should strip that away," Shadow said, "but I agree that it would be best if she didn't return."

The others nodded, all except Reece, who had drifted over to stand before Angel's armor. Armor none of us had been able to bring ourselves to touch yet. I watched as he reached down and pressed his hands to the gold-and-bronze piece, and then it vanished. I had no idea where he'd sent it, but I hoped back to the wall in her home. That was where it belonged.

Reece's eyes met mine, and even though his face was expressionless, his eyes were fire. He wasn't okay, even if he was hiding it somewhat better than me.

"We should go now," Shadow said, giving us all the distraction we were searching for.

He opened the portal into the Grey Lands, which really needed a new name. Since my rebirth, where I'd risen with the Nexus, it had been slowly returning to its former glory.

With not a scrap of grey in sight, these lands were now a run of golden fields and mountains, cut through by red rivers. Beautiful and powerful... It felt whole again.

"How is it that you don't need to stay here in the Nexus?" Lucien asked me. "Your rebirth created you into another Nexus goddess, right? Are you bound to it now?"

"No," I said, knowing the truth of it. "I still belong to multiple worlds. It's what makes me different to Dannie and allows me to exist in multiple places. I may need to return here at times to keep it all in check, but this is not my only home."

Earth, Honor Meadows, the Library of Knowledge. All equally as important as this land we stood on now. "There is no other like Mera," Shadow said, his eyes locked on mine. "And there never will be."

Even my broken heart flip-flopped at the depth of emotion in his voice.

We moved closer together, and our hands joined as we made our way up to the Nexus itself, still at the top of a gently sloping hill. As we closed in on it, a sense of calm and peace washed through me. The relentless hammering pain I hadn't been able to lock away eased just enough that I could take a deep breath and not feel like my lungs were being compressed.

Shadow's constant presence at my side helped as well, and I found myself pressing harder into him as we crossed under the beautiful stone gates. As we stepped to the other side, the Nexus power flared, which I felt intimately within myself.

"Dannie is returning," I said with a sigh. "I feel her power."

The others took it seriously, spreading out in a circle around the streaming lights emerging from what I was coming to think of as the Nexus birth pool. It was in the middle of a grove, gold and red blossoms surrounding it. As the air grew heavy and thick, a figure shot up into the air, coated in the Jell-O-like substance, bright fiery wings shooting out from either side of them.

None of us broke formation or relaxed, waiting to see which version of Dannie we were about to get. Would it be the power-hungry, angry, untouchable version who would have destroyed us all in her need to control? Or would it be the Dannie I'd known before the stone?

And would it make a difference either way?

The light around the figure was bright and blinding, and even with my preternatural sight, I couldn't manage to make out what version of her was landing. It wasn't until I caught sight of fire-touched wings, which looked an awful lot like mine, that I faltered. The Dannie from before could shift into a phoenix, but she'd never worn her wings as I did.

The flutter in my chest hit me, and I took a stumbling step forward. "It's not Dannie," I whispered, my throat closing over as I started to run. The light faded, the Jell-O disappearing as soon as I slammed into Angel, and she wrapped me up tightly. We remained like that forever, and as our pack and family closed around us, I finally pulled away. "How?" I asked, unable to say more.

She smiled her beautiful smile, and I took a moment to examine her. Her eyes were the same, only slightly more fire-touched. Her hair too, which was now heavily streaked with red and gold. And the wings—the largest change of all—were still angelic in shape, with some fire and phoenix in there as well. Those wings wrapped around us, hiding her naked form.

"I was reborn," she trilled in the musical voice I'd never expected to hear again. "Honor Meadows have their own afterlife, but I never went there. I went to yours because of our bond."

Shadow made a sound over my shoulder. "It makes sense," he said. "You're warned never to bond with one outside of your brethren, no doubt because it can disrupt the natural order of life, death, and... your afterlife."

Angel nodded. "Correct. And Mera is so powerful that it was her world I was pulled into, instead of my own. But it allowed me the choice of rebirth. A choice that any who are born of the Nexus are given."

I shook my head. "I can't believe this." My voice broke. "I was just given my greatest wish, and yet I did nothing to deserve it."

Angel hugged me tightly again. "You deserve it, my friend. You were willing to sacrifice yourself as well. All of us were."

As she pulled away, she wove clothing across her body, tucking her wings behind her to reveal the most human outfit I'd ever seen on her. Jeans, a shirt, and sneakers.

"I think my wings can even—" she started before closing her eyes, and there was a pop as they vanished in the same way mine could. For the first time, she almost seemed petite without the statuesque angel wings.

"Wow, you were reborn," I said with a chuckle.

"At least our bond remains," Angel said with a true smile. "You will always have me as family, and I've been given a second chance at life, reborn from the sins and tragedy in my past. I will never forget my family, but I don't wear their deaths around my neck any longer."

It might have been my imagination, but I thought that her eyes flicked toward Reece's for a split second before both of them cut the contact. Angel looked around at all the others then, finally realizing we were all at the Nexus. "Wait! Did you all know I would be reborn?" she asked.

"No," Lucien said with a shake of his head. "We were waiting for Dannie. Seeing if she chose to be reborn."

Understanding crossed Angel's face. "Ah, right. Well, you have nothing to worry about. Dannie has chosen to remain as part of the Nexus; her energy was dispersing as I exited, and with this one act, she'll keep the balance better than she ever could have in a vessel."

I wasn't the only one to sag in relief, but I did make sure I wrapped my arm around Shadow to offer whatever comfort I could. "I'm sorry, beast man," I whispered to him. "I loved her too."

He returned my hug, holding me long enough that I knew it hurt him to lose his mother, no matter what she'd done to deserve it. Thankfully, she had made the decision, and now we could try to remember the best parts of Dannie.

Chapter Fifty-Eight

O ur group was quiet as we made our way back to the library, following Shadow through his Solaris System pathways. There was a lot that had to be done in the Shadow Realm still, but all of us were exhausted, needing some rest before we stepped back to ensure that world finally had a chance to reach its full potential.

I, for one, needed sex, sleep, and sustenance. In that order.

I was banking on the fact that I would still need to eat food after my rebirth, because that was a soul deep bond too... right?

Shadow was first through the doorway into the library, and I was second, both of us grinding to a halt. "What in the hell?" I muttered.

Beings were everywhere, standing no more than a few feet from the door, filling the space between the shelves and even pushed right back into the middle of the library.

As our pack crowded in behind us, equally as confused, I was about to start stressing that something else had gone wrong in our absence. Until the room burst into loud applause, everyone shouting and calling to us.

"Thank you!"

"Long live the gods!"

"Our saviors."

The many beings from all the different worlds heaped praise on us as their cheers continued.

"How did they know?" Angel asked, close behind me.

Gaster pushed his way to the front then, wanting to be the first to greet us personally. "The entire Solaris System knew that our fate hung in the balance," he said, nodding his head respectfully to us. "The Great Council arrived to prepare us for what might be left if you all didn't win."

I'd never heard of the Great Council, but it sounded fancy.

"We've been waiting for you to walk through the door," someone shouted from back in the group. The rumble told me it was a Brolder inhabitant. "And if you didn't, we knew that all hope was lost."

Cheers rose up again, and it was clear that they were settling in for a night of revelry to celebrate our victory.

Shadow held his hands up, and I was pretty sure he was the only being who could have shut them up so quickly. "We'll have a grand feast in the dining hall later tonight," he called loud enough for all to hear. "Bring your friends and families, for we have much to celebrate."

"The balance remains," Reece added.

This time, the noise was deafening, allowing none of us to get a word in, but my spirits lifted with it. As Gaster hugged me tightly, there was even more joy in my heart, and it was maybe at that moment I finally recognized that we'd won.

We had beat the freaking Nexus Goddess. I hadn't let that sink in until now, as I'd been too filled with grief and pain. But with Angel back at my side, I could allow the joy to take hold.

This was finally the life I'd always dreamed of, not that bullshit in Torma Dannie had tried to sell me. Speaking of...

"We need to deal with Torma," I said to Shadow, deciding that I was ready to let that part of my life go for good. "Before we can celebrate, that's the final thorn in my side."

His lips met mine, and it felt like the first kiss all over again. Power and life and sex filled the energy, and I wanted him so badly, my legs trembled as my panties tried not to drown.

"Later." I growled against his lips. "Torin has already had too long to sow the seeds of his destruction. It's time to reap that fucking bastard."

I think my words only worked to arouse the beast further, as his chest rumbled, and he deepened our kiss. When we managed to pull apart—with great difficulty—I turned to where Angel waited, looking somewhat amused.

"You're going to Earth?" she said.

I nodded. "Yeah, I have a pack to deal with and friends to ensure are okay. Do you want to come with us?" I was having a Shadow possessive moment, not wanting to let her out of my sight.

She shook her head. "I think I should head to the Honor Meadows and finalize a few pieces of unfinished business."

As much as it hurt me to let her go, Angel was a grown-ass warrior who definitely didn't need a babysitter. "Okay, friend," I said, wrapping my arms around her. "We'll meet you back here for the big celebration dinner, right?"

She smiled, and it was more real and more content than any smile I'd ever seen from her. "I wouldn't miss it for anything." A secret twinkle hit her eye, but before I could press her to reveal her thoughts, the rest of our friends pushed closer.

"We'll keep the system running until you get back," Reece said, slapping his hand on Shadow's shoulder in a manly gesture of friendship before he leaned down and kissed my cheek. Lucien, Alistair, and Galleli all did the same before each of them disappeared into the library.

When it was just Shadow and I, he led us through the bowing and cheering crowds. No one touched us, of course, as they still feared the beast in charge, so we had a clear—and noisy—run toward the hallway to Earth.

"Do you think Len and the mists are okay?" I asked, worried that they weren't here waiting for us.

"They're fine," he assured me. "Inky got a message through saying they're staying a little longer until all the securities were in place."

"Oh, fuck," I said quickly, the word "message" reminding me that I'd lost the parchment I was supposed to use to communicate with Simone. Not to mention the stone Len had given me to protect my mind.

When I told Shadow, he just laughed. "You died, Sunshine. You were lucky to keep your life. Don't worry about the other parts." He pressed lingering kisses to my cheeks and down my face, and I forgot everything but the taste of my mate.

Somehow when his lips hit mine, the world went silent and cool, and I knew we'd entered the white hallway. Finally alone after being surrounded for so long by others. "I missed you," I said stupidly, since we'd never really been apart.

Outside of that dying thing.

"You'll never need to miss me again," he promised. "We've paved the path to our future, and it's bright, Sunshine."

I chuckled. "Yeah, I caught that cute play on words."

Shadow grumbled before he dragged me along the hallway. "Just like old times," I said with a sigh.

He didn't bother to reply, but he did throw me over his shoulder, sending my heart into a racing pace. He was recreating our first memory together. The moment my life had changed.

Through Shadow, I had found a true mate, and a true pack in Angel, Simone, and the rest of our merry band of assholes.

"I almost feel bad that I'm heading into Torma to strip the pack away from their lands," I said to Shadow, resting against him and enjoying the sensation of my body jolting against his. "Torin's rejection is what set this all in motion, giving me the best fucking life, while he's still a sad sack of dog balls."

"My vote is to kill him," Shadow said with a shrug, lifting me higher. "But out of respect to you, and your right to enact punishment over them, I'll accept whatever decision you make."

Leaning back, I wrapped my arms around his neck in an awkward hug. "You're so sweet, mate. And while some of them deserve death, it just feels so limited. They'd suffer for a minute, maybe less. What a waste."

Shadow's shoulder lifted again as he chuckled. "Oh, sweet Mera. I can show you ways to drag their suffering out for as long as you need to."

I joined him in laughter, wondering if we might not both be a little psychotic these days. In truth, when had either of us ever been normal? Normal was overrated, and while I might not hold the same bloodthirsty streak as Shadow, I also wasn't letting Torma get away with their sins any longer.

"I think I've decided," I said softly, and like a true mate, he didn't ask me what it was, just accepted that when the time came, he'd be at my side to inflict this punishment.

Chapter Fifty-Nine

Torma looked exactly the same as the last time I'd been there, but somehow, it was also vastly different. Maybe it was that I had changed and now looked at it with a different perspective, turned what had once been a beautiful and strong mountain community, into one that was rather tired and outdated.

The alphas had not been keeping the town or pack as they should have been. Money went into the pack house and lands, with little returning to build up everything else. I'd always known the school was a pile of crap that needed to be demolished, but I hadn't really seen it everywhere else. No doubt because most of the time, my focus had been on hiding and surviving.

I was seeing it all with new eyes today, and I was determined that this time, Torma would change for the better. If it was the last thing I did.

As Shadow and I stepped into the pack lands for what would probably be the last time, my power spilled from me, washing across my form until I was over six-feet of badass winged wolf-phoenix. Shadow followed my lead, his Anubis beast form making an appearance, and I had no idea what the shifters thought when we strolled into the main street, the ground literally trembling beneath our feet.

Did we look like gods to them? Their awed and fearful expressions said yes.

One could grow addicted to that sort of power, if one hadn't seen firsthand what craving power could do to a being. I would never be Dannie. I refused. Thank the gods for my friends and family, who would keep me in check if I ever lost sight of that.

"What's your plan, little wolf?" Shadow rumbled at my side as gasps and cries rang out around us. Seemed the townsfolk were not sure what to do about the twin Egyptian-looking gods, covered in flames, standing in the middle of the main street.

"It's time to call the Torma pack to their final meeting," I replied, in an almost as impressive rumble of a voice.

I tilted my head back and howled. It was the howl I'd accessed that first night I'd shifted, when I'd called the Shadow Beast. A howl that was connected to my Nexus side, even if I hadn't known it all the way back then. It was also a howl connected to the shifters, and with it, I could call and control the packs.

Shadow had the same ability, of course, since he'd kind of created shifters, but this was my fight. My true mate stood at my side, and not in my way.

By the time my howl had died off, shifters were already making their way toward where we stood in the middle of the street. There were thousands of them, my call leaving no stone unturned, as even ones I hadn't seen for years found their way to where we waited.

Torin, Jaxson, Sisily, and a few of the other higher members of the pack pushed their way forward, each of them meeting my gaze with varying degrees of fear and anger. The pack enforcers were there as well, holding weapons, but none of them were stupid enough to try to take us on. They knew their place here, and it was finally my turn to be feared.

Simone was one of the last to arrive, but she got a spot up front as well, and I was beyond relieved to see her looking whole and healthy and happy. Somehow, she knew it was me, even with my new form, as she waved and smiled and bounced on the spot. I looked around for Sam as well, but the gorgeous brunette was nowhere to be seen.

Where's Sam? I mouthed at Simone, and she sobered a touch.

With her pack, she mouthed back, and I was about to panic, until she waved both hands at me. *She's fine,* she added. *Tell you later.*

I let out a relieved breath, nodding a few times before I faced the crowd again. Simone and I would catch up soon, and I'd find out all the things. But, for now, I had judgement to impart.

"My name is Mera Callahan," I said, my power projecting my words out to all those silently waiting. "And when I lived in Torma, you all made my life hell. I was punished for crimes that were not my own, and for that alone, each of you will face my judgement."

For the first time, there were gasps and sobs, as many of them started to beg, falling to their knees, praying for my mercy.

I hated it. "I'm not a god," I continued, my voice calmer, "and thus, the life and death of the Torma pack is not a decision that rests with me."

"It rests with me," Shadow muttered, and I hid my smile.

"However, *corruption and darkness* runs deep in this pack," I said with emphasis. "Each of you will be assessed, and if you have abused your privilege of being a shifter, of having a pack, of sharing the wealth and power that Torma contains, you will be stripped of your wolf soul. You will become a human, with all the frailties of a human, and there's no appeal to change this decision."

Shadow was staring at me now, his gaze heated, and when I turned to meet his eyes, the smallest of smirks tilted his lips. "Well played, mate," he said sounding pleased. "Well played."

The noise that had exploded after my last revelation didn't ease until Shadow's flames shot up above them, and he snapped, "Enough!" The bite of his power had every shifter shutting their damn mouths.

Torin was the first to step forward, and it might have been the most alpha thing he'd ever done. "I am the alpha here," he said, as if he were reading my mind. "My people are innocent. You should judge me and me alone for the sins of Torma."

I moved toward him, our eyes meeting since I was now his height. "Torin," I said softly. "Bet you regret rejecting me now."

He shrugged. "Not really. You're weird-looking in this form, and I don't know if I could get into the feathers."

I sighed, not offended by this rodent. "Thank the fucking fates we aren't really true mates. My mate—"

"Would like to destroy you," Shadow said casually, his flames growing larger so Torin was forced to move away.

"Shadow Beast," Torin choked out, showing him the fear that he was too stupid to show me.

"Torin Wolfe," I snapped, "for crimes of being a dumbass and a really shit alpha, you're stripped of your shifter soul."

Shadow was the one who would take back his gifts, touching Torin's shoulder to retrieve his shifter side. As Torin lifted his head and howled into the world one more time, a brilliant light left his body, and the former alpha collapsed forward, landing on his hands and knees. He remained there for many minutes, rocking back and forth as he adjusted to the change.

The loss of his wolf soul.

Sisily rushed forward from the crowd, wrapping her arms around Torin. The devastated look on her face told me that maybe... just maybe their relationship was actually real. No doubt that had been half the issue when it came to my bond with Torin. The other half was his dickhead of a personality.

"Take my wolf too," Sisily snapped, lifting her head toward me, the hatred she'd always felt spilling from her eyes. She had no reason to hide it now, and I appreciated her honesty way more than the fake bullshit from last time.

"You don't want to wait for judgement?" Shadow asked her.

She shook her head, looking determined and far stronger than usual. "Torin has always been my chosen mate, and I won't give up on us now. If he's a human, then so am I."

I managed not to snort out the derisive laughter, because she would have lost her wolf no matter what, but now she got to dramatically sacrifice herself for Torin. Ugh, whatever. They could have their second rate, sad-ass love story. Mine was a million times better.

Shadow's power shot out and locked around her, lifting her up to his level. He touched her briefly, and there was the same burst of light as her wolf was removed, before she dropped to her "mate's" side.

Torin managed to pull himself together enough to wrap an arm around her, as she was the one now rocking back and forth and crying.

"You will live a normal, full life as a human," I said, crouching down to their level. "Be grateful for your second chance, and don't waste it. Don't waste your human life."

Torin and Sisily lifted their faces toward me, tears painting their cheeks in lines of sorrow.

"My wolf... He's gone," Torin choked out.

My heart ached because I could empathize, but he had brought this on himself. He'd had so many chances to do better. Literal years since his father had died, where he could have grown up and taken Torma to the place and prestige it deserved.

Instead, he'd remained a spoiled, entitled asshole. Just like his father, he'd abused his power, and now he faced the consequences of that.

Jaxson hurried forward and he lifted the pair, dragging Torin and Sisily away from us. They disappeared, but I wasn't too worried. I knew Jaxson, and he would be back for his judgement. One thing he never shirked was responsibility.

Shadow's power dragged the other powerful members forward first, and we both placed our hands on them. This was the way I could see their actions over the years and pass judgement. Some of them were easy to decide, with corruption and depravity the truest part of who they were, while others I really had to weigh up if they were deserving of this level of punishment.

Dean Heathcliffe sneered when he got close, and I absolutely did not want to touch him. "You deserve death," I said without inflection, even if my eyes were telling him to drop dead.

Jaxson returned at that moment, and I was struck with the urge to touch them both. To see the truth of what Jaxson had been trying to tell me.

Shadow dragged them forward and held them in place so I could put a fingertip on both of their temples, digging straight into the past, searching for the time when my life had changed for the worst.

A room swirled before coming into focus, a familiar face sending a pang of grief through my chest. It was my father in one of the pack meeting rooms, with Dean and Victor. They'd been arguing, it was clear by the looks on their faces.

"Taking her friends away only makes it worse," my father snapped. "You killed her damn bunny and she almost burned the town down."

Dean laughed. "You birthed her, you deal with it. I'm protecting my family by ensuring my son is no part of her life. I'll break him if it's the last thing I do."

The scene changed, and then it was Dean and Jaxson. The father was slamming his fist into his son's face and chest and stomach, over and over, until a young Jaxson was limp and unresponsive. Torin was the one to rush in between the beta and his friend, holding both hands up.

"He won't see her again," a young Torin shouted. "She's a traitor. We both know she's a traitor and we'll ensure that everyone treats her as such."

Now my chest hurt, and Shadow must have sensed that, because he broke through the memories, separating me from them. It was fine, though; I'd seen enough.

Jaxson and Torin hadn't been lying or exaggerating when they'd said that Dean would have killed his son before he let him be my friend. Fuck, it had been going on before my father had lost his shit and gotten himself killed. And I could no longer blame those two when they'd been doing the best they could.

I had suffered so much, but they had too, and in some ways that allowed forgiveness in my heart. Torin still didn't deserve to be alpha, but Jaxson could keep his wolf. He was worthy of a second chance. Dean, on the other hand...

Shadow rumbled loudly beside me, and as I turned toward him, he struck out, plunging his hand into Dean Heathcliff's chest and ripping out his heart.

Ah, now that was a fitting punishment. "Your sins have finally caught up with you," I said to the former beta, and when Dean's body hit the ground, no one made a sound.

He would not be mourned in death, just as he wasn't respected in life.

A legacy all of his own making.

Chapter Sixty

B y the time we were done with our judgment, half of the pack was spared. Those shifters would be able to remain in Torma and rebuild their life. I sincerely hoped they did more with it than the first Torma pack.

At the end, Jaxson made his way toward me again. "Hello, old friend," he said.

Pain finally hit me, right as Jaxson reached out and grasped onto my furred and feathered hand. "You look amazing, Mera," he said, and I could tell he meant it. "Strong and beautiful. Powerful in a way that I always knew you could be." His words were the polar opposite of the disgust Torin had shown over my new form, and once again, I was content with my decision.

Jaxson released me then, turning to Shadow. "Thank you for saving her when I couldn't do it."

Shadow crossed his arms, staring his Anubis nose down on him. "She saved herself. And me."

Jaxson nodded, like he should have thought of that. Returning his gaze to me, he asked, "Why didn't you strip my wolf?"

I met his eyes. "Your soul is pure, even if you have been led astray at times."

He quickly glanced at his dead father, still untouched on the ground, not a single shifter taking his body away for a true burial. "It's a liberating feeling to finally be free. Kinda sucks that it comes with having to lose you. Will I ever see you again?"

"Fuck yes, you will," Simone said, finally having exhausted her patience in waiting, barging through the remaining crowds to reach me. We hugged hard, my fire wings popping away just in time so no one got burned.

"I missed you so much," she cried, "and you're in deep fucking trouble for not sending me any more messages."

"I'm so sorry. I kind of lost the parchment," I said against her shoulder.

She grumbled but didn't call me out on how I'd lost it. Best she didn't know about my *almost* death.

"I missed you so much, Sim," I said when we finally pulled away. "It's been so hard knowing you were here, with Torin and those others."

She shrugged. "Shadow gave me a few extra skills. Every time Torin tried to come near me, he was hit with a strike of electricity. A magical taser, if you will. It's been brilliant."

I snorted, side-eying my mate, who was still standing in awkward silence with Jaxson.

Turning back to Simone, I sighed at how happy I was to see her face. "Tell me about Sam going back to her pack?"

Her expression grew grim, and my smile faded away. "She didn't have a lot of choice. They called her back to deal with unfinished pack business."

A trickle of unease ran down my spine. "Are you sure she's okay? They didn't treat her very well, which is why she tried to get out in the first place."

Simone nodded. "Yes, I've spoken to her on the phone every day, and she says it's all going okay there. Just dealing with some shit because her true mate wants to try to make it work."

"The true mate who rejected her?" I confirmed.

Simone grimaced. "Yep, that would be the bastard."

My unease didn't disappear, worried that Sam was in a situation that could turn to shit very fast. Would she ask for help if she needed it?

"She's not in any immediate danger," Shadow told me, tilting his head as if he was sensing her out in the universe. Sometimes it was scary how powerful he was, especially when it came to shifters. "Her emotional state is subdued, but her physical state is good."

I made a mental note to check in on her myself soon. I'd made the mistake before with Dannie, trusting she was okay, only to find that Shadow's definition of okay was not exactly the same as mine. This time, I would ensure the safety of my friend, but as long as she was in no immediate danger today, we could clean up our other messes first.

Simone started to circle me, examining my form from all angles. "The wings," she said, "are fucking awesome. Where do they disappear to? Do they really fly or are they just show pieces?"

My wings reappeared and I shot up into the air, and those of the Torma shifters still around clapped and laughed as I zoomed around like a showoff. When I landed back at my mate's side, we were once again all business.

"There're some rather large holes in Torma's power structure now," I said, staring at the scattered shifters.

"Who is the new alpha?" someone nearby asked, having heard my statement.

Shadow looked at me, but I shook my head. "I don't know who's worthy, outside of Simone."

My friend in question held both her hands up as she shook her head. "No. Nope. Absolutely not a fucking chance. I'm not vibing that sort of power play and responsibility."

I snorted. "And why am I not at all surprised?"

Simone shrugged, and we both laughed. Jaxson cleared his throat, interrupting, and I was suddenly worried he would suggest himself as alpha. He had the power, and the control, but it would take more than that to strengthen this pack. Thankfully, he just said, "Why don't you allow us to rebuild slowly, and maybe a worthy alpha will emerge? We can have a true selection by the pack... a vote."

Shadow didn't love that idea, if the annoyed huff he exuded was any indication, but he didn't argue. My ancient mate probably just hated his traditions being messed with. "I think that's a plan to work with," I said, trying to hide my amusement. "We'll periodically check in on you all, and hopefully by then, you'll have figured out who is alpha enough for Torma. Until then, Shadow will protect you from other packs, right, mate?"

He tried to kill me with his eyes, but unfortunately for him, he'd fallen in love with me and now he was stuck forever dealing with my shit. Sucker.

"Right," he growled.

Simone snorted out some laughter before shaking her head. "What about me?" she said. "Now that Mom and Dad got the old heave-ho back to human they go, I'm not sure where I fit."

"I'm sorry about your parents," I said quickly. That had been a tough decision for me, but there was no denying their complicity in all the bullshit that had gone on in Torma. A lot more than I'd even known about until I touched them and saw into their souls. It was dark in there, even if a lot of it was initiated by Victor. But they'd never tried to fight his corruption, and for that, they'd lost their wolves.

She shrugged. "They had it coming, in more ways than one. Mostly I want to know when I will see you again. Can I visit the library?" She took my hand. "You're my family, Mera, and I refuse to live this life away from you."

Gods, my friends were legit going to kill me today. Between Angel almost dying and Simone hitting me in the feels, I was maxed out on emotions.

Wanting to have this conversation in my normal form, I released my power and returned to the human-Mera. Shadow handed me clothing that he had to have created in about a second, and once I was dressed, I was able to hug my friend again without feeling like I was a giant compared to her. "You can visit me whenever you want," I said, sniffling at how happy I was. "I want to see you all the time, talk to you every day, and we will figure out a way to make that happen."

Shadow didn't tell me it was impossible, which gave me hope that there was a way.

"We're pack," I said, pulling away. "Family. Always."

"You know it," Simone choked out with tears in her eyes. "And we have so much to catch up on. I need to know everything that happened. How you turned into a fire bird wolf goddess. Is Dannie gone now? Did anyone else get... hurt?"

I think we all knew who the *anyone* was in that situation. "Dannie's dead, she chose not to be reborn, and all of us made it through mostly alive. Lucien is fine."

She sagged in relief, her face a complexity of emotions that spoke of memories I still wasn't aware of. A lot had happened in the library and Valdor between those two, and one day very soon I wanted to know all of it.

"Do you want to see him?" I asked her gently.

She shook her head. "Not... yet. It's too hard to know the truth of what can never be. There's a shit ton of backstory there, and I will spill it all when we meet up next for our weekly PJ and margarita girls' party in Shadow's room. Deal?"

"Deal!" I said, right around the time Shadow wrapped an arm around me and hauled me back against him. He was still in his huge flaming form, and as the warmth surrounded me, I sighed in pure contentment.

Torma was dealt with. The pack had one final chance. And now it was time for us to head back home. We had a dinner to attend.

Chapter Sixty-One

My heart was slightly heavier as we left the Earth realm, returning to the long hallway. "I'll bring Simone across soon," Shadow said, frowning at what was no doubt a pouty look on my face. "You won't have to miss her for long."

I forced my lips into a smile. "Sorry, I'm actually really happy. We saved the damn world. Our main threats are eliminated, and we're together. I couldn't have asked for a better ending and yet I'm a little melancholy that everything might change now."

"It won't," he said. "Unless you want it to, and then I will ensure that everything changes."

"As simple as that," I shot back.

He kissed me suddenly, leaving me breathless and horny as fuck. "As simple as that, Sunshine."

Before I could think up another smartass reply, he swung me up and over his shoulder, and then he started to sprint through the hallway. Inky and Midnight, who had been guarding the entrance, rushed toward us. "They're back," I said, and now I was feeling much happier because this all felt normal.

Like a future I'd been dreaming of but had never expected to happen. I'd been forcing myself to accept the reality. We'd been fighting against a power we shouldn't have beaten. To know it was over... It had taken me a bit to get there, but finally, I could be happy.

Our mists surrounded us, lifting our bodies off the ground in their version of a hug. "Hey, buddy," I said to Inky, who started to spark.

All good in Faerie? I asked Midnight through our bond.

All good. The stone is safe.

That was all we needed to know at this point. Len would no doubt fill in the rest of the blanks when we saw him next.

"You two keep watch," Shadow said. "Mera and I have some business to wrap up before the great feast."

The mists jiggled before they wrapped around us one more time and then zoomed off together looking all cute and best-friend-like.

Shadow slapped a hand across my ass then, and I moaned, wiggling against him. "Business?" I got out.

"We have an hour until the dinner," he rumbled "Maybe even a few hours, because no one is monitoring when we arrive. Imagine what we could do in hours."

Well, when he put it like that... Now I was laser-focused, urging the beast on like I was riding a fucking racehorse. Of course, I planned on riding this particular "horse" very soon and for that to happen, he needed to move faster.

When I kicked his side, he growled at me, jerking his head up to see what the fuck I was doing. I shrugged, holding both hands up. "What? It works for racehorses."

That got me another slap on the ass, and I jerked against him, desperate to be naked and fucking my mate. He was still in his huge Anubis-like form, and that gave him extra speed and strength, so we made it along the hall and through the library in record time. Like, I barely even saw anyone as we dashed through, and when we entered the lair, everything inside of me was thrumming with excitement. My nerve endings were buzzing, and Shadow had better hurry the fuck up—

We didn't make it into the bedroom as his chest shook and he ground to a halt, dropping me down so he could tear my clothing from me. He was still Anubis, and I had no issue fucking the beast in this form. He was still almost completely humanoid with a little extra fur, and really, what was some body hair between shifter gods?

Before I had to question my moral compass, Shadow shifted back, his cock jerking between us as he thrust up and planted himself deep inside of me. He moved hard and fast, fucking me in the middle of the shelves, both of us too horny to make it to the room. I screamed out my pleasure, clawing at his chest while he slammed up into me as well. Both of us moving like our lives depended on it.

It was too much for me to not come immediately, and when the explosion of pleasure rocked through my gut, I was unable to do anything except hold on and ride it out.

"Sunshine, this time is going to be fast," he said, burying his head against my shoulder, his teeth biting down as he tasted me. "But that's only the beginning."

"I'm going to die." There was no denying it any longer. I was about to die via Shadow Beast dick, and I couldn't even be mad about it.

"You cannot die," he reminded me, lifting his head and shifting our position so he could tilt me back, hips pumping harder as he thrust into me. This time, his teeth closed over one of my nipples, and when he bit down, I screamed again, and he groaned, jerking into me as he came as well, sending me into my second orgasm.

"I think I can die," I wheezed, unable to catch my breath to speak clearly. "Dicked to death. It's a thing, even for immortals. Look it up."

Shadow shook his head, straightening as he licked across the teeth marks on my breasts, soothing them. The marks were gone in a moment, but I enjoyed the small pain he'd inflicted. He remained hard inside me as he started to walk us deeper into the lair. He didn't head for his room this time, but instead took us into the area around the fire, with all the comfy sofas.

We were already naked; he was still buried deep inside me and as he walked, his cock rubbed right across my G-spot, sending delicious sparks of pleasure through me with each step. On instinct, I ground myself against him and he groaned, moving with me, and all too soon we were moving together as we had before. Slower this time, though.

Shadow took us close enough to the fire that the heat surrounded us, which added to the pleasure. I expected him to lay me on the ground or maybe against a nearby shelf—the beast did love to fuck against hard surfaces—but he surprised me when he sank back into a nearby chair, leaving me straddled on his lap.

Our eyes met, this position intimate in a way that I'd only felt a few times before. I was on top, and I was moving against him, riding him slowly as I allowed my body to do what felt good. Shadow groaned again, one hand landing on my hip, while the other went to my ass, and he played with me, tracing across my skin.

"Sunshine," he rumbled, and I looked up, my body tightening at the sight of fire burning in his eyes. "I love you."

My body jerked and I almost came, but I was determined to try to hold out until I could ride him to orgasm. "I love you too," I whispered, leaning forward and pressing a gentle kiss to his lips. That lasted all of three seconds before he took control and our kiss deepened as I continued to ride him, moving against him with just enough speed that we were breathing heavily, but not enough to push us over the edge yet.

The hand that had been on my hip lifted to my cheek and he cupped around the back of my head, his thumb brushing my face as he held us close. His energy was all around me, and the fire we felt was from more than the one burning in the nearby fireplace.

My pace picked up, my hips dipping and swaying against his body as I rode his cock faster and faster. It felt like parts of Shadow were deeper inside of me than they ever had been.

And it wasn't just his dick, but his freaking soul, as wisps of his magic entered my brain. The mate bond was thrumming, strongly, and we were cementing it, piece by piece, brick by brick, as our souls intertwined.

My heart was pounding as I desperately tried to hold back my orgasm, wanting to bring him there first, but there was never going to be a chance of that. Not after he'd just come. I would have to be content with having multiple orgasms while I got to spend a few hours riding my mate.

Together. Always. Just like this.

Chapter Sixty-Two

Inky and Midnight were once again waiting for us when we finally emerged from our sex afternoon. It had been one of the best afternoons of my life because there had been no stress in the back of my mind. We got to screw our way around the lair, without worrying the world would end while we did.

"What do we do now?" I asked as we strolled through the Library of Knowledge.

He looked down at me. "What do you mean?"

I shrugged. "Like, day to day, year to year, century to century. How do immortal creatures prevent boredom?"

His lips twitched. "Lots of sex. It's really the only cure."

A snort of laughter escaped me. "We should run with that theory and never look back. But seriously, outside of the sex, what else will we do?"

Shadow took my hand, and we were back to being couple goals as we strolled through the shelves. "We'll always be busy with the Solaris System and our friends," he warned me. "It'll take me many years to restore the balance in Shadow Realm, and you have the Nexus and your creatures to watch over."

Yeah, that was true. "Our friends often have dramas?" I hadn't missed that not-so-subtle warning.

"Like you wouldn't believe," he said with a short laugh. "On a smaller scale than my mother, but there's always something. Each of them is powerful and important in their world, and with that comes a ton of drama."

I thought about it for a moment before shrugging. "Is it weird that I'm excited to see what will arise? It's weird, isn't it?"

I was no longer afraid of the future or the next big bad. I was certain that together, nothing would be a real threat to us.

"You're brave and loyal, Mera," Shadow told me. "You don't fear for your safety and you will always help out a friend. Your excitement makes sense, but it terrifies me."

I scoffed. "You're not terrified of anything, Shadow Beast."

He stopped me suddenly, wrapping his arms around me as he held on with a desperation he rarely showed in public. "I almost lost you. The way that felt, the choices I made... The world would not survive it again. *I* would not survive it."

I held on with everything I had, holding his broken pieces together. "This helps," he whispered into my hair. "It really helps."

"Then I will hold you forever," I declared.

I felt the brush of his lips against my neck and then he lifted himself up. "Are you okay?" I asked him seriously. "I mean, really okay? With Dannie and everything that happened. I'm sorry about your mom, Shadow."

He took a moment to answer, like he wasn't quite sure. "I will be okay, if that makes sense. It's just going to take time and having you at my side is all I ever wanted. A true mate."

"I didn't even know I could ask for something as amazing as this," I said, serious for once. "You are a gift that came from nowhere, with your grumbling, growling, snarling, asshole of a personality. Not to mention one huge dick. Like, that is such a bonus—"

It was at this point, laughter spluttered from between my lips as

Shadow shook his head, his expression amused and exasperated. "Ah, Sunshine, life is certainly never boring with you."

"I pride myself on that," I said as we finally continued walking toward the dining hall.

When we entered the hall I got why the library had been all but empty before.

Everyone was in here for the celebration feast.

Cheers went up as we stepped through the long rows, and even though Shadow didn't do much more than nod and walk along looking broody, I found myself thanking them all and smiling a lot, even after my cheeks started to hurt.

Thankfully, we reached our section before I whipped out the queen wave, our pack having commandeered three tables. Angel was in her usual spot, and I fell in beside her, able to land easily since my wings and hers were both tucked away. "Is that really weird for you?" I asked before wondering if it was rude to be so blasé in mentioning her lost appendages.

Thankfully, she was used to me and didn't miss a beat. "I fall over more than I stay straight at the moment," she told me. "My wings were always there, and I feel both cold and naked without them, but I'm testing not having them out all the time. I blend better in this form."

"You're never going to blend, my friend," I said, resisting the urge to hug her again because she was probably over that by now. "But I do understand. How was Honor Meadows anyway?"

She smiled. "Peaceful. We have a few layers remaining in our land, and so far, no one has tried to declare war on us and steal it. I'd call it a win."

"We'll destroy any who try," Shadow said, and he meant every word.

"They will learn to respect us as a pack," Lucien added, leaning forward, "wine" in his hand as he took a sip. "The entire Solaris System will learn."

I didn't argue because there had to be a hierarchy in these worlds, a pecking order, so to speak, to keep everyone in line. I preferred us at the top because I trusted every being in our pack.

Len leaned forward as well, and I was so happy to see him, that one would think it had been weeks rather than hours since he'd left us to go to Faerie.

"Did you get *you know what* hidden away?" I asked him. "Safely. With, like, seventy layers of protection?"

His smile was sad, and I hated to see him sad. "It was destroyed. We have the means to do that, and once the power was drained and released back into the universe, we made the difficult decision to let that stone go. It was just too powerful."

Did you keep the grains of stone? Galleli shifted in his chair, his huge wings tucked neatly behind him.

Some of Len's melancholy lifted. "Of course I did. If we ever need a really awesome boost in our spells, that shit is Grade A. But it can never be used in the same weapon-like manner again. And that's the most important part."

Galleli placed his hand on Len's shoulder, and whatever he said was meant for the fae alone. By the time he was done, they both looked much happier. Spirits lifted. The loss of the family stone would take Len some time to get over, but the fae appeared to be dealing with it as best he could. Unlike Reece, who wasn't even here.

"Where's our favorite desert deity?" I asked the group.

Angel shifted in her seat behind me; I felt the movement, but when I looked her way, she was unmoving, her expression blank.

Shadow answered me. "He said there was some unrest back home that he needed to deal with. He's not sure he'll be back for a while."

I narrowed my eyes on Shadow and he leaned in. "He needs some time," he murmured. "Your death and Angel's death didn't sit well with him. He'll be back when he sorts himself out."

Reluctantly, I let it go because Reece needed to do what he needed to do. That was true of all of us. He was allowed to deal in his own way, but I would be getting the full story about him and Angel out of somebody very, *very* soon.

The food arrived then, and that allowed a sense of celebration to creep back into the atmosphere of the room. Drinks were brought out as well, and just like the first time I'd ever seen this group of friends together, Shadow and the other four enjoyed a dark amber liquid in crystal glasses. He offered me a sip of his, and I almost died at the first blast of *liquid death* in the glass before politely declining another taste.

The food was much better than the drinks, and when the table was literally groaning under all of the dishes, I started eating and didn't stop.

"Everything tastes the same since your rebirth?" Angel asked, shaking her head at my skill level of shoveling food into my mouth.

I had to swallow before I could speak. "Yep, if anything, it all tastes better than ever. My senses are strong, but they regulate themselves, so I don't have a freakout overload. It's nice."

"You know you probably don't have to eat now, right?" Shadow said from my side, only shutting up when I tried to murder him with my eyes, mouth full as I slowly chewed and swallowed. "Never mind," he added, lips twitching.

They'd pry food from my cold dead hands, and even then, I'd demand a last meal.

"I wonder how it will taste for me now?" Angel said, looking down at the food in front of her, which consisted of a creamy chicken pasta, with spices and dried tomato and lots of vegetables. In my opinion, it was one of the best dishes that had come out so far. Others might have disagreed, especially those around the table filled by a huge fish carcass, which smelled a tiny bit rotten. They clearly did not eat in the same food pyramid as I did, but that was cool. As long as they stayed downwind, no one needed to judge.

"Here we go," Angel said, a pasta curl sitting on her utensil.

I found myself holding my breath, hoping that someday soon, she would need to eat in the same manner as myself. She popped it into her mouth and started to chew. Over and over, her brow furrowed, and I was about to hand her a napkin to spit it out when she swallowed.

No one spoke as we stared.

"It's good," she said suddenly. "It tasted good."

She smiled broadly at me before near bouncing in her chair, acting nothing like my centuries-old friend. This new joy had come with her rebirth, and in a way, she felt younger and more vulnerable. No less badass, of course, but more emotional.

"Do you require food for energy now?" Shadow asked her as she ate another forkful of pasta.

"Both," she told him, her eyes locked on the food. "I found I could meditate in Honor Meadows for energy, but an empty feeling persisted that's only easing now as I eat."

"Just like me," I said happily. I'd never had admitted it to anyone, but I had been mildly concerned that food would no longer taste good to me after my own rebirth. Thankfully, I'd worried for nothing. "Twinning at its finest."

Angel dropped the utensil into her bowl, turning to me with a sudden serious expression. "I'm honored to be your twin," she said.

I blinked at her. "There's some sort of context here I'm missing, isn't there?"

"Twin souls, separated at birth," Shadow said from beside me, still just sipping his lethal drink.

Turning back to Angel, I reached out and grasped her hand, squeezing it tightly. "Twin souls. I'm honored as well."

This made her happy and even though I still really didn't understand the significance, sometimes it was enough to just make them happy.

Happiness was all I wanted for Angel, and all the rest of our friends.

I tipped my head up to see Shadow, enjoying the way his eyes locked on mine, burning into me with their intensity. I remembered that moment on the lounge when his body had been buried deep inside mine, but more than that, it felt like his energy had filled me as well.

"Here's to the beginning of our new life," I said, clinking my respectable water with his glass of swill. "Thanks for kidnapping my ass. It was the best thing that ever happened to me. And you, of course, because... Shadowshine."

He leaned over, and I felt his breath brush across my cheek, sending shivers down my skin. "You belong to me, Sunshine. Now and forever."

As his lips met mine, all I could think was: Where's the lie?

Shadowshine.

He'd been worried that one was too dark and the other too light with only destructive storms between us, but that was no longer the case. Now we were both filled with dark and light, and together, we were the storm.

NOT READY TO LEAVE SHADOWSHINE AND the Solaris System behind? Make sure to pre-order the first spinoff in this world: Deserted (A Shadow Beast Shifters story).

Books2read.com/Deserted

Keep reading for a sneak peek of the first chapter.

Deserted

Angel

The air in the Library of Knowledge was cooler than usual as I stepped through from the Honor Meadows. Or maybe it was simply that the meadows themselves were going through their warm transitional months, heading toward the wet season. It was not like Earth, where their wet season consisted of literal rain for many days. In the meadows, it was about the energy flow. The hotter it was, the less the free power was distributed, and when it cooled down, we all got a boost.

It had been a long time since I'd had to care about such things, but after the battle in the Shadow Realm, where I'd all but stripped my family powers in an attempt to help my best friend defeat the Danamain, our shared family power was at its lowest. I was already waiting for the cooler days to replenish our stash.

I had no regrets about using my power, of course. I'd been willing to die to make sure my family and the rest of the worlds had survived. The fact that I'd been reborn, without the scars of the past dragging me down, was a bonus I hadn't seen coming. I'd also underestimated the way my Earth-raised best friend would turn all of our lives upside down, bringing her family together for all the occasions we'd missed out on experiencing.

Mostly because they were Earth customs, which in and of itself didn't make them bad—I was actually really looking forward to today.

As I hurried farther into the great library, the usual sense of awe filled me over this room, which contained all of the knowledge of the worlds. When I reached the center of the space, I finally understood why it was so chilly in here today. Mera wanted snow.

"Angel! There you are!" my goddess of a best friend snapped, as she appeared between some shelves. Her red hair was messier than usual, piled on top of her head, with green tinsel threaded through the strands. She looked festive... and a little crazed.

As she dashed toward me, I tried to figure out how she was moving so fast for someone in her very pregnant state. I shouldn't be surprised, though... I'd learned to never underestimate this particular being. She'd started life as a shifter before evolving into a goddess. A goddess who'd tamed one of the most formidable and scary beings in our worlds.

Shadow Beast.

Truth be told, no one could ever tame him, but Mera had definitely softened some of his harder edges. The beast and I had always had a tenuous sort of relationship, but thanks to Mera, we actually considered ourselves more friends than frenemies now. She was also the reason I used words such as "frenemy" these days because why the hell not? I was embracing this new side of myself, a side that did not carry the burdens of the ancients.

"Hello," Mera tried again, waving her hands in front of my face. "Are you here to help me set up or what?"

I chuckled, unable to help myself. Since learning she was pregnant, she'd been extra fiery. "Are you actually getting crankier? How long until the baby is due?"

Mera sighed, all but sagging against me, her frame too fragile for someone who was technically indestructible. "Fucked if I know.

Shadow keeps telling me it's best if we don't discuss how long and just enjoy the experience." She trailed off into a ton of curses and colorful phrases regarding the *Shadow Bastard*, finishing with, "Easy for him to say since he's not the one growing a demon spawn, or experiencing these insane cravings. Or dealing with my insane mate. You know that today is the first time in eight months he's left my side? He keeps growling at anyone who steps near me like the caveman beast he is, but today he had to head to the Shadow Realm because it just couldn't wait. And he left me with six fucking bodyguards. SIX!"

The moment she'd said "six," I was hit with an urge to run and run fast. There wasn't much in this world that scared me, not after everything I'd seen and done, but one of those six bodyguards was one of the few beings to knock me off-kilter.

Reece of the desert lands.

I'd known him a long time, and once, very long ago, we'd been friends. Now we were bitter enemies, and for some reason, recently, that bitterness had grown near out of control, making it difficult for us to be around our common friends.

I wasn't sure why he was acting so weird, and I didn't have the energy or inclination to dive into his hatred for me, but I knew that it was only a matter of time before we had no choice but to sort our shit out the old fashioned way.

I'd lost a lot of who I'd been in the rebirth, but my fighting skills were still as strong as ever, honed by daily training. It would do him well to remember whom he was constantly challenging. A reminder was in his near future if he didn't start sorting himself.

"Come on," Mera said, tugging my arm as she led me deeper into the great library, dodging shelves and other worlds' inhabitants, all of whom bowed respectfully to both of us. Mera barely noticed, though, her focus on the winter wonderland she was establishing in the center of the room.

"It's Christmas in two days," she said in a rush. "Two freaking days. My baby's first Christmas. I'm just not ready."

"Your baby is not exactly born yet," I said tentatively because she was unpredictable right now. "I don't think they'll mind if it's not quite the perfect Christmas."

She paused, and I braced myself for her yelling, but instead, she sighed. "I'm being overbearing, aren't I? Shadow told me I was, but I just thought it was his usual asshole personality rising to the surface."

She rubbed a hand over her stomach, and despite the way she frequently and loudly complained about the trials of pregnancy, she already loved her child with a desperation that should warn any meaning it harm to stay far away.

She wasn't the only one, either. Shadow was downright scary these days and when this baby was born, he would be the literal beast he was named after.

Who was I even kidding? This child would be the most protected being in the Solaris System, and I'd be the first in line if any came at us with ill intent. For Mera, Shadow, and the baby—my family—I'd fight the gods themselves... and even put up with a dust-weaving asshole.

An asshole who looked really good tonight, his warrior body showcased in a simple black shirt, black pants, and his usual scowl as he watched us approach. Reece's skin shone bronze in the low twinkling lights strung around the snow-tipped Christmas tree. The blue of his eyes was searing, and what had once been my favorite color was now my least, no matter how pretty he made it look with those dark lashes framing pools of cobalt.

"Mera, you're not supposed to run off like that," he admonished, removing his glare from me to glare a touch less at her. "Sticking us with stringing up the lights was not a good distraction, but luckily, I knew you didn't leave the room."

She poked out her tongue, hip-checking him gently. Their relationship was so easy and caring, and I had no idea how she'd achieved that with the being who was basically as reticent and cold as Shadow had been. But that was Mera's way. To tame the angry soul. A way I did not possess, but that was okay. I made up for my lack of people skills with exceptional blade skill, and I had no doubts of which was more important.

Only one would protect my family when the time arose. And it *would* arise... There was always something evil lurking in the wings. That was just how our worlds worked.

"Angel, come on," Mera called, dragging me right into the midst of her winter wonderland.

She'd gone all out for the library's first Christmas, the tree dominating the space, while underneath it was stacked with what seemed like hundreds of wrapped gifts. She'd been in the room of need for days choosing the exact right gifts for us all, and maybe it was her child-like excitement, but I found myself with swirls of anticipation in my stomach. An emotion that I'd thought I could no longer feel.

Rebirth might have taken from me, but it had also given so much back.

Shadow's energy entered the library then as he stepped back from the realm. He would have to go there more and more as he helped to rebalance a world that had spent centuries under the rule and control of evil beings. It would take years to repair the damage, but they were heading in the right direction.

Despite Mera's complaints before, her head snapped toward the direction of her mate as soon as his power was felt. When he appeared, her face lit up, and they came together in a way that was hard to watch. Not because I wasn't happy for them, but because their pure love was the same sort of love my parents had shared.

A love I knew nothing of, and doubted after this many years, I would ever know.

"You weren't long," Mera said, after he kissed her senseless, and she dragged him toward the tree.

"And yet somehow you found the time to completely redecorate the library," Shadow said dryly.

Mera lifted an eyebrow at him, her warning expression. "You don't like it?"

Shadow's lips twitched. "It's perfect, Sunshine."

Mera paused then, her little nose twitching as she started to sniff before she turned suspicious eyes on her mate. "Hand it over," she snapped, and this time, Shadow actually fucking laughed.

To see that stoic bastard tip his head back and laugh like that was super unsettling. Sometimes I wondered if Mera wasn't the long-fabled lost witch of Solaris System. She had that way about her.

"Shadow," Mera growled. "You do not want to fuck with a pregnant person."

"You really don't," Len called out from nearby, his voice filled with concern. "Can someone seriously tell us how much longer she'll be pregnant?"

Mera had enough at this point, all but jumping on her mate before using her powers to hold him down while she searched his pockets. Shadow let her, his eyes eating her up in a way that was probably dangerous to any of us standing nearby.

Finally, she found what her nose had sniffed out, pulling free a white paper bag, her hands near trembling as she hugged it to her chest. "You found one," she sniffled. "Aw, mate, I love you."

She kissed him then before wiggling her way down, both of them careful of her stomach.

Shadow pulled her close as she opened the bag and removed a weird green... stick? "What the hell is that?" Reece asked, in his usual asshole, tactless way.

"Deep fried pickle," Mera said, still tearful. "I swear to fuck I've been desperately craving these and no one in the dining hall has a clue what I'm talking about."

She took a bite and then moaned, and as flames sprang into Shadow's eyes, I knew my friend was about to disappear from the room. Sure enough, after Mera's second bite and second moan, Shadow's energy whipped through the space, and by the time I blinked again, he was gone. Taking his Sunshine with him.

"The only surprise there," Alistair said, letting out a warm laugh, "is that she wasn't pregnant the first day they met."

"Those two stubborn souls had a lot of shit to sort out," Len said, twirling more lights across the tree, using sparks of fae magic. "Fuck, if it doesn't make me happy to see them like that. I think Shadow's turning us all soft."

Lucien punched Len, a solid hit on his shoulder. "Speak for yourself. Nothing soft about me."

It sounded a lot like Len coughed out *Simone*, but before a war broke out, Reece let out a low, rumbling huff of air. As much as he pissed me off—and why the hell was I still standing in the same room as him?—I knew that sound well enough that I had to look his way.

What is it? Galleli asked, so at least I didn't need to.

Reece shook his head. "The desert lands are uneasy; their sands of time drift through my energy. They're calling me into the depths of the Delfora, and I can't get a straight answer from any of the other dynasties about what has been unearthed."

"When is your next meeting of the lands?" Lucien asked, and once again, my question was answered without me even having to say a word. Lest Reece think I give a single fuck about him.

I'd do about anything to ensure that never happened.

"It's in a dozen red moons," he said shortly. "And I have a favor to ask. Will you all accompany me? There's betrayal afoot, and I think it's best if I bring backup. We must ensure there's never another dynasty war." His eyes met mine briefly, his blue embers of fury. "The last one near destroyed us all."

"Of course, you don't even have to ask," Len said, slapping a hand on Reece's shoulder. "As Mera said, we're a pack now, and pack sticks together."

"She used that emotional blackmail to get us to hang up her damn Christmas lights," Reece said with a laugh. "But I'll take it. I know Shadow won't want to bring her while she's pregnant, but I think with all of us there, she'll be safe. I'll speak to him tomorrow."

That had me standing a little taller. Truth of the matter, I was more than a little curious about this meeting of the dynasties. Especially if there was trouble afoot in their ancient and sacred Delfora lands, but I'd had no intention of taking part in it. At least not up until I'd known Mera would be there.

Where Mera went, so did I.

This time, I was the one to slam my gaze into Reece, and there was a moment of truth between us. I would be in the desert lands with him in a dozen red moons, back to the place where our shit had all gone down.

A place that held our past hurts and losses.

The place where Reece had destroyed my heart and soul, and I wondered if finally, I might be able to dig it up from the red soil. Dig it up and let him and our feud go.

For good.

STAY CONNECTED

The best way to stay up to date with the Shadow Beast Shifters world and all new releases, is to join my Facebook group here:

www.facebook.com/groups/jayminevenerdherd

We share lots of book releases, fun posts, sexy dudes, and generally it's a happy place to exist.

Next best place is my newsletter at www.jaymineve.com and

www.facebook.com/JayminEve.Author

I'm also getting a lot of questions about what book to start next.

If you're looking for the same sexy supernatural style story, my recommendation is Supernatural Prison or Supernatural Academy. These are set in the same world but can be read standalone. Both are recommended for 18+ readers. :)

I'll post links and blurbs below for you.

[Image: upe aca fb (1).jpg]

http://smarturl.it/SupernaturalAcademy1

Maddison James is about to discover some truths about the world.

Firstly ... supernaturals exist.

WTF?

Secondly ... she is one, even though no one seems to know exactly what kind.

Double WTF.

Thirdly ... she's about to go back to school.

Well, things just got a little more interesting.

The Supernatural Academy is where shifters, vampires, magic

users, and fey are educated. Where they are taught about their abilities, and how to function in the human world. Maddison already has the human part down, but this supernatural thing is an entirely new dangerous game.

Example one: mean girls who can actually turn you into a frog.

Example two: Asher Locke, a god at the Academy. Not literally ... well, who knows for sure. He certainly acts the part, as do all of his minions who worship him.

Asher drives her crazy, because apparently gorgeous and arrogant is her thing. Sparks fly between them, and the more they're thrown together, the more Asher is determined to figure out what's been blocking her abilities.

Until the moment the truth is revealed, and they find out nothing in this supernatural world is what they thought.

Including each other.

[Image: facebook group 3 sps.jpg]

http://smarturl.it/DragonMarked1

It's time for the dragon marked to rise...

Jessa Lebron doesn't have a lot to complain about. Her father is the alpha of their wolf pack, she lives in Stratford, a protected supernatural prison town, and her best friends, the Compass quads, are the strongest dudes of the four races: shifter, vampire, fey, and magic user.

Yep, life is pretty much exactly how she wants it. Until the fateful day, just after her twenty-second birthday, when the mother who abandoned her returns to the pack bearing secrets that change everything.

The biggest secret of all: Jessa's dragon marked, a designation that places her in grave danger.

For a thousand years, every supernatural child born with the mark was eliminated to prevent the rise of the dragon king, a fearsome ancient warmonger. In a bid to learn more about her fate and how to avoid the hunters, Jessa finds herself locked in Vanguard, the notorious supernatural prison.

Thankfully she's not alone. Braxton Compass, the most feared of the dragon shifters, is right there with her. Together they'll have to survive long enough to free themselves and the other dragon marked.

Before the king rises.

The rest of my books can be found here: https://www.amazon.com.au/Jaymin-Eve/e/B00E1URI2I/ or join my group for all the reccs.

ALSO BY JAYMIN EVE

JAYMIN EVE

Shadow Beast Shifters (Urban Fantasy/ PNR)

Book One: Rejected

Book Two: Reclaimed

Book Three: Reborn (March 31st 2021)

Royals of Arbon Academy (Dark, complete Contemporary Romance)

Book One: Princess Ballot

Book Two: Playboy Princes

Book Three: Poison Throne

Titan's Saga (PNR/UF. Sexy and humorous)

Book One: Releasing the Gods

Book Two: Wrath of the Gods

Book Three: Revenge of the Gods

Supernatural Academy (Complete Urban Fantasy/PNR)

Year One

Year Two

Year Three

Dark Legacy (Complete Dark Contemporary high school romance)

Book One: Broken Wings

Book Two: Broken Trust

Book Three: Broken Legacy

Secret Keepers Series (Complete PNR/Urban Fantasy)

Book One: House of Darken

Book Two: House of Imperial

Book Three: House of Leights

Book Four: House of Royale

Storm Princess Saga (Complete High Fantasy)

Book One: The Princess Must Die

Book Two: The Princess Must Strike

Book Three: The Princess Must Reign

Curse of the Gods Series (Complete Reverse Harem Fantasy)

Book One: Trickery

Book Two: Persuasion

Book Three: Seduction

Book Four: Strength

Novella: Neutral

Book Five: Pain

NYC Mecca Series (Complete - UF series)

Book One: Queen Heir

Book Two: Queen Alpha

Book Three: Queen Fae

Book Four: Queen Mecca

A Walker Saga (Complete - YA Fantasy)

Book One: First World

Book Two: Spurn

Book Three: Crais

Book Four: Regali

Book Five: Nephilius

Book Six: Dronish

Book Seven: Earth

Supernatural Prison Trilogy (Complete UF series)

Book One: Dragon Marked

Book Two: Dragon Mystics

Book Three: Dragon Mated

Book Four: Broken Compass

Book Five: Magical Compass

Book Six: Louis

Book Seven: Elemental Compass

Hive Trilogy (Complete UF/PNR series)

Book One: Ash

Book Two: Anarchy

Book Three: Annihilate

Sinclair Stories (Standalone Contemporary Romance)

Songbird

AFTERWORD

You did it! You all made it to the end without killing the author. ;)
Seriously, thank you, I really appreciate you only trying to murder me
with your minds. And I don't blame you one bit... those cliffys were
rough.

But we got there in the end, and I am feeling a touch emotional about
the conclusion of Shadow and Sunshine's story.

I never expected it. I really didn't expect them to capture me body
and soul, every word flowing in a way that I'm not sure I've ever had
in a series before. There's something special about these characters
and this world, and to have them embraced by you all so thoroughly.
Honestly, it's the best gift you could have ever given me.

Thank you! Thank you so freaking much.

Thank you to my family for allowing me to escape into the
libraries and worlds, and to my PA Jane, who legitimately made the
most incredible teasers for this series, that I think she's a little magic
as well.

Thank you to my cover artist who might be fae, with her ability to
turn my vague ideas into words of art. And to my editors, who worked
tirelessly polishing my words.

Thank you to my review team, the bloggers, and all the readers who
have made my life so much fun with their love and enthusiasm for

this series. I can't name you all, but know that I'm grateful for each and every one of you.

There's more to come in this world, because I can't let it go, but know that Shadow and Mera will always hold a special place in my heart. As do all of you. Xxx

CPSIA information can be obtained
at www.ICGtesting.com
Printed in the USA
LVHW090907240723
753027LV00094B/298/J

9 781925 876246